PRAISE FOR

THE PRIVATE LIFE OF JANE MAXWELL

"Gott aims true in this action-packed, emotionally resonant series opener about hope and heroism in the face of overwhelming loss."

—*Publishers Weekly* (starred review)

"This is a fast, fun book. . . . [A] queer homage to superhero television."

—*Tor.com*

"*The Private Life of Jane Maxwell* did a great job of drawing a line between the comic book reality and the reality of good fiction."

—*The Lesbian Review*

WHO'S AFRAID OF AMY SINCLAIR?

JENN GOTT

HOPEFULS #2

WHO'S AFRAID OF AMY SINCLAIR?

Copyright © 2019 by Jennifer Gott

Cover design by Jenn and Graeme Gott
Cover images: woman © quadshock/Shutterstock;
blue hallway © Drew Graham/Unsplash;
man adjusting cuffs © Alvin Mahmudov/Unsplash;
wedding aisle © Shardayyy Photography/Unsplash;
state capitol building © Michael/Unsplash;
rainbow crosswalk © Tayla Kohler/Unsplash

ISBN 979-8-4256-3227-2 (hardcover)
ISBN 978-0-9908914-8-2 (paperback)
ISBN 978-0-9908914-7-5 (ebook)

For Stefani
Because some people come into your life exactly when you need them.

WHO's AFRAID OF
AMY SINCLAIR?

NEARLY THREE YEARS AFTER THE DAY SHE DIED, CLAIR
Maxwell was getting married again.

Sort of.

The truth is complicated. Forget shades of gray—the reality of
Clair's life now was an ever-shifting mosaic of color, each shade
so close to its neighbor that at first it doesn't look like there's any
change at all, until you step back and suddenly an entire rainbow
of nuance reveals itself. For example: does it count as getting
married "again" if the two of you were never technically married
on the parallel world you lived in now? And does the answer
change if *one* of you is physically from your original world, where
it did actually happen, but the *other* is the living consciousness of
the you who went through it, now reborn into the body of your
parallel self that *didn't*?

These were the kinds of questions Clair was choosing to avoid
as she navigated the rented beach house on the morning of her

second wedding to the same woman. She laughed, dodging the bustling groups that passed through the packed house. "Is someone going to get the doorbell?"

"Looks like you are!" Donna, Clair's mother, said as she passed by Clair. Her arms were overloaded with a stack of presents, and she blew a thank-you air kiss at her daughter. "And don't forget—dining room in five."

"Wouldn't miss it," Clair said. She was already moving off down the hall, her bare feet soaking in the warm, vacationy vibes that saturated the slats like wood stain. This was a good rental, a happy little beach house on a happy little beach front— and though traces of the occasional family fight still lingered in a room or two, overall the place filled Clair with a sense of openness and possibility, like everything was brand new. She'd toured half a dozen of them before settling on it.

On the front porch, a faceful of pollen and perfume assaulted her. An enormous display of white flowers toppled forward, a loud "whoops!" rippling through the bouquet as Clair lurched to catch them. Petals lapped against her skin, whispering to her their history of being lovingly tended, a soft-spoken widower pruning dead leaves every morning. Clair shut her eyes, just for a second, letting her mind fill with the peaty smell of the greenhouse.

Memory that wasn't her own took over her senses, memory from the gardener who'd tended to the flowers. His back became her back, aching and curled from a lifetime of pruning. His hands, her hands, release the stinging smell of ointment, purchased from the grocery store at the insistence of his sister, who swears it's the only thing that'll help with arthritis. He'll try anything by now—he's been running this shop since the fifties, opened just after he and his wife got married, god rest her soul. The gardener glances up, catching a wink from where her picture hangs over the register. The photo was from the grand opening, and in it his wife is done up like a movie star, hair in perfect curls, skirt blooming around her flawless legs. The gardener's chest hurts just looking at her. His granddaughter is almost that age now. The ghost of his own reflection catches in the glass, such an old man by now, but what would he have left if he retired?

"Whoa there, sorry about that!" a voice said, ripping Clair from the depths of memory. She found herself blinking in the morning sunlight spilling in through the front doorway. A young man wrestled the bouquet out of Clair's arms, then frowned at it when he realized he was *supposed* to have handed it over—just not so clumsily.

Clair stretched her arms out, and the man passed her the heavy pot once more.

"Sorry," he muttered. "I swear I'm not usually this much of a klutz."

"I know you're not," Clair said. *Jimmy.* The name came to her as she looked at his face, familiar now from years of visits and school photos wedged into the old gardener's wallet. He was a good kid, reliable even when he grumbled about working in his grandpa's shop after school.

She knew this, just like she knew the history of the flower shop, just like she knew the joy this particular beach house had brought to so many people, just like she knew her friend Stacey was somewhat confused by Clair's actions ever since Clair had assumed her doppelgänger's life over a year ago.

Stacey never *said* anything, of course. That was the whole point—she didn't need to. The powers Clair's parallel self had left behind told her more than enough. And Clair tried to be mindful of the confusion she had caused. She'd done her best to soften the changes, but there was only so much she could do. This world's version of Clair, the one who'd never shortened her name down to "Clair," but still went by "Amy" instead, had never come out as a lesbian. In some respects, it would have been easier if Jane and Clair had waited to get remarried, but Clair had been dead long enough by now. It was time to move forward. The two of them settled on a lie: that they'd been together in secret for years by this point, only just coming out in time for their wedding.

Now here it was. Clair shifted the pot of flowers so it rested against her hip like a baby. Jimmy was still standing there, boggling at the swirl of activity unfolding in the beach house behind Clair. She couldn't exactly blame him—not yet eight in the morning, and already the household was in full swing. Hordes of guests and stylists had descended over the past three days, and now they prowled the rooms in organized packs, looking for faces that hadn't been prettied, dresses not yet zipped, hair not yet pinned tight and sprayed to within an inch of its life. Caterers had commandeered the kitchen, overseen by Estella, Clair's half of the wedding coordinator tag-team the Maxwells had hired to ensure that *nothing* went wrong today. Except that, apparently, a whole arm of Jane's family had a fish allergy they had only just now thought to tell people about. Clair didn't know the details. She wasn't supposed to know the details—by now, all the major decisions had been made, and Clair's role was reduced to a simple mandate: show up and look beautiful.

Jimmy gave a low whistle, taking it all in.

"I'm sorry, are you waiting for a tip or something?" Clair asked.

"Huh?" Jimmy's eyes shifted, reluctantly, away from the edge of the living room, where several relatives had unabashedly set up camp to change. Hints of slips and stockings were visible even in Clair's peripheral vision, and she held her free hand up to her face, hoping to block the view.

"A tip?" Clair asked again, trying to keep things moving. Though where she'd find the cash, she had no idea—she was still in her robe-and-pajama set that Jane affectionately called Clair's "grammie jammies," a name that was only appropriate considering Clair's great-aunt Amelia had given them to her as a wedding present. Clair certainly didn't have her wallet on her, and her mind flailed, trying to remember where she'd seen it last.

Jimmy's face softened, as if he was reading all this off Clair's own. "Nah, don't worry about it. I get it—deaths are hard."

The taste of ash settled thickly on Clair's tongue. "What'd you say?"

Surely it was impossible for him to know, wasn't it? The circumstances of her death and subsequent rebirth into the body of her parallel self were closely guarded secrets. Even more than her empathic powers, even more than her superhero persona in the Heroes of Hope. If somehow this guy *knew*, if he'd picked up something . . .

But Jimmy only blinked in confusion. "Um. The flowers . . . ?"

"They're for a *wedding*." She sounded annoyed, though really, relief was already settling over her. Just because Jimmy was a good kid didn't mean he wasn't a dumbass sometimes. Of course he'd make assumptions about why he was delivering his grandpa's flowers. She wanted to laugh at her own paranoia.

"Oh." Jimmy shrugged, already moving on. "Okay. In that case, good luck today!"

"Thanks, Jimmy," Clair said as Jimmy turned and sauntered across the porch with a jaunty wave over his head. If he'd noticed that Clair shouldn't have known his name, he did not show it. A green pickup truck idled in wait for him, its bed piled high with shrubbery, *Thursday Florists* stamped on the driver's side door.

Clair shook her head. She hooked the door with her foot, nudging it shut. A few moments later, she was lugging the heavy pot into the dining room, where Donna and a small circle of Clair's half of the wedding party had assembled.

"There she is!" Stacey called. Her high voice carried easily across the room, a slight squeak to punctuate the end of her sentences. "The woman of the hour!"

Clair rushed to set the flowers down on the sideboard. "You didn't start without me, did you?"

"Nonsense," Donna said. She carried over a tray of mimosas, as bright as sunshine.

"In fairness, I wanted to," Stacey cut in, "but Hannah wouldn't let me."

Hannah, Clair's cousin, stood up from the dining room table, where she'd been checking her phone. "Good thing, too. The last thing we need is for people to be buzzed before we even hit the reception."

"Oh, well, then I'll just take yours," Clair said. She plucked one off the tray without being asked, and did not wait for the toast before taking a long drink.

"Hey hey hey!" Hannah said. "Save some for the rest of us!"

Clair grinned. Her mimosa was still half full, but she grabbed a second right out from under Hannah's nose. "Bride's prerogative!"

Stacey laughed. "If that's the rule, we're going to need to send a tray over to Jane. Double trouble and all."

Donna shook her head as she passed out the remaining glasses. Stacey, Hannah, Clair's aunt Penny. "There's plenty for *everyone*," Donna said. "Just don't drink so much you can't say your vows."

Clair leaned over, kissing her mother's cheek. A swell of motherly pride transferred at the contact; the sight of Clair when she was little, sitting on the battered living room carpet of an old apartment, singing to herself as she brushes the hair of her Little Mermaid doll. Clair's heart warmed as she and her mother shared a matching smile at the memory.

"Don't worry," Clair said. "*Nothing* is going to keep me from getting married today."

Donna hip-checked Clair. "You'd better. I've always wanted another daughter."

Clair's mouth gaped as she put her hand to her chest, mock annoyed. "I wasn't enough?"

"After four more boys? You'd wish for a second girl, too. Now, everybody gather 'round."

A quick shuffle, as the party rearranged itself. Donna held up her glass.

"It is a truth universally acknowledged," she started, and a series of groans and giggles passed through the room, "that a mother in possession of a daughter getting married must surely be in want of some tissues." She pressed her hand to her chest as she raised her glass higher, her eyes sparkling with tears. "To my Clair. I'm so proud of you."

A starburst of tropical drinks met above their heads. "Clair!"

They drank up. Clair shut her eyes, letting the tang of the juice and alcohol settle the last of her rattled nerves. A sniffle from Donna made her open her eyes, just in time to see Hannah reach down into her bra—she was the first one fully dressed, hair and makeup already perfection—and pull out a Kleenex.

"What?" Hannah said as Clair laughed at her. "It's a wedding. I come prepared for weepy mothers."

At this, Hannah shot a significant look across the table at her own mother. Aunt Penny, halfway prepared for the day in gray slacks and a lilac blouse but no jacket or makeup, her hair still wet around her shoulders, gave the room a look of mock incredulousness. "I have no idea what she's talking about!" she said, but then she glanced at Clair, and immediately waved toward Hannah. "But I'll take one of those, too. Just in case!" she added, talking loudly over the room.

"So, Clair," Stacey said a moment later. She reached over, throwing her heavy arm around Clair's shoulders. "It's the big day. Any last-minute jitters?"

Hannah rolled her eyes. "That is such a reporter question."

"Hey, I *am* a reporter, okay?" Stacey said as she brushed a lock of red hair out of her flushed face. "I'm allowed."

"It's fine, it's fine," Clair said. Stacey shoved her half-empty glass in Clair's face like a microphone, and Clair laughed, grabbing it and leaning in. The joy and happiness Stacey felt for Clair's wedding seeped into Clair's fingers as she said, "First of all, I'd like to thank the Academy, and my wonderful friends and family for their continued support."

Stacey yanked her glass away, giving Clair a playful smack. "This isn't a speech, dummy—that comes later."

"Honestly, though," Hannah said. "How are you feeling? Can you believe it's really here?"

Clair paused, considering this. All throughout the rest of the house, the careful storm continued to swirl—even now, voices and laughter and shouts could be heard from every corner—but here in the dining room, they'd managed to carve out a pocket of calm for themselves. She looked at the faces surrounding her, all the sparkles of tears looking back.

How was Clair feeling?

Like every breath she took was a miracle, because it was. Clair was never supposed to be here. Everything about this life was a gift—one her parallel self had given her, one Clair had no intention of ever taking for granted.

Clair grinned until her cheeks hurt. She raised her glass high. "I am so ready!"

The room whooped with her, laughing and drinking. They still had fifteen minutes until Clair would be whisked away to dress and have her hair and makeup done, and in this bubble a sense of endless possibility filled the space. Clair did not even need her empathic senses to feel it.

"Okay, no, but seriously," Stacey said, "love and 'grats and everything all around, but *someone* needs to tell whoever sent this latest bouquet that this is a happy occasion."

She jerked her thumb over her shoulder, pointing back to the flowers Clair had brought in with her. Clair had been so busy juggling them and handling the delivery guy that she hadn't stopped to pay much attention to what the bouquet actually looked like, but she did now. A ceramic green pot, overflowing with blooms. The bottom layer of petals brushed the counter. But it wasn't so much the size of the bouquet that rankled Stacey. The flowers themselves, while lovely beyond words, and obviously tended to with the greatest care, were nothing but white lilies.

Deaths are hard . . .

A splinter of discontent shot beneath the thumbnail of Clair's happy mood. She'd thought Jimmy was just being an ignorant kid, but now she understood where his confusion came from.

"It *is* a weird choice for a wedding," Donna said.

Clair set her glass down. "Yeah . . . the delivery guy seemed to think so, too."

"Maybe it was misdelivered?" Stacey offered.

"Is there a card?" Hannah asked.

"I don't think so . . ." Clair walked over to the flowers. The petals were soft beneath her touch, full of nothing but the old man's nostalgia and pride. "No, wait . . . here's something."

At the base of the pot, a battered white envelope was pinned and staked into the dirt. It didn't have the same tender care as the rest of the presentation, and in fact it didn't seem to fit with the flower shop at all. Clair hesitated, just for a second, before picking it up. The paper was rough in her hands, but oddly lacking in emotional depth. Just the vague hint of something sour, like the lingering taste of blood.

Clair stepped aside, out of the watchful gaze of her mother, away from the curious glances of the others. *For the Bride . . .* , the envelope read. A drawer in the sideboard held silverware, and Clair helped herself to a butter knife. She sliced open the envelope and set the knife back down, drawing out the card.

She was greeted by a picture of Jesus. A familiar painting, the same one her great-aunt Amelia had in her bedroom. He stood there on a bed of clouds, beatific, one hand raised, the other over his heart, eyes toward the heavens. Clair frowned, flipping the card over.

On the back was a printed prayer, chapter and verse stamped on top, but it wasn't the words of comfort that immediately drew Clair's attention. Instead, her eyes slid down, widening as she spotted two lines printed in flowing italics.

In loving memory, it said, and then beneath that:
Amy Ophelia Sinclair, 1985–2018

THE WIDE SWEEP OF A CITY SKYLINE. SKYSCRAPERS DOT an otherwise inky-blue backdrop, their lights a man-made galaxy tied down to the earth with steel and concrete. Beneath that, a series of streets drawn at sharp angles, the panels divided by slashes, as if the viewer is flying down them like a bird. Smudges blur the edges, providing a sense of speed. You see, in pieces: the entrance to a nightclub, neon lights contrasting the despair of the homeless man collapsed in the nearby alleyway; a sleepy construction site, spied through a chain-link fence, lumbering yellow beasts nestled down for the night; a police car, parked in an alley, its driver's face slack-eyed and lit by the screen of his speed trap; a dark shape, being beaten upon by a larger dark shape, a red purse held tight in the attacker's fist.

Jane put down the red marker, and reached underneath her glasses to rub her dry eyes.

She wasn't supposed to be wearing glasses right now. Her stylist had already been through, transforming Jane in a whirlwind of activity that made her feel like she was spinning around in a phone booth. The glasses, it had been deemed, would catch too many reflections, and send the wrong aesthetic to the photohungry media. Using contacts again, she was told, would not kill her.

A perfectly valid argument, except that contacts irritated Jane's eyes something terrible, and what no one knew is that Jane was *already* wearing them on a regular basis—every time she donned her uniform and went out as Captain Lumen, in fact—and with the number of hours she'd been putting in recently . . .

Jane sighed, and retrieved a bottle of dry-eye drops from the pocket of her jeans, currently in a heap on the bathroom floor beside her. She put her sketchbook on the edge of the tub, hooked her glasses across her knees, and leaned back, squeezing the drops in and blinking through the blurriness.

As she put the bottle away, she shook her head at the ridiculousness of the situation. Look at her: in a bridal dress worth over five grand, sitting on the lid of a toilet, surrounded by white. The only colors in the room were ones she'd brought in herself— her sketchbook, her markers, her normal clothes on the floor, her overnight bag sitting on the counter. Jane tried to picture how she'd draw it, if she was still writing about the Heroes of Hope, if her life was still nothing but a story she'd once sold to Quantum Zero Comics. She'd frame herself in the lower left corner, the room looming around her. The detritus of her life drawn in greater detail than the room or her dress, to ground the reader in what was real and what was fake.

A sharp knock rapped on the door, Mrs. Maxwell's voice filtering through. "Janie? Ten minutes, honey!"

"Okay!" Jane called. She drew herself carefully to her feet. Everything she did was careful these days. Between her secret identity in the Heroes of Hope, to her origins on a parallel world, to the truth of Clair's death and rebirth, her life was a delicate balance of lies layered upon lies, and even the smallest slip would send it all crashing down.

Jane scooped up her art supplies. Her dress rustled as she straightened up. She'd just started toward the sink when something out the window caught her attention. Jane stared down at the lawn, gawping. A moment later she was digging into her overnight bag. She found her phone, her fingers dialing without needing direction.

It rang only twice before Clair picked up. "Hey, stranger."

Jane thought Clair's voice sounded a little funny, but she brushed it off as an effect of the speakerphone. Jane didn't dare hold the phone up to her face, not in this much makeup.

"Oh my *god*, Clair," Jane said. She was back at the window by now, holding herself on her toes to see above the high sill. "We've created a monster."

This time, there was no doubt as to the smirk in Clair's voice. "That bad?"

"You'd think I was his single biggest PR hit. He's outside right now, talking to reporters! The ceremony's starting soon. Doesn't he have anything better to do?"

"In fairness, you *are* his single biggest PR hit."

"Not helping, Wife."

"Not meant to, Wife."

Jane sighed. She couldn't argue with Clair, though. In this version of reality, Jane's father had become mayor of Grand City, and when Jane and Clair had first adopted these new lives, she'd had no idea how the public would react to his daughter coming out as a lesbian. Apparently, the Jane Maxwell who was born here never had. Jane herself had never lived a life of public scrutiny before, not *really*. The media attention she got as the creator of a runaway-hit comics franchise was nothing compared to being the daughter of a prominent politician, where every choice was vetted by three different consultants and half a committee. And while Jane and Clair would go public *regardless* of what it would do to Mayor Maxwell's poll numbers, a part of Jane had hoped they'd take a hit.

They hadn't.

Instead, due to a quirk of fate, it turns out this world's politics ran slower than the already glacial pace of the one Jane was used to, and so the state only *just* voted to allow same-sex marriage the month after they arrived. The previous attempt—the one that had worked six years ago for Jane and Clair's world—had been shot down by a narrow margin, and the citizens of Grand City were not too happy about it. They'd been a cornerstone destination in the LGBT+ community for decades by that point, a city at the early forefront of the movement, and a huge part of Mayor Maxwell's voter base had been urging him to take a stronger stand on the issue.

And so: a gay daughter, a lesbian wedding. Mayor Maxwell's press office couldn't be happier.

"Just tell me it's worth it," Jane said, her voice a small echo in the enormous bathroom.

"Oh, Jane," Clair said softly. "You know it is."

It's true, she did. They both did. Memories of their first wedding, so different from this one, surrounded Jane as a familiar embrace.

Another knock hit the door, harder than any of Mrs. Maxwell's. "Jane!" called Francine, Jane's half of the wedding coordinator tag-team. "Photos! No more stalling!"

"Gotta go," Jane said to her phone. "The wolves are at the gate."

Clair laughed. "Okay, Xena. Slay a few for me."

"Will do," Jane said with a smile. "Love you to pieces."

"Love you back together."

A moment later, Jane was at the door. Instantly, Francine's attention ran across her, noting each tiny flaw. She tutted as she took in the few rumples Jane's escape had wrought. Jane hadn't put her contacts in after all, but really, what difference did it make if the world was a little blurry today? It's not like the wedding required her to read off a script, or drive a car, or fight crime.

Francine stepped Jane forward, yanking and tucking at the layers of fabric surrounding her.

"You can't just treat this dress like it's *nothing*!" Francine said.

Jane snorted. "Excuse me for thinking clothes can take me *sitting down* in them."

"This isn't *clothing*," Francine chided. "It's a *wedding dress*. You want to trash it later for pictures, fine—though the trend is passed by now, so don't go posting them on Instagram, okay? But in the meantime, will you please *be careful* with it?"

Jane rolled her eyes. Her gaze caught briefly with Mrs. Maxwell, who stood by biting down on a laugh. At least Jane didn't have to lie to *her*. The two women had long ago come to an understanding: Jane wouldn't pretend to be her *real* daughter, if Mrs. Maxwell didn't pretend to be Jane's *real* mother. Jane's *real* mother was still back on Jane's original world, and thanks to superhero techno-wizardry, Jane got to hop back and visit her several times a year. This woman, the one sculpted and maintained by diet coaches and plastic surgeons, merely had to put on the public face, to preserve the lie that Jane and this world's Jane Maxwell were one and the same.

So far, it had suited them both fine.

But that didn't explain why Mrs. Maxwell's soft gray eyes filled up as she looked upon Jane now.

"Oh, sweetie. You look gorgeous."

Jane shifted uncomfortably. Her dress was strapless, a decision Jane had *not* accepted easily, and now she wished she'd fought harder against it. She cleared her throat. "Thanks."

Thankfully, in that moment, Francine tutted again, breaking the mood, and Jane snatched the skirts out of her meddling hands.

"Let's get this over with," Jane said. She cut through the bedroom of the master suite, heading for the hall. The sound of preparations already met her ears—the whirl of hairdriers, the laughter of women, the squeal of the flower girls. The whole of the upper floors were bedrooms, and they'd all been taken over for the process. It had been underway for four hours already. As Jane walked by, she took stock of exactly how much was left to do. It had seemed endless at first, but now, somehow, they were down to the last bit of professionally styled hair and makeup, as Jane's not-exactly-a-sister sat in the chair of honor. A mirror of what might as well have been Jane's own face reflected back at her as Allison caught a glimpse of Jane, and Jane quickly looked away. There was no "Allison" on her original Earth, no sister at all in fact. And even though Allison knew about Jane's origins, and even though that *should* have made it easier, things . . . still weren't great between them.

"Smile!"

A camera flash went off in Jane's face as she ducked into the hall. She threw her arm up, but too late. Not that she needed to shield her eyes. Her superpowers, manipulating the electromagnetic spectrum, gave Jane the ability to see through almost any type of light or darkness—she could even look at the sun, though she still had to be careful not to keep it up *too* long. Still, it was important to maintain appearances.

A rainbow phone lowered itself, revealing the spiky pink hair and sharp angles of Blue Hamilton's grinning face. "Girl, don't look so happy," Blue said, studying the photo she'd taken. She swiped at the screen, and raised it up again. "Let's try this again. A real one this time!"

Jane stuck her tongue out.

Blue snapped the picture anyway.

"Close enough," Blue laughed, tucking the phone into the spring-green wristlet that matched her dress.

"Glad to be of service."

Blue threw her arm around Jane's shoulder. "Oh, sweetie, cheer up." She pinched Jane's cheek. "You've got your dream girl, *and* family support for your wedding. There is literally no reason for you to be grumpy today. It's not allowed."

Jane took a breath. That may be so, and yet . . . there was so much about the wedding that wasn't really *them*, this time. It was easy, being in the midst of all the production and the chaos, to forget about what it was all for.

"Okay," Jane said. "Okay, I'll *try*."

Blue grinned, cracking the gum in her mouth. "That's my girl."

Carefully, Jane leaned her cheek against Blue's shoulder. For the most part, Jane felt her double from this Earth had made terrible life choices—certainly becoming a supervillain and rejecting her version of Clair had been huge mistakes, as far as Jane was concerned—but one thing she'd gotten right was this: Blue Hamilton was a delightful best friend. One Jane could only hope wouldn't be too upset when she finally learned the truth of Jane's identity.

Because Jane *was* going to tell her.

Eventually.

Jane's mouth soured. She straightened up, putting some distance between her and Blue. It was easy to forget, in times like this, that Blue still thought she was the *other* Jane. So easy that, when Clair had convinced Jane a few months ago to finally launch a new comics publishing company, Jane had asked Blue to be her business partner, and the two of them had spent a good five hours geeking out over all the ideas they had, before Jane realized that *maybe* this wasn't such a great idea, given the circumstances.

But that was a problem for another day. Today, Blue was right:

Jane had no reason to be grumpy. Today, Jane had photographs to pose for, people to dance with, drinks to drink. Today, she promised herself, she would put all of it aside and just be a bride.

Today, she would marry Clair again, as genuinely as if it was the first time.

CLAIR DIDN'T TELL ANYONE ABOUT THE PRAYER CARD.

In fairness, she'd meant to tell Jane. When Clair's phone rang, Jane's laughing face appearing on Clair's screen, she'd felt a surge of relief. But then Jane had needed calming down, and how was Clair supposed to segue into something like that? *Oh, by the way, I got a funeral card implying I would die soon,* wasn't exactly a pick-me-up. It was just as well that Jane was called away for more bridal prep. They didn't need something so grim clouding their big day. Later, when everything was over, Clair could bring it up.

Yes. That was a plan, and all Clair needed to work on was putting it out of her mind. She stuffed the card into the back of her phone case, keeping it safe but out of sight.

Now, waiting for the ceremony to start, it would be a lie to say she'd forgotten about it. But it didn't dominate her thoughts anymore, so that was something. Clair sat in the limo, waiting for her signal, when her phone buzzed again. She glanced down. A selfie from Jane, cloistered away in her separate car, out of sight but not far away. The Jane in the photo was Hollywood-beautiful, barely recognizable: her skin smoothed out so much it could have been airbrushed, her brown hair curled and drawn into a thousand complicated loops, her makeup colored and styled in a way she'd never choose for herself. Even for her photoshoot with the *Grand City Times*, when she'd announced the launch of her comics company, she had never transformed herself so thoroughly. Clair studied the photo, trying to spot her wife behind all the false layers of glamour.

Isn't it bad luck for a bride to be seen before the wedding? Clair texted back. It was difficult to type in her wedding gloves—lace, but full-fingered, so her contact with the screen was patchy and kept dropping out as she swiped across the keyboard. At least they should keep her moderately protected from the impressions of the world today. Clair stared at the little bubble of her comment, waiting for a reply.

The poop emoji popped up on her screen, and Clair laughed.
For the GROOM to see the bride, Jane texted. *Aren't you lucky?*

The door to the car opened, Hannah's head ducking inside. "Ready?"

Clair nodded. She tucked her phone into the pockets she'd had specially tailored into her dress, and gathered her skirts as she navigated her way free of the limo.

Outside, the air smelled like jasmine and fresh-cut grass. A sea-kissed breeze fluttered by, toying with the trailing ends of Clair's veil and dress as Estella fussed once more, making everything perfect. Clair brushed the edges of her flapper-bob away from her cheek. The sky above was a glorious blue, the grass electric green in this unseasonably warm autumn. A string quartet played nearby, optimistic notes drifting overhead.

The first time around, Jane and Clair had rejected the idea of getting married at Charlotte's Landing. It was too expensive, too fussy, too staged, too much like Jane's father. But now, looking out toward the bluffs in the distance, the sparkling water beyond, Clair wondered if they'd been too quick to dismiss the idea. Not that she didn't enjoy their other wedding, held privately in a small gallery in the Grand City Museum of Fine Arts, but there *was* something nice about the formality here, the tradition. Clair followed Hannah to a spot behind a trellis, where her half of the wedding party was already assembled. She and Jane were going to appear at the end of separate aisles, coming straight across the front of the guests and meeting at the altar in the middle.

Nerves shot through Clair as she stole a peek through the vines. The crowd beyond the trellis was huge: even jammed in thick, they sprawled across the entire lawn. Visions of their guest lists and the RSVP stack flew through her mind, trying to put context to the mass in front of her. She sought out whatever familiar faces she could find. Donna and Simon were easy to spot, right up front, and Clair's chest loosened just a little as she watched Donna lean across Simon to whisper something to the oldest of Clair's younger brothers. Through some miracle, all four of them had made it. Even Adam, fresh out of boot camp and on special leave from the Navy—he'd arrived the night before, was leaving first thing in the morning, but he was *here*. The only person missing was Nicole, and she wasn't exactly family yet, not until her and Kevin's own wedding.

Unfortunately, the row of her siblings was about where the comfort ended. To Donna's other side, they'd seated Clair's Actual Grandma, and it just looked weird to see her and Donna together. Clair tried to remind herself that the seating choice was Donna's decision, but somehow it didn't help. With all the media attention, Donna had been doing everything she could to make their family seem normal next to the Maxwells, but it just didn't feel right to Clair. Aunt Amelia was two rows back now, despite the fact that she'd taken Donna in after Donna had gotten pregnant with Clair, and been way more of a grandmother than Actual Grandma ever was.

Beyond that . . . well, there was a reason they'd opted not to demarcate the guests down the middle, Hers and Hers. People from the department store where Donna worked were sprinkled into the crowd. But who was there to represent *Clair*? Even the coworkers Clair spotted from the museum, this version of them, had a longer history with Amy.

At least the rest of the Heroes of Hope were here. Clair spotted each of them in turn: Keisha, her husband and children in tow, was whispering sternly to one of the boys as her husband, Dominick, fussed with a spill on their youngest girl's dress; Devin sat by himself, his curls caught in a tight bun, his knee bouncing as he played with his phone and ignored the crowd around him; Marie had come alone as well, and was currently ducking her blond head as she fixed her makeup in a compact mirror; Tony had brought a date, a slim brunette who clung aimlessly to his side as he tried, and failed, to rub elbows with the chief of police. They were scattered throughout the rest of the guests, no two of them even so much as acknowledging the other. Not that it was likely for anyone to recognize them sans-uniform, outside of their superhero personas of Pixie Beats, Windforce, Granite Girl, and Rip-Shift, but it never hurt to be cautious. The last thing they needed was someone to draw comparisons, put two and two together.

The notes faded to nothing. The pause that followed was just long enough to get people's attention. Clair pulled herself back before anyone spotted her.

It was time.

Estella, hidden behind the trellis with Clair, gave a stiff nod and thumbs-up. The string quartet struck up a robust, joyous tune. A pair of young cousins, borrowed from Jane's family, set off, followed by Hannah, followed by Stacey.

There was nothing left to it, then, but to get married. A grin burst out of Clair. What did it matter, really, what guests were where? The most important person—the only important person—was waiting for her, just across the way. Clair clutched her flowers tightly in her gloved hands, and only good feelings worked their way through. The music swelled. Clair and Jane stepped into view, perfectly in sync.

That's when all hell broke loose.

SHE CAME FROM THE SKY IN A BOLT OF LIGHTNING.

It was a perfect image, a spread Jane couldn't have done better herself. A short panel along the top shows the waiting altar, its bright colors full of optimism, the officiant behind it drawn in hazy, undefined lines. A lightning bolt splits the page: it starts in the bleed, cutting through the idyllic "before" image, landing in the middle of the panel beneath. An explosion rips the scene apart as the altar bursts into a thousand shards. The officiant is knocked aside, the trellis is knocked aside. On the next page, a woman rises from the smoke. Chairs are scattered and overturned in the foreground, flung close enough to make the reader flinch. It's a chaos that contrasts against the woman's wickedly controlled grin as she unfolds herself and straightens to her full height.

The woman gleams. She is *designed* to be seen. Her look is crafted, something straight out of a comic—though not one of

Jane's. Her silver catsuit, complete with boob-window and spiked heels, and the dyed white hair tumbling porn-style across her shoulders, places her much more in line with the old-school drawings of Quantum Zero Comics's tent-pole franchises, the ones that have existed since the days of the Depression and World War II. This is a woman who *wants* the spectacle, who *wants* to be noticed. Even her face is unobscured, no masks or greasepaint or tattoos to hide her features. She commands the frame as she steps forward from the rubble.

"My, my," the lightning woman says, spreading her arms wide. "What a fine day for a wedding."

This was the last clear view Jane got. Strong hands yanked her back. Allison dragged Jane into a huddle rapidly forming behind a cluster of folding chairs. As if such a feeble fort would hold off a woman like that, but there was no time for Jane to argue.

Besides, they were hardly the only ones. Everyone, it seemed, had dove for the closest excuse for shelter, no matter how weak. They huddled among the mass of overturned chairs, their suits a wrinkled mess, grass stains already ruining their knees. One of the guests made the mistake of running, and the lightning woman thrust her arm out, a burst of electricity downing him before he'd even made it halfway back.

Jane's heart leaped to her throat. She craned her neck, trying to see through the mess—trying to see Clair—but Allison pressed down hard, protecting the bride. All Jane could get were fragments, the white legs of folding chairs cutting her world down to tight shots scattered across the page like the cut-out letters of a ransom note. Bouquets spilled across the front aisle. The arch of a flower girl's back as she curls in on herself. A paper program, trampled into the grass. A lost shoe.

Her father's face. Mayor Maxwell's eyes on her. Then down to the grass. They shut, just for a moment, as he gathers himself.

He rose to his feet.

"Paul!" Mrs. Maxwell shouted. Her arm shot forward, as if she could snatch his picture off the storyboard, but he did not stop. Fear and purpose carried him forward.

"Hey!" he said as he drew closer to the altar. "Hey, I'm talking to you!"

The lightning woman turned. One eyebrow cocked high, and she put her hands on her hips as she regarded Mayor Maxwell's approach. "Yes? Is there something you'd like to say, Sunny Jim?"

Stay out of it, stay out of it, Jane thought to herself, even though she knew there was no chance of that. She watched, cringing at Mayor Maxwell's bravery. Stupidity. Either/or.

Mayor Maxwell came to a stop. Squared his shoulders. No doubt he was hoping the guests were recording this. "I want you to leave my family alone." His voice boomed out, his speech voice.

The lightning woman smirked. "Do you, now?"

"Yes. Whatever grudge you have against me, they're innocent in—"

"You?" The lightning woman laughed. She threw her whole head back, a burst of laughter cracking once toward the clear blue sky. "Oh my, your ego really is everything they say, isn't it? Well. Hate to break it to you, Mr. Mayor, but I'm not here for *you.*"

She turned, and Jane's heart leaped as the lightning woman's attention affixed squarely on the huddled mass that was Clair.

"Oh, look!" the lightning woman said, glee dancing in her voice. Her grin cleaved the wedding in half. "Here comes the bride."

"No!"

Jane's muscles surged. Despite Allison's government-agency training, she spilled off Jane, thrown like water from a dog's back. Jane burst forward, a fury of white lace and pure rage.

"Don't you dare touch her!" she shouted. Jane reached the edge of the altar, bursting by Mayor Maxwell—who used the opportunity to slink back, toward Allison and the rest of the cowering guests. Jane's powers roared to life inside of her. She could feel the waves of the electromagnetic spectrum around her, the light and heat and wireless signals that blanketed the wedding. All of them would bend to her will, if she let them.

Should she let them, though? That was the question, the flutter of hesitation that stilled her just for an instant. There was no question she *would*, that she was *willing*—Jane would do anything, to keep from losing Clair again. But to do so, openly, in front of cameras and her entire Maxwell-level wedding spectacle would be admitting to the world who she was, who she went around the city dressed as, and there was no going back from that moment.

Jane pulled her hand back. Ready to strike.

This is when a lightness landed on Jane's shoulder, breezy as a butterfly.

"Stand down, Captain," a miniature Keisha, uniformed as Pixie Beats, said. "We've got this."

Jane's muscles twitched. She wasn't much for standing down, especially not since stepping into Captain Lumen's hero-red boots, but no sooner had Pixie Beats uttered her reassurance than a rip appeared in the air above the lightning woman. A tear in the fabric of reality, shimmering like a slice of heaven. Tony, as Rip-Shift, bedecked in black leather like something out of *The Matrix*, leaped through the rip, Marie right beside him. Her skin had hardened to stone, her camo pants and black tank top lending her a military bearing, and before Jane could even blink, Granite Girl landed the first punch against the lightning woman.

Pixie Beats leaped from Jane's shoulder, the vibrant colors of her tulle skirts enlarging in the middle of a twisting pirouette. She had a martial arts all her own, created from the ballet moves she'd learned as a child. Her foot connected with the lightning woman's side, painted sneakers sending the woman careening toward the edge of the platform. A burst of air coursed up from across the guest chairs, carrying a blue-and-white skydiving wingsuit, and Devin, as Windforce, joined the chaos now erupting at the altar.

Jane didn't wait for a second opportunity. Her hand found Clair's, and she yanked, hard, to one side, the both of them racing fast for the aisle.

The rest of the Heroes seamlessly divided themselves into two teams: Granite Girl and Pixie Beats kept the lightning woman busy in combat while Windforce and Rip-Shift cleared a swift path for Jane and Clair. A rip appeared in front of them and Jane didn't think, she just did. Leaping through, pulling Clair along with her. They tumbled out several dozen yards away, spilling onto an empty expanse of lawn just downhill from the wedding venue. The heel of Jane's shoe sank into the grass, and she tripped forward, into Clair's arms.

"Are you all right?" Clair asked, and Jane ran the back of her finger quickly across Clair's cheek, hoping it would carry her answer faster than any words could. She yanked off one shoe, then the other, as Rip-Shift appeared next to them, breathing hard.

"Don't stop!" he said as he sliced first one more tear in front of them, and then a second, acting as a connecting point, down on the beach. The smell of the ocean poured through, stronger down at the coast. Jane's hand clamped tight in Clair's, their pulses echoing madly between their palms. It was all that mattered.

The brides leaped forward as one, the flare of their white dresses stretching out like capes behind them.

CLAIR LANDED AGAINST THE BEACH WITH A FACEFUL of sand. For a moment, she had no concept of what was happening—her whole world flipped upside down, and now Jane's hand had slipped up to Clair's exposed wrist, and a rush of anxiety and adrenaline that wasn't her own flooded her veins. Clair was slipping, losing herself, when a thunderclap tore through her, as loud as the apocalypse. Clair blinked. Sand stung at her eyes, the briny smell of the ocean assaulting her. Jane was rolling away, springing into a defensive crouch. Their beautiful day disappeared, a low-rolling cloud layer obscuring the sky. Lightning split the air, the woman appearing on the beach as if stepping straight from a nightmare.

"Hello, Mindsight. Miss me?"

Electricity crackled around the lightning woman, sparking and dancing across her silver catsuit, her hair, jumping the shifting gaps between her fingers. Amy's memories stirred, deep in Clair's subconscious. Too far to reach. Clair pushed herself to her feet, swaying as her heel sunk into the uneven sand.

A flash of light burst from Jane's hand like a sunbeam, momentarily blinding the lightning woman. Now that they were on the beach, there was no one from the wedding to see what was happening, but fear still shot through Clair like a drug. "Back off!" Jane shouted. She threw herself in front of Clair, her body becoming a shield. Rip-Shift glanced at her, and Jane gave him the smallest nod.

He disappeared, leaping through a rip that sealed up neatly behind him.

"Jane, don't!" Clair pleaded in Jane's ear. She grabbed Jane's arm.

Lace did nothing to shield her from the intensity of Jane's emotions. Memory assaulted her. Clair's death, witnessed from the outside—she is looking down on herself, through Jane's eyes, as a grief more real and powerful than anything she could imagine cracks her down the middle. Clair, Jane. When accessing someone else's memory, the walls between them break down, and for a moment there is no difference. Sobs rack their joined chest, their shared heart breaking, as a pair of loving arms takes them by the shoulders. *Shh*, a voice says, motherly and loving, but it barely reaches them, it does nothing. There is nothing.

Clair staggered back, releasing her hold on Jane's arm. *Never again.* The memory of her death was gone, but a certainty remained charged in her system, a fierce protectiveness that manifested itself in front of Clair: her wife, in a wedding dress. In an instant, Clair knew that Jane would tear the world apart to save her, and what was one supervillain when faced against a determination like *that*?

Unfortunately, the lightning woman did not seem to be taking the hint. She blinked heavily, clearing Jane's blast from her vision. She was already laughing, even as she said, "Are you *kidding me*? Captain Lumen? Really? Of all people, you really chose *Captain Lumen*?"

"Leave her alone!" Jane shouted. Her arm was still raised, palm out in a defensive position. "You got a problem with her, you deal with *me*, is that clear?"

The lightning woman clucked her tongue. "Aw. That's touching. Stupid—but touching."

"Stop!" Clair grabbed Jane's arm again. She bit down against the wave of emotions. The beep of a hospital monitor. The stale air of the funeral home. Clair shoved through them, shoved Jane's arm aside. She wedged herself in front of Jane, even as Jane seized her waist, dragging her back. "What do you want from me?" Clair called over the struggle.

"Like you don't know."

And that's the thing—Clair *did* know, or . . . she should know. A restless feeling clawed through her, something struggling to burst free. She just . . . couldn't . . . quite . . . grab it. But it was *there*. Somewhere, beneath the layers of fog that shrouded Amy's memories. She knew. She knew.

It didn't matter if she knew. Within an instant, a breeze kicked up that had nothing to do with the ocean. Windforce was back, gliding in to land at Jane's side. A rip appeared beside him, Pixie Beats and Granite Girl spilling out in fast succession. Another rip, and Rip-Shift himself returned, his heavy boots landing hard in the sand. Jane pushed herself forward, the whole of the Heroes forming a human wall between Clair and the lightning woman.

She had to know she didn't stand a chance. Simple odds put her at a five-to-one disadvantage. And while *technically* Jane didn't have the same amount of training as the Jane from this world did, she'd fought harder than Clair had ever expected over the last year or so, making up for lost time until the difference was almost imperceptible. The Heroes of Hope had an impressive track record, and this woman had just kicked up a hornets' nest that she probably was not expecting.

Clair watched the calculations run rapid-fire behind the lightning woman's eyes. *Don't be stupid, please.* Could she see Clair, begging her to accept defeat?

The lightning woman looked right at Clair. Narrowed her eyes. She raised her hands in a disarming way, then reached through the boob-window of her suit, into her bra, and slid out something small. Another prayer card—she flicked it in the Heroes' direction, and it landed in the sand by Jane's feet.

"Don't think we're done, Mindsight," the lightning woman said. "You will pay for your sins before this is over." Then a burst of lightning collapsed her, and with a flash to the side, she was gone.

THE FIRST TIME AMY DIED, SHE WAS FIFTEEN YEARS OLD.

That's technically an exaggeration. Marie would point out later that they hadn't *died*, look, they'd gotten up and walked away from it, so what did you think happened, dummy? Tony and Devin and Cal piled on, bro-laughing it off, teasing Amy for being so "easily" scared. Even Jane was dismissive. Keisha was a little more sympathetic, rubbing Amy's arm as they walked their bikes back toward the main part of town in search of a pizza joint. None of them wanted to admit what had happened at the abandoned factory, when they'd gotten too close to the generator and the green orb that Amy would later swear they'd all seen, even as the rest of them denied its existence.

But Amy remembered. And so, years later, Clair remembered, as well. A nestle of thoughts and feelings, images that were and weren't her own. They lived just beneath her skin, never far out of reach. They came to her in chunks, like finding seashells on the beach. She remembered it now—the orb, the current that sent them flying, the cold breeze of death against their skin. The way they'd all forgotten. All except for Amy.

Amy was the one who'd spotted it, though, so maybe it made sense that she would be the one who remembered.

It had been late, their excursion a bust. No one wanted to admit how much time they'd wasted, biking outside the city limits, their legs pedaling hard, their heads full of visions of how cool they'd become if they found such a great place to hang out. They had arrived full of hope and enthusiasm, sure that this time, this place would put them on the social map.

And the building had looked so promising. An imposing slab against the night's sky. Giant white letters, half faded, the words *ChemWerks Industries* splashed across the brickwork like ghosts. They could see how awesome it could become, the kind of parties that could happen inside these walls. They abandoned their bikes at the road and raced through the tall grass, the shifting blades *shushing* against their shins. Without even meaning to, they ran in pairs: Keisha and Devin, Marie and Tony, Cal lagging behind. Jane and Amy, right in the middle of the pack. This was just before Jane's family moved her out of the city and up to snooty old Charlotte's Landing, just after the last girls-only sleepover the two of them would ever share. Jane's arm brushed against Amy's as they ran, heat and sparks seeming to trail up from wherever their skin touched. The need to tell Jane how she felt filled Amy to the brink, her emotions sloshing all over the trampled grass. She'd almost done it at the sleepover. Almost.

Instead, too soon, they reached the walls of the boarded-up factory. It didn't take long for them to realize there was no way inside, though accepting it took a little longer. The boys fought over who got to try breaking the lock, and Keisha gave the door a couple of good, solid kicks—her legs, toned from years of ballet lessons, were so strong—but nothing helped. The windows, if there were any, were too high to be reached, disappearing somewhere in the darkness above their heads.

Left with no other viable options, they turned back toward the road. Grumbles drifted between them, muttering about how nothing cool ever happens around here anyway. They were leaving Amy behind, their silhouettes disappearing into the dark.

That's when Amy had spotted it.

"Hey, guys!" she called, before she'd even figured out what she was looking at. "Over here!"

They didn't follow her, not at first. That was fine. She was used to her suggestions being overlooked, her opinions ignored. Only on the rare instances when Jane sided with her did anything change, the collective verdict always swaying toward her will. Jane was always their leader, even before she had anything to lead.

So Amy ran over by herself. She'd been taking one last look back, the factory a monument to their disappointment, when the faintest trace of green light caught her attention. She didn't know what she expected to find, but when she rounded the back of the building and the generator came into sight, this wasn't it.

This is when the group's collective memory grew murky, recalled only years later, and even then, only in fragments. A mysterious green orb, pulsing like something out of a science fiction movie. A feeling of weightlessness as Amy approached, all the hairs on her arm standing on end. The shouts from the rest of them, exclamations about how cool this was. They barreled past her, and then . . .

"It was just an electrical short," Keisha said to Amy later, after they'd woken up, after they'd hightailed it back toward the suburban outskirts of Grand City. By now, they'd reached their destination, and the bell overhead was already chiming as the horde of them crushed through the door to Grand Slice Pizza. Amy knew she should accept the group's explanation. It was logical, after all. And no one could really remember, exactly, what had happened before they'd been thrown back, before they'd all blacked out for a while. Before they'd died.

"Oh, for the last time, will you *drop it*?" Marie snapped. They were in front of the counter now, twirling on stools or running over to play the outdated arcade machine while they waited for their order. Grand Slice was little more than a hole in the wall, a dark room with a soda machine and an arcade, and a swinging door with a thick rubber mat leading back to the kitchens. Marie, choosing the stool just to reach the same height as the rest of them, glanced over her shoulder to make sure the pizza boy had gone into the back room so they wouldn't be overheard. When she turned back, she lowered her voice. "Look, we did not *die*. And anyway, do you really want to blab about it? What if Donna finds out, hmm? Or Simon?"

"It's a good point, Samey Amy," Cal said. He'd come up behind her, just a minute before, tickling her ribs as he made a zappy sound, which had caused Amy to yell and nearly burst into tears. "Come on, buck up. If any of our parents found out, then we'd *really* be dead."

"We should make a pact," Jane said. She swiveled outward from her spot at the counter, reaching her hand between them. "We don't talk about it again. Ever. To anyone."

Amy swallowed. The others wandered back over, slapping their hands easily on top of Jane's in solidarity. Jane looked over, right at Amy, her face an open dare.

What was Amy supposed to do? Even at fifteen, she was too in love to deny that face. She cast her eyes down, noting the scuffs on the toe of her Keds. But she shuffled over, dutifully, and she laid her hand on top of the others, dutifully, just long enough for them to pump them down and then fly up in release, their youthful fingers spread like they'd just tossed their vow into the depths of the universe for safekeeping.

So it was done, the deal was struck. Amy stuffed her hands into her pockets, and later, digging out some crumpled bills, she paid for her and Jane's share of the pizzas. The rest of them grabbed the boxes and ran out, leaving Amy to count up the money they'd thrown at her. The pizza guy frowned from across the counter, as Amy came up a dollar short and had to break into the emergency ten Donna always sent her out with.

Her hands were still shaking as she passed the money over. The pizza guy's skin was rough against her fingers, annoyance at their noisy group leaching off of him in waves.

"You want a receipt?" he asked, all but snorting out the question.

Amy shook her head. "No, thank you." She stuffed her hands

back in her pockets, turned to go. But just before she did, she hesitated. "I'm sorry for your loss, by the way."

The pizza guy frowned at her. "What?"

Amy looked up. "Your mom," she said simply. "That must really hurt."

"How the hell did you know about that?"

"I—" Amy started, but then her words died in her throat. She stared at the pizza guy for a long moment, neither of them speaking. He was wearing a stained T-shirt, Grand Slice's logo painted over the breast. He was maybe twenty, if that. She knew nothing about him, had never met him before, barely exchanged words. "I—" she started again, as the door chimed open behind her.

"Hey, Ames!" Devin called, a hint of his repressed Puerto Rican accent slipping through. "Come on, we're hungry!"

"I'm sorry," Amy muttered. She turned away, her cheeks burning in embarrassment, as she ran to catch up with her friends.

"OKAY, SO WHAT DO WE KNOW?"

Jane blew into the room, a whirl of white lace and barely controlled fury. The question was out before she was even through the door, projecting ahead of her as a herald of her arrival.

The rest of the team looked up. Jane and Clair were the last to arrive. It had taken ages for the police to get to the venue, ages for them to appear satisfied enough with their statements to let them go, ages for Jane and Clair to escape the clutches of concerned friends and family. The others had disappeared fairly quickly, and so Jane had assumed they'd already begun an investigation. She strode over to the old conference table, slapping her palms down on the surface as she towered at the head of the group. The table—the whole room—was smaller than Jane had imagined it, smaller than she'd drawn it in her old comics. Not that Jane had drawn the original headquarters in Charlotte's Landing often; only in backstory issues, and even then, not in excessive detail. When she'd first arrived on this world, she'd been shocked to learn it actually existed.

It was still strange to think about, even now. The way Jane's comics had been *real*, all along, running silently just one step to the side of her reality. Clair could remember parts of it, through Amy, but all Jane had to go on was the backstories of her own comics, reimagined to include herself in their midst. She tried to picture it: how she'd have sought out the rest of them, one by one, the childhood friends who had shared a near-death experience, now scattered to their own lives; how she must have known they were all starting to exhibit odd symptoms, flashes of power they couldn't explain; the vision she gave them, the idea that they could become something greater than themselves.

In the early days, in the comics and reality both, they met in the subbasement of the Maxwells' mansion in Charlotte's Landing. Once the nuclear bunker of a wealthy arms dealer, the rounded cement tunnels and reinforced walls provided a perfect space to experiment with the abilities that none of them really understood at the time, much less knew how to control. She could practically see the ghosts of their younger selves, as the Heroes fell into old patterns—Tony crashed in a pile of beanbag chairs stacked high in the corner, Devin and Keisha on a ratty old couch along one wall, Marie pulled up to the table, already at work. Though these days, Marie was seated with an array of tablets spread out around her rather than tapping furiously at the clunky old computers that had filled Jane's drawings.

Jane didn't like coming here, much preferred their proper headquarters back in the city, but practicality in this matter would always win out over Jane's personal distaste. She looked around at the rest of the Heroes, gathered in their rumpled formalwear like prom-goers at the end of the night.

"Well?" Jane asked, annoyance already flooding through her. She snapped her fingers repeatedly, both hands together. "Come on, there has to be something about this woman in a database somewhere—FBI, ARRO, GCPD, something. Let's have it. What are we dealing with?"

"Honestly?" Devin said. "We don't know."

Jane shook her head. "No. That's not acceptable. There's always data to work with. What about the prayer card she dropped? That's got to be a start."

"Not really," Marie said. She tapped one of her tablets. "Her prints aren't a match for anything in the system. The card itself . . . it's pretty standard. Paper and ink are common brands, could have been printed anywhere—even a home computer."

"So then we thought, okay, what if we approach this from a different angle?" Devin added. "Maybe the answer isn't in the *who*, but the *why*. Fact is, the attack was targeted—it's not like she just crashed a random wedding. That means there's a reason."

"We went over the footage from the attack," Marie said. She swiped her tablet, throwing projections into the air. Shaky video footage, scoured from hacked phones and social media accounts, filled the space above the conference table. "Trying to see if she said anything, did anything, that might give us some clue as to her motive."

"Yeah, but that doesn't make *sense*," Jane said. She put her hands on her hips, classic Captain Lumen. "There's no reason to target Clair. She has literally *no* enemies."

"Not Clair," Devin said. He stood up, laid down the prayer card on the conference table. Grit fell from the cardstock, shimmering like glitter. "Look at the name."

Jane didn't want to look at the name, didn't want to look at the card at all. She made herself do it anyway, her eyes immediately falling on the italic script along the bottom. *Amy Ophelia Sinclair.*

Jane's throat went dry. "Amy . . ." Something uncomfortable slithered over Jane's skin, and she hurriedly looked away. She was acutely aware, suddenly, of Clair's presence somewhere behind her, hovering at the edges of the room like a shadow. Clair hadn't said anything since they'd left the wedding venue.

Keisha, still on the couch, cleared her throat. She was fiddling with the end of one of her tight braids, a sure sign she was anxious. "Actually, it's got to be *Mindsight* that has the hit out. That's the name the woman used. And I hardly think Amy *or* Clair has done anything as themselves that would put her in the crosshairs of a person like that." She glanced to the corner, a soft smile on her face. "Unless you have a secret life none of us know about?"

"Okay, whatever," Jane said, waving this idea off before Clair had to deign herself to answer the joke. "It doesn't matter *who* they intended to target. They're after Clair now."

Sighing, Tony unfolded himself from the stack of beanbags. "Look, with respect, I think it *does* matter. I'm going to say it, even if no one else will. If *Mindsight* is being targeted, and it brought this woman to *Amy*, or Clair, then it's safe to assume we're all in danger."

"He's right," Marie said. "If she can find out Amy's identity, it won't be long before the whole team is compromised."

"You think someone wants to take out the rest of us?" Keisha asked.

"You don't?"

It's a question none of them wanted to answer, not even Jane. She turned, hoping to catch Clair's reassuring eye, but Clair was looking at the hovering images from the attack, studying them as if there was some deeper truth hidden in the set lips of the lightning woman's face.

Jane's chest tightened. Clair's wedding dress was torn along the skirt, the whole thing covered in bits of sand and flecks of grass. A green stain marred the knee, but nothing—*nothing*—took away from her beauty. Her Roaring Twenties bob may be windblown, her eyes may have been glassy with fear, her lips red from being chewed, but she was still a perfect picture of a bride, still *Clair*. Jane looked at her, and all she saw was the way her face had been, in the moment of her rebirth. The way Clair's smile had slid, slightly lopsided, into place. The recognition that had sparked in Clair's eyes. It was how Jane had known she was really back. The look of a wife.

There was nothing Jane wouldn't do now to keep her safe. She turned back to the table, and the nervous faces of the Heroes. "Fine. So we take her down."

"Oh, brilliant!" Marie clapped her hands together. "Golly, why didn't *we* think of that? Seriously, did . . . did nobody else think of that? *I* sure didn't think of that!"

"Cut the crap, Marie," Jane said. "I know it won't necessarily be easy, but the bottom line is our objective is simple. We need to track down the woman who attacked us."

"Yeah, but we *can't*," Marie said. She shrugged, even as she tapped at her tablet. "Weren't you listening? There's just *nothing* on her. Facial recognition can't even find a hit on traffic cams. It's like she's a ghost."

Clair cleared her throat. "I can find her."

All the attention of the room jumped toward her, pinning Clair in place. She straightened up, brushing some semblance of order back into the skirt of her wedding dress.

"I can find her," she repeated.

"You mean with the prayer card?" Keisha asked. She shook her head, her braids dancing down her back. "Clair, I just don't think there's enough emotional connection for you to trace her."

"I don't mean with the prayer card, or my powers," Clair said. "I mean *I* can find her."

"Clair," Jane said, "what are you talking about? We don't even know who she is."

A fragile smile tugged at Clair's lips. She took a breath, turning to look straight at Jane. "Yeah, but that's the thing. I *do* know her. Her name is Electric Fury, and I think . . . I think she's my lover."

"THERE'S NOTHING IN HERE ABOUT MINDSIGHT HAVING A LOVER."

The journal landed on the bed, right beside Clair's legs. She glanced down at it, then up at Jane. It was the most recent one available, though it would have been better if they still had the one Clair was writing in up until the day of her accident. But that one had been destroyed in a confrontation with UltraViolet, so they had to settle for the next best thing. Boxes of journals filled the living room, taken from Jane and Clair's apartment in their old world, locked away in storage since the move. Jane had just spent the last six hours pouring through them, searching for . . . something. Evidence, maybe. Next steps.

From the looks of it, she wasn't having much luck.

Clair looked at the journal. A velvety green cover, the image of a tree embossed over the front. Raised branches spread across the upper half, roots across the lower. Years ago, when Clair had bought it for herself, she'd liked the symmetry of it, the way both roots and branches mirrored each other. She thought it was deeply meaningful.

Now she just wanted to burn it, burn the whole pile of journals. She used to record her dreams, every morning as soon as she woke up—or even in the middle of the night, padding out to the living room so as not to disturb Jane, if a dream was particularly vivid. Sometimes they were just dreams, but more often than not they were images of this place, this life. Amy's world, bleeding through into Clair's. Whenever Jane was stuck on her comic, Clair would tell her pieces of her dreams, and the two of them would hash out a storyline that matched up disturbingly similar to what Clair had written down. It wasn't until long after Clair's death, after Jane got swept up into this parallel world, with these people from her comics who were somehow real, that Jane worked out the connection which must have always existed between Amy and Clair.

Clair didn't write down her dreams anymore. Usually, she didn't even remember them. Jane had never questioned her on it, but that afternoon, after getting home from what should have been their second wedding, Jane had dug the boxes out and spread the journals across the living room floor. She wanted Clair to look through them, and Clair had asked her, in the way only a wife could, if Jane would do it instead. Clair didn't think she could face it.

Only now, as Jane took her glasses off and rubbed at her tired eyes, Clair wondered if maybe it was a burden she should have shouldered after all. Jane's hair was still sprayed and pinned, though large chunks of it were coming loose, tumbling in exhausted waves across Jane's shoulders. Her eyes were red, and it was only just occurring to Clair that Jane had been crying.

"Jane?"

"Nothing," Jane said, answering the next question, the one Clair hadn't quite spoken yet. She shoved her glasses back on and went over to the dresser as if everything was normal, as if this was any other night, and it was time to get ready for bed.

Clair slid her ring back on. While Jane went through the journals, Clair was supposed to have been trying to dig up more of Amy's memories, but she'd come up oddly empty. Like the thoughts didn't *want* to be found. So Clair had spent the last half hour turning her ring over in her hands instead, wondering how it was that something so small had managed to encompass something as big as her entire life. Some days, it didn't seem possible. Like this was all some sort of elaborate trick.

But that didn't matter now. She hauled herself up, knee-walking across the mattress. Clair did not reach out to Jane, did not draw her close, though she wanted to. But they'd made a pact, in the first few days after Clair's rebirth—she was not allowed to read Jane when Jane was upset, not without express permission. And so Clair was forced to stifle her instincts, to keep a cold distance from her crying wife. She balled her fists, because what else could she do?

"Talk to me," Clair said. The only thing she could offer.

Jane shook her head. "It's nothing. It's stupid. We should just go to bed."

"I don't care if it's stupid. I want to hear what's bothering you."

"You really don't."

"I really do."

Only the silence of Jane's back answered.

Clair sighed. She wanted to do this, but she didn't want to do this. The weight of Jane's distress threatened to drag Clair down, the last anchor needed to tether her to the seabed of the second worst day of her life. "Jane, please. I can't help you if I don't know what's wrong."

"Don't you, though?" she asked, as she finally, finally turned back around. "You really can't figure it out?"

A test. Clair felt Jane's uncertainty, even from here—nothing to do with Clair's powers, everything to do with her heart. There was weariness in Jane's eyes, and judgment, too.

Could Clair figure it out?

Of course Clair could figure it out. Clair has been in love with Jane all of their lives. Clair had studied Jane's face for so long that she held two doctoral degrees in Jane's moods. Clair could tell Jane's emotions by her breath, or . . . she used to be able to. A cold seized Clair's heart, as she tried to remember the last time she surprised and infuriated and delighted Jane all at once, by knowing what she wanted before she realized she wanted it. Had it happened, even once, since she'd "come back"? Suddenly Clair wasn't so sure.

Time was passing. Jane was still watching.

Clair made room for her on the bed.

It was a sly tactic, and one Clair wasn't at all sure would work: she moved the journal aside, smoothing out the blanket in its place. The hours Jane spent with the journals had saturated them with her feelings, thick as an old lady's perfume.

Ordinarily, Clair would never stoop to such a level. Since gaining Amy's powers, Clair had fought hard to respect Jane's privacy, especially because it was so easy for her to invade it. When Jane's dreams became Clair's dreams, when Clair accidentally answered an unspoken question after borrowing Jane's shampoo. When the two of them watched TV, Jane tucked under Clair's arm, and a seemingly random moment onscreen would bring up a memory of Clair's own funeral with such intensity that even she began to weep.

But Clair needed to get this *right*. Clair Maxwell, the original one, the Clair who'd poured her soul into her wedding ring to be reborn here, the one she hoped she still was now, would get this *right*. So Clair pushed the twinge of guilt aside, and allowed Jane's feelings to soak in through her skin.

Jane sank heavily into the mattress. She curled on her side, her knees drawn up. A good three inches still separated her and Clair, a distance Clair couldn't help but feel had to do with more than just her empathic powers.

"You're jealous," Clair said.

The truth was so much more complicated than that, but yes, this much Clair knew. Jealousy burned hot through the cover of her journal, leaving a vaguely metallic taste.

"No," Jane mumbled as she turned her face in to a pile of blankets, but this was a lie. Clair didn't even need her powers to tell her that.

A sick feeling twisted up Clair's stomach. "Jane—"

"How much do you remember?"

Jane spat this question out fast, like she'd been chewing it for ages and was *finally* ready to be rid of the taste of it. Clair wished the asking would have brought Jane the peace she obviously hoped for, but it didn't. Her whole body was rigid, braced for an answer she wouldn't like.

"Nothing," Clair said. The truth. "It's more an impression than a memory."

"But you're sure it happened?"

Yes. "No."

Jane rolled over. On her back, her mussed-up wedding hair haloing on the blankets beneath her. Her face was carefully blank as she asked, "You want to try that answer again?"

Guilt propelled Clair to her feet. "This is ridiculous," she said as she paced to the closet and back again. "I didn't do anything."

"No?" Jane sat up. "Only you, and only me. That's how it's always been, Clair."

"And that's how it still is!"

"Except you *remember* someone else! You can fight it as much as you want, but on some level you remember. Which means it happened."

Clair crossed her arms. "*You* slept with Cal."

"That wasn't *me*," Jane said, disgust and insult strewn all over her face. "That was the *other* Jane."

"And this was Amy!"

"Oh, like there's a *difference*!"

Clair's breath disappeared.

Jane's regret swept in, immediate and obvious. She put her hand to her mouth, like she couldn't believe what she'd just said. Perhaps she couldn't. She had told Clair about her time in the parallel universe before all of this, how confusing it was for her to interact with the "other" Clair, the Clair that was still Amy. Sometimes even Clair got flashes of it. Amy's memory of seeing Jane. Silent heartbreak, and guilty wild hopes.

"Clair—"

Clair held up her hand. "Don't."

"I didn't mean—"

"I know."

Did she, though?

Did Jane?

* * *

DONNA ANSWERED HER PHONE ON THE SECOND RING.

"Clair?"

"I don't want to ring the doorbell," Clair said. "Can you let me in?"

"Can't you just use the key?"

"It's not where you leave it."

"What do you mean?" Donna said. "I put it back under Mr. Stubbs this morning."

Oh. Of course, the emergency key could easily be in a different spot in this reality. In the one Clair remembered, Donna stopped using Mr. Stubbs (a hideous lawn ornament Clair had made in pottery class in the fifth grade) when Steve accidentally ran over him with the mower, the first summer he was old enough. At least, he claimed it was an accident.

Phone still to her ear, Clair glanced over. The lawn was dark, a silent pool of grass, but there in the moonlight was the peak of Mr. Stubbs's hat. "I'll be right in."

"I'll be right down."

Clair hung up, and slid the phone into the pocket of her jacket. It was too cold out for the thin layers she was wearing, but everything else carried emotions she did not need right now. This jacket was relatively new, a slip of a raincoat that folded up into a pocket-sized bundle, bought at the checkout of the grocery store on a whim. It meant nothing to anyone.

Her feet padded silently over the damp lawn. Traces of her youngest brother's anger pricked Clair's toes as blades of grass worked their way around her sandals. She squatted down in front of Mr. Stubbs.

He was supposed to be a rabbit, a rabbit in a wizard's hat, though there had been considerable debate in the years since then about what he *actually* looked like, because nothing in nature is that lumpy and misshapen. Clair picked him up and flipped him over, where a tiny fold in his base—a flaw, the clay turned over when it wasn't supposed to—created the perfect hiding spot for a key to tuck into. Even now, decades later, the chipped paint of his back was infused with motherly pride, and it made Clair's throat close up as she hastily set him back on the lawn. She held the key in the grip of her knuckles, pinched between the knitted fabric of her fingerless gloves.

Inside, she was greeted by both of her parents. They came out of the kitchen together, Donna draped in a thick Snuggie, her hands tucked into oven mitts, Simon holding a spatula. He pointed to the kitchen, an unspoken question, as Donna shuffled forward, arms outstretched, kicking the length of Snuggie aside with each zombie step. Clair nodded at her father as her mother embraced her in a carefully padded bear hug.

Jane and Clair shared a whole host of similarities, but here was perhaps one of the sharpest differences: Jane made a very clear delineation between her Real Life and this parallel world they'd adopted for themselves. In her view, this world's Paul and Olivia Maxwell were *not* her parents, and even Jane and Clair's friends, even the Heroes, were not the counterparts the two of them grew up knowing. Clair understood Jane's perspective, and she did not blame her for needing the separation—for one thing, Jane's life actually *was* different here. Between her parents' divorce never happening in this reality, and the presence of a sister she never used to have, it only made sense to Clair that Jane would form a solid line of demarcation to help her cope.

No such line existed for Clair.

Clair used to worry it was only because she still had Amy's memories that this "version" of Donna and Simon were familiar to her, when they shouldn't be. But it ran deeper than that. Clair and Donna had been a team for the first nine years of Clair's life, Them Against The World, and nothing, not even a parallel reality, could change the way Clair felt about her mother.

So both Donna and Simon knew the whole story. The super-powers, Amy had told them about when the Heroes of Hope first formed, but even this, even Amy's fate, Clair's rebirth . . . Clair had never considered keeping it a secret from them. She was nervous about broaching the subject, more nervous than she'd been since she and Jane came out, worried that her parents would never be able to look at her the same way again. That they'd always see Clair as a scrappy version of the daughter they used to know, never truly *theirs*.

They didn't. And if Clair ever harbored any doubts, Donna and Simon dispelled them that night.

Neither one of them asked a single question. Simon made Clair a grilled cheese with tomato and basil, which Clair ate on the couch, curled into the padded fold of Donna's arm. The oven mitt stroked the top of Clair's head, over and over, as she finished her sandwich, as she cried in silence, as she drifted off to sleep.

Clair didn't remember falling asleep, but it was the only explanation. One moment, her thoughts swirled through her mind, shapeless and murky, only the pillow of her mother's lap to soothe her. The next, Clair jerked awake. The living room was silent around her; she felt her parents' decision to go back to bed, clinging to Clair's cheek from the cushion where Donna had been sitting. Clair sat up, momentarily confused, as the day tried to reorder itself in her mind.

She was not alone.

Clair knew this, the way a child knows there are monsters beneath her bed. Cold dread, stealing her breath. Her ears, pricked for the slightest sound. Her skin tingled, hyperaware.

"What's the matter?" a voice said, light and mocking. "Afraid of the dark?" Clair recognized the voice, but did not accept it.

She squeezed her eyes shut instead. Maybe she was still dreaming.

"Now, that would be convenient," the voice said. As if she could hear Clair's thoughts. "Of course I can hear them," she continued. "They're *mine*, after all."

"No they're *not*," Clair said, aloud, as she opened her eyes. She was not at all surprised to see the figure before her, leaning against the mantle of the fireplace as if she belonged.

Well, she *was* surprised. But not as much as she should have been.

Amy Sinclair gave her a dry smirk.

She looked exactly like Clair. Which, obviously, but—*exactly like* Clair. The clothes she was wearing, the smudged makeup from crying, the bit of Clair's bangs that Clair could feel sticking up from her forehead. She reached up, touching them. The hairs were stiff from the hairspray of her abandoned wedding.

A dozen possibilities dangled before Clair, some more defined than others. Another parallel world? Time travel? A shapeshifter? Delusions spun by an Enhanced? Perhaps she was just plain crackers—that answer would have calmed her more than the larger explanation, the one sitting heavily in the forefront of Clair's mind: that Amy was telling her the truth.

That these thoughts really were hers.

"Of course they are. Why would I lie about a thing like that?"

"How are you even *here*, though?" Clair didn't want to ask, didn't really want to know, but was there any point in hiding from her?

Amy shook her head. "Oh, Clair, Clair, Clair. Don't you know? I'm *always here*. You're living in *my* mind, remember? What? Did you think I would just *go away*?"

"No, but . . . you . . ." Now Clair shook her head, a perfect mimic, call and repeat. "Amy, you died."

"So did you."

"Yes, but *you died*. You absorbed the essence of me, and you *died*."

"Yeah," Amy said. A soft smile toyed at her face. "That's what I thought, too."

A dull pain began to drill into Clair's temples. She leaned over, massaging her forehead. Trying not to be sick.

"This isn't possible," Clair moaned into her knees. "You're not really here. You're a hallucination. You have to be."

"'Fraid not." Amy pushed herself away from the fireplace and came around until she was right in front of Clair, and sat down on the coffee table. Close enough to touch. Clair watched Amy's knees, inches from hers. Identical to hers.

Hers. Not hers. Nothing in this body was Clair's, nothing in this reality was Clair's—except for Jane. And the ring around her finger, tucked beneath the weave of her glove. Clair balled her fist, holding it tight.

Amy saw the motion. Tentatively, she reached out, and Clair stiffened as she approached. What would happen if Amy touched her? Did she have any kind of substance and form? And then, a still more horrifying thought: the ring gave Clair life, but likewise, could it take it *away*?

Clair jerked her hand out from Amy's reach. Clutched it against her chest, cradled by her other hand.

"Don't you dare touch that."

Amy rolled her eyes. "You don't think it could really be that easy, do you?"

"I think we'll let that remain a mystery."

"Fine," Amy said. Then, before Clair could even blink, Amy grabbed Clair's chin. She pinched down hard, so hard that Clair winced, as she held Clair's face inches from her own. Eyes of steel bored down on Clair, flooding her with terror—but whose? "Don't think for an instant this is over, *Clair*. I will get my life back, if it's the last thing I do."

Clair cried out as Amy released her, shoving her against the back of the couch. Clair's hands flew out, her heart thundering in her ears. She scrambled into the corner of the couch, instinct making her flee, but when she glanced up a second later, Amy was gone.

The papers on the coffee table laid undisturbed. As if Amy had never been there at all.

5 A.M.

A square narrative bubble, hanging in the upper left corner of the panel, marks the time. The panel itself is filled with nothing but Jane's hand, finger extended, overlapping lines indicating motion as she rapidly pounds the doorbell. Large, shrill letters of various sizes fill the background, a repeating string of *ding-a-ding-a-ding-a-ding-a-ding*, until, in the next panel, the door is ripped open, and Clair's sleep-dazed face fills the frame.

Jane threw herself at Clair. Arms wrapped tight, Jane's face pressed unabashedly into the exposed skin of Clair's neck. Jane held nothing back, as she let Clair absorb the feelings she was too jumbled and scared and ashamed to express. She tried to picture everything she'd been sitting with all night: sour memories of the way Jane had handled things, mingling with images of Clair in her hospital bed, mingling with memories of their first wedding, their real wedding, mingling with the first morning after Clair's rebirth. The memories are shaded by the depth of a thousand ordinary days, and Jane tried to wrap her love around Clair even harder than her arms.

What was jealousy, in the face of this? That was the question that had haunted Jane, all night, that had propelled her here before dawn had even broken.

"I am so, so sorry," Jane whispered. Unnecessary, perhaps, with everything Jane let spool out into Clair, but she needed to *say* it. "I love you so much."

When Clair's arm unfroze and gripped hard around Jane, Jane knew she'd been forgiven. "I love you, too," Clair whispered, and Jane laughed, giddy with a relief that weakened her knees. They rocked together in the open doorway, laughing and crying, until a voice broke in from the stairs behind Clair.

"What is *wrong* with you two?"

Clair's youngest brother, Mike, stood on the landing halfway down the steps. Scrawny legs stuck out from a pair of gym shorts, a Star Wars T-shirt self-consciously covering the lack of hair on his fifteen-year-old chest. He blinked sleep from his eyes even as he scowled at Jane and Clair, their early-morning ruckus.

Before either of them could answer, Donna appeared behind him, saving them the trouble. One glance at the doorway, and a knowing smile crept up her face. "Go back to bed," she told Mike, ruffling his hair as if he was still five. Mike scowled, grumbled something indecipherable as he shoved past his mother. His oversized feet thumped heavily on the stairs and the curl of his hair, mussed from sleep and motherly affection, waved goodbye as he disappeared.

"I'll leave you be," Donna said a second later, following the path of her son.

A silence fell in their wake, fragile as a baby bird that's tumbled out of its nest. Jane and Clair unhooked from each other, the polite distance that was necessary these days reasserting itself between them. Jane hated that distance, but she hated the imbalance that being close now created even more.

Clair stepped aside, offering a tentative smile. "Breakfast?"

she asked, motioning for Jane to come in. Even if Jane hadn't just opened herself up like that, it would have been safe to assume she hadn't eaten since last night.

They went back to the kitchen, where a frying pan and a spatula rested to the side of the stove, and Clair covered both of them with a towel as if she didn't want to see them. Jane sat at the table, feeling uncomfortably like a guest, as Clair began the tidy rituals of breakfast.

"Clair . . . ," Jane said a minute later. Clair's back was turned, busy cracking eggs into a bowl. Her hair caught the slant of light from the window, deep brown with lighter brown highlights that only showed up in the morning sun. Jane's heart ached. It was a bad time for this conversation, but it wasn't going to get any better by putting it off, either.

Clair's shoulders stiffened. She took a step to the side, tossing the eggshells. "You don't have to say it. I saw what you're thinking about. And you're right, I probably should get tested. I can't guarantee how careful Amy may or may not have been."

"It's probably something we should have done from the beginning," Jane said, rushing through the words. "Just as a matter of course. I don't know why we didn't think to."

"I do," Clair said. She'd washed her hands off while Jane was talking, and now she turned around, towel in hand, as she dried each finger one by one. Her gloves sat on the counter beside her, untouched. She studied Jane for a minute before she spoke, and when she did, her words were as considered as if they'd been scripted in a speech bubble. "It's because you can't imagine any circumstances where I'd want to be with someone else. Even if it wasn't really me. Even if you weren't really you."

Denial rose in Jane's throat. The words "no, you're wrong," or "it's not that" fought their way toward her mouth; who would get there first? She washed them down with a glass of water Clair had deposited in front of her as she'd been getting out their breakfast supplies. That was the problem with having a spouse who'd known you since you were both young—so much time to learn how you tick, so much insight into the uncomfortable workings of your subconscious.

"Can you blame me?" Jane said instead, a moment later, after she'd wrestled with her indignance and fought her way back to a place of maturity. "I mean, could you? If you were me?"

Clair's phone pinged. "I don't have to imagine it," she said as she pulled it from her back pocket. The kitchen was still semidark, and the phone lit up the underside of Clair's face as she swiped at the screen. She didn't look up as she spoke. "Jane rejected Amy, remember?"

"I'm not sure that's a fair assessment of—"

"Hang on," Clair said. "It's from Donna." Clair reached into the cabinet near the sink, retrieving the remote for a small TV in the corner. Her phone rested on the table near Jane, and Jane twisted her head to read it:

JIM, channel 86, NOW.

Jane's lips curled back in disgust. "JIM," the terrible acronym for GCN's *Jillin' the Morning!* news show, practically gave Jane hives. The few times she'd been forced to watch it were torturous —how could *anybody* be that perky and passionate to argue at five in the morning?—but Donna was a devote follower of lead anchor Jill Jones.

"Do we have to?" Jane asked, but Clair had already found the station. She turned the volume up, the green bar expanding along the bottom of the screen.

"*—have to ask ourselves what's being* gained *by the switch,*" one of her co-hosts was saying. "*Listen, I wasn't the biggest fan of Bryson, either, but this guy? Who is he? What's he ever done for Grand City?*"

"*I think he's damn cute,*" another one added. The youngest, blondest, and probably a guest, now that Jane stopped to look. She didn't seem familiar.

Jill Jones raised a pen—her signature move, her signal for quiet. "*Let's let the viewers decide. Gus?*"

A video clip took over, labeled from the evening before. Jane rolled her eyes, already turning away, as their longtime senator, Bob Bryson, leaned in too far over his outdoor podium. The bay sparkled behind him, the breeze lifting the edges of both his white hair and his red-blooded-American tie. *BRYSON WITH-DRAWS,* read the scroll-text along the bottom, but even that wasn't enough to hold Jane's interest.

"Can he even do that?" Clair asked. She was still watching, her arms folded over her chest, the remote hanging loose in one hand. "The primary's over, but—there's still the general. I didn't think—"

"Who cares?" Jane muttered as Bryson droned on from the TV. Though even she knew this was a game-changer. She pinched the bridge of her nose, imagining the jubilation that must have been flowing through Mayor Maxwell's office last night. No wonder Mrs. Maxwell kept trying to call her—they'd been looking at an uphill slog, her father against the Republican juggernaut that was Bryson. But now . . .

"I know a lot of you are going to be disappointed—even angry—at me for it. But I urge each and every one of my supporters: do not give up hope. For today I step down, but a new voice is rising to take my place. A younger voice. A stronger voice. A voice I am confident will pick up my banner, and champion to make sure that you"—Jane glanced up as here Bryson pointed to the audience and the camera—*"are heard in Congress. That* your *concerns, not the liberal media, not big government, not PC handwringers, will be brought to the floor."*

"Hang on," Clair said, "is he giving his spot to someone *else*?"

Jane could only manage a shrug.

"Is that even allowed?"

"Shh," Jane said as the roar of the audience died back down and Bryson continued.

"My friends . . . my neighbors . . . You deserve a stronger champion than I, to continue this fight. You deserve fresh blood. You deserve a hero. A symbol. In fact, more than anything, I know what you really need . . . is a Good Man."

Could Jane sense, somehow, what was coming, even then? The hairs on the back of her neck raised as the camera panned back, widening the shot. The glint of blond hair and the flash of a smile catch the light as Bryson's replacement bounds up onto the stage beside him.

Cal Goodman waved to the assembled crowd. *"Thank you!"*

Clair's hand went to her mouth, but all Jane could do was stare.

More than a year they'd been searching for Cal. Ever since UltraViolet's defeat at the Grand City Museum of Fine Arts.

He'd betrayed the rest of the Heroes by siding with Jane's "evil twin," but in the midst of everything that went down in the end, had managed to slip away. Since then, the Heroes have had every ear to the ground, every favor called in—not to mention an elaborate spy algorithm discreetly running on *several* government databases. So far, nothing. Not a whisper, not a ping.

He went to ground so hard that it was difficult to believe he'd ever lived at all.

Now here he was.

Waving.

Grinning.

Cal took Bryson's hand and raised them together, like running mates doing a victory wave. Bryson looked across at him, the way a proud father might regard his son on his wedding day.

"Thank you!" Cal said again. He turned, just as the screen froze, the replay finished, his eyes catching the camera. They locked in, piercing straight through the lens, straight through time, as if he was looking directly at Jane. Jane took a sharp breath, her stomach seizing in a cold fist. His lip was curled just the slightest bit up, the faintest smirk. It was a look Jane knew well, one she'd seen too many times to let it pass. It was the same look he'd given her when he forced a kiss upon her and then laughed at her refusal, the same look he'd given her when he'd had her trapped in UltraViolet's clutches.

It was the look of power, of danger, of someone willing to ignore every "no" thrown in their face.

Jane felt like she was going to vomit.

"Turn it off," Jane whispered, and now, finally, Clair complied. The screen went blank, but Cal's image stayed there, burned into the darkness behind Jane's eyelids.

Jane steadied herself against the kitchen table, relishing the heavy feeling of the oak beneath her palms. She stared at the woodgrain, the faint scratches, the light spray of crumbs along the edge of one place mat. "How the *fuck*," Jane said, "did this happen?"

Clair shook her head. She was already busy on her phone, swiping through news feeds and hashtags. Jane dug her own out. This had been what, yesterday evening? So why, she asked herself, were there a grand total of zero calls or texts from any of the rest of the Heroes? Sure, Jane had been distracted, too busy with Clair's journals to bother checking in with the world. What excuse did the rest of them have?

A soft gasp drew Jane's attention. Clair stared at her phone, eyes wide.

"What *now*?"

Silently, Clair turned the phone around for Jane to see. A photo dominated the screen, taken at the same rally where Bryson had made his announcement. In it, Cal's smarmy face grinned wide, one hand raised in a peace sign as if Cal was a rock star and not a newly minted political candidate.

Tucked beneath his other arm was a woman.

She was objectively attractive, styled for TV, though compared to the bright sun of Cal, she looked a little drab. Mousy-brown hair in loose waves past her shoulders, fresh highlights catching the sun. A white blazer and gray miniskirt, sunglasses held loose in her free hand.

Instinctively, Jane let her gaze fall to the caption. *Cal Goodman and his wife, Louisa Gaines-Goodman, shortly after his introduction as replacement for Senator Bob Bryson.*

"He's *married*?!"

Clair shook her head. "That poor girl."

"But . . . *how*?" Jane took Clair's phone, clawing through the news article where Clair had found the picture, searching in a hopeless frenzy. "All that intel . . . there's no way he could have pulled this off without us knowing it. *None*."

"I don't know," Clair said. She drummed her fingers on the kitchen table. For a second, it looked as if her attention was caught by something else, like she'd spotted someone entering the kitchen, but when Jane turned her own head, checking, there was no one.

Perhaps Clair was just jumpy. Perhaps they both were.

Jane squared her shoulders. She stood up, slapping Clair's phone back into her palm. "Come on," Jane said. "We're not going to fix anything by just sitting here."

"Where are we going?"

Jane grabbed her jacket off the back of the chair. Hero red, the iconic outer layer to Captain Lumen's suit. Jane wasn't supposed to wear it out as "herself," but it had been the first thing to grab as she'd raced out of the apartment that morning. Now she slid it on, tugging the front straight. With her hands on her hips, the morning light spilling in from the window, she was the picture of a hero, tall and proud, and way more sure of herself than the knot in her stomach let on. Jane let the confidence of the pose fill her up. In the drawing of her mind, it isn't even quite her own face that stares back at her, but the subtle difference of life rendered in solid lines and bold colors. Captain Lumen juts her chin forward, just a little, meeting Clair squarely in the face. "To meet up with the rest of the team," Captain Lumen's booming voice said. A close-up of furrowed eyes, heavily shaded to mean business. "It's time we paid a visit to an old friend."

AMY KNEW CAL BETTER THAN THE REST OF THEM.

Clair could have, too, if she'd taken the time, if she hadn't been so all-consumed by her obsession with Jane. She and Amy shared most details of their past, after all, and so her parents and Cal's parents, in both versions of reality, had all gone to the same church together. Clair and Amy had both known their respective versions of Cal since before kindergarten, had both gone to the same Sunday School classes, both sang in the same children's choir with him.

But it was Amy, not Clair, who actually got to know him.

"Did you get it?" she asked.

Cal nodded, a huge grin splitting his face.

"Oh my god, let me see, let me see."

"No way!" Cal said. He lunged aside, dodging Amy's grabby fingers, though they both knew he wouldn't hold out for long. He laughed as he stretched the pack of trading cards high over his head, flapping it in the autumn breeze.

A few months ago, a year ago, Amy might have leaped for it. The two of them had grown up like puppies, after all—wrestling and tagging and tumbling across the trampoline the Youth Group rented at the beginning of summer each year. But something had shifted recently. It was hard for Amy to put her finger on it, exactly, except: little things, things she never would have questioned before, just felt *weird* to her now. Sharing a popsicle, getting a ride on Cal's back, leaning against each other on the couch. They were ten years old. This past summer, Cal and Tony and Devin had started making whooping noises at the girls they'd pass on the beach.

So Amy took a step back instead. She ducked her face, tucking her hair behind her ears. "Are you gonna open them, or what?"

"Maybe I shouldn't," Cal said. He loped off to the side, leaning against their favorite tree on the front lawn of the church. "They're worth more in mint condition, you know."

Amy rolled her eyes. "Yeah, Star Trek trading cards are going to be worth a fortune."

"Hey, don't knock Star Trek!"

"You know I'm not." Amy raised her hand into the Vulcan greeting, two clamped sets of fingers and a thumb sticking out the side. "But you're not exactly gonna buy a mansion with them."

Cal grinned. "Yeah, I'm messing with you." He ripped the pack open, the cards slipping free.

In the nineties, in any group of nerds, there lay a fierce divide: Star Trek or Star Wars? Amy and Cal fell firmly into the Trek camp, while most of the others sided Wars. Jane thought the whole debate, and both franchises, were kind of dumb, and Amy's cheeks flushed whenever she went on another rant about the flaws of each. But that didn't stop Amy from watching each episode, faithfully gripping the remote so she could stop and start the recording to cut out commercial breaks. She had almost every episode of almost every series, lined up on shelves in her parents' living room, the tapes hand-labeled with the timestamp of each episode for easy fast-forwarding.

Star Trek nerdery, then, was largely relegated to Sunday mornings, when Cal and Amy were neatly separated from the rest of the group, their friendship a little soap bubble that hung off the larger bubble of everyone else. Every week, they'd wait for church service to let out, and while everyone else wandered downstairs for coffee and cookies and the social hour following, Cal and Amy spilled out onto the front lawn.

At the base of their favorite tree, Cal split the handful of trading cards in half. Star Trek trading cards weren't exactly common, but Cal usually managed to find a few packs when his dad brought him into the city, and they'd stop at Cal's favorite comic book store. This pack was a set from *The Next Generation*, season three, and Amy pawed eagerly through the four in her hand. As soon as Amy flipped them over, she was met with a headshot of Dr. Beverly Crusher—an apt name for the character, as Amy had been mooning over her since she was seven.

Amy blushed, tipping her head to let her hair fall across her face as she quickly shuffled the card to the back of the pile.

"So . . . did you see it?"

Amy flipped the next trading card over, pretending to read the back. "Yeah." She did not feign ignorance. Making Cal admit what he was talking about would only drag the conversation out longer.

What he was talking about, of course, was the latest episode of *Star Trek: Deep Space Nine*. It had aired nearly a week ago by then, last Monday night, but between Cal being home sick from school for the first few days that week, then all of the catch-up he and the rest of their friends had to cover on Thursday and Friday, he and Amy hadn't gotten a chance to geek out together yet.

Not that Amy was particularly looking forward to discussing this episode, but traditions were traditions—and besides, *not* talking about it felt, in some ways, even more dangerous than talking about it. Because why would a straight girl be uncomfortable seeing her first lesbian kiss on TV? Okay, so there were probably a lot of reasons, homophobia chief among them, but to Clair, age ten, so deeply closeted that she didn't even understand the concept of coming out, the situation felt impossible to navigate correctly. It was, perhaps, the first time she fully understood Donna's favorite phrase: "damned if you do, damned if you don't."

So she looked at the back of the trading card, though none of the squiggles looked like letters, much less words, much less trivia facts that conveyed actual meaning. And she tried very, very hard not to jump when Cal sat down next to her.

"My dad didn't let me watch it," Cal said. "But they forgot to turn off the timer on the VCR, so it recorded, and I snuck it out and watched it at Tony's house."

Amy nodded. "Okay."

She said this like it was nothing, like it was cool. Cal's parents were a lot stricter than Donna, who instead embraced the philosophy that any topic was a good topic for Discussion, and no questions were too taboo for Amy to ask. *You can always tell me anything,* were some of Donna's favorite words, but that didn't make true. *She* might be willing to listen, always supportive, always an open ear, but that didn't mean Amy was comfortable talking. Besides, now there was Simon, and all the changes he'd brought in the last two years—the marriage, the new baby—and, well . . . it's not that Donna was *ignoring* Amy, she'd never *ignore* Amy, but obviously she was distracted.

And what would Amy even say? If the very *presence* of a same-sex kiss on their favorite TV show was cause for outrage, banning, and angry letters to the studio, what kind of reaction would people have for *her*? Sure, Donna always tried to prove how "cool" she was, but there had to be limits somewhere. There had to be.

"Hellooo, Earth to Amy."

"What?" Amy snapped, too harshly. She tried to fight back the heat in her cheeks as she turned to him. "I'm listening."

But Cal didn't say anything. For a long time, Cal didn't say anything, and the longer he didn't say anything, the harder it was for Amy to just sit there and watch his carefully slack face. She was still holding the trading card, but now her palms had gone sweaty, and she had to put it down soon for fear of ruining the finish. Maybe it was her imagination, but it seemed like he was studying her, debating something in his head. Trying to make up his mind. Cal had always been less of a doofus than the rest of their friends assumed, and the longer he watched her, the more convinced Amy became. The more her stomach threatened to spill out her throat.

Cal took a breath. "Amy—"

"We should go." Amy stood up from the roots, not even bothering to brush herself off. Her feet thundered against the cold dirt with the same furious beat as her heart. It was only once she got inside that she realized she'd crumpled the cardboard trading card in her fist.

A FLOCK OF PIGEONS KEPT THEM COMPANY ON THE ROOFTOP.

It was crawling into the afternoon, and Clair and the rest of the Heroes had been at it for hours now. They'd arrived in the morning, most of them still slurping coffee even as they hunched on rooftops or hung out in side alleys. Surveillance was standard procedure, Superheroing 101, so the team broke into their typical groups and spread out without being told to. They couldn't make a move on Cal, not yet. Not when he was surrounded, the center of all attention in the city. So they held their distance, keeping an eye on him. Through meet-and-greets and TV interviews. Through speech after speech. Through strategy meetings and a quick rally. Cal spent his time in full campaign mode, as if he'd been prepping for this for months already. He walked from door to door, a trail of reporters and cameras at his back. He waved to crowds. He shook hands. Once or twice, he literally kissed a baby, grinning as the flash of cameras captured each iconic moment. Somehow, he already seemed to have a crowd of supporters wherever he went.

But by the time the sun dragged itself up to and beyond the apex, Clair could tell most of the Heroes were getting restless. And why shouldn't they? They'd been watching Cal for hours now, and so far the most sinister thing he'd done was jaywalk as he bounded up to greet the owner of the diner where he'd had lunch.

Still. Jane had made her decision, and when Captain Lumen makes a decision, the rest of the team falls into place. Originally, with the first Jane, it had been only natural—she was the one to reunite them, after all, these friends who'd long ago scattered to the winds. When Clair's Jane appeared, there had been no plans for her to stay, no assumption that she'd ever become a regular part of the team. But that was before Clair had been brought back, that was before Jane had wrestled control of her powers.

Clair only had vague memories from Amy of the moment Jane fully came into her own—Amy had been flaring pretty badly by that point, and fear and stress tended to wash clean a lot of her experiences from Clair's mind—but she did remember this: Jane Maxwell, *her* Jane Maxwell, stepping through a network of laser beams without breaking them. Even UltraViolet had been caught off guard.

So when they'd decided to stay, Jane just naturally assumed an air of authority, and the rest of the Heroes had fallen into listening to her without much balking. Jane was a leader by nature, after all, and had been bossing this particular group of friends around since elementary school; deciding on what games they'd play, defining the rules, assigning roles and settling disputes. By this point, following Jane was instinctive.

"I just don't know how you can be so goddamned calm," Jane said eventually. "I mean, *you're* the one he's targeting."

Clair glanced up. She was sitting against the lip of the rooftop, her legs stretched out in front of her and crossed at the ankles. A chill bit the air, but Clair was fairly warm; her trench coat and gloves helped her in cooler weather, even as she cursed them in the summer. Clair had her phone out, reading the concerned texts and posts and comments that had come flooding in in the wake of her wedding. She hadn't brought herself to reply to more than a handful yet, and she still wasn't. But there was something comforting in reading them over. Knowing that people cared, even if they didn't really know the truth of who exactly they were caring for. Stacey in particular seemed extra shaken by what had happened, but then, she'd been there. Seen the chaos for herself.

Jane was still standing over her, pacing, hands on her hips. In her iconic red suit, eyes hidden behind a mask, hair caught in a high ponytail, she looked every bit the Hero she'd been training to be.

Clair squinted in the sunshine. "It might not be Cal. Behind the attack."

"Oh, please. You've lived a spotless life, Clair. Who *else* could have cause to want you dead?"

Electric Fury's face flashed through Clair's mind, but outwardly, all Clair could bring herself to do was shrug a shoulder.

She glanced across the rooftop, wondering if Amy might appear —but it stood empty behind Jane, nothing but the pigeons cooing from their roost on the air conditioning duct work.

"Mindsight's got to have made enemies," Clair said, her attention still off in the distance. "I don't know why you think Electric Fury isn't working alone. It seemed personal to me."

Jane shook her head. "It's Cal. It has to be."

Clair didn't say anything. There was no sense in arguing this with Jane, not right now. Instead, she shifted her weight. Her butt was getting numb against the hard surface of the roof. "How much longer do you think he'll be, anyway?"

Jane snorted under her breath. "Who knows? You never could rush him. Damn, though, what I wouldn't give to just charge in there. Or, I don't know, ambush him the next time he's alone."

"He's not letting himself be alone."

"True." Jane stepped a little closer to the edge of the roof. From Clair's perspective, she looked *mostly* whole, but Clair knew Jane was bending the light around her, masking her from anyone looking up from the street. Abruptly, Jane turned away, pacing. "He's got to be alone *sometime*, though. Maybe if we caught him on his way to the bathroom—"

A laugh burst out of Clair. It startled the pigeons, who cooed indignantly as they took to the sky. "Sure," Clair said, "because *that's* the image we want going viral today."

Jane's lips twitched in a repressed smirk. "Okay, maybe that's not the greatest idea. But it's not like he has a superbladder. He's got to go sometime."

"I agree that he urinates, I'm just saying I doubt it's a prime suspect-questioning opportunity."

"Fair enough," Jane said.

Jane's original point was a valid one, though, and one Clair still didn't understand: she *should* be more anxious than this. The attack wasn't even quite twenty-four hours ago. That hardly felt like enough time to have recovered from the trauma. And it . . . it *was* traumatic. Surely. It must have been. Perhaps this was shock. That felt like the safest explanation, at any rate, and so Clair would go with it.

Clair jolted as her phone buzzed. She glanced down, her heart racing. Despite the stack of old messages, she wasn't supposed to get any new ones. Clair always turned on Do Not Disturb mode while they were out on a mission, only Jane's and Donna's numbers allowed through, and she always sent a coded message to Donna so she'd know—the emoji of a four-leaf clover when she left, a unicorn once she was safely back. For Donna to be texting now, the circumstances would have to be dire.

"Oh, shit," Clair said as she read the message in front of her.

Jane turned. "What's wrong?"

"Nicole." The girlfriend-slash-kinda-fiancée of her brother Kevin. The highly pregnant girlfriend-slash-kinda-fiancée. She'd been having no end of pregnancy-related health issues, and had been on strict bed rest for the past three weeks. She was, to date, the only person who'd been glad Jane and Clair had needed to reschedule their wedding, even if the reason was terrible. Clair bit her lip. "They took her to the hospital."

"She's in labor?"

"No . . . Some kind of chest pains, I don't know."

"Go," Jane said.

Clair looked up. "Jane. I can't. We're—"

"Not doing anything—not right now anyway. *Go.* Seriously, Clair. The rest of us can handle it."

Clair didn't argue a second time. She was already halfway to her feet by the time Jane stopped talking. She stuffed the phone into her pocket, brushing against the holster on her side as she reached under her coat. She gave Jane a fast kiss. "Thank you. Love you to pieces."

"Love you back together," Jane said. She held her hand out, and Clair took the Heroes' comm device from her ear, passing it over. Officially "off the clock." Jane pocketed it immediately, then jerked her chin toward the rooftop door. "Be safe."

"Back at you," Clair called over her shoulder as she moved for the access door.

Jane watched her go. Watched the door slam shut behind her, watched the imagined version of her race down the stairs. Panels of Clair's trip slotted themselves neatly into Jane's imagination, a coping mechanism that made it possible to let Clair out of her sight. More than a year since Clair's resurrection, and Jane still couldn't shake the feeling, whenever Clair left, that she wouldn't come back. And why should she? It had happened before.

A deep breath, and then another, and Jane forced herself to turn away. She peered back over the rooftop, watching the churning crowd. There was still no sign of Cal.

She didn't know how long she stood there, waiting, watching, not really paying attention, before her phone buzzed angrily in her pocket. Three short bursts, repeating against her ribs—an alert from the app Marie had developed, to hook into the mainframe of the Heroes' computer system back at headquarters. Jane's powers snapped on. Her mind went wide as the frequency shifted down, down, down beyond visible light and into microwaves, and the wireless spectrum. She tapped into her phone without taking it out.

The jolt that went through her might as well have been electrical. *Enhanced attack in progress,* the message read in her mind. *Downtown, Saga Street Bank.*

Jane tapped the comm device in her ear. "Guys?"

"Yeah, we got it, too," Windforce replied. "Orders?"

"Standard approach," Jane said. "We'll meet at the corner of 54th and Staples to assess." She turned away from the edge of the roof. "It looks like Cal will have to wait."

THIS WAS THE STUFF JANE LIVED FOR.

That she loved being a superhero as much as she did was a surprise even to her. She remembered when she'd first arrived on this Earth, the terror she'd felt at even the idea of going up against a single villain. Her powers scared her. The other Heroes scared her. Even the masks scared her—what they represented, the hidden identities, the *need* for an alter ego. Everything about this life was terrifying. If you had told her then that she would choose to stay of her own volition, that would have been enough to get her to laugh in your face. That she would learn to *enjoy* it? That her heart would pump with excitement as she zipped up her suit? That these powers would fill her up, as if the light she controlled was inside of her, purging all the darkness and fear and anxiety from her soul?

It would have felt as impossible as getting Clair back.

Yet here she was. Clair *was* back, and every bit of Jane's life finally felt exactly the way it should.

And so: Captain Lumen's sports car zoomed up in front of the bank, turning at just the right angle to skid to a stop near the ring of patrol cars. This world's Captain Lumen used to come speeding in on a motorcycle, but Jane had never quite managed to master that. She did her best to make it look cool enough that hopefully no one would stop to notice. In the comic of her mind, the panels lined up perfectly: the swing of the car from above, as it came to a stop; the door, kicked wide; a low-angled shot of Captain Lumen's red boots striking the ground. Below, taking up nearly the full page, is the classic Hero Shot, Captain Lumen herself in all her suited glory, fists on her hips as she took in the situation. Though she doesn't wear a cape, you know it would be flowing triumphantly in the breeze.

Marie, her skin hardened into full Granite Girl mode, gave a messy huff from behind Jane. "Christ. You're doing that *thing* again, aren't you?"

Jane frowned. "What thing?"

"You know," Granite Girl said. "The one where you're turning us all into comic strips. You realize you always get a weird look on your face, don't you?"

"It's *comics*," Jane said as she straightened the cut of her jacket. "Not comic *strips*. And anyway, no I wasn't."

Granite Girl rolled her stony eyes. "Whatever you need to tell yourself, Captain."

"How do you even see like that, anyway?"

"Seriously?" Granite Girl said. She pointed at her upturned face. "You're only just *now* asking me?"

"Guys," Pixie Beats said. She bloomed up in front of them, returning to full size. "Can we focus, please?"

Jane squared her shoulders. "Right. *Comic strips*," she muttered, shaking her head.

She marched up to the perimeter of the scene. Windforce blew in, landing in stride beside her; Rip-Shift appeared a moment later, sliding his black sunglasses into place as he stepped through a tear. Jane couldn't help but smirk, because damn if they didn't look *cool*, and they knew it. Marie could make all the snide comments she wanted, but even she put a swagger in her step as the five of them approached the line of cops.

"Lieutenant!" Jane called as they drew near. She stood with her feet planted wide, her arms crossed in a way she hoped was assertive. She nodded her head at the bank as she asked, "What's the situation?"

A courtesy question. Marie had already hacked into the GCPD's computers, and Tony had gone down to the precinct en route for a quick debriefing from Captain Daniels. Three Enhanced had stormed into the bank thirty minutes ago, armed and raving. They'd quickly overpowered the bank's own security personnel, and taken everyone inside hostage. Still, the thing about working with the police is you have to let them *think* they're in charge, even if you plan to disregard every single thing they told you.

It was a lot like dealing with men, in that regard.

The lieutenant glanced over her shoulder at them. *Crap.* Why hadn't their intel included the fact that Collins had been put in charge of the situation? Jane cut an accusing glance sideways at Granite Girl, but the tightening of her stone fist told Jane well enough that Granite Girl was just as surprised to see Collins as she was.

Reluctantly, Collins drew herself away. "I should have known you'd show up."

"Yes," Jane said. "You should have."

Jane knew what would come next. Collins had hated the Heroes ever since she'd joined the police force. The barbs would fly for a minute or two, each side trading insults with the other. Then, eventually, Collins would have to yield to the Heroes' plan. Either because circumstances blew up in their faces and she lost control of the situation, or because an order came down from on high, it didn't matter. Collins would swallow the loss, adding another rock to the pile of resentment in her stomach. It was a dance Jane had written dozens of times, and seen firsthand several more. She steeled herself for it, taking a deep breath.

But instead of insults, this time Collins only grimaced. She gripped her belt, talking more to the holster at her hip than to the Heroes. "Actually, you're just in time. We . . . need your help."

Jane did her best not to be too outwardly startled. "What seems to be the problem?"

"See for yourself." Collins stepped aside, sweeping her arm toward the bank.

Really, Jane should have spotted it earlier. Saga Street Bank was a corner building (and not, technically speaking, on Saga Street), a grand design with huge plate glass windows that swept up to a corner peak three stories tall. Ordinarily, the architecture drew in enough light that lamps were rarely needed in the lobby, especially during banking hours. Jane had sketched it a few times, sitting in the café across the street, just because it was such an interesting look; you could see all the way back to the row of TVs behind the tellers, all the way to the hallways that led to the vault and offices and back rooms.

Only now, every square inch of every window had gone dark. Not just black—a boundless void, as if all the light had been sucked up from the room. It looked more like a 3D render of a building, one where someone had forgotten to texture the glass or add transparency.

"What the . . . ?" Pixie Beats said.

Windforce whistled through his full-face mask. "Did someone paint it black?"

"Even black isn't that dark," Granite Girl said, motioning at her tank top, the mask around her eyes.

"Ordinarily, no," Windforce said, shrugging. "There is something that would work, though. Remember a few years ago, I showed you pictures of this new paint-like stuff they'd developed? It looked just like that."

"Yeah, and how exactly would someone get their hands on enough of it to paint a *building*?"

Jane shook her head. "It's not a coating." She squinted, shifting her vision through the different bands of the electromagnetic spectrum. Visible light revealed nothing, infrared revealed nothing. But as soon as she skipped into the lower frequencies, where radio signals and wifi devices reigned supreme, the background bubble of the world sprang to life. The inside of the bank came into focus, as the shifting fields of the people and objects inside resolved themselves, the different materials allowing greater and lesser amounts of the fields to pass through. A ghostly picture developed in front of her, like watching an old Polaroid slowly emerge from the darkness. "Okay," Jane said after a moment, "so that's your problem."

"Exactly," Collins said. For the others, she added, "The building was stormed by three Enhanced, about a half hour ago. Eye-witnesses outside the bank reported they held up the building, and then one of them did . . . *this*. Naturally, we tried sending a team in with night vision goggles, but—"

"Let me guess," Granite Girl said, "whatever absorbed the visible light also absorbed the infrared?"

Collins nodded. "I don't know if your team is going to have any better luck than they did, but . . . frankly, at this point, Captain Lumen's powers are our only shot at knowing what's going on inside."

Rip-Shift turned to Jane. "Captain?"

Jane could hear the slight quaver in his voice. She could only guess that he knew some of the team who'd been sent in, or at least feared he might. "Well, no one seems to have been killed so far," Jane said, and everyone, including Collins, seemed to give a slight sigh of relief. "But it looks like your team has been added to the hostage pile."

"We figured as much," Collins said.

"Was there any demands?" Pixie Beats asked.

"No. They won't even answer us when we use the bullhorn."

This didn't surprise Jane. Inside the bank, everything seemed to be in a holding pattern. A row of figures sat huddled on the floor in front of the teller counters, including what looked like the captured police team, judging by the number of electronic devices they had strapped to themselves. One person stood in front of them, hands held as if they were cradling a rifle of some type. Presumably, this had to be the person who was causing the darkness, because presumably, they were the only person who could see through it.

Jane squared her shoulders. "Right, then. Wish me luck."

"You're going *in*?" Granite Girl said.

Jane shrugged. "Someone's got to."

Rip-Shift grabbed Jane's arm. "Captain. We don't go in alone."

"Sure, and I'm all for that," Jane said, "unless there's an environment where only one of us can manage."

"But—"

"Listen," Jane said. She turned away, blinking hard to shift her vision back to normal. The world glared brightly around her, all the colors popping like an oversaturated movie. She waved, and the Heroes formed an impromptu huddle around her. Jane lowered her voice. "I appreciate your concern, but we don't have time to figure out another angle. I can see what's going on in there—you can't. I know I'm . . . not as trained as I could be, but I'm telling you, guys . . . I can do this."

The rest of the team looked at each other. Pixie Beats behind her lavish masquerade mask, Granite Girl hidden in a face of stone, Rip-Shift behind his mirrored sunglasses, Windforce blocked by a spandex mask and reflective ski-goggles. They didn't need to see each other's faces to read their expressions, not by this point. Jane may not have been with them as long as the others, but even she recognized the moment when the decision was made. She did not need them to turn to her and agree; she turned away instead.

She'd only taken a few steps toward the bank when the radio on Collins's belt crackled. A man's voice, deeply accented with the gruff tones of Russia. It carried straight to Jane.

"That's far enough, Captain. One step closer, I start shooting hostages."

THE TRAIN SWAYED BENEATH CLAIR AS SHE TEXTED HER mom. *We still don't know anything?*

She's in with doc now, Donna replied. *Should know more soon.*

Clair bit her lip. She stared at the screen, trying to take comfort in the circular profile photo of Donna that hovered beside her message bubbles. Clair's finger swiped along the keyboard. *OK. I'll be there in 15.*

An optimistic time frame, given Grand City's infrastructure, but one Clair needed to cling to. She leaned her head against the window, shutting her eyes at the view of the city slipping past. It didn't do much good. The glass itself had made a popular headrest, and many of the denizens who'd stolen a few moments of respite against its cool surface could picture the view outside as clearly as if their eyes were still open. The memories drifted through Clair's mind, jumbled like cut-out pictures from a dozen different magazines: the city in spring, in summer, in winter, the way it used to look back in the seventies. Longing and excitement and bone-deep weariness stained the glass in equal measure.

She drew herself upright. All things considered, it was better to focus on her own emotions right now. Ordinarily, she'd put her fingerless gloves back on, the better to shield herself from the world, but she was still in Mindsight's signature trench coat, with Mindsight's signature hair, and Mindsight's retro-red lipstick. Sure, she'd taken off the hat and black mask, but did she really want to risk adding back the gloves? Clair sucked her lips in, scraping some of the lipstick off with her teeth. Normally, she removed it before venturing back out in public as herself.

Normally, she had time to.

Her stomach gave another squirm, thinking this. She glanced at her phone, but it showed nothing it hadn't thirty seconds ago.

She still couldn't believe her brother had gotten himself into this situation. She remembered the night he'd told the family. It was the angriest Clair had ever seen their father. Simon was not prone to outbursts, and so, once Kevin had broken the news, all Simon had done was grab him by the shoulder and take him to the upstairs office. Donna and Clair had glanced at each other, mother and daughter, and silently decided to head to the basement to put away the long-lingering Christmas boxes. The yelling started a moment later, and followed them down. They busied themselves in the work, pretending not to hear.

It was . . . weird, in a lot of ways. Donna had been sixteen when Clair was born. Simon *was* Clair's biological father, but because she'd been the result of a summer fling, he'd never known about her until Simon and Donna reconnected when Clair was almost nine. Phrases like *raised you better than this*, and *can't believe you're willing to repeat my mistakes* rained down like the cut of sleet. Clair's brothers had all been born after her parents' reunion, so she supposed it was easy for them to think they'd always been a normal family. But Clair remembered the early years, her and her mom and sometimes Aunt Amelia in one tiny apartment, Donna working her ass off to make sure Clair could eat and go to the doctor and have clothes that fit.

Kevin had proposed to Nicole a few days later. It wasn't that Simon regretted his part in Clair's birth, he'd always assured her, but rather the years he'd "wasted" not knowing her. All the milestones he'd missed. He'd always told the boys, growing up, that they were never going to be absent fathers to their children, not *ever*, not if they knew what was good for them.

In truth, Clair wasn't sure this was a good enough reason to marry someone, especially not when you were only twenty. But she'd given both Kevin and Nicole hugs anyway, congratulating them, and tried to be welcoming to Nicole ever since.

The lights of the train flickered as Clair turned her phone over in her hands. Clair looked up. No one else seemed to think anything of it. And maybe it was nothing, just a blip in the power, but a restlessness crept up in Clair's chest. She craned her head, looking first up and then down the length of the train car. Nothing appeared to be amiss. Just passengers, keeping to themselves or the small groups they'd boarded with. Clair was just sitting back, trying to convince herself not to worry, when a bolt of lightning struck the train.

The train bucked like a stallion, throwing passengers from their seats. Clair landed hard on her side in the middle of the aisle. Thunder shook her bones. A tumble of strangers' screams and smells and memories assaulted her senses. The lights snapped off and then on again, buzzing brighter than before. Another flash, and Electric Fury's spiked silver boots appeared down the aisle from Clair.

Panic flooded the train car. Like adrenaline and fear had been pumped into the sprinkler systems, and now the fire of Electric Fury's appearance triggered their release. Several of the other passengers scrambled over Clair, trampling her with both their feet and their thoughts; an elbow to the head, the memory of an assault to the heart. Clair groaned, curling herself like a beetle until the worst of the storm had passed. Only then, lying exposed on the ground, with the rest of the passengers huddled in the back, did Clair dare to peep open her eyes.

Electric Fury was standing over her. She leaned in for a closer look, cascades of white hair swinging past her shoulders. "We meet again."

Clair rolled away. Electric Fury stomped down, her pointed boot landing firm on the sweep of Clair's coat. Clair slid out, goosebumps springing to life down her bare arms. She whirled around, still in a crouch. Raw surfaces threatened her skin from every angle, and there was no way Clair could afford to be distracted right now. She did, at least, still have her gun, strapped to the side of her ribs—but did she really want to be using such a weapon here, in this tight of quarters? Besides, the train was still somehow barreling forward, the car rocking underfoot, and Clair wasn't anywhere near as good of a marksman as Amy had been. Even the muscle memory Amy had left behind would only get her so far, in a shaky environment.

Electric Fury squared her shoulders. "No one here to protect you this time."

Clair drew herself to her feet. "Who says I need protecting?"

"Bonus points for badassary," Electric Fury said with a smirk. "Still won't do you any good."

She thrust her arm forward. A bolt of lightning leaped for Clair, and Clair leaped for safety. The lightning raced past her skin, and a shot of rage coursed through her, so intense that for a split second she thought she'd been hit. She stumbled, collapsing against the seats and catching herself on the glass of the windows.

Clair lost herself as impressions flooded her mind. A young man, eager to get home to the guy he'd just started sleeping with—an old woman in tears after a particularly fraught appointment with her lawyer—the nervous flip of someone's stomach as they struggled with recent revelations about their non-binary gender identity—the plot of a woman's intricately woven science fiction novel, as she'd been untangling it on her commute.

A strong hand grabbed her arm. Clair startled, breaking the surface of the memories. "Duck, you idiot!" Amy shouted, and together they fell, a single unbreakable unit hitting the floor of the train car. Landing right on Clair's coat.

* * *

JANE TURNED. COLLINS HAD ALREADY UNCLIPPED HER radio, passing it over before Jane even reached for it. Probably, Jane could have just tapped into the radio waves themselves, transmitting a signal with her voice straight through the open air, but that felt a bit showy for her purposes. She pressed down on the button instead.

This is one area where Jane hadn't practiced. Sure, there'd been bantering back and forth with UltraViolet when she'd first arrived, and sure she'd exchanged barbs with enemies here and there as she'd taken them down since. Who wouldn't look for an excuse for a sick burn or two? But this . . . people trained for years to negotiate in hostage situations. Lives were on the line. And Collins had just handed over her radio like it was nothing, and why? Because Jane wore a costume that hid her identity? Because her team had rescued a few people from burning buildings, taken down a crime ring, stopped robbers?

It didn't matter. She had the job now, whether she wanted it or not. "Hello. This is Captain Lumen."

Crackle. "I know that. Do I look like idiot?"

"I have no idea. You're in the dark, remember?"

"How you say—'bullshit'? You see as well as I, Captain. Which means you see gun I am pointing at hostage's head."

It was true. The figure standing over the group of hostages had shifted, one hand raised with what appeared to be a radio, judging by all the waves pouring in and out of it, while the other had leveled the barrel of the gun toward the head of the nearest hostage.

Jane held down the button. "What do you want?"

"You. To keep distance."

"There has to be something more than that. Why take hostages, if you're not going to make demands?"

A second of silence. Then: "I was told you were smart, Captain. This is not smart."

Jane gritted her teeth. Fine. They wanted smart?

She took a moment, studying the lobby of the bank. It was *possible*, she supposed, that her powers could help counteract whatever was suppressing the light here, but somehow Jane doubted this person's powers were actually like her own. If he had free range of the spectrum, then why wasn't he suppressing the lower bands? Why just light and infrared? It also didn't *feel* quite the same, though it was hard to explain why. With Jane . . . she had a connection to the waves and fields most people walked through without a second thought. They . . . well, they "listened" to her, in a sense. They'd bend to her wishes, or vibrate at different frequencies, or narrow their focus, for example. This was more like a black hole, everything sucked down into an abyss before it had a chance to escape. But the bank hadn't gone dark until after the attack was already underway, which meant there was every reason to assume that disrupting this Enhanced's hold *should*, theoretically, let the light go back to its usual behavior.

This still left the problem of how to disrupt his control in the first place. Typically, an Enhanced's powers needed some degree of mental focus—Clair's being the obvious exception—so if they could somehow get, say, Granite Girl in there, to deliver a hard enough knock upside his head . . .

The comm piece in Jane's ear gave a soft click as it came on. "What's your thought, Cap'n?"

Jane nudged the device with her powers. They grabbed the wireless signals, twisting and manipulating them to carry a string of words to the rest of the Heroes' comms, without the bother of Jane actually speaking aloud. It seemed better, not to give the attacker inside the chance to know she was communicating with her team. *"I think I can keep him distracted long enough for Pixie Beats to sneak inside,"* Jane "said" to the others. *"Shrink down with Granite Girl, so she can knock him on his ass and disrupt his powers."*

"Not that I won't love to," Pixie Beats said, "but did you forget the part where I don't know where I'm going in there?"

"Yeah," Granite Girl said, "or that someone else could get hurt if I just swing blindly?"

"Don't worry about that—I'll guide you through. Both of you. Rip-Shift: once they're in, it's going to get wild in there. I want to get the hostages out as fast as we can. On my signal, I'll need you to create a rip, about . . . twenty feet in from the front window, and maybe dozen in from the left."

Rip-Shift sighed. Loud enough for Jane to hear him, even outside the comms. "I know this is where you're going to tell me to trust you, but I just want to reiterate how *incredibly dangerous* it is for me to rip a hole in the universe if I can't see exactly what I'm doing."

"I know." Jane hesitated, just a second, before she added, *"But please trust me, okay? I won't let anyone get hurt. I promise."*

She only hoped it was a promise she could keep. Already, the effort of managing both her covert communications *and* the extra-intensive method of keeping an eye on the bank was wearing on her. One or the other, okay, fine. Both together was more of a strain than she'd anticipated.

"All right, Pixie Beats, Granite Girl, get ready. Windforce, if you could trigger the automatic doors with a stiff breeze, I'd appreciate it. Maybe give the others a lift through, yeah?"

After that, there was no more arguing. Pixie Beats and Granite Girl retreated behind a police van, so no one inside the bank could witness their shrinking act. A few moments later, a breeze kicked up out of nowhere.

Jane raised her radio. "All right. You seem like a man who appreciates honesty. I know your team is robbing the bank. You should know we're going to stop you."

The bank's automatic doors slid open. Two signals, so small that Jane could only track them from the bubble of wireless activity coming off their comm devices, floated through just before the doors shut.

"Move left until I tell you to stop," Jane told them.

Jane's radio crackled in her hand. "Brave words. Foolish words, but . . . brave."

"Keep going. You're doing great."

"In credit, you may be able to stop us," the attacker continued. "Is not impossible to imagine. But let me ask: if you do, will you still have time to save comrade?"

An audible scoff escaped Jane's lips. Classic baiting. If she didn't need him distracted, she never would have stooped to it, but it was as good of an excuse as any to keep him talking. Her finger depressed the button again. "What comrade?"

"Okay, stop. Forward."

She was so busy watching Pixie Beats and Granite Girl's progress that she almost missed the answer: "Mindsight."

Jane froze. Her concentration slipped, and for a second, the bank plunged into impenetrable darkness. Her hand gripped down on the radio, the sound of her bitter snarl echoing through the bank. "If you hurt her—"

"Don't be silly, how am *I* supposed to hurt someone miles away?" he asked. "No, she need not fear me. My *friend*, on other hand . . ."

Jane turned away. She dropped her radio, letting it clatter to the pavement. The attacker's laugh filtered out from the tinny speaker, his words chasing after her. "Go ahead, Captain. Call her."

He did not need to tell her. Her fingers were already digging into the pocket of her suit—she did not trust the control of her powers to stay steady, not now.

"Captain . . . ," Collins started, but one look from Jane shut her up. Jane pressed the phone to her ear, listening to it ring . . . and ring . . . and ring . . .

When Clair's prerecorded voice clicked on, cheerful and oblivious to the danger, it took every ounce of self-control not to throw the phone across the street. Jane stormed back, snatching the radio from the ground. "What did you do?"

"Nothing," the attacker said. "As I said, I sent friend. You should still have time to help her. If you leave now."

"Captain!" Pixie Beats's voice sounded in Jane's ear, small and frantic. "I think we reached him!"

With a blink, Jane's vision refocused. Sure enough, the bubble of wireless signals from their comms were positioned right at the attacker's boot. Jane glanced to the side, and Rip-Shift gave her a subtle nod.

Jane did not hesitate. She reached up and tapped her comm. A mask-shaped panel squat in the middle of a black page, nothing but the heavy lines and thick shadows of her glowering eyes. A single speech block hovers in the corner: "Go."

CLAIR SANK HER FINGERS DEEP INTO THE FABRIC OF HER coat, and rolled into a crouch. The coat came with her, ripped from beneath Electric Fury's boot like upending a table setting.

Electric Fury staggered back—just enough time for Clair to wrap a thick bundle of coat around her hand and retrieve the gun from her holster. The grip was way too bulky with fabric to fire it, but Clair had no intention of using her weapon in the traditional sense. She rose to her feet in a spin, leading with the gun raised high over her head. Sure enough, Electric Fury had regained her footing; a lightning bolt was already flying at Clair. It leaped across the cramped expanse of train car—caught the metal of the gun, yanking it off-course—skipped to a metal pole by the seats.

A good portion of the coat still trailed from Clair's fist. She whipped her hand, snapping the fabric through the air. Like herding a bull, Electric Fury stepped back, and Clair pressed forward. Another snap, another step in the dance. Electric Fury's startled eyes tracked Clair's movement. She tossed another handful of electricity, and Clair knocked it aside like confetti. Clair's coat sizzled, and sparks rained down as the current hit the overhead lights; they flickered once, twice—died.

Like a heavy blink, the train plunged into semidarkness. Outside, clouds had blotted out the sun, and daylight had just begun to sink beneath the skyscrapers. In this breath, Clair grabbed the pole beside her for stability, flung the trail of her coat aside, and kicked hard at Electric Fury.

A cold grip found Clair's ankle. Clair knew what was going to happen, too late to do anything about it. Current arced across her. Toes to fingertips. Electric Fury to the pole of the train. Clair's body jerked upward, a bridge between contact points. Every muscle contracted, every cell rattled with electricity and rage. Clair's scream was a demon leaping free of the cage of her chest.

Clair's mind retreated. A flash of white, and then Jane's face resolving itself from the haze. Her smile beneath the sheets. The soft glow of morning sun against her skin. Fingers running up Clair's spine, a warm laugh against her collarbone. Death wasn't so frightening, not really. Clair had already done it once, and when the brush of the curtain teased her ankle again now, she did not kick it away. There was a certain peace in nothingness. It was *this* she didn't want to leave: the taste of Jane, the feel of her hair tangled up in Clair's fingers. The way Clair's heart raced, still, all this time later, whenever Jane walked into a room after being away. The sound of Jane's voice as she whispered words meant only for Clair. As she whispered her name. *Clair . . . Clair . . .*

"Clair!"

Clair's eyes jerked open.

She lay on the floor of the train, the ceiling spinning above her. Jane's voice was gone, but dimly, Clair could hear the notes of Goo Goo Dolls' *Iris*, the ringtone that played whenever Jane called. Clair turned her head toward the sound—or she tried to, but her neck was too stiff, her whole body pummeled as if she'd had the worst workout of her life. Clair cried out, but she couldn't even clutch the offending muscles, in part because there were too many of them and in part because that meant lifting her arm, which was tensed worse than anything else. She settled for a low groan as she collapsed back to her starting position.

Her own face appeared above her, her brow creased with worry. "Jesus, Clair," Amy said as she took in the sight of her. "Are you trying to get us *both* killed?"

Clair couldn't answer. A hand squeezed down like a vice on Clair's shoulder, fresh pain ringing through as someone hauled her to her feet. "How does it feel, bitch?" Electric Fury snarled into Clair's ear.

She threw Clair across the aisle.

Clair landed hard against the seats. Her hands flung out, trying to catch herself. None of her muscles were working right. She had no choice but to slump into the padding of one of the seats, and even that effort exhausted her. She just sat there, looking up at Electric Fury.

"Please stop," Clair whispered. She reached up to massage her forehead. Her powers crackled inside her, every sense amped up to eleven. She could taste the fear in the air, and the underlying gratitude from the other passengers that Electric Fury was ignoring them. Electric Fury's own hatred pooled off of her, strong enough to give Clair a headache. Clair had to get control of this. A quiet panic had begun to stir in her chest, and when she looked up again, Amy was staring at her, naked terror on her face. Amy's hand was at her chest, the same point of pain Clair pressed at on her own. *Oh no.* It was as familiar as heartache, and it took

Clair only a split second to recognize it. A flare was building, as strong as the one that had wiped out Amy.

Clair staggered back to her feet. The train swayed, and she caught herself against one of the hanging grips. "You have to get out of here!"

Who was she talking to—the passengers, or Electric Fury, or Amy, or herself? No one, not even Clair, seemed to know. Curious glances flew through the train, but only for a second. Electric Fury bristled, her spine straightening.

"I'm not going anywhere," she said. She raised both hands. "You are."

"No," Clair whispered. No, she wasn't going, not again. Not ever again. Her chest ached, a stitch as her heart skipped a beat. Power ripped through her. She grabbed her head with her free hand, her nails digging into her scalp.

"Clair!"

Someone yanked her head up. Amy, her fingers tight in Clair's hair. Clair drew a sharp breath, and time seemed to suck down into her lungs with it. For a second, everything hung around her, exactly as it was: Electric Fury, a bolt of lightning just beginning to spark from her open palms; Amy, so close that her body heat warmed Clair's shoulder; the passengers, stuck at the back of the train as witnesses to this spectacle; the pain in Clair's chest, leaping, furious, itching to be used.

Clair frowned. Fine, then. Her powers wanted to be used? She would use them.

A single touch, pressed to her heart. The pain leaped to her finger, and Clair pinched down tight. Time snapped back as she flung the sensation away, ripping it free of her chest.

It was hard to say, exactly, what happened then. Can a flare burst outward? Clair was hardly an expert, and there was still so much about superpowers that even the rest of the Heroes didn't know. An explosion of power, at any rate. It ripped from Clair, blossoming out in rippling energy waves, like something straight out of Jane's comics. Reality itself seemed to blister and twist, snapping the bolts that held the seats together. It tore through the train car, the metal cracking and sparking as the waves raced toward the oncoming bolt of Electric Fury's lightning.

The forces met in the middle, and burst outward tenfold. The blast was an uppercut to Clair's chest, lifting her and throwing her against the door at the front of the train car. Her lungs burned on impact; her head knocked hard against the metal. Clair's vision blurred, spots threatening to drag her down, but not before she saw the chaos in the rest of the train car—the bodies flying, the windows cracking. Not before she saw Electric Fury hit a side exit door, the whole thing blasting off its hinges. The wind whipped in. The wind whipped out. It dragged Electric Fury with her, nothing more than a shriek and a flash of her silver catsuit as she disappeared through the empty doorframe.

"*No!*" A jolt like a current across her heart sent Clair lurching forward, a single zombie shuffle toward the gaping hole in the side of the train car. Pain flared in her ribs and she stumbled, catching herself on a support pole. She clutched at her side and sucked in lungfuls of air, trying to catch her breath. But the flash of concern that had sent her moving didn't belong to her, not really. Not anymore. Clair looked around; at the upturned seats, the broken poles, the missing windows. At the only other figure left standing, the perfect mirror of herself.

JANE WAS THE ONLY ONE TO SEE THE PUNCH.

In the upper corner of the page, an inset panel as Pixie Beats's hand releases Granite Girl's. Inside the box is filled with black, a faint silvery-blue outline sketching the outstretched fingers, the fist that's already increasing in size. But it's the center of the page that really draws the eye: concentric silhouettes as Granite Girl's black-and-silvery form grows larger and larger, her arm an upwards battering ram; it collides, at the top, with a chin that's knocked off-center, an impact which splashes both light and color across the rest of the page, spewing like blood from a wound.

Chaos broke free.

What would be chaos, to the untrained observer. Like soldiers charging across a muddy field to war, the police and the rest of the Heroes stormed into the bank. A rip already hung in the middle of the lobby, towering over the scene as Pixie Beats and

Rip-Shift hauled hostages through. Granite Girl continued to spar with the attacker, keeping him off balance, keeping him from ripping the light from the lobby once again. Traps snapped and popped to life along the ceiling—green pods that sprang wide, spitting acid as a sadistic sprinkler system.

Jane dropped to her knees, turning her run into a slide. She whipped beneath one of the financial advisors' desks as acid spat and hissed through the papers that had been left sitting on top. A quick glance revealed that most of the hostages had already gone through Rip-Shift's tear by this point, so that was something— but now the entire team, plus at least a dozen officers in blue, were stuck cowering beneath various pieces of furniture that were slowly dissolving above their heads.

The comm device came alive in Jane's ear. Granite Girl's angry voice: "Any more bright ideas, genius?"

But they didn't need Jane's planning, not this time anyway. Windforce had already reached out, dragging in a current from outside. It blasted in, shattering the windows, and raced up toward the ceiling. There it spun, trapping the acid as it fell.

It was a temporary solution. Even as Jane scrambled out from beneath the desk, the acid was building into an ominous cloud, and stray droplets were still flinging down into the lobby. Still, it should be enough. Enough to capture the original attacker, enough to flush out his cohorts from the back. After that? Well, one problem at a time.

Speaking of problems: the floor shook beneath Jane. Once, then twice. Jane glanced down. Rubble skittered across the marble as it shook again. Again. A series of thuds, like cannon fire, the steady drumbeat of an oncoming war. The thudding grew louder, closer, and Jane turned her head toward the back of the bank, the vaults beyond, following the sound. It was too steady to be an earthquake—more rhythmic, organic. Like a heartbeat, or . . .

Jane went cold. Or footsteps.

"Duck!" Jane shouted, seconds before the wall exploded into the lobby. Chunks of wood and marble went flying. Plaster dust choked the air. Jane scrambled back to her feet, shaking debris from her shoulders. Her red suit was dusted white, like she'd dipped herself in flour.

A voice echoed through the lobby, loud as a megaphone. "Got some trouble here, Pitch?"

Two figures emerged from the cloud of dust. Vague shapes at first, the bigger of which loomed massive over the rest of the lobby. "Holy sh—!" Jane started, but then speech failed her as the figures came fully into view. She ducked back, hiding behind a particularly large chunk of wall. "You failed to mention that one of the attackers was *fucking enormous!*" she shouted at Collins, who was taking cover behind a stone planter nearby.

Collins glared at Jane. Her gun was raised, held ready beside her head. "He wasn't, when witnesses first reported it!"

"He is now!" If anything, that was an understatement. Jane stole another glance around the chunk of wall, then wished she hadn't.

He wasn't monstrous. Simply gigantic. As if someone had taken a body builder, muscles bulging from steroids and bench presses, and pinch-zoomed to scale him up. As he straightened up, unfolding himself in front of the hole of his own making, his nineties-era flat-top buzz cut nearly brushed the vaulted ceiling. Jane's eyes went wide just trying to take in the scale of him. Panels could not contain him. He cricked his neck, left and then right, and flexed his arms, as if anyone had missed those. He wore no shirt—which, given his size, Jane couldn't really blame him for—and loose black martial-arts pants that only reached his knees.

The sight of him was so imposing that it was easy to miss the woman standing beside him, but Jane made herself take note. Willowy and small (Jane thought, though it was hard to tell with her sense of scale all messed up by the gigantic dude), with an acid-green suit, makeup, and hair. So if Jane had to guess, she was probably to thank for the spray-bombs, still gathering in the wind overhead. Gold spikes from a crown poked up from her green hair, lending her slightly more height, and a cape like a royal robe trailed from her shoulders.

Jane ducked back. She sucked in a breath. "Okay," she said, more to herself than to anyone else, though she was broadcasting over the comms. "Okay, new plan. I'm going to try to take over for Granite Girl with the first dude"—Pitch, she'd heard the huge one call him—"so Granite Girl can try her hand at dealing with Giant Jackie Chan over there."

"Watch it," Windforce cut in. "That's racist, Captain."

"What? He's *Asian*. And we're in the middle of a thing, here!"

"Still."

Jane sighed. "Fine, Mean Hagrid, then. In the meantime, Pixie Beats, with your stealth and dexterity—"

"I'll handle Acid Bitch."

"I was gonna go with Lady Acid, but sure, apparently *naming them* is the priority right now!" Jane sighed low under her breath. They had to put a cap on this, fast. Clair was still in danger, and Jane didn't even know what kind of threat she was up against. "Rip-Shift and Windforce, I need you to try to figure out a more permanent solution for that acid. We can't just drop it all over the bank once we're done."

"Way ahead of you," Rip-Shift said. "One tear, and we drop it in the sewers. Easy peasy."

"What?" Windforce said. "That's a terrible idea! You realize the damage that'll cause to the pipes?"

Rip-Shift sighed. "Fine, Mr. Science Wizard. What's your great idea?"

"Guys!" Granite Girl shouted. "Don't know if you've realized this yet, but we've got a massive fight breaking out over here!"

As if to illustrate the point, a chunk of marble went flying over Jane's head. It crashed through what little was left of the windows, and bounced onto the street like a lost soccer ball. Jane tapped her comm. "Okay, go!"

They threw themselves into the fray. Jane ran, dodging flying debris as she made her way toward Granite Girl and Pitch. The police, meanwhile, had apparently decided Mean Hagrid was their top priority, which Jane couldn't argue with. They had him under a barrage of fire, but so far their bullets pinged off his skin like bees hitting a window.

Not Jane's problem at the moment. She vaulted over an overturned desk, and fired off a tightly bound laser beam at Pitch, just as he swung a punch down at Granite Girl. The heat of it made him rear back, sucking the back of his hand like a baby. He turned, eyes narrowed, as Granite Girl ran for her new target.

So now it was just them. Jane raced up. She threw herself underneath the swing Pitch launched at her, countering with an elbow to his ribs as she came up behind him. In the light, he looked a lot less intimidating, borderline cliché. Dark pinstripe suit. Dark hair, combed down tight against his head. A classic mobster.

Jane tried to tell herself this was nothing more complicated than the routine sparring matches the Heroes engaged in. She bounced up, fists raised, drawing a mental picture around herself. The training room back at headquarters, and she in her workout pants and snarky tank top. Clair sits on the chairs along the wall, one leg tucked up in front of her, as she calls out notes of encouragement and critique. Pitch takes a wide step forward, away from her, bringing his other leg with him as he turns, and Jane's mind sketched out his movements. Weight balancing on his right foot, a circular arrow beside it to show the pivot.

He was trying to create distance, and Jane couldn't let him. She stepped forward with him, but not quite fast enough—his free foot darted out, as if he'd anticipated this, and hooked Jane's ankle. The swing of his fist came with it, but Jane was already off balance, and she let herself dodge by falling. She hooked his elbow with hers. She'd intended to drag him down with her, but his balance was anchored to the ground, and Jane used him as a support pole to pull herself back to her feet, even as his opposite fist whaled against her shoulder, her ribs. He swung high next, aiming for her head, and Jane quickly spun around, behind him again. Their arms were still locked together in a violent do-si-do, and Jane let her momentum carry her own punch around, up. She clocked the back of his head, and he jerked forward, slumping, dazed.

In Jane's mind, Clair bounces to her feet, cheering, as the image dissolved and the real world sprang up to take its place. Two police officers detached themselves from the firefight to rush up toward her. She pulled Pitch's arm back and they grabbed the other, cuffing him in an instant, knocking him to his knees. He was still awake, but barely coherent, spitting blood and slurred Russian insults as he hit the floor.

Jane turned to the rest of the fight.

It wasn't exactly going to plan. Windforce and Rip-Shift still hadn't managed to deal with the acid situation yet, drawn into the rest of the battle going on around them. From what Jane could tell, Windforce was trying to drop the acid cloud just enough to catch the swinging fists and bobbing head of Mean Hagrid; Rip-Shift, meanwhile, was creating tears just large enough to catch whatever streams Acid Bitch was shooting in her battle with Pixie Beats, adding them to the swirling cloud up above. Granite Girl was doing her best, pummeling Mean Hagrid's calves, trying to climb or leap up onto his torso, but he was simply too solid, too massive, too goddamned bulletproof. Even the acid was only irritating his skin, rashes appearing like patches of sunburn.

The situation couldn't hold. Wouldn't last.

And Jane was right—it didn't. She'd barely finished thinking this when a batch of the acid cloud broke loose, right in Mean Hagrid's face. Perhaps it was on purpose, or perhaps Windforce was just having trouble controlling the mass of it by this point, but either way: Mean Hagrid wailed, his bellow shuddering the building. Jane lurched to the side, grabbing hold of a sofa for support, as Mean Hagrid staggered, stomping forward. His hands flailed out. It was hard to tell, in the split second when Rip-Shift made his decision, if Mean Hagrid was off balance and falling, pinwheeling his arms, or if he was making a conscious effort to snatch Windforce out of the air; but regardless, if he did, the whole bank would get doused with all the acid that had piled up near the ceiling.

A tear split the floor beneath Mean Hagrid. Jane sucked in a breath, terrified, as the mass of him took a split second to catch up with the gravity of his situation. His arm was nearly to Windforce by that point, fingers outstretched—but then he fell, his legs immediately dropping out through a matching split in the ceiling. Instinctively, Jane glanced at the ground below him. She was running before she realized it, throwing herself toward the handful of police officers who were in imminent danger of being crushed. Jane toppled into them like a bowling ball, the whole mass of them tumbling into the gutters. Jane squeezed her eyes shut as she slid to a stop along the floor, bracing herself.

Only, the crash Jane was expecting never came. Instead, when she peeped her eyes back open, she found something she didn't anticipate: Mean Hagrid had caught himself against the floor, his massive hands scrambling for purchase, and now he hung in two places at once, half in and half out of Rip-Shift's tear. His arms grabbed at the floor while his legs flailed from the ceiling, kicking into the acid cloud, sending fresh sprays to rain through the broken windows and into the street.

The team swarmed in, the police right alongside them. Everyone ran for Mean Hagrid, and maybe they would have reached him, and maybe they would have found a way to contain him, had the light of the room not suddenly been sucked away, snapping off like a switch.

Jane skidded to a halt. She felt the itch of her powers, wanting to shift her view again, but that wouldn't help anyone else, and she needed their full support this time. So instead she took a breath, focusing her energy inward. Clair had always said Jane was the light of her dark times. Well—now it could be literal.

There was so much about Jane's powers that were complicated for her, even hard to understand. This wasn't. This was primal, instinctive. This was tapping into the raw energy of her powers, and letting them out without interference. Jane scooped them up, cupped in her hands, and threw them open as light burst from her skin. For one brief and glorious second, her light filled the entire lobby, a glow that revealed everything Pitch was trying to keep hidden.

And then, in an instant, it was gone.

Jane swore. She'd never gone up against anyone with abilities that were even remotely related to hers before (UltraViolet notwithstanding, and their powers seemed to cancel each other out anyway), and unfortunately, she didn't really know what to do in the face of it. She scooped another surge of power from her core, sent it bursting out through her skin. It swept away just as easily as the first. Like a candle being snuffed out. Pitch's power sucked up the light as fast as Jane could generate it.

"Captain!" Granite Girl shouted, not even bothering with the comms. "Could really do with a little better about now!"

She didn't need to tell Jane that. In the darkness, the sounds of gunfire and fistfights had fallen away, but the lobby still roared with the whirlwind above their heads, the hiss and spit as flecks of acid wormed free or brushed the ceiling. She could still hear the grunts as Mean Hagrid clawed his way free of Rip-Shift's tear. The screams from outside, as acid spilled out onto the streets. Not to mention that every second they spent on this was one more delay in tracking down Clair.

"Okay," Jane whispered to herself. "Focus. You can do this."

She opened her powers again—only this time, she did not fling the light outward in a single great burst. This time, she fed the light out slowly, letting it fill her up, a glow that poured out in a steady stream.

It still whisked away as fast as Jane could generate it, but Jane pushed back, amping up the levels, until eventually she reached a sort of balance. Sweat broke out along her skin. Light billowed out from her, flickering as it fought against the black hole of Pitch's power. He just kept stealing it, but Jane just kept feeding it. It wasn't a steady source of light by any means, more like an old movie projector than anything else, but it was enough for the police to resume their attack on Mean Hagrid, and it was enough for Windforce to regain control of the acid cloud. And it was enough for Pixie Beats to race across the lobby, enough for Jane to see the roundhouse kick she aimed straight at Pitch's head.

All the light he'd been sucking up burst out of him, a hundred flashbangs going off at once. He collapsed onto his side, and Jane sagged against a planter as glorious daylight stained the lobby shades of orange once again.

It felt, for a moment, like a victory, but a victory short-lived. Mean Hagrid yelled in triumph, the last of his footing finally caught back on solid ground. He leaped up, and Windforce only just managed to dodge his grip. Somehow, if such a thing was possible, he looked even larger than he had before he'd fallen through the tear. Anger and sweat darkened his face as he stormed a group of nearby police officers—Jane flinched, looking away, as screams and a sickening squish filled the lobby.

"Now what?" Pixie Beats shouted, but Jane had absolutely no idea.

She didn't need to.

"Hey!" Granite Girl called over the comms. "Rip! Remember that summer we spent playing *Portal*?"

Jane looked over. Granite Girl had backed up, away from the raging mass of Mean Hagrid, who was currently sweeping his way through more ranks of police officers. Even on Jane's original world, Tony and Marie had wiled away their time on video games, and Jane remembered the Portal Summer as a particularly strong addiction. She'd heard the stories of Portal Summer from this reality, too, though it had taken a somewhat different turn than her own. In short: it was a video game that worked a lot like Rip-Shift's powers, planting gaps in the world where you could walk through one place, and drop into another. In the game, the tutorial showed you that momentum was not affected by a player dropping through the portals, and so, as the game explained, "speedy thing goes in, speedy thing comes out."

Rip-Shift met Granite Girl's eye. He gave her a solid nod.

"Everybody back!" Jane shouted, and Pixie Beats immediately came over to help her. They dragged the police officers away.

In the corner of the lobby, Rip-Shift tore a slice in the floor, right in front of Granite Girl, and another several yards above it. According to the team's stories, this was a move they'd practiced a lot that summer, though not one Granite Girl was particularly fond of. As Jane watched, she suddenly understood. Granite Girl stood on the edge of the tear, taking a breath as if preparing for a dive. Which, well, she was.

She jumped into the rip along the floor. Fell out of the rip above it. Fell through the rip in the floor. Fell out of the one above it. Over and over again, faster and faster, a sickening reel of an endless fall, until finally she was going so fast she was nearly a blur, just black and gray and blond and camo blended together like granite.

That's when Rip-Shift flicked his finger. The tear on top sealed itself, and a new one split the skin of the world, dangling like a thread in front of where the windows had been. Granite Girl plunged into the one on the floor, and came literally screaming out of the one standing upright.

She shot like a cannonball across the open lobby. Her stony fist led the way.

The collision of her punch and Mean Hagrid's chin shook the entire bank. A double-page spread, the explosion nearly filling the frame, everyone else flying back like flecks of debris. Jane hit the ground on her shoulder, sliding until she was nearly through the broken windows. She groaned, dragging herself to her feet.

In the center of it all, Granite Girl lay on her back. Her skin was rapidly returning to its usual fleshy peach, a single neat cut above her mask. "Owwwwww," she moaned as Jane reached down and hauled her up. She was positively covered in plaster dust and debris, and wavered a little, unsteady on her feet, when Jane let go.

It was worth it, though. Mean Hagrid lay unconscious at her feet. He'd shrunk back down to normal size, a hell of a goose egg already swelling up on his jaw. Jane nudged him with her toe, just to make sure he was really out of it, even as the remaining police officers swarmed in to contain him.

They still needed to do something about the acid, of course, and it looked as if Acid Bitch had slipped away sometime in the darkness and the chaos, so it wasn't a complete win. Still—two out of three wasn't bad, and Jane was confident in Rip-Shift and Windforce's ability to move the acid out safely. They were already working on it, conferring in the corner of the bank as they sorted out their plan of action.

Which meant the worst of it was over, which meant she was finally free to check up on Clair. Jane's heart spiked, and no sooner had she thought this than her phone started ringing in her pocket. Clair's song. Jane turned away, and all but ripped the phone from her jacket, swiping it like her life—or her heart—depended on it.

"Clair? Oh, thank god!"

Clair gave a nervous laugh. "Don't start going to church yet," she said. "There's . . . a bit of a situation here. I need your help."

IF AMY WAS DISTRAUGHT BY WHAT HAPPENED TO
Electric Fury, she didn't show it. She stared open-mouthed at
the bodies slumped at the back of the train car, the empty hole
where Electric Fury used to be. "What the hell just—?"

"You think I know?" Clair shouted as she raced to the back
of the train car. "These are your powers, not mine!"

She winced as she ducked down, still clutching her ribs. Clair
had intended to quickly check the pulse of a few passengers,
but she didn't need to—before she'd even quite touched the first
neck, a swell of impressions rose up to meet her. Thoughts and
memories, dreams, a sense of identity. Clair ripped her hand
back, as if she'd been burned. She actually looked at the pads
of her fingers, but the skin was pale and clammy, not at all the
angry pink she'd been expecting. She ran her fingers together,
as if the memories had been sand that could be brushed off as
easily. Her stomach soured with uncertainty.

So that was a problem for another time, then, but at least the passengers were alive, if unconscious. Clair hauled herself back to her feet. Her empty holster knocked against her battered ribs, and she took the time to collect her revolver from the singed tangle of her coat. She patted her pockets. Her phone . . . she could find her phone later.

At the front of the train car, the door was locked. Not such a surprise, really—if the rear door had worked, no doubt the passengers would have used it to escape, so the discovery of the front door also being inaccessible made sense. Clair turned. Amy was still gawping at the whole situation, her arms wrapped tightly around herself as if she'd just been hauled out of freezing water.

Clair reached over, swatting Amy's shoulder. "Hey. I don't suppose *you* can get through these doors, can you? Find out what's going on in the rest of the train?"

Amy frowned, seeming to come back to herself. "I'm not a *ghost*."

"Don't get mad at *me*," Clair said. "How am I supposed to know?"

So apparently that was out. Clair bit her lip, regarding the walls around the door. Maybe there was some kind of emergency button, or an intercom to the driver's compartment? It seemed like a prudent safety measure, and anyway, didn't even old-timey trains have those ropes you could pull to hit the brakes? Or was that only in movies? Clair had never been big on Westerns.

"Okay, stop," Clair muttered to herself. Instinctively, she ran her fingers along the seal of the doorframe.

And maybe it was her hyperactive powers, still popping and jumping beneath her skin, or maybe it was the aftereffects of the explosion that had knocked everyone else back, or maybe it was something else entirely, but suddenly a flash of the next car up leaped out and grabbed Clair by the throat. Then the next car. Then the next. The next. All up and down the length of the train, unconscious passengers, collapsed in their seats, one and another and another, straight up to the front—straight up to the driver, passed out over her controls. The nose of the train met a gentle turn, and the force slid the driver's body. Her elbow hooked the throttle, dragging it along, and Clair's stomach gave a lurch as the increase of speed caught up with her.

"Shit." Clair dropped her hand, turning around. Her eyes swept the floor as she scrambled onto her hands and knees. She reached beneath the seats, swishing her hand through the dust and debris and god knows what else.

Amy came over, crouching beside her. "What are you doing?"

"We can't handle this on our own," Clair said. A jolt of triumph coursed through her as her fingers seized upon her target. "Got it!" She sat up, pulling her phone out from where she'd lost it. The screen was cracked, the case covered in dust, but Clair's heart soared as it lit up beneath her touch.

It took only a second to dial Jane's number. Clair bit her lip as the phone started to ring. Out the window, the buildings of Grand City whipped past at speeds well beyond what they should be doing within city limits.

"Clair?" Jane said. Her voice was frantic, almost strangled. "Oh, thank god!"

Clair gave a nervous laugh. "Don't start going to church yet. There's . . . a bit of a situation here. I need your help."

"Tell me."

Clair moved to the front of the train car. She laid her fingers on the doorframe. "Long story short? I'm fine, but currently stuck on a speeding train with no way to get to the controls."

"So, not so fine, then."

"Yeah," Clair said. "No, I guess not."

Jane sucked in a breath. "Okay. Okay, Granite Girl, Pixie Beats, and I will be there as soon as we can. You've still got your tracker?"

Clair checked the inside strap of her holster. A tiny pin, blinking green, sat nestled against her blouse. "It's here."

"All right." Jane's voice wavered, like she was already running. "Can you maybe call Olivia, get her to report the train as a runaway? We need authorities clearing the tracks. I would handle it, but—"

"I've got more time on my hands," Clair said. "I get it. Consider it done."

The slam of a car door echoed through Jane's phone, followed immediately by the purr of an expensive engine. "Good. I'll be *right there*, do you hear me? And Clair?"

"Yeah?"

"Stay calm. I'm not going to let *anything* happen to you."

Clair squeezed her eyes shut. The hot sting of tears spilled onto her cheek.

It was supposed to be reassuring, Clair knew, and yet. That wasn't what she'd wanted Jane to tell her. Not that the danger of her situation hadn't registered with her, and not that Clair didn't fully believe in Jane's intention of using every available resource to save her.

But Clair knew better than anyone that death wasn't something your loved ones "let" happen to you. It wasn't a choice—save the day, or allow fate to unfold as it will. And no one, not even a superhero, could make the kind of promise Jane was making.

Clair nodded, even though Jane couldn't see it. "I love you."

"I love you, too. I'll call you when we get there."

"You didn't tell her about Electric Fury," Amy said as Clair hung up the phone a moment later.

Clair turned away. She brushed her cheeks dry with the back of her hand. "No," she said. She drew up her contact list, already hunting for *Olivia Maxwell*. "I didn't."

"ARE YOU FUCKING KIDDING ME?" GRANITE GIRL SAID. "First a bank robbery, and now a speeding train? What, are you pulling this shit straight from your dumb comic books?"

"Left here!" Pixie Beats shouted. The car was only a two-seater, so she was currently standing in Jane's cupholder, a miniaturized phone in her hand as she followed the directions from Clair's tracker.

Jane slammed on the gas pedal, surging in front of the other traffic and cutting a sharp left. The tires shrieked beneath them, the tail of the car whipping through the intersection. Pixie Beats yelped, and Granite Girl's hand slammed hard against the window to keep her balance.

"Christ!" Granite Girl yelled. She yanked at her seatbelt, to keep it from choking her. "Do you want to get there fast, or do you want to get there *alive*?"

Jane shifted gears, ignoring this. "How much farther?"

"Not much," Pixie Beats said. "It looks like Clair's on the Blue Line, but . . . Jane, they're moving *fast*. I hate to say it, but you're going to need to give it more ga—aaah!"

"Again!" Granite Girl yelled. "Fast, or alive?"

Jane didn't answer. She wove between the thick traffic of Grand City, slipping through impossible gaps, jumping the sidewalk, cutting across red lights and moving intersections alike. In speed, there was peace. Everything else fell away as Jane's focus narrowed. There was no time to worry about what would happen once she stopped, what was happening even now. There were only the obstacles in front of her, the path she needed to track around the other moving cars, the directions Pixie Beats kept shouting from her spot near Jane's elbow. Jane didn't care that it was reckless. She didn't even care, particularly, about their lives, for what was life if she lost Clair again? The only thing that mattered was reaching the train in one piece, in order to save it. What happened beyond that was minutia Jane simply couldn't bring herself to care about.

"There!" Granite Girl shouted. She pointed up, to the elevated tracks that cut across the heart of Grand City. They were almost beneath them by now, and sure enough, up ahead, a fast-moving shadow galloped across the road. Jane swerved hard to the right, narrowly avoiding a pedestrian that had just started to cross. The papers he was carrying went flying in their wake, chewed up by exhaust.

"So what's the plan?" Pixie Beats asked. She'd tucked her phone into her jean jacket now that their target was in sight. "How are we supposed to get up there?"

"Easy." Jane reached over, punching the button for the glove compartment. A variety of weapons were housed inside, any spares the team might need while out on the field. Mostly it was extra bullets, but there was a pair of pistols, a tactical knife, a zip cord . . . and a wrist-mounted dart gun, a spare to the ones Cal used to have integrated in his suit. They'd never bothered to remove it.

Jane grabbed it, tossing it onto Granite Girl's lap. She held out her arm, wrist up.

"Strap it on me," Jane said. "And then shrink down and get ready for the ride of your life."

Granite Girl jerked back in her seat. "I think she meant something a *bit* less suicidal!"

"I don't care!" Jane drew her arm back, spinning the wheel hard as she dodged around a particularly slow dump truck. She stuck her arm out again. Her eyes never once left the road, the traffic, the train up above, but something in Jane's voice made it clear she'd be glaring at Granite Girl right now. "The two of you are going up there, and you're *going* to find some way of stopping that train, or so help me, I will go even more supervillain on your asses than UltraViolet ever did. Do I make myself clear?"

A moment of silence filled the car. Jane tapped the steering-wheel-mounted sunroof controls with her thumb. Wind came rushing in, beating down on their chances to argue.

"I suppose I could grab on and try to act as an outside brake," Granite Girl said, shouting to be heard over the noise.

Pixie Beats nodded. She was gripping hard to the walls of the cupholder to avoid being sucked out with the wind. "I'll make my way to the front. See if I can't get the real brakes to work. These things usually have a dead-man's switch, maybe I can figure out why it didn't trigger."

"Sounds like a plan!" Jane flexed her wrist impatiently.

Granite Girl bit her lip, clearly hesitant. But a moment later, she was sliding the dart gun onto Jane. Jane nodded as Granite Girl snugged up the straps, locking them in place.

"This is probably too late to ask," Granite Girl said as Pixie Beats held her miniature brown hand out toward her, pink palm upturned, "but are you sure you know how to fire that thing?"

Jane jerked her head. "Only one way to learn."

"Jane . . ."

"There's no time!" Jane snapped. "Now get your tiny asses on this dart!"

Granite Girl scowled. It was clear she wanted to argue, but what other choice did they have? Clair aside, there was a whole train full of civilians up there, and the Heroes were better equipped to handle the situation than anything emergency services could throw at it. Granite Girl glanced at Pixie Beats, and Pixie Beats gave her a steady nod, and then Granite Girl gave her her hand.

A second later, the two of them were climbing onto the mount on Jane's wrist.

"It's okay," Jane said to them as she raised her arm. They were almost directly underneath the train by now. From the sidewalk, they'd have a clear view of the wall of the train. Jane leaned on her horn and then veered hard, hopping the curb. Thankfully, everyone had either seen the chaos speeding toward them, or news of the car barreling through downtown had made its way to the airwaves and social media channels, because a straight shot opened up in front of Jane. Jane pointed toward the train, finding her sightline along the length of her arm. She squeezed one eye shut. "I've got you," she said and then hit the trigger.

As soon as the dart released, Jane snapped her attention back to the sidewalk. She skidded off, back into the roadway, as she, and the tracks above, began a long right turn. The train would take longer, tacking a much wider angle between the buildings. Jane had to make do with a series of sharp right-lefts.

"Holy. Fucking. Shit," came a voice on Jane's comms. Granite Girl. So they were still alive then. "I am *never* doing that again in my fucking *life*, do you hear me?"

Jane smirked. "Roger that."

"We're in the back car now," Pixie Beats said. "I'm going to shrink down and make my way forward. Granite G—"

A crash sounded over the comms. A second later, Jane spotted a piece of debris flying off the train. She whipped her head around as it crashed to the street—a door.

"Okay," Pixie Beats said, "I was gonna say Granite Girl should pry the back door open, but I guess we all need stress relief sometimes. We'll update you as soon as we know anything for sure."

The comm went dead. Jane tapped another button on her steering wheel. "Call Clair."

A buttery-smooth computer voice chimed. *"Calling Clair."*

Her phone barely rang. "Jane?"

"We're here," Jane said. The turn over, she slid into line with the tracks again. "Pixie Beats and Granite Girl are up there now. They're going to do what they can."

As if on cue, a series of sparks lit up the back of the train as the whole thing gave a lurch above the street. Jane didn't have a clear enough view of Granite Girl to see what was going on exactly, but she could picture it. Marie, her skin hardened to stone as she grabs hold of the back of the train and digs her heels into the tracks; Keisha, shrunk to the size of a pixie and clinging like a desperate butterfly to the outside of the cars as she heads toward the front compartment. Vague imagery began to swim through Jane's mind, looking for places to slot it onto a page spread, but her thoughts were too chaotic, too desperate. Finished panels dissolved into loose storyboard sketches, and storyboards collapsed into graphite snakes that fell in a writhing lump to the bottom of the page, unable to be contained. Jane jerked the car to the side, narrowly avoiding a taxi, and the mental image disappeared completely, like shaking an Etch-a-Sketch.

"I'm sorry," Clair said. Jane could picture her: tucked into a corner, her head dipped as she spoke softly into the phone. "I shouldn't have left the group. I shouldn't have—"

"Stop it. We're not doing this."

"I just . . . I want you to know—"

"No." Jane's throat squeezed tight as she swerved around a delivery truck. "You are *not* saying goodbye to me, Clair. I won't have it."

"What if I need to? I didn't get the chance, last time."

"You won't need it," Jane said. "I won't—"

A loud burst of cursing broke through Jane's comm, so strong that she grabbed her ear.

"Marie?"

Granite Girl's voice was garbled, breaking off and collapsing into static as she spoke. "—lost my grip . . . —can't catch . . . —fucking hate comics!"

Jane went cold. She glanced up, letting her vision slip into infrared, and sure enough: Granite Girl's heat signature had disappeared from the back of the train. Jane spotted it, briefly, as a fleck in her rearview mirror as she and the train sped away.

"Jane?" Clair asked tentatively over the phone. "What's going on? We've sped back up."

Jane's fingers tightened on the steering wheel. "I'm handling it." She was grateful that Clair wasn't hooked up to the comms at the moment. She punched the mute button on her steering wheel. "Keisha? I hate to rush you, but—"

"It's okay, I'm here," Pixie Beats said. Sounds of movement filtered through Jane's earpiece. "It looks like the dead-man's switch shorted out somehow. I've got the throttle. I just . . . can't get it . . . moving."

"Jane," Clair said. She'd turned to her stern Wife Voice. "I don't like this silence. Talk to me."

Jane ignored her. "Keisha?"

"The damned thing's stuck!"

Of course it was. Somehow, Jane wasn't even afraid, hearing this news. As if she'd always known it would come down to this. The plan didn't so much unfold in her mind as reveal what was already there, like whipping away a drop-cloth to reveal a finished painting.

"I'll be right there," Jane said.

"What? Captain, no. *How?*"

"That's my problem. Keep trying. I'll join you soon."

"Captain—"

"This isn't up for debate!" Jane ripped the earpiece away, tossing it onto the empty seat beside her. She just couldn't, not right now. She was already turning fast down a side street, already putting together the path she'd need to follow. Already pressing down on the gas.

She pushed the mute button again. "I have to go," she said. "There's been some complications, but we're going to fix them. Clair. We're going to get you back home. I promise."

"Don't. Don't promise."

"I promise," Jane said again. "But listen, I have to go. I'll see you soon."

"I don't—" Clair started, but Jane's thumb hit the button to end the call.

Silence filled the car. That was fine—Jane needed all of her concentration if there was any hope in hell of pulling this stunt off. She did not let herself think more than a single step ahead as she cut through the city, drawing farther and farther ahead of the train. As she found what she was looking for.

The brakes squealed as she pulled the wheel hard to the left. Jane barreled into a parking garage, the gate splintering to pieces behind her. If she was right, it should be empty by this point, so the chances of running into anyone should be fairly slim. Should. Jane kept a careful eye out, as careful as she could while careening up the spiral from one level to the next, shooting through the dark, spiraling up to the next. Dimly, she was aware of the fact that this was an outrageous stunt. That she'd definitely seen too many movies, read too many comics. That she might well die in the attempt.

Those thoughts slipped from her as fast as they formed, trailing behind her like exhaust. There was only Clair. Her smile and the birthmark beneath her right eye and her laugh and her ringtone, looping on repeat in the car with Jane.

Jane broke onto the roof of the parking garage. Her car skipped a little on release, skidding on impact as she threw the wheel sideways. If she could pause to think about what she was doing, she might have been able to talk herself out of it, but she didn't. Action/reaction. Adrenaline pushed her forward, as sure as the gas in her tank. A quick infrared scan through the roof, assessing her line of approach. Jane looped around once, gathering speed, and then shot forward.

Terror blanked out her memory of the jump itself, and that was just as well. An endless moment where her car careened through the air, and Jane was sure she was going to die. She didn't need to remember it. She came to as the impact hit her bones. The car landed hard on the tracks, and shimmied sharply to the left. Jane's heart leaped to her throat as she jerked the wheel, narrowly swerving the car back on course. She hit the brakes. The car skittered forward, wheels fighting for purchase. When she lurched to a stop a moment later, she wanted to leap from the car and kiss the ground in gratitude. Jane set the parking brake, then slammed open the glove compartment and the sunroof at the same time. The zip cord was in her grip by the time the seatbelt slid from her shoulder. Jane got her feet beneath her and hauled herself up.

She popped through the open sunroof like a gopher. The cold wind stung against the sweat of her skin. Headlights appeared in the distance, washing the front of Jane's car. Jane scrambled up. Onto the roof of the car, into a crouch. She hooked the zip cord onto her belt, cinching it tightly in place. By the time she looked back up, the train had seemed to leap forward, barreling down on top of her. Jane's eyes widened, soaking in the headlights as their reflection grew.

"Shit," Jane whispered. "Forgive me, Clair."

Jane huddled down. She drew in a breath, clearing her mind down to the comfort of empty panels. Her muscles coiled, then sprang as she leaped into the air.

Color and ink embraced her. Lines slid along her skin, brush-strokes nudging her spine into the proper arch. She spread her arms wide as the panel bloomed out around her. The first, running full-width and twice as tall as the others in the stack: the length of the train as it crashes into Jane's car, shards flying in all directions; the light of the explosion catches and highlights the scrap of red as Captain Lumen leaps, backflipping through the air, above the front train car. This is her Hero Shot of the issue, the one Jane clings to as her fingers fumble with the zip cord, as she hangs weightless and waiting to splatter like a bug. She has to believe it, has to feel it in her core. Quickly, now: stacked below, a tight shot as the end of her zip line pierces the roof of the train, a second as her boots land with confidence on the metal. The first panel of the opposite page has her face rising with determination.

The lurch in her stomach as her zip cord struck true brought her back to reality. Jane dry-heaved, her whole body whipping like a rag doll as she slammed against the roof of the train. Every muscle ached at once. Her grip slid, her fingers scrambling for purchase against the slick metal. Her heart raced like a rabbit as she managed to grab hold of a rail, a random piece of metal running along the train that seemed, at the moment, to have been placed there simply to catch her.

In the comics she hurries forward in a crouch, a series of tiny panels that cut from close to distance and back again: her boots, mid-leap between cars; the train cutting through the nearby buildings, Captain Lumen reduced to a dark smudge; a shot from the front, Pixie Beats's nervous face seen through the window as Captain Lumen finally reaches the roof over the driver's compartment.

Jane slithered forward on her belly. The zip cord ratcheted tighter and tighter beneath her as she followed the line up the train. Wind stung at her face, forcing her eyes closed. Did she even need to see? The zip cord would guide her, her panels would guide her. Sheer bloody-minded determination would guide her.

When she finally reached the arrow-tipped end of the line, she both did and didn't believe it, but she did not dare question her luck. She drew her knees up, dragging herself until she knelt on the roof of the train. Her power did not even need to be asked. She called up a laser beam, feeding the light along the index finger of her drawing hand as she cut a fast hole in the roof.

Metal clattered to the floor of the driver's compartment, Jane following fast on its heels.

Pixie Beats shrieked. "Jane! Shit, we thought you'd di—"

"I'm fine," Jane said as she staggered to her feet. She lurched forward, wrapping her hands around Pixie Beats's around the throttle. "Pull!"

Pixie Beats didn't need to be told twice. The two of them threw their weight into it, hauling the throttle down. She was right, it was good and stuck—but there was no force on earth that would stop Jane from making this work. Not now. Not after everything. Jane pulled at the handle, and Pixie Beats put one of her strong legs up on the console, pushing back, and together they worked until Jane's muscles were straining against her suit and screaming as loudly as she was, as loudly as the squeal of the brakes just catching their grip. Inch by inch they pulled, and inch by inch the train began to slow beneath them—almost imperceptible at first, the change so subtle that Jane didn't dare let herself believe it.

They lurched to a stop.

Jane collapsed, as every ounce of strength and determination and sheer stubborn need that had been propelling her forward retreated all at once. She did not even try to fall with grace. Her legs simply buckled beneath her, her arms falling wherever across her body. Her head clonked to the floor, and Jane didn't even flinch at the pain.

Pixie Beats's shadow fell over her. She put her hands on her hips, regarding Jane as she lay broken on the floor. "Damn, girl."

A strangled laugh escaped Jane's chest. "Yeah," she said, because what else was there to say? Jane shut her eyes. Her muscles were so beaten they almost didn't hurt anymore, just laid there in a puddle on the hard floor of the train, and Jane couldn't argue with them. She couldn't argue with anyone.

Damn, girl.

CLAIR LEFT HER SINGED COAT WITH JANE AND PARKED herself in a Starbucks about a block away from the scene. Close enough to see the perimeter of gawkers and reporters jamming in for a look, far enough that hopefully no one would be paying attention to her wind-tumbled hair, the slightly frazzled look around her eyes. She hugged a cup of tea against her chest. The warmth helped. She'd put her fingerless gloves back on, a thicker pair than she normally wore on the job. Thankfully, the cardboard of the cup was fairly indifferent, only the faintest trace of boredom from the barista who'd prepared her drink. Clair's powers were still sparking, but they had finally begun to settle down as the Heroes worked to evacuate the train's unconscious passengers.

Her phone chimed on the table in front of her. *Good news,* Jane's text said. *The passengers are waking up fine, and they seem to have no memory of their encounter with Mindsight.*

A sigh slipped out through Clair's lips. She should be there, too, but Jane had insisted she find a place to sit, collect herself, try to calm down. She'd been through an ordeal, Jane said. Jane would handle everything. Clair tried to argue that leaping onto a train was plenty of an ordeal, too, but Jane had waved her off, insisted she was fine; she'd pop into HQ later, slip into a rejuvenation pod for half an hour to restore her battered muscles. Clair didn't know if she believed that, but she was too tired to argue by that point. She unlocked her phone, tapped out a quick *Thanks*, and hit Send. The team would still need to silently hack into the passengers' phones, make sure no one had taken any videos while Clair had been dealing with Electric Fury, but she could breathe a little easier already. Whatever had knocked them out in the first place must have been strong enough to cause short-term amnesia.

"Well, that's lucky," Amy's voice said, and when Clair looked up, there she was. Sitting across the table, a mirror of Clair's tea steaming from her hand.

"Very." Clair tried to keep her voice down, so as not to look like she was talking to herself, but would anyone even notice? They'd probably just assume she was on the phone.

The two of them sat in silence for a moment. Clair sipped her tea. Amy appeared to do the same. As usual, she was the perfect match to Clair's appearance, right down to a singe along the lapel of Clair's blouse, which she only noticed when she spotted Amy's. What was that about, anyway? If these visions really were Amy, wouldn't she be able to look however she wanted?

Amy's face soured. "I'm afraid it doesn't work like that. You're still in the driver's seat, Clair. Everything I am is at your mercy."

Clair set her cup down. She leaned forward, elbows on the table. "Yeah, except I'm not buying it. Don't get me wrong, whoever or whatever you are, I'm grateful for your help earlier. But you're not Amy. You can't be. That's not how these powers work."

"Can't I?" Amy cocked an eyebrow. "You're awfully certain, for someone who's only been living with them for a year."

"More than. But it's not a matter of experience," Clair said. "You were flaring. You absorbed my essence. I'm sorry, but it doesn't just squash you down to make room. It's like overriding a file. Amy's gone."

Amy sat back, crossing her legs. She leaned onto the backrest of her chair, twisted just enough for one elbow to rest along the top. "Okay. Humor me for a second, though, will you? Who, exactly, are you getting this information from?"

Clair blinked. "Um. Marie, I suppose, for the science of it? And Jane, of course."

"Who isn't exactly an unbiased party in all this."

"What's *that* supposed to mean?"

Amy twirled a hand through the air. "Just that you shouldn't necessarily take her word for everything, Clair. When it comes right down to it, in a contest between you and me . . . who do you think Jane would really choose?"

Clair's fingers tightened around her cup. "That's not fair. It's not up to her."

"Isn't it?"

"No," Clair said, though her voice was a hair less confident than she wished it would be. "And I don't appreciate you saying that."

"The truth often hurts," Amy said with an indignant shrug of her shoulder.

"You mean like the truth of how you knowingly had sex with a supervillain?"

Amy narrowed her eyes. "That's not relevant."

"No? Because the way I see it, you didn't start showing up until after Electric Fury targeted me. I don't think that's a coincidence."

The expression on Amy's face flickered, just for a second, before she regained her composure. "Maybe I just realized you weren't capable of keeping my body safe anymore."

"Or maybe there's more going on here than you're willing to tell me. Who is she? Why is she so determined to see me dead?"

"How am I supposed to know?" Amy snapped. "She's a psychopath, obviously. They do weird shit."

Clair snorted. "You keep telling yourself that." Her phone chimed again—the ride share Jane had ordered for her was here. Clair stood up, pocketing her phone from the table and taking the rest of her tea with her. She leaned over the table, until she could whisper in Amy's ear. She did not even care, just then, how it looked. "In the meantime, just remember I'm on to you. And I won't stop until I've figured out what's really going on here."

Amy's eyes cut to hers. So close that Clair's own reflection stared back at her from the glassy void. "That would be a mistake, Clair."

Clair shrugged. She straightened up. "Then it'll be my mistake. Because it's *my* life." She turned away, throwing her cup into the trash as she reached the door. When she glanced back over her shoulder, Amy was gone.

IT WASN'T PART OF A SUPERFIGHT, SO IT WAS EASY enough for their meeting to go unnoticed. Four years ago. Before the new Janes, before the emergence of UltraViolet. Mindsight was out scouring for clues about a villain named the Ruinator, hitting up one seedy bar and then another. Her job was simple: get inside, shake some hands, rub some elbows, literally anything that would let her get a read on the clientele. If she picked up traces of the Ruinator's name or face in the corners of anyone's mind, she'd signal Pixie Beats, currently riding shotgun in the roomy pockets of Mindsight's trench coat. Pixie Beats could then tail the suspect, and if that didn't work, Keisha knew plenty of martial-arts moves that would leave thugs in a painful twist, more than enough to get the average scumbag to crack.

In truth, Amy hated when the team used Mindsight like this, but who was she to argue? She'd never been a physical force to be reckoned with, certainly not compared to Marie or Keisha or Cal, and even her marksman training at the shooting range was not enough to pass Cal's Marines-inspired tests. Plus, Jane had made up her mind a long time ago, and, well . . . once the captain had spoken . . .

Four hours into her search, more than a dozen bars prowled, and Mindsight hadn't managed to turn up anything of substance.

She let the door shut behind her, cutting off the pitiful wail of the dive bar's falling-apart jukebox, and replacing it with the scream of sirens, the bark of a dog, the shouts of a nasty fight coming from the apartment building across the street. South Shits, as this part of the city was known, wasn't exactly prime real estate, but on nights like tonight, the weight of everything the Heroes *hadn't* managed to fix in Grand City dragged heavily on Mindsight's mind. Each crash of glass, each cry of a child, felt like a personal slight against Mindsight and everything the Heroes had fought so hard to accomplish.

A gentle weight shifted in Mindsight's pocket, and a second later the faintest *whoosh* of air announced Pixie Beats returning to her full size beside her. Pixie Beats fell into step effortlessly, the slap of her sneakers and the jangle of her bangles lending some small comfort to the night. She held out a bottle of Purell, and Mindsight's palm was already upturned, waiting for it. Mindsight's signature fingerless gloves were stashed into a different pocket of her coat for the evening, allowing her better contact with the sweaty palms of Grand City's dive-bar patrons. Mindsight spent several long moments rubbing in the hand sanitizer, reveling in the cold of the alcohol, the sterile bite of meaningless liquid against her skin.

"So, we going to regroup?" Pixie Beats asked, and Mindsight nodded. It had been more than long enough to determine that they weren't going to find anything this way. Plus, the team still had several other avenues to explore, so there was no harm in packing it in.

After a cheery little wave, Pixie Beats shrank back down, heading off. Navigating the city was easier, she said, when she could dart along railings and hitch rides on the back of people's coats, hopping from one shoulder to the next. Plus, even if she stuffed her masquerade mask away and unclipped the green braid from her hair, the fluttery skirts, bright tights, and bedazzled jacket of her uniform weren't exactly inconspicuous. Unlike Amy, who only needed to remove her hat and slim black mask, turn down the collar of her trench coat, stuff her hands into her pockets.

Sometimes, though, the simplicity of Mindsight's uniform made it hard for Amy to tell where her persona ended, and *she* began. Especially since she never got a break from her powers—unlike the others, who could simply choose not to use them, Amy's empathic awareness was a constant undercurrent to her life. *Was* there a difference, she sometimes wondered, between Amy and Mindsight? Or was it merely two sides of the same coin, flipping endlessly through the air?

It was the kind of question she'd like to ask Jane, but *that* wasn't exactly an option these days. The two of them hadn't been close since they were young. Even once Jane had come back into Amy's life, forming the Heroes, reconnecting with her old friends, there was something . . . missing between the two of them. At first, Amy had just chalked it up to the fight they'd had as teenagers, and the time and distance that had followed—people grew apart, she told herself, it happened, it's life. She couldn't expect Jane to still be ruled by childhood sentimentality. Just because *Amy* was still hung up on the mad crush of her youth, that didn't mean *Jane* owed her anything.

It was a testament to how wrapped up in her own thoughts Amy was, that she almost walked straight into the mugging happening at the corner. She should have spotted it half a block away, but she didn't, and only the startled cry of a voice that sounded disturbingly like Jane's made her look up.

The voice wasn't Jane's, of course, but that didn't matter now. Amy had walked right into the situation, and she'd be a lousy hero indeed if she'd stood by doing nothing.

"Hey!" she shouted.

The muggers looked up. Two men, white, brushing twenty if that. The streetlight at the corner caught their faces, and the sneer they turned upon Amy glowed like torches in a mob. They did not wear hoods or hats, they did not wear ski masks. They were brazen in their attack, emboldened by the knowledge that no one would bother coming after them. They wore Adidas T-shirts and designer jeans. They did not need the money, they were not desperate. This mugging was a game, their victim a plaything.

A slice of fear coursed through Amy. The daily drum of every nervous mother and tutting opinion piece marched through her head: *stay small, stay quiet, run away, why aren't your keys tucked between the fingers of your fist, are you wearing anything too revealing, why did you interfere, you're next, you're next, you're next, it's all your fault.*

It was a familiar tune, one Amy had long ago made peace with. She let it run through her, took a deep breath to cleanse the toxicity. She was a Hero, she reminded herself. She had helped take down villains of all shapes and sizes—hell, once they all fought off a monster from another *planet*, which had fallen through some interdimensional portal at the Grand City Public Library. *You've got this,* she told herself. Hours of hand-to-hand combat training with Cal flitted through her mind as she took a step forward.

Plus, there was always the revolver she had strapped to her side.

The muggers grinned.

Amy's stomach gave a nervous twist. Monsters be damned—there was nothing in the universe scarier than a man looking at a woman the way these two looked at her now.

The time for posturing was over. Amy's hand flew to her revolver as the muggers took their first steps forward. For a second, a flicker of hesitation did seem to pass between them. But then, like a pack of piranhas, they rushed her.

It happened too fast to track. Amy's revolver fired, one of the muggers shouted, a predatory hand found a fistful of Amy's hair. A flood of bitterness, entitlement, superiority, pride, ego, fear, rage, repression, too much to process, hatred so pure that it drowned out all thought. Then a flash of light broke the scene, and for a second she was convinced Captain Lumen had come to rescue her—that *Jane* had come to rescue her.

But it wasn't Captain Lumen's iconic red suit that stood now between Amy and the muggers, and it wasn't Jane's brown ponytail flying out as her savior whirled, landing fist and heel upon the muggers as easily as if they were training dummies. Flashes of silver and white crackled through the alleyway.

Shame replaced relief. Whoever this mystery woman was, she clearly did not need Amy's help, but Amy would not just stand there like the kidnapped secretary of a 1940s B-movie, whose only role was to scream for help and swoon over the hero.

She snatched her gun from where it had fallen on the sidewalk, took aim, but . . .

The number one rule of both heroing and self-defense: you do not escalate a fight yourself. Looking at the muggers now, their asses getting repeatedly handed to them by the deft moves of the woman in the catsuit, they looked almost pitiful.

Back into the holster went Amy's revolver, and instead, she marched up and threw a solid punch across the jaw of the remaining mugger. He pivoted, thrown off balance, and fell comically over the heap of his compatriot.

"Nice!" the mystery woman laughed as sirens screamed in the distance. The last thing either of them needed was to be found at the scene. Amy rushed over to the woman who'd first been attacked. Her fingers brushed against the back of the woman's neck just long enough to determine she was fine, not seriously injured, just shaken up, when a cold hand clamped down around Amy's wrist. "Leave her!"

What happened next was an experience Amy was never able to describe, no matter how many times she tried to sort through it in her mind.

The world collapsed.

Not literally, perhaps, although it was impossible for Amy to tell at the time what was real and what was perception. A jolt that crossed her skin and seared her heart, and then the world as Amy knew it smashed into her, folded her up, and there was nothing for an instant except an endless stretch of *speed*. Rage carried her forward. Crackling and electric, wild and free, a fury so strangely intense it was almost euphoric. Nothing could hold it, not time or space, not physical form. It raced across the city, carrying Amy on a burst of anger that was at once familiar and unexpected.

It was over so fast. Too fast. When she finally burst back into herself, she was so stunned that she couldn't breathe. She collapsed, straight onto the woman who'd intervened in the alleyway, the woman who'd apparently brought her here.

Amy rolled off, sputtering apologies. She threw herself onto shaky legs, a new lamb not yet dry of its mother. Her heart pounded as hard as if she'd just outrun a murderer.

The woman laughed. She pushed herself up onto her elbows, grinning up at Amy. "That was fun. I have to admit, I was a little worried. I've never tried to bring someone along for the ride before."

Amy gaped. "You . . . you mean you didn't even know if it would *work*? What if I'd died!"

"Then you wouldn't be around to complain about it, now would you?" the woman said as she drew herself to her feet. She brushed off her silver catsuit, fluffed her white hair. "Oh, come on. You know you loved it."

Denial slipped up Amy's throat. She opened her mouth, intending to release it, except: nothing came out. She frowned instead. "I suppose I should thank you for your help. With the muggers."

"No problem," the woman said with a wink. She turned, stepping up onto the ledge of the roof like she was prepared for a dive. "See you around, Mindsight."

Then she raised her arms, leaped, and with a crackle of lightning that shot from the building, she was gone.

THE BANK LOOKED BETTER IN THE DAYLIGHT.

Despite the glass that crunched beneath Jane's red boots. Despite the bloodstains that swept the marble floor. Despite the ring of police tape circling the building, the numbered place cards marking pieces of evidence. It was an after shot, sure, and a mess some poor shmuck would need to clean up later, but there was a peace to be found in the crisis being over.

Or maybe it was just that Jane felt a lot better having Clair by her side this time.

"Okay, so . . . what are we looking for, again?" Clair asked.

"Anything," Jane said. "Some indication as to what they were after, or any clues the police might have missed."

Clair raised one eyebrow above the line of her mask. "You said the police report showed they broke into the vault? Call me a fool, but I'd guess they were after money."

Jane shook her head. "No. There was more to it than that. I know there was."

She knew Clair didn't believe her. That was okay—Clair didn't need to believe it. Jane had asked Clair to do her a favor, and so she'd do the best damned job she was capable of, belief or not.

In truth, Jane wasn't sure she necessarily believed it, either. On the surface, it certainly looked like a straightforward robbery. There was nothing in the thieves' actions yesterday that pointed to some larger conspiracy, some nefarious plot. That was kind of the problem. Jane had done some digging last night, after Clair had gone to bed. In her comics, no group of Enhanced this organized or experienced would have hit up a place like this as a petty crime. People with new powers, sure, all the time. Even those who'd had abilities for a while, if they had a niche power, or never really got a handle on how to use it properly. Banks were a popular target for rookies—a training ground, of sorts. Hit up a few, maybe a jewelry store. See if you were ready for the big leagues.

But once they gained a level of notoriety, and certainly once they'd begun to team up and make costumes and give themselves code names, they tended to start setting their sights higher. It was almost like the powers themselves gave Enhanced a calling, a sense that they could be something larger and greater than they were before. For some, this led to acts of heroism. In others . . .

There was no evidence, of course, that real life would necessarily follow the pattern of Jane's comics. All of the truly uncanny details had come from Clair's dreams, and a lot of the remainder was just stuff Jane had made up to fill the pages and drum up more interesting storylines. Still. In her home office that night, she'd booted up her laptop and connected to the Heroes' private server, had a look through their database. All the old criminals they'd helped put away. The pattern certainly seemed to hold, and that was enough to get Tony on board, using his badge to get Jane and Clair, as Captain Lumen and Mindsight, access beyond the police tape.

It's also possible Jane had just woken up bitter, having been ripped from sleep by an alert on her phone. Both of the Enhanced they'd captured at the bank yesterday had "mysteriously" escaped police custody overnight. Lots of fingers were being pointed, but so far, there was no obvious culprit. So a trip to the bank, retracing their steps, felt like an appropriate investigatory measure.

"So this is where the hostages were being held," Jane said now, motioning at the teller counters.

Clair nodded. She stepped over, gingerly avoiding the spent bullet casings, the bloodstain on the marble. Since yesterday, she'd picked up a new copy of Mindsight's trench coat from headquarters, all evidence of what had happened on the train swept aside. But Jane could still see it, every time she looked at her. Hovering like ghosts around Clair, everything that might have happened. Dreams of Clair's funeral had plagued Jane's sleep. She'd tried to keep some physical distance between her and Clair in bed last night, hoping not to bother her with the images; but Jane could tell, from the way Clair looked at her this morning, that she'd picked up on it. Well, why wouldn't she? Jane had probably left fear all over their sheets, like sweat stains on an August night.

Jane went around the back of the teller counter. She and Clair were far from the only people in the bank that morning. Forensics and at least one detective milled through the lobby, as well as a handful of uppity-up bank staff, their expensive suits a sharp contrast to the uniforms and grubby jackets the police sported. In the teeming activity, two superheroes almost blended in.

"—as soon as we can, but you have to understand, this is a major crime scene," one of the officers was saying to the bankers as Jane regarded the mess sprawling across the marble floors.

Jane held her phone up, arms-length away. A picture of one of the attackers was on her screen, and she panned it across until she found the spot where he'd been standing. Another bounty from the Heroes' database: she now had aliases and clear faces to put to the three of them. It wasn't much—they were fairly new to the crime scene, little known about their backgrounds or abilities—but it was something. Acid Reign, a.k.a. Natalie Nelson; she was the only one they had a proper name on, because she'd already built up a rap sheet for petty thefts and carjacking. The prince of darkness actually called himself PitchBlack, not just Pitch; no idea where he came from. Which left Megacrush, who'd apparently already hit up a convenience store or two in recent weeks, though no one had recorded his size as reaching quite the heights he'd managed yesterday. She swiped through their pictures, moving them around the lobby of the bank like paper dolls on an imaginary stage. Her fingers itched for a pencil, her sketchbook. If she could better visualize what had happened here, would she be able to figure out what their game was?

"I doubt it," Clair said. She'd come up to the teller counter while Jane had been distracted, and now she rested her arms on the low surface, regarding the basket of lollipops in front of her.

Jane looked over sharply. "What?"

Clair picked up a lollipop. She stuffed the wrapper into her pocket, the candy into her mouth. "What's 'what'?" she asked, though it came out more like "wuh wuh?"

"Why did you say that?"

A puzzled frown disrupted Clair's forehead. The lollipop clicked against her teeth as she shifted it around her mouth. "I don't know. Don't get me wrong, I like the creative thinking. But I just don't think you're going to crack this with a comic." Clair paused, her expression growing wary as she watched Jane. "What's wrong? Why are you looking at me like that?"

Jane pressed her hands down flat on her side of the counter. "I didn't *say* any of that."

"Yes, you did. I heard you."

"No," Jane said. "I *thought* about it. But that's all."

Clair pulled her lollipop out. "You must have been muttering to yourself, then."

"I wasn't."

"Well, you *had* to be," Clair snapped. "Because whatever else you're implying, you can stop implying it." She stuffed her lollipop back in her mouth, snapping her lips shut like the matter was final.

Jane took a breath. "I just—"

But before she could finish, Tony rushed up. He glanced at Clair, the lollipop in her mouth. "Hey." He pointed at the basket. "Um. Should you be eating those?"

"It's not exactly evidence," Clair said through her mouthful.

Tony shook his head. For a second, Jane thought he would argue with her, but he didn't. Instead, he held out his phone. "You two need to see this."

Jane took it. She held it over the counter, so that both she and Clair could see the video Tony had pulled up for them. Jane's stomach was already cinching before she even hit play, just seeing Cal's face paused on the screen.

"*. . . and look, I'm not saying it's their fault,*" Cal started. He was already midspeech; the video looked like it had been captured at a rally or something. Cal had a mic in his hand, his suit coat off, his tie loosened, his sleeves rolled up. He stood in the middle of a circle of chairs in some shitty community room somewhere. An American flag hung on the wall behind him as he gestured toward the crowd. "*I don't want to criticize them. I know they think they're doing good—and plenty of people, across all Grand City, have stories that attest to the lives they've saved. No one is questioning that.*

"*But you have to ask yourself, and you have to be honest . . . would these criminals* need *to resort to using such extravagant powers if the Heroes weren't around to crush anything less? It's simple physics. Every action has an* equal and opposite *reaction. The Heroes get powerful enough to stop ordinary criminals. Suddenly the criminals have to get* extra *ordinary, just to keep doing the levels of crime they were before! Which makes the Heroes up* their *game, which means the criminals need to get still* more *powerful. Think about it. We're stuck smack dab in the middle of an arms race. And who are the ones to suffer, when they get caught in the crossfire?*" He pointed, first to one audience member, then another. Then another. "*All of you. Good, ordinary citizens.*"

"Oh, bullshit," Clair said, though she seemed to be in a minority opinion. Jane's blood chilled as, in the video, Cal waited to let a wash of applause pass over him.

"*Which is why,*" Cal continued, "*if I'm elected, my first priority in Washington is going to be a series of comprehensive, anti-superpower legislation. We need to cap this madness, here and now, before it escalates to the point where it's unstoppable.*"

There was more, but Jane couldn't listen. Her thumb slammed the pause button, and she handed Tony back his phone. "Please tell me you've been doing something more useful than browsing social media."

Tony frowned as he slipped his phone into one of the many pockets of his police uniform. "Excuse me for thinking you'd find this important," he said. "But since you asked *so nicely*, there was something else. We've been working with the bank to identify what, exactly, was stolen."

Clair glanced at Jane. "Not money?"

"Some money, sure. But if you're going through the effort of robbing a bank, you'd think they'd have made off with more than they took. There's still plenty of bundles just sitting there, and frankly, banks don't really hold as much cash in their vaults as TV makes it seem."

Jane bit her lip to keep from smirking in triumph. Clair rolled her eyes.

"Okay," Jane said. She was decidedly *not* going to say *I told you so*. "So what's the deal?"

Tony put his hand to his chest. "Well, surely I, as a lowly beat-cop, wouldn't know. But . . . I do have it on good authority from a certain superhero I'm fairly close to, who shall remain nameless, that they hit up the safe deposit boxes before they left. And I, um. I may have found this on the floor."

He held out a slip of paper, pinched between his fingers.

Clair took it, before Jane could. A box ID code was written in Tony's cramped handwriting.

"Found it on the floor, huh?" Clair said.

Tony shrugged. "Possibly. Who can really say, for certain?"

Clair smiled as she tucked the paper into her trench coat. "Good work."

"It's a start," Jane said. "We still need to identify the owner of the box. And see if he'll tell us what was in it, or else try to learn that on our own. And figure out why *that* may have been important enough to knock over a bank for. And—"

"Yes, Captain," Clair said. She reached across the counter, running her hand up and down Jane's shoulder. "We know. But as you said, it's a start."

Jane caught her breath, swallowing down the litany of tasks still left ahead of them. She shut her eyes instead, focusing on the comfort of Clair's touch on her arm. Clair was right, of course. She was always right.

A buzz brought Jane back to herself. Her phone, stirring angrily in her jacket. Jane had felt, through the tether of her powers to the phone's wifi, that she'd been receiving messages and voicemails all morning, but she'd been studiously ignoring them, because they'd all come from Mayor Maxwell. Now that they'd switched over to Mrs. Maxwell, though, Jane figured it couldn't hurt to find out what was going on. She sighed and took her phone out.

"Ah, crap," Jane said a moment later. She tapped Clair's arm. "Come on, we have to go."

"What's wrong?"

Jane rounded the counter. "There's a terrible foe needing to be vanquished, and it's going to require every ounce of strength I have left to defeat it," she said. She glanced at Clair. "We're late for my 'father's' campaign photoshoot."

JANE DROVE. BOTH HANDS ON THE STEERING WHEEL,
in three-and-nine position. Textbook-perfect signaling. Excellent corners. Jane slowed to a complete stop at every stop sign,
accelerated smoothly, obeyed all posted speed limits.

Clair wasn't driving anymore. It was an unspoken agreement
after she'd come back. Three days after her resurrection, the first
time either Jane or Clair ventured out from the hotel room they
were staying in until they figured out what they were doing
long-term. They'd finally put on pants, combed their hair. At
the door, Jane didn't even hesitate before she grabbed the keys.
Normally, Before, Clair did most of the driving; but Clair didn't
argue then, and she hadn't argued a single day since.

Jane it was, then. Since they'd moved, she'd spent hours,
days—whole weekends, even—at a private track just outside
the city, learning with retired race car drivers. For acting as a
Hero, this had the benefit of letting her pull stunts like she'd

done yesterday, in her race to rescue Clair. But while she was a speed demon whenever she wore the suit, the minute she took it off, she became one of those moms who puts a Baby on Board sticker in the window. She routinely putted along just under the posted limit. In truth, Clair sometimes felt a little stifled by the overboard obsession with safety, but who was she to judge?

Clair leaned her head against the window. Patchy sunshine struggled to break through the clouds. They drove to the northeast corner of the city, into an odd little neighborhood called Howard Park. Howard Park was notable as the site of Grand City's famous A. B. Steelworker Protests in the 1870s, which made it historically interesting and gave it a certain gravitas, but moreover: it was notoriously a pain to get into. All public transport ceased just outside the perimeter, and the roads were a hellish nightmare of one-ways, roundabouts, and cobblestones. It took Jane only twenty minutes to get across town, and then another ten to navigate to the Maxwells' city residence. The Grand City Mayor's Mansion, according to Allison, was only allowed to be used for city business, and so campaign activities were strictly off-limits.

At the gate, security waved them through. Box shrubs lined both sides of the circular driveway. Jane pulled the car in beside Mrs. Maxwell's sleek black town car, and a vintage blue convertible with Maryland plates that presumably signaled Allison's presence.

Jane and Clair had been to the house a handful of times, but Clair still couldn't get used to it. Something about the deep red bricks and pitch black roof, the numerous chimneys jutting toward the sky, the point of the circular corner tower, struck Clair as vaguely sinister. This, despite (or perhaps enhanced by) the forcibly infused cheer of Mrs. Maxwell's numerous flower boxes, and the creeping ivy blooming all over the south wall. It didn't help that by now the sun had disappeared completely, the blue of the sky retreating like a shy bride, drawing a curtain of gray over the city. They walked up the front porch beneath a splash of yellow lamplight.

Mrs. Maxwell opened the door herself. As always, she looked impeccable. Clair knew that Jane often resented this version of her mother, and any little difference—the surgically de-aged face, the tailored clothes—was a point for scoffing and silent judgment. Privately, though, Clair admired Mrs. Maxwell's elegance. Not that the version Clair had grown up knowing was a slob, by any means, but just *once* Clair wished this Mrs. Maxwell would invite her to see her closet. Clair bet she had a whole room just for her shoes.

Somehow, though, Clair doubted that invitation would come today. The line of Mrs. Maxwell's lips tightened as her attention settled on Jane and Clair. "You're late."

"Hi, Olivia, nice to see you, too," Jane said. She breezed into the foyer, shouldering Mrs. Maxwell aside.

Mrs. Maxwell grabbed her arm. "Do me a favor and try not to make things worse today, Janie. He's already annoyed enough as it is."

"Don't call me Janie," Jane said as she pushed her glasses up with her free hand. "And as for the mayor, I'm 'sorry' if my work keeping the city safe interferes with his precious timetable, but—"

Mrs. Maxwell's grip tightened, cutting her off. "Keep your voice *down*," she said through gritted teeth.

Jane pulled her arm free. Half-moon impressions from Mrs. Maxwell's nails faded against Jane's skin as she moved silently into the depths of the house. Mrs. Maxwell watched her go, her attention lingering in the hall, and Clair bet she was counting to ten in her mind.

By the time she turned back to the door, her face had been wiped clean. She motioned for Clair to come inside, her composure and charm reasserted in full force. Her voice sparkled as brightly as her diamond earrings. "Clair, my dear. Thank you so much for joining us on this."

"Thank you for asking me to," Clair said. She stepped up, gracefully allowing Jane's behavior to pass behind them. "I know the wedding got disrupted, so I'm not *technically* part of the family yet, but—"

"Oh, nonsense," Mrs. Maxwell said with a dismissive wave. "Even if we both didn't know the real story, I think it's safe to say you've *always* been part of this family."

This was kind of her to say, though not, strictly speaking, *true*. Not in this world, anyway. The memories Clair could dig up were still patchy in so many places, but she knew with absolute certainty that there had been a number of years, as they finished high school and most of college, when Amy and Jane didn't speak at all. Even before then . . . well, the Jane that Amy knew had never been *Clair's* Jane, that was for sure.

Clair didn't argue with the sentiment, though. Instead, she slipped inside the house, wiping her shoes carefully on the mat. They were a recent thrift-store find, contented patent leather heels in traffic-cone orange, a Mary Jane strap across the top held down with cheerful daisy buttons. Her suit, cobalt blue, consisted of a pencil skirt and cap sleeve blouse, cinched together with a wide lavender belt that matched her lace gloves. She'd based the color palette on a photo of a sea anemone, something about the peace of the deeper ocean instantly settling her nerves.

Jane was already in the doorway to the study by the time Clair caught up with her. Her own dress was a sleeveless A-line, done in basic black like she was going to a funeral. Dark gray stockings traced her legs, though Clair had talked her into maroon flats instead of black ankle boots. They'd thrown their outfits together in record time, Clair still twisting Jane's hair into a bun as they'd power-walked to the car. *"Hold still,"* Clair had muttered through a mouthful of bobby pins, though Jane either hadn't heard or had pretended not to understand. *"God, Jane,"* she'd added once they were in the car. *"You could at least try to care. You* want *your dad to win, after all, if Cal is the alternative."*

"He's not my dad," Jane had said, checking her mirrors and starting the car.

Now, Clair reached up, fixing a loose tendril on the back of Jane's head, which had either been missed or wormed its way free in the meantime. Through the doorway, you could see the camera crew packed in as thickly as teen girls in line to see a boy band. A nest of lights filled all available space, trying to brighten the stolen daylight—there was even a false backdrop someone had hung outside the window, a clear blue sky that wasn't fooling anyone in real life, but would probably look convincing enough out of focus in the background of a political ad.

Mayor Maxwell sat in the middle of it all, a king at high court. The ease that pooled off of him was a dead-ringer for the real thing. Only the slight tightening of his fist in his lap gave away that he'd noticed the arrival of his daughter and would-be in-law. The ruby of his ring caught the light—class of '75, Sutton University. Jane sometimes criticized him for hanging on to it for so long, longer than he'd worn his wedding ring on their own world. It only made sense, then, that Sutton is the first and only place his campaign had suggested for the upcoming debate.

"I'm Paul Maxwell, and I approve this message," Mayor Maxwell said. He paused, giving the camera a moment to capture the full extent of his sincerity. Some makeup artist somewhere had made sure to leave the crinkles around his eyes. Then, without missing a beat, he tried it again. "I'm Paul Maxwell . . . and I *approve* this message."

"Good," said a guy standing behind the cameraman. He had his arms crossed, a pair of glasses on a cord around his neck, and a studious expression like he was a blockbuster director and this was his shot at finally nailing an Academy Award. He stepped back, studying the arrangement of the furniture. "All right, now why don't we try bringing in Olivia for a moment, and then—"

Mayor Maxwell shook his head. "Dave, give us a second, okay? I'd like to speak to my daughter, please."

Dave nodded, just the tiniest pinching of his brow. "Sure, good. That gives us time to fix this lighting. I know we can do better . . ."

Annoyance rolled through Jane, shooting up Clair's fingers before she could pull away. Instantly, Clair left the Maxwells' house behind. Gone were the cameras, the old-world charm of the study, the warmth flickering off the fireplace. When Clair blinks, she finds herself in the Maxwells' old backyard, in the shade of the oak tree down by the river. She recognizes the moment from her own memory, though the pain that surges through her chest now is decidedly Jane's, as are the hands folded neatly in her lap as she stares down at the lump of used tissues. *It's my fault, it's my fault,* Jane keeps blubbering, and Clair keeps rubbing her back, the feel of her hand strong and reassuring. *No, it's not. It's not, Jane.*

Nothing is going to change Jane's mind, though. Clair knew it at the time and she knows it now, feeling it over again from Jane's perspective. The night before, the two of them had finally come out to each of their parents in turn, finally admitted the true nature of their relationship. That morning, without a word, Jane's dad had come down the stairs with a suitcase in his hand; he wouldn't even look at her as he went out the door.

The ache of Jane's chest stayed tight in Clair's as she came back to herself. Clair pulled her hand away from where it had rested on the back of Jane's neck. The warmth in the hall felt too much now, stifling in a way that had previously been cozy.

Mayor Maxwell stepped out of the study. His face shone from sweat and camera makeup, and a hidden microphone still clung with desperation at the inside of his navy-blue suit jacket. He did not say anything, just crossed the hall to the library, expecting to be followed.

"Nice of you to finally show up," Mayor Maxwell said, as soon as Clair closed the door behind them.

Jane shrugged. "I was busy."

"I *texted*."

"I was *driving*."

"Like that's ever stopped anyone."

"You know, if it was really so important, you could have tried Clair's number, too."

Mayor Maxwell's eyes flicked over. He hadn't so much as said "hello" to Clair—and it wasn't just the distraction of the filming, or his annoyance with Jane. Clair knew that, he knew that. Jane sure as hell knew that.

"That's not the point." He did not even begin to address the fact that he didn't *have* Clair's phone number; that, despite the publicity and good face for the voters, he'd barely spoken ten words to Clair since they'd announced their second engagement.

Jane sighed. "Look, I'm sorry I'm late, okay? I didn't mean to—"

"God*dammit*, Jane, this has nothing to do with you being late! Do you really not understand that you've been targeted by *assassins* recently? When you didn't answer your phone, we thought—"

He cut himself off. Clair's heart tugged as he turned his head, running his hand over his shaved face as if to gather himself together. She glanced at Jane, but Jane remained as impassive as ever.

"I'm assigning you police protection," he said, turning back.

Jane blinked. "What? No! Dad, I don't need—"

"Yes, you do. Or did you not notice the disaster at your own wedding?"

"Yeah, well, maybe if you'd stuck around after the attack, instead of running off to deal with your precious public image, you'd know I wasn't the target."

Mayor Maxwell sneered. "I'm well aware of that, Jane." He did not look, not even once, in Clair's direction, but the absence of a glance was somehow even more telling. "But what makes you think you're not next on their list? Why bother coming after just *one* of you? Perhaps Amy was merely—"

"*Clair.* Her name is *Clair.*"

"Clair, yes, whatever," Mayor Maxwell said with a wave.

"No," Jane said. "No, it's not 'whatever.' She's going to be my wife—your daughter-in-law!—and you can't even be bothered to get her name right?" She shook her head. "You're unbelievable. You haven't changed at all."

Clair glanced nervously at Mayor Maxwell. Technically, both Jane and Clair knew this version of him wasn't the same man who'd walked out on Jane and her mom all those years ago. Even that one, they'd never found out his reasons for sure—he was, after all, already having an affair by that point. Uncertainty had softened the guilt Jane felt at first, before curdling into an anger so deep that Clair doubted Jane would ever let it go.

Still. Wouldn't this version of Mr. Maxwell have done the exact same thing, if circumstances had unfolded that way?

"How dare you speak to me like that," Mayor Maxwell said. His voice was not angry, per se, and yet. The evenness of it, the control. The *quiet.* "Do you have any idea how much I have done for the gay community in this city?"

"If you're looking for a cookie, you're asking the wrong lesbian."

Mayor Maxwell shook his head. "Unbelievable."

They were saved by a soft knock on the door. It cracked open before anyone had a chance to answer, and the assistant mayor stuck his head inside. He glanced briefly at Jane, pressing his lips into a tiny smile of sympathy before he turned to the mayor. "Sir? We really should keep things moving."

"Thank you, Dominick. I'll be right there," Mayor Maxwell said. He turned to Jane. "This discussion isn't over."

"Oh, goody."

"Watch it, young lady." Mayor Maxwell raised a finger. His ring caught the light again, red as blood. "Now, you're going to go in there, and you're going to pose with us like a family, and you're going to look happy about it, do I make myself clear?"

Jane opened her mouth, taking a breath, but Mayor Maxwell did not bother waiting for an answer. He turned to Clair. Held out his hand, as if to usher her through the door. "And of course, we wouldn't want to forget my favorite in-law. Clair, you'll be just to the other side of Olivia."

Clair swallowed. She knew Jane hated being used like this, as props for the narrative Mayor Maxwell wanted to present. Still, what other choice did they have? This was part of being a Maxwell, and if there was one thing Clair had been desperate to get back to, it had been that name. Clair pulled her lips wide, the practiced smile she used in presentations and board meetings at work. "It would be my pleasure."

THE REST OF THE SHOOT TOOK HOURS. STAND HERE, stand there. Look at Clair, look at the camera, look at the mayor. Sit, stay, shake. Smile, smile, smile. *We're the Maxwells!* Flash, snap, click.

By the time they were done, Jane's teeth hurt. Whether from smiling or the saccharine-infused Americana being peddled by Dave the director, or both, she couldn't tell. All she wanted was to go home, crawl into a hot bath, and forget everything.

Allison smacked the back of Jane's head. "Come with me."

"Ow," Jane muttered. She glanced back, but Clair had stepped out to take a phone call, so there really was nothing stopping Jane from following.

Allison cut through the main hall, heading toward the kitchen. Jane's stomach rumbled. There was a big family brunch scheduled for before the photoshoot, but they'd missed that part. Jane followed the flick of Allison's highlighted hair as it graced the top of her shoulders.

The kitchen door swung shut behind them.

"So," Allison said as she crossed the tiles.

"So."

Allison reached into an overhead cabinet and pulled down a bulbous wine glass. She kept her back to Jane. "Don't play dumb, Jane. You know what I want to talk about."

"How concerned you've been for your dear, devoted sister since her wedding?"

Allison didn't even deign that one with a response. She grabbed a bottle from the counter, and popped the cork. Poured herself a glass.

Jane side-eyed the mountain of leftover boxes sitting neatly on the counter. "Look, I don't know what you expect me to say."

"Bullshit," Allison said. "Cal's back."

"Yes."

"You and I both know his arrival can't be a good thing—for us, or the city."

"Yes."

Allison turned around, the curve of the glass cradled in her hand. "Then stop being obtuse and tell me *what you're planning to do about it.*"

"Doesn't seem to be much I *can* do about it," Jane said. "Bryson resigned, and this is a free election. Cal can run if he wants to."

Maybe. Jane still wasn't entirely sure that switching candidates after a primary followed any sort of rules, but the media wasn't complaining, and Mayor Maxwell hadn't so much as whispered the word "lawsuit," so what did Jane know?

Allison rolled her eyes. "And that's a lovely sentiment, but since when did you and your friends ever care about technicalities like whether or not something was *legal*?"

Jane bristled. "Hey. We're not criminals."

"You're not 'bad guys,'" Allison said. She literally raised her free hand, hooking her fingers for the air quotes. "Last I checked, vigilantism was against the law."

"The city's never enforced that."

"You mean *Dad's* never enforced that." Allison set her glass down, probably harder on the counter than she'd meant to. She turned back to Jane, crossing her arms over her chest as she leaned against the edge of the sink. "And why is that, do you think? Jesus, Jane, you've got his wife *and* the assistant mayor on your side. You realize how sinister that looks, don't you?"

Jane adjusted her glasses, unconcerned. "It's not my fault Keisha's husband chose a career in politics. Dominick's choices are entirely his own—and for that matter, I certainly never asked Olivia to get involved in anything. Not that the mayor would ever listen to her, anyway."

A laugh burst out of Allison. Sharp as glass breaking. "You don't really believe that, do you?"

But a burst of noise from the hall saved Jane from having to answer. Squeals and happy greetings, the ricochet of small footsteps racing around.

Allison glanced at her Apple Watch. "Ah, crap."

Jane was going to ask what was going on, but her question was answered just as she took the breath to say it. The kitchen door burst open, a sugary-blond head careening into the room. "Mommy!" the girl shrieked as she pelted Allison's legs.

The shift was instantaneous. Gone was the snarking, sassy older sister, the cranky member of a top-secret government task force. Instead, Allison's face bloomed, all smiles as she crouched down and allowed for a more equal hug. "Hey, baby! How's my girl today?"

"Libby threw up in the car!" the girl said as she and her mother broke apart. Which wasn't an answer, not really, though Jane supposed it was as useful as Allison was going to get.

"Oh, no!" Allison said. She brushed a stray piece of hair out of the girl's face. "Was Daddy able to clean it up?"

A nod. "Uh-huh." But then the girl's attention shifted, turning. She spotted Jane, where she'd slowly wedged herself into a corner by the microwave. "Aunt Janie!"

"Oh, no, honey—!" Allison started, but too late. The girl

slipped from her grasp, and now it was Jane's turn to brace herself against the force of the incoming hug-missile.

"Uh . . . hi . . . ," Jane started. She glanced over the girl's head, where Allison was already mouthing *Gracie* at her. "Gracie," Jane said. "Hi, Gracie."

Gracie giggled, squeezing her tentacle-like arms tighter around Jane and rocking back and forth. Jane was a terrible judge of children's ages, so she didn't even try. Somewhere older than diapers, younger than the roils of full adolescence. Gracie's head landed against Jane's hip, the angelic slope of her curls leaning against her. Her arms clamped Jane's legs together in a way that threatened to topple her.

"All right, that's enough," Allison said, darting forward. "Give your aunt some room."

"Why?" Gracie asked. There was a distinct whine in her voice as Allison hooked her arm, dragging Gracie away from the embrace.

"Because Mommy said so," Allison said. "Honestly, who raised you? Monkeys?"

"I want a monkey!" Gracie said.

Allison grabbed her glass of wine from the counter. "I bet you do."

The door opened again, and in spilled a whole cluster of people, Mrs. Maxwell leading the way. "I think we have some in here," she said, her head twisted back to address someone behind her. She let the door slide from her fingers, where it was instantly caught by a man in his late thirties or early forties. He, then, held the door open as Mayor Maxwell followed, carrying what Jane could only assume was Allison's other daughter— the infamous car-puker, Libby. Clair brought up the rear, trailing into the room almost as an afterthought.

Mrs. Maxwell turned, then drew herself to a stop. "Oh! Jane, Allison. That's where you disappeared to."

"I didn't know we were lost," Jane said, but her comment was washed over as the man Mrs. Maxwell had been leading stepped over to kiss Allison on the cheek.

"Sorry we got held up," he said as he slipped his arm around her shoulders, sandwiching Gracie between them.

So this had to be Allison's husband. He did look vaguely familiar, now that Jane thought about it, from photographs scattered around the houses and Mrs. Maxwell's office. A forgettable face, a genial smile. Jane chewed the inside of her cheek, trying to remember his name, even as his attention fell on her, even as he released his wife and stepped forward.

"Hey, Jane," he said. Jane tried not to be too startled as he gave her a hearty bro-hug, one thump on her back. "Sorry," he whispered fast, "I would shake your hand, but people might think it's weird if I introduced myself to my sister-in-law."

Jane nodded as he stepped back in line with Allison. His arm found Allison's shoulders again, so easily Jane got the impression it lived there.

Mrs. Maxwell, meanwhile, ignored the reunion as she dug into the cabinets for something or other, and Mayor Maxwell was listening to a long, rambling story told by the girl in his arms. Clair took the opportunity to step forward, lining herself up with Jane, and Allison's husband's face instantly lit up.

"You must be Clair!" he said, extending his hand. "I'm Alex. It's fantastic to finally meet you—long overdue."

Clair smiled. "Likewise." She accepted his handshake with ease. Jane glanced down, noticing the way Alex avoided Clair's exposed fingertips.

Allison brushed the top of Gracie's head. "Gracie, say hello to Clair. She's going to marry Aunt Jane."

Despite it all, Jane's heart swelled. Okay, so she may not get along great with the parallel sister she'd never had on her world, but the fact that Allison introduced their gay marriage like it was nothing softened Jane's feelings.

"Hi," Clair said. She smiled at Gracie, gave her a friendly wave, but made no attempt to hug her, or even shake her hand. Children's emotions were so intense and unguarded that they tended to give Clair what she once described as a "sugar headache," saying she felt it in her teeth.

Gracie, for her part, regarded Clair carefully, her thumb wedged deeply in her mouth. "Hi," she said finally, shyness whisking away her voice.

An awkward beat fell next. How long it would have gone on,

it was impossible to say. Libby, still in Mayor Maxwell's arms, gave a high shriek as he began to tickle her stomach.

"Dad," Allison said with a sigh, "you're going to wrinkle your suit."

Mayor Maxwell shifted Libby's weight, and shrugged with indifference. "It can be ironed. Can't it?" he said, addressing his comments only to Libby now. He tickled her stomach again, causing her to writhe so hard with giggles that it was a wonder he could still keep a grip on her at all. "Yes, it can!"

All Jane could do was stare. *This* was her father? This laughing, joking, unconcerned grandpa? The word "jolly" floated through Jane's mind, bumping abrasively against her understanding of her dad. The two concepts did not seem like they should exist within the same universe, and yet here they were, right in front of her: Mayor Maxwell was the same man he'd always been, had done the same things he'd always done; Mayor Maxwell was holding one granddaughter in his arms, but was already crouching down to let the other climb onto his back like he was a jungle gym. Gracie's head clonked against his, mussing the careful combing of his salt-and-pepper hair, and he didn't even bother to fix it.

"Goodness gracious, you two get heavier every time I see you," he said as he accepted the weight. He glanced at Allison and Alex. "What are you feeding them?"

"Peanut ballast and jelly sandwiches," Alex said, and Mayor Maxwell gave him a nod of approval.

"Dad, don't hurt yourself, please," Allison said, exasperation weighing down her words.

Mayor Maxwell let out a laugh that ended with a grunt as he began to stagger to his feet. "Calling me old, Allie?"

"You know I'm not. But, seriously, you're in the most important campaign of your career, don't you think—"

"I think my grandkids are only going to be young once. Besides . . ." He paused, his attention shifting, just for a second, toward Jane. "These are probably going to be my only ones. Unless you've got more surprises planned for me."

Allison rolled her eyes. "Hardly."

"Then let me have this," Mayor Maxwell said. He shifted,

adjusting each of the girls' weight. "All right, who's ready for takeoff?"

"Meeeeeee!" they screamed, in unison, so loudly in his ear that it would be a miracle if he didn't have hearing loss later.

"All right, then!" Mayor Maxwell said. He hitched Gracie higher, securing her legs. "Here we go!" Then he made one circle through the kitchen—Jane had to leap back, avoiding the chaos—and trundled through the door, disappearing in a whirl of laughter and motor noises.

Mrs. Maxwell shook her head. "Well. Now that *that's* out of the way." She handed a pill bottle over to Alex, who accepted it with a grateful nod.

Allison frowned. "Again?"

"It's fine."

Allison bit her lip. She studied him for a moment, like she didn't quite believe him, but clearly she wasn't prepared to make a scene.

Whatever was bothering him, though, it couldn't have been that bad—he tucked the pill bottle into his pockets, his attention already shifting, his grin already back in place. "Hey, listen, you two, I'm really sorry the girls and I couldn't make the wedding— even if it ended badly, we should have been there. But Libby . . . I suppose you've figured out she doesn't travel well." He shook his head. "What can I say? The life of a SAD is never glamorous."

Jane frowned. "SAD?"

Alex's grin grew even broader. "Stay-at-home dad."

"Wouldn't that have an 'h' in it?" Clair asked, but Alex only laughed.

He shook his head. "Nah. Then I'd have to pronounce it 'saad,' and that sounds Middle Eastern, which would probably just come across as racist out of someone who looks like me." He pointed to his white face, flushed slightly pink from either drink or laughter or the sun.

Allison frowned. "You don't need to apologize," she said. "Jane didn't come to *our* wedding, and she didn't have an excuse."

"Mine was *two days ago*," Jane said.

Allison shrugged. "Still."

"Hey now." Alex laid his hand over Allison's. "Honey, that's different and you know it. This Jane isn't to blame for your sister's mistakes."

Silence fell in the kitchen. Even Mrs. Maxwell, previously content to let the younger generation speak among themselves, glanced up in alarm.

"Oh, it's okay, we're cool," Alex said. "I know. Allison tells me everything. There are no secrets in our marriage."

Jane raised an eyebrow. "You work for a top-secret government spy organization, and there are *no* secrets between you?"

Allison rolled her eyes. "It's not a *spy* organization, and obviously I don't share anything *classified*."

"*I'm* not classified?"

Allison's brow wrinkled, a little uncertain. "I'm not going to keep secrets about my family."

Jane's cheeks heated. She looked away, Allison looked away.

"Have you seen her?" Jane asked a second later.

Allison glanced up. It was the first time since Jane had decided to stay on this world that either of them had openly spoken of the *other* Jane, the one who'd turned supervillain. There was no protocol for this sort of thing.

"No," Allison said finally. She smoothed her already-smooth hair away from her face. "You?"

Jane shook her head.

Not that UltraViolet was being kept in a typical prison, with visiting hours and phone privileges. Still, Jane didn't think that would stop someone like a Maxwell, like Allison. When Jane had asked, as UltraViolet was being carted off, Jane was told information on the prison was available on a need-to-know basis, and clearly (at the time, anyway) there was no reason to think Jane would ever need to know. Now, though, she wondered. She thought she should at least have the option of checking in on her alternate self. Not that she wanted to chat, or anything. Just . . . she was still *Jane*, wasn't she? Didn't Jane owe her . . . something?

"Well," Jane said. This conversation had clearly gone on long enough, as far as she was concerned. "Um. If we're done here, I really should be getting back to work. After all . . . I have a campaign to stop."

DONNA SET THE CUP IN FRONT OF CLAIR, AND SLID INTO the chair opposite. "Here we go. One strawberry shortcake triple-ripple, as promised."

"You really didn't need to do this," Clair said, though a smile fought against her lips even as she spoke.

Donna just shrugged. "Hey, you take your baby girl to the doctor, you get her ice cream on the way home. I don't make the rules."

"You kind of do, though, since *you're* the parent."

"And who am I to argue with me?" Donna handed Clair one of the two plastic spoons in her hand, then dug the other one through the chocolate sauce pooling around her own sundae.

Clair smirked, half of her face winning the battle. "Thank you."

"You're welcome, Bug."

Though it made Clair feel a little silly, she was glad her mother had been available to go with her this afternoon. Clair had gotten a call while she was at the Maxwells, her doctor's office getting back to her; they'd had a cancellation, and would be able to squeeze Clair in for the STD tests Jane had suggested. By that point, Jane was itching to go join the rest of the Heroes, who'd resumed tailing Cal. Clair wasn't about to bother Jane with something like this, especially not now, but she hadn't wanted to face it alone, either. And while your mother might not be the *first* person you'd think to turn to for this kind of appointment, Clair and Donna's relationship had never been conventional. Donna didn't even blink when Clair asked her to meet. *"Well, that makes perfect sense,"* she'd said after arriving, when she and Clair were in the waiting room and Clair explained what they were doing there.

So now that was done, though Clair would need to wait for all the results to come back. In the meantime, then, the ice cream shop. Strawberry shortcake triple-ripple, and an old-fashioned banana split. They were the go-to flavors Clair and Donna used to get on Mondays when Clair was little and Donna would work a double shift at the jewelry counter every weekend. Before her promotions, before Simon. They'd catch up on Monday, Donna's day off, after school. They didn't even come home first. Clair's backpack would hang off her chair, and she'd ramble on and on about her friends, about Jane, about homework and tests and lunchroom dramas.

"Do you want to talk about what's bothering you?" Donna asked now. She licked the back of her plastic spoon. All her attention was on the task, the ribbons of chocolate lining each divot in the plastic.

"I don't know," Clair said with a sigh. "Maybe?"

This was a lie. Clair *did* want to talk about it—desperately wanted to talk about it. There was so much in her head these past few days, and Clair hadn't gotten to release much of any of it. Between the attacks and the Maxwells and Cal and the election, Clair hadn't even had a moment to breathe, much less process her experience, much less talk about her feelings.

And normally, Donna would be one of the first people she'd want to talk it over with. But somehow, right here, ice cream sitting between them . . . a lever of doubt moved in Clair's chest. She shifted in her chair. Sure, Donna had always been great about the transition, but . . . if she told her about the Amy visions, would she still be okay with it? Or would that be one step too far, one leap of love Donna might not be capable of crossing? What if she believed them? What if she wanted her "real" daughter back?

It wasn't a risk Clair was willing to take. Not yet.

"I'm just worried Kevin's mad at me," Clair said finally.

Donna glanced up, eying Clair over the top of her plastic cup.

"Because I didn't show up last night," Clair added.

Donna nodded. Clair didn't need her powers to know Donna was only humoring her, allowing this topic to act as a shroud for her real feelings. "Well . . . Sure, he *is*. But it's not like he'll never forgive you for it. And it's not like you could have actually done anything for them, anyway. Besides, Nicole is going to be fine. She's still stuck on bed rest, but she'll be fine."

"I know, but I still should have been there for them."

"You were trying to. That counts for something."

"Not if they don't know that."

Donna shrugged. "You've always made it a policy to keep your activities to yourself."

"Maybe I shouldn't."

A silence fell on the table between them. Cold as the ice cream.

Clair glanced down. She dragged her spoon through her untouched sundae. "I'm sorry," she said. She took a breath. "Things are just . . . they're hard right now. I don't know how to balance myself."

There was no hesitation. Donna reached out, laying her hand carefully over the back of Clair's glove. She gave her a gentle squeeze, solid and maternal. "It's okay, honey. You'll find your footing again. You always do."

"You mean Amy did."

Donna's hand stilled.

Clair pulled herself back, sliding out from underneath her mother's grip. She didn't know why she'd said that. Wasn't the whole point of not talking about it to keep things normal between them? Clair picked up her ice cream cup. Marbled red cut through cheerful pink ice cream, while whipped peaks crowned heaps of pale yellow sponge cake. Everything was so much simpler when she was a kid, when they'd come here after school, when the only things Clair had to worry about were math tests and homework.

"Clair," Donna said. "I don't know how much of . . . *this* version of your life you remember . . . but you have to know I love you, right? No matter what you're going through, you've been through worse. These powers can be hard, but you've always managed to figure it out. I promise: you'll figure it out again. Just . . . give it time. Trust me."

Trust me. Clair bit her lip, nodding. She couldn't bring herself to look at her mother, but she trusted her mother to understand. Donna would always understand, even when Clair herself could not.

They left a short while later, tossing their cups into the trash can on their way out. Clair was just pushing open the door, sunlight flashing off the glass, when she spotted a reflection of her blue blouse hovering over her shoulder. But when she looked back, of course, there was nothing.

Only the memory.

EIGHTEEN YEARS AGO, AMY RANG THE MAXWELLS' DOOR-bell with a knot in her stomach and a present held loosely in her sweaty hands.

The door swung open. "Why, Amy! Don't you just look a peach!"

Amy blushed, suddenly uncomfortable. She knew Mrs. Maxwell was just being sweet, but honestly, the last thing you want is your crush's *mom* telling you you're pretty. She stood on the front stoop, shifting her weight back until she balanced wholly on the thick-chunked heels of her shoes, her feet level in front of her.

The shoes were part of her warrior plan: rustic leather clogs with two-inch heels, studded with simple pewter stars around the opening. They were, by far, the most badass and therefore the sexiest pair of shoes fifteen-year-old Amy had ever owned, and hopefully by the powers of transference and the age-old maxim of "fake it till you make it," they would grant her the strength she needed to accomplish her mission that day.

"Thank you, Mrs. Maxwell." Amy's weight shifted, her toes slamming back against the doormat as Mrs. Maxwell stepped aside. "And thank you for inviting me."

Mrs. Maxwell smiled and waved this off. She was dressed "down" today, a painfully soft blue sweater and pressed gray pants, the sparkle of a necklace dotting just beneath her throat. "Oh, don't be silly. I may not have known who else to invite, but *you*, my dear, were always at the top of the list."

Amy feigned a smile. Reserved, polite. She knew how this sort of thing was supposed to work, knew how to be a good party guest, but honestly . . . this whole evening was just *embarrassing*. For Jane, and everyone else involved.

In and of itself, there was nothing wrong with a going-away party. Under different circumstances, it could even have been cool, finally elevating Jane and her friends to a level of popularity they'd always sought. That was, if Jane had planned it herself. If she'd even *wanted* it. The fact that Amy had received an actual *invitation*, and not just an email or heard wind of it at school, had been the first indication that something about this party was seriously effed up, but now, stepping into the foyer, she knew the full depths of the disaster.

Nothing about the event had a trace of Jane to it. Instead, the whole house dripped with the overdone enthusiasm of a child's birthday party. Straight ahead, through the open doorway to the kitchen, Amy spied bowls of chips and Cheetos and M&Ms, sitting beneath a bunch of cheerful streamers and balloons. The so-called party itself was to the left, in the Maxwells' formal living room. Inside, the plastic had been removed from the furniture, the curtains thrown open, the piano dusted. Though Jane was clearly doing her best to deal with the situation—Pink's *Most Girls* blasting too-loudly from the stereo—even that reeked of too little, too late. Like air freshener sprayed thickly to cover up a stench, the girl power of the song instead choked the air with cloying desperation.

Amy hovered at the threshold, uncertain how to proceed. She

could count on one hand the number of times she'd been in this room—mostly parties, much like these, back when they were actually a good time. More often it was seen from the entrance hall, perfectly preserved, roped off like the bedrooms in one of those dusty old houses Simon sometimes brought the family to tour because someone famous used to live there. Everything inside was perfect: pristine, off-white wallpaper with just the subtlest vine texture running up and down it; thick gray-blue carpet adorned with permanent vacuum lines; cream-colored couches and chairs covered in a floral pattern, their cushions looking so plush and inviting even though Amy knew, from personal experience, that they were uncomfortable and hard to sit on without toppling. It was a world away from her own house, where no room went unused for more than a day, where every surface was covered with toys, books, and Donna's craft supplies.

There was no avoiding it, though, and so Amy took a breath and plunged in. The party, such as it was, was already underway. A handful of girls sat around chatting—on the uncomfortable couches, cross-legged on the floor, backward on the bench of the piano. The faces weren't ones Amy was terribly familiar with, but she did recognize a girl from her algebra class, Brittany, and a slightly older neighbor from two doors down who'd sometimes helped to babysit them. No one really seemed to know what they were supposed to be doing. Jane and Marie were at the Maxwells' stereo in the corner of the room, flipping through a portable CD case, ignoring everyone else. "Hey, can you burn me a copy of this one?" Jane said, leaning down as she held out a CD, and Marie nodded.

This was a mistake. Panic clawed up Amy's throat, remembering the determination she'd felt as she'd put on her outfit, done her makeup, combed her hair. What had she been *thinking*? She hadn't been thinking. She'd been desperate, knowing her time with Jane was coming to an end, not wanting it to end without saying *something*.

But it was too late to bail now. Brittany looked up, and Amy's arrival was finally noticed. "Hey, Ames," Brittany said, waving from the corner of the couch.

Amy forced a polite smile. Her fingers tightened around the package in her hands. If she'd known what this party would be like, she'd have never added to it by showing up with a present. What was she supposed to do now? She glanced around the room, looking for a place to sit, a spot to drop her present off like it was no big deal, but nothing felt appropriate, everything was wrong, this whole plan was wrong, and she was the only one who'd worn a skirt, shit shit shit, and what was Jane going to think *now*, and—

And then Jane turned around. Drawn, perhaps, by the sound of Amy's name. Their eyes met across the living room, and Amy's heart flipped over, and—was it her imagination, or was there a hint of a smile playing at the corner of Jane's mouth? Certainly, her own lips were twitching upward, a doofy grin that Amy bit her cheek to contain.

Amy looked down quickly, before she gave it all away. Already, she could feel her whole body flushing, and so she crossed the living room, hoping movement would make her less of a spectacle. The stereo was along the far wall, hidden behind the L of the couches. Amy looped around and handed Jane her present before she could back out. Their fingers, thankfully, did not brush as the exchange was made. Quite apart from the touch itself, Amy really didn't think she could deal with the possibility of picking up stray emotions right now. This . . . sense she'd developed, ever since the night of the accident, was still blurry at times, coming and going in unpredictable patterns, but somehow Amy knew it would be present today. She'd purposefully worn long sleeves, thick tights, even though it was a fairly warm autumn. She kept her head down, the curtain of her shoulder-length hair hiding her face. Their legs shifted awkwardly, reflected in the glass front of the stereo cabinet: Jane's in dark jeans, wide cuffs pooling out over her bare feet; Amy's hidden behind the khaki-green of a cargo skirt. Crap, if Amy had thought faster, she might have been able to stuff the present into her pockets and avoid this whole situation.

Jane cleared her throat. "Hey, thanks." Her voice was light, breezy, just a hint of irritation. She brushed past Amy, rounding the couch and flopping down into the cushions. A swell of conversation immediately enveloped her, and Amy heard her present land on the coffee table.

Amy swallowed. The final lyrics of *Most Girls* swept away, and the longing opening notes of Savage Garden started up in their place. Amy looked toward the CD player that took central position in the stereo system. A clear jewel case sat on top, fitted with an inkjet-printed cover. *Road Trip Mix*, the cut-out-letter font read, behind which sat overlapping pictures of cars, open sky, and girls lying around on the grass on clear summer days.

"That's mine," Marie said, unnecessarily. Marie was known for her mixtapes, one for every occasion. She used to snag songs off the radio, carrying her tape recorder with her everywhere, holding it up near the speakers, silencing everyone in the room with a strict gag order. It was a relief to all of them when she discovered Napster.

"It looks great." Amy picked up the CD case, flipping it over to read the track listing. Nothing more complex than Marie's professional pride stained the plastic. Marie was peering up at her with a funny expression, one Amy hoped to distract her from, so she laughed and pointed to one of the tracks at random. "Oh man, I love that one, don't you?"

"Yeah, duh," Marie said, rolling her eyes. "Seeing as how I made the mix and all."

Amy nodded, trying to play it off as intentional.

The rest of the girls arrived over the next twenty or so minutes. A whole gaggle of them, filling the Maxwells' formal living room with the smell of perfume and the high-pitched drawl of their fake Valley Girl accents. Almost none of them were Jane's actual friends, but all of them had turned out to witness this odd little farewell to the girl who'd suddenly gotten rich. If Amy was feeling kind, she would assume it must have felt like watching a princess in a fairy tale, the king suddenly handed his throne, and the castle awaiting her. Though the change wasn't quite as dramatic as all that, in truth: Mr. Maxwell had been commuting into the heart of the city so long that he was nearly a stranger in his own home, and the new promotion was long overdue. The money wasn't so much *new*, as recently acknowledged. Amy still wasn't sure how moving to Charlotte's Landing was supposed to help his career, since it was even farther from Grand City, but apparently a partner at a prestigious law firm like McAlister and Roth (and *Maxwell*, Amy reminded herself) couldn't live in a modest three-bedroom in the suburbs.

She didn't blame them for being curious, then, though their interest was so vapid and obvious that it hurt to look at.

No, Amy realized, as she hovered off the corner of the group, the person she was annoyed at was *Jane*. Jane, for embracing the attention even if their motives were shallow. Jane, for playing the perfect hostess, despite the fact that Amy *knew* she hated several of these girls now hanging near her elbow.

Jane, for not fighting this change harder. An irrational anger, to be sure, for it's not like there was anything a fifteen-year-old girl could do if her parents decided to move away. Still . . . when Jane had told Amy she was moving, she hadn't even looked up, just announced it as she leaned in toward her mirror, one of her brand-new contacts posed on the tip of her finger. The news had hit Amy so hard that she'd had to sit down on the end of Jane's bed. But Jane hadn't seemed upset then, and she didn't seem upset now. Look at her: laughing, showing off a stack of photos of her new bedroom, telling them about the pool and the gym and the beach.

Amy's stomach twisted. If Jane felt the same way at all, surely this would be harder for her, wouldn't it? In which case, this whole plan was a bad idea from the start. She'd just started to lean forward, hoping to swipe the present from the coffee table while Jane's attention was on the photos, when Mrs. Maxwell came back into the room.

"All right, girls, I'm just about to order some pizzas—who likes what, for toppings?"

Amy jerked back, cheeks burning. She grabbed a chair that had been dragged in from the dining room, and quickly sat down. Maybe it would just look like she hadn't been sure where to sit? But when she glanced up, her heart beating wildly, Jane was watching her from across the coffee table, a slight frown between her eyebrows.

"Good, then we're settled!" Mrs. Maxwell said, and Amy realized there'd already been shouts and comments floating past that she hadn't even noticed. Mrs. Maxwell had her hand up in the air, four fingers raised to remind her of each of the pizzas she'd be ordering. She nodded, satisfied. She'd just turned to go when she noticed the present Amy had brought. "Oh! Jane, what's this?"

Amy bit her lips. She stared at Jane, desperately hoping she'd downplay it.

Jane shrugged.

"Amy brought it," Brittany said, and Amy's flush deepened as Mrs. Maxwell looked to her with a gleaming smile.

"Oh my, isn't that just the sweetest," Mrs. Maxwell said. She picked it up, holding it out to Jane. "You should open it, Janie. It isn't polite to ignore a gift."

Jane snatched it from her mother's hands. She crossed her arms, stuffing it into her armpit. "I'll open it later."

Mrs. Maxwell put her hands on her hips. "You will open it now, young lady. A friend has taken the time to select something kind as a going-away present, and I will not tolerate rudeness."

"Actually, it's—" *fine*, Amy wanted to say, the word already on her tongue, but one sharp glare from Mrs. Maxwell shut her mouth. Amy swallowed down her assurance, letting it settle in her stomach like hot iron.

Mrs. Maxwell's attention went back to her daughter. Jane sighed, loud and exaggerated. Her back had curled deeper as she'd been sitting there, and now she was almost fully engulfed by the cushions as she uncrossed her arms and began to rip the paper violently from Amy's present.

Amy's stomach jumped. This wasn't how it was supposed to go at all. She sat up a little straighter, squirming on the plastic of her chair. She wanted to snatch the present back, rewind this whole afternoon, eject the tape, bury it under her mattress. Her earlier optimism felt Pollyanna-ish now, the foolish dreams of a child. She sucked in a breath as Jane dropped the wrapping paper, as her fingers lifted the white cardboard cover off the box.

Jane's face went still.

The one small mercy of this whole situation was at least Amy hadn't chosen anything *overtly* romantic. She'd thought of it; standing in Delia's, her fingers trailing the rows of necklaces like they were forbidden treasure. She'd bought plenty for *herself*, over the years, and even one or two joint friendship necklaces, their pieces interlocking in increasingly complicated ways. But this was different. Amy had never bought a present *for a girl* before, not like *that*, and it was a careful balance. Too forward, and she risked not only outing herself to *everyone*, but also what if Jane wasn't actually interested? The last thing Amy wanted to do was offend her by the suggestion. But if she didn't choose something meaningful *enough*, then it really would just be a present between friends, and what was the point?

When Amy had found it, finally, tucked away in the back of the display rack behind a pendant shaped like a computer and another with a peace sign, she knew she'd nailed it.

She knew it again, now, just watching Jane's face.

The necklace was held on a dog-tag style chain, the ball links just a little more polished than usual. The pendant was about an inch and a half wide, three comic panels in a row, showing a flower as it sprouted from the ground, budded, and finally bloomed wide. The panels were filled in with glossy paint, blue sky and green ground and cheerful pink petals. It had cost Amy twelve dollars.

Mrs. Maxwell squealed. Somehow, while they'd all been distracted, she'd moved around so she could look over Jane's shoulder. "Why, Amy, isn't that just perfect! Jane, don't you think that's perfect?"

Jane's ears were bright pink. She reached up, as if to adjust her glasses, then realized she wasn't wearing them anymore, so she untucked her hair and patted it flat instead. "It's nice, sure. Yeah. Thanks."

Mrs. Maxwell frowned. "Janie."

"I said *thank you*!" Jane snapped. "Okay? Mom, can you just order the pizza, please, for the love of god?" She threw herself to her feet, stuffing the necklace into the pocket of her jeans. She stormed around the corner of the couch, making a beeline for the stereo once more. When she got there, she knelt down on the carpet, her finger trailing the line of CDs on the rack beside it.

She did not look at Amy.

Not even once.

CAL'S LAST EVENT OF THE DAY WAS A RALLY IN THE
ballroom of a local hotel. A televised speech, in which he reit-
erated his desire for legislation that would curtail the use of
superpowers. He stood on a stage in front of everyone, bright
lights glinting off his wolfish teeth, and whipped up a frenzy
against the very thing he used to believe in. Jane watched with
her fists clenched. Her pulse thundered in her ears, a thousand
angry horses storming to war. It took every ounce of restraint for
Jane to keep herself from bursting out of the shadows, charging
up to the stage, and taking down Cal where he stood. But that
wouldn't exactly help her case.

So she'd waited. Through every vile line, every twisted truth.
Seething with unspoken fury as he accepted waves upon waves
of applause, as balloons showered over him once he was done.
As he grinned and hammed it up for the cameras. As he shook
the hand of each and every person who'd attended. As the crowd

finally, *finally* began to break up, sometime after midnight. The whole event had the air of a victory party, like the election was already done and won.

The last to leave were a cluster of three bro-types that would have appeared equally at home in a frat house or a prison cell—beefy arms, crew cuts, and tattoos, their speech slurring as they shouted their way out of the ballroom. Most of Cal's supporters, actually, had been men, and most had sported a similar look, which didn't exactly help Jane's opinion of them or their candidate of choice. But at least now they were gone. The doors shut behind them with a weighted clunk of finality.

Only Cal and Louisa and a single staffer remained. Cal stood center stage, looking back at the enormous screen of himself. For a moment, he was so still that it may as well have been a photograph: the level plane of Cal's shoulders, the sharp corners of his suit, the cropped blond hair, buzzed tighter in the back than anything he ever used to sport. Cal reached up and ran his hand along the back of his head, over the stubbled remains of his blond locks, as if he was noticing this himself, as if he was wondering over the transformation. His wedding band, gleaming brand-new, shone brighter and a thousand times larger on the screen.

The staffer bounded up onto the stage beside him, a smaller slice of his profile in the corner of Cal's image. He was young, fresh-faced, a faint sheen of sweat blotting on his ruddy forehead. Cal did not even glance at him as the staffer said, "I have to say, that was *quite* the success. I didn't think anyone could pull off that kind of rally on such short notice, but you, sir . . ." He shook his head. "That was somethin' else."

At last, Cal turned around. The smaller reality of him, backed by the blinding white of his grin on the screen. You'd never be able to tell he was exhausted unless you'd known him for years, but Jane had. She was not fooled, even as Cal nodded approvingly at the staffer, even as he clapped the young man's shoulder.

"Thanks, Aaron," Cal said. "Couldn't have done it without you. Now, though, I'd like to have the room alone for a few minutes. You too, Lou," he called over his shoulder. "I'll be up soon."

Color shifted as Louisa unfolded herself from the corner by the curtains. "There's no rush." She moved in long, confident strides as she breezed across the stage, but when she went to pass by Cal, he grabbed her wrist and, like an obedient dog, she stopped. In the image on the screen, she nearly managed to block the sight of Cal, and so it was a close-up of her grinding teeth Jane saw most, as Cal leaned in to whisper something affectionately into her ear. Too low for Jane to hear what he said, even with the mic attached to Cal's lapel. Pixie Beats might have caught it, though—she'd been shrunk down and tucked into the podium all evening, staked out behind Cal's water glass. Jane would have to remember to ask her about it, later.

Louisa did not look at Cal as she was released and set off again. She gathered the staffer in her wake, the two of them heading down the steps and across the trampled scraps of confetti and napkins and *A Goodman for Senate* signs. Cal's grinning face beamed up at them from the posters, even as the heel of Louisa's shoe impaled him between the eyes.

Cal waited for them to leave. He watched their progress, watched the door. In the silence that followed, he stepped up to the podium, staring out at the empty sea of the ballroom, where all those faces had been not long ago.

He looked straight into the camera. In the screen behind him, his gaze seemed to pierce the entire room, as if he was looking *right at* Jane, as if he knew where she was, as if he could peer behind her mask and directly into her soul, all of her secrets nothing more than noise to him.

Jane squared her shoulders.

"Did you enjoy the show?" Cal asked.

In the empty chamber of the ballroom, his voice carried even more easily than it had when all those bodies had been packed in. The question echoed out, drumming into the walls, drumming into Jane.

"There's no sense in pretending like you can't hear me. I know you're here. I've known all night." He snapped his fingers, pointing into the depths of the balcony, cloaked in shadow. "Windforce"—point—"Rip-Shift"—point—"Granite Girl"—down to the podium—"Pixie Beats." He paused, just for an instant, and then the line of his finger stretched toward the far-thest corner of the ballroom, finding Jane like an arrow. "Captain Lumen."

Was there a point in denying it? The comms were silent, each member of the team seeming to weigh the merits of stepping forth and revealing themselves.

Jane took a breath. "Wait for my signal," she told the others, then made the call.

She let the spotlights catch her as she moved up toward the center of the open ballroom, pulling the light in her direc-tion. With the view drawn from the balcony, they pin her in place. Her back catches the light, the red of her suit shining brighter under her control. She stands before the open maw of the stage, Cal rendered in sharply contrasting shadow like the villain he is.

Cal laughed, motioning toward her approach. "Aaaaand, there she is! Ladies and gentlemen, my good friend, Jane Maxwell!" He raised his hands in applause, as if egging on an invisible audience. Jane could practically see them in her periph-eral vision, loose sketches of admirers ready to throw themselves at Cal's feet.

"Enough." Jane snatched at the air, crumpling the image in her fist. She did not shout, but the acoustics of the empty room carried her voice almost as well as it carried Cal's. She knew he'd heard her, though he continued his charade for a moment or two longer, pointing into a crowd that wasn't there and nodding encouragement to individual members.

Only once she was about halfway up the room, did he stop. Abruptly, he dropped the game, shoulders slumping in overdra-matic defeat. "Aw, come on! You're no fun at all anymore. Can't you pretend you're even a *little* happy to see me? For old times' sake?"

"There are no 'old times' between us, Cal. You saw to that."

Cal's expression turned inside-out, a hurt puppy droop of his features that filled the screen behind him. "It's because I held you captive once, isn't it? You really should learn to let things *go*, Main Jane. The past is passed."

"You've certainly done a good job of leaving it behind."

"Ah," Cal said. "Yes, I can see how my speech might not look great for our friendship. But I swear, the legislation, it's . . . nothing *personal*."

"Nothing *personal*? You're trying to turn us into criminals, and you say it's nothing *personal*?"

"Not *you*. And if you'd read my proposal, you'd know I'll allow any such persons with history of superheroic activity immunity for any acts committed before it goes into effect."

"Yes, that's so magnanimous of you," Jane said, her speech bubble dripping with a heavy crosshatch of sarcasm.

"Look, Jane." Cal loosened his tie. "I hate to break it to you, but the city *wants* this legislation. I know it hurts to hear, but it's true. If it wasn't me, it would be someone else. Superhero containment is going to be the hot-button issue over the next *several* elections. You're going to have to get used to it."

"You can't honestly expect me to fall for that."

"It's the truth," Cal said. He put one hand to his heart, the other held aloft as if he was taking an oath. Standing there, boy-scout perfect, he looked like a trading card, Upstanding Citizen Cal Goodman. "Honestly. Jane, for all my teasing, I'm a reformed man. I mean to do good by this city."

"Cut the crap, Cal. This was never about the city. This is about you, and me, and the Heroes, and you know it."

Cal shrugged. He reached into his breast pocket. Jane's muscles flexed, ready to spring—she was so sure that he was going for a gun, but instead all he drew out was a silver comb. It caught the light as he raised it to his head, monogrammed initials glinting in the metal.

He took his time, smoothing out his shorn hair. When he was done, he tucked the comb away with precision, patting the fabric above his breast pocket.

He smiled at her. "And what if it is personal?"

That was it. Whatever reserve Jane had when coming into the room, it fled her now. He may as well have admitted he was behind the attack on Clair's life, as far as Jane was concerned. Rage stained her panels with the tint of blood. "You *bastard*."

She lunged forward. Not thinking, not thinking. Her powers were already springing to life inside of her, itching her to attack, to fight, to *maim*, and Jane let that voice propel her the rest of the way up the ballroom, vault onto the edge of the stage, raise her arm.

They only stopped when Cal laughed.

Just a hesitation.

Just enough.

"Go ahead," Cal said. He spread his arms, the crisp white triangle of his shirt a perfect target against the deep blue suit that framed it. "There are cameras everywhere—or had you forgotten that this whole rally was televised? You'd only be proving my point."

Jane glanced up. At the enormous screen flanking Cal, mirroring his every move. The cameras littering the edges of the stage. They weren't transmitting anywhere—her powers told her that much—but that didn't mean they weren't still recording. Watching in silence.

Training told Jane that the fight wasn't worth it. That the risks were too great. That she should back off, back down. But then she looked back up at him, at the smug face enlarged and plastered on the giant screen behind him, and, well, training be damned. He wanted it to be personal? He'd damn well made it personal.

She'd just started to surge forward when a pair of stony hands grabbed her elbows, stilling her in place. Jane jerked, but Granite Girl's hold was unbreakable.

"We can't," Granite Girl said. "As much as I hate it, he's right. The last thing we need is a video of you attacking an anti-superhero candidate."

"We can't just let him go!"

"He hasn't done anything *wrong*."

"Hasn't—! Did you hear a *word* he said?"

"I did," Granite Girl said. "And believe it or not, we're not just sidekicks, Captain. We can't deal with him here—not like this. We need to back down. We need to be *smart*."

Jane's fingers twitched at her side. In point of fact, she really didn't need her arms to be free to conjure and direct the beams of light, it just made them easier to handle. She chewed on the inside of her cheek, considering, comparing the various issues that would follow this sequence, and maybe Granite Girl could see the debate waging there, because her grip on Jane's arm tightened. She shook her stony head, back and forth, just once.

The muscles in Jane's arm slackened. "Fine," she spat. She turned back to Cal, pointing to his face—Granite Girl did release her arm enough for that. "This isn't over, Cal. I promise you, whatever you're planning . . . we'll stop it."

Cal grinned. His aw-shucks grin, his boys-will-be-boys grin. His victory grin. "Why, my dear Jane"—he leaned in, close enough for Jane to smell the bite of his aftershave, and lowered his voice—"I wouldn't have it any other way."

THE TEXT WAS STRAIGHTFORWARD: *HAVE IMPORTANT INFORMATION. PLEASE MEET.*

Below that, a string of GPS coordinates and a timestamp for eleven p.m. Clair had stared at it when it first came in, confusion wrinkling her brow, wondering why on earth Stacey would be acting so mysterious. It took her a minute to realize the message had come in through the app Marie had installed on all their phones, which bounced the signals through a series of hacked satellites. The end result is the Heroes could pass out randomly generated phone numbers to key contacts without needing to go through a dozen burner phones a month, and without needing to carry around multiple phones all the time. It also meant the message Clair had received wasn't so much for *her*, as it was for *Mindsight*.

Clair ran her thumb along the edge of her phone. It was just before ten. Jane was still out, tracking down Cal, but Clair was already in her pajamas, gloves off, a fuzzy blanket tucked around her as the light from the TV washed over the room. Did it make her a bad superhero, that she didn't immediately leap up from the couch? The truth is she'd never embraced the job as much as Jane had. Still, she owed it to her friend to find out what was so important. And Jane shouldn't be back for a while yet—Clair could slip out, meet with Stacey, and probably still be back first.

An hour later, Clair checked her watch as she stood waiting in the empty parking lot of a Tycho's Tacos that closed down years ago. Fifteen minutes early. In uniform, as in life, there were some habits she just couldn't break, and so: early was on time, on time was late, and late was unacceptable.

"We shouldn't be here," Amy said.

Clair turned her head. She kept her face angled down, the tilted fedora obscuring her features. Beside her, Amy's own face was also hidden. The same black mask around the eyes, the same shadows. Except, somehow, Clair couldn't help but feel like Amy *fit* the persona better. That the version standing beside her, which only Clair could see, was somehow the *true* Mindsight.

She looked away. "No one invited *you*."

"That's not very grateful. Don't forget, 'Mindsight,' I'm your only backup here."

"I don't need backup," Clair said. "It's just Stacey."

This was a relationship Amy had cultivated way back in the first year of being a superhero. Stacey had just graduated with a degree in journalism, and by all typical metrics, was a complete nobody in the field. That, plus the usual barriers of sexism and fatphobia meant she was staring down the beginning of a very long, very difficult road in her career of choice. She'd never understood why the Heroes chose her—why Mindsight chose her—to be their contact within the journalism community, but she was also smart enough not to question her luck. She'd been given an incredible gift, plucked from the depths of obscurity and granted exclusives, inside access, a front-row seat to the very beginning of the Heroes' rise to prominence. All the Heroes asked for in return was information to help them pursue their cause, and who was Stacey to deny that?

Amy sighed in annoyance. "Did you seriously forget everything I learned in the field? Never assume things will go according to plan. I don't care how simple it looks."

Clair shook her head. "You're too paranoid."

"And you're not paranoid enough. Maybe that's why you're the one who died properly, instead of me."

The squeal of brakes. Panic closing up her throat. The reaction was automatic, faster than Clair could process. One second she was beneath the broken taco sign, the next she was upside down in her car as the tires let go. She remembered the way the road had mirrored in front of her, everything familiar but unrecognizable, like an abstract painting. Panic and disbelief had slowed time, and in that moment Clair released both the steering wheel and her breath.

She swallowed down the taste of vomit. "I can't believe you just said that."

Amy shrugged.

"Mindsight?"

Clair cut herself off, just as she took a breath to start. She scrambled in the pocket of her trench coat, finding the trigger that controlled her voice changer. The button clicked beneath her thumb.

Identity safely obscured, she turned around. Her emotions were fluffed around her like an angry cat's coat, and she tried to settle herself as she regarded Stacey.

"Miss Hutchinson. What do you have for me?"

Stacey was standing at a distance, watching Clair—watching Mindsight—warily. Shit, what if she'd heard something? What if, after all this time, all the care Amy had put into protecting her identity, Clair had gone and ruined it right out of the gate?

But Stacey just stepped forward. She held out a thumb drive.

"This is everything I've managed to find out about Electric Fury."

Clair stared at the thumb drive.

"Who . . . who asked you to do this?"

Stacey snorted, a sound that squeaked out higher than she'd probably like. "Nobody needed to *ask* me. She attacked my best friend's wedding."

Heat threatened Clair's cheeks. "Oh. Of course."

"I didn't discover much, unfortunately," Stacey continued as she handed the thumb drive over. She stepped back, slipping her hands into the pockets of her flowing sweater. "Electric Fury's good. There's almost nothing to go on. But I *did* manage to discover she was part of the Ruinator's efforts to build the fermion oscillator four years ago."

Clair looked up sharply. Her eyes flicked over Stacey's shoulder—but Amy was gone, disappeared as thoroughly as a lost dream. Clair tightened her grip around the thumb drive, caught in the middle of her gloved palm. She wasn't ready to get a read on it yet. "Really."

Stacey nodded, flicking her red bangs out of her face. "Yeah, it's all there. Listen, I don't know what someone like that has against my friend, but whatever it is, it can't be good. What if she's trying to continue the Ruinator's work? If she manages to build another . . . it could make the destruction of Woolfolk Tower look like a sparkler accident at a Fourth of July party."

Clair didn't need to be reminded of the danger. She remembered the Ruinator well. He was the last supervillain the Heroes had taken down before Doctor Demolition had entered the scene to carry out UltraViolet's shadowy will. The fermion oscillator was a doomsday device, one designed to split open the skies above Grand City and recreate the Rift that had activated the Heroes' dormant superpowers. Rumor was that he believed the Rift was a portal not just to another world, but a whole other dimension, one where time and space and energy recombined in infinitely complex ways. The Heroes had managed to capture him before he did any lasting harm, but . . . Clair frowned. Her memories after that—Amy's memories after that—went oddly dark.

"Thanks for this," Clair said. "I'm sure it'll be helpful."

Stacey started to turn away. "I'll let you know if I find anything else."

"No!" Clair reached out, catching herself just before she grabbed Stacey's sleeve. "That is . . . you shouldn't pursue this any further. Electric Fury's too dangerous—especially if she's up to the Ruinator's old tricks. You should leave this to us."

One of Stacey's eyebrows cocked high. "I'm not going to let something like this go."

No, of course she wouldn't. And why should she? Clair didn't need all of Amy's memories to know Stacey had never been asked to drop an investigation before, at least not because it was "too dangerous." Stacey was studying Clair now, peering beneath the shadow of Clair's brim as well as she could in the dark. Clearly, she was wondering why the change. What was so special about Electric Fury.

Join the club, Clair thought darkly, because she sure as hell wanted that answer, too. And in truth, she couldn't even explain *why* she was trying to get Stacey to back off. She only knew that Stacey needed to—that Clair needed her to.

Clair reached into her coat pocket. The folded scrap of paper Tony had given her was still there, and she drew it out, handed it over. Stacey opened it without a word.

"Can you find out what was in that for me?"

"A safe deposit box?" Stacey asked, and Clair nodded.

"It was stolen during the attack on Saga Street Bank. No one's been able to identify the contents yet, or even who it belongs to. If you want to do good . . . figure that out for me. I'll handle Electric Fury."

Stacey rubbed the paper between her fingers, considering this. The subtle scritch of the two halves was like the whisper of leaves in autumn. "All right," she said finally, pocketing the paper, the number. She held out her hand, and Clair hesitated only briefly before taking it.

Stacey's grip tightened, pulling Clair close. Panic flared in Clair, just for a second, as Stacey's eyes narrowed on her. She stared beneath the brim of Clair's hat, peering into the eyeholes of Clair's mask, and Clair had to fight every instinct to look away.

"I'm trusting you on this, Mindsight," Stacey said. There was something cold in her normally high voice, a steely resolve that made Clair's stomach squirm. Stacey shook her head. "Don't let me down."

LIFE WAS SO MUCH SIMPLER INSIDE THE BORDERS OF A COMIC PANEL.

In her mind, Jane could see a hazy montage of the way the day should have gone. Tony at the precinct, digging up more intel on what might have been stolen from the safe deposit box. Devin and Marie back at HQ, pouring over security footage they'd hacked from the bank. Clair, tucked away safe at home. Jane's pencil drifted loosely over the notepad in front of her, vague shapes that didn't feel like taking form yet. She kept trying to focus on the team, and it kept failing. Instead, her own panels filled her mind. She tried not to see them, but they came to her just the same, sharper than the others. Her face tucked behind sunglasses as she faked her way to Cal's floor of the hotel where he'd set up his temporary campaign headquarters. A tight shot of her closed fist, Cal's chin knocked aside, a spray of blood from his mouth. Bitter speech bubbles, demanding answers.

Jane set her pencil down. She took off her glasses, holding them up to the light to check for smudges. It was only natural that she feel stifled, Jane told herself. Cal was still at the top of Jane's list for who put out the hit on Clair, after all, and tracking him down was better than what she was doing now: stuck in a conference room in a swanky law firm, waiting for their overpriced lawyer to finish a phone call in his office so they could begin the meeting that had been scheduled to start ten minutes ago. And sure, maybe her motives didn't exactly come from the most "heroic" impulse, but did that mean she needed to be *benched*? Seriously?

Apparently it did, or at least the rest of the Heroes thought so. They insisted Jane "cool off" for the day, that they could handle things. Cool off, sure. Like this would do it. She'd considered trying to pull rank, but . . . staring at their faces that morning, the way they'd surrounded her. Somehow, she wasn't sure it would work.

Besides, there were five voicemails waiting on Jane's phone when she woke up, all from Blue, all about their new company. It wouldn't do, to ignore her new business forever.

"Tell me why we're here again?" Jane asked as she slid her glasses back on. Time to set Captain Lumen on the shelf. Back to Jane Maxwell, Businesswoman.

Blue sighed from beside her. She snapped her gum, the smell of artificial fruit making Jane's mouth water. "It's negotiation red tape. The Shapiro estate's asking for more money."

"How *much* more?"

"Too much," Blue said. "Hence the negotiation."

"Jesus Christ." Jane swiveled in her seat, leaning back. She tried to spot their lawyer through the glass wall of the conference room, but his own office was conveniently opaque—nothing but the shut door and the clack of the receptionist's keyboard filled the empty space outside. "I don't know why we're even doing this."

"I told you. The distributors aren't interested in taking on the risk of a complete nobody. If we buy up Sharp Eye Comics' old intellectual property—"

"Then all we're doing is recycling old ideas," Jane said. "The whole *point* was to publish something new. Fresh voices."

Blue spread her hands patiently on the table in front of her.

Her fingers were stubby and squarish, the nails trimmed down so far that there was not a trace of white left. "Which we're going to do, Jane. Even this IP, there's nothing demanding that we stick completely to their old origin stories and themes. But it'll show people we're serious. Meanwhile, we publish your 'new voices' right alongside them. We establish ourselves, and build up our own image at the same time."

Jane frowned. She adjusted the front of her blazer. Another nod to the establishment. Just because it was layered over a silk-screened T-shirt she'd bought from a street vendor, that didn't make her any more punk. She was losing her edge. Fast.

"How are we coming with hires?" she asked, hoping to change the subject.

"Good." Blue drew a tablet out of the bag by her feet and passed it over to Jane. When Jane swiped it awake, it was already set to new artist portfolios, as if Blue had been waiting for Jane to ask.

Jane flicked through the options. Each image was presented individually, no artist names or details attached. The idea was to cut down on preconceptions and biases. Jane would double-tap the drawings she especially liked, and if she flagged more than three by the same artist, their contact info would get added to the list for Blue to call.

The art soothed Jane. She took her time, studying each piece. Character sketches and concept art were mixed in with finished paintings, comic pages, even the occasional photograph. Nothing, and no pitch, was too left-field for Jane's new company—that was her mandate.

Blue cleared her throat. "Since we're here—"

"No."

"You don't even know what I was going to say!"

Jane double-tapped the current drawing, then swiped it aside. "You want me to ask my father for money. This is his lawyer, and you think if you get him on board with my 'vision,' he'll help convince the mayor."

"His name is still on the door," Blue said.

Jane looked up, though she didn't really need to. *McAlister, Roth, and Maxwell* was stamped in silver across the glass.

She turned back to her tablet. "We'll find another way."

Blue sighed. She ran her hands through her hair, bubblegum-pink spikes poking out between her fingers. "Jane, I don't know if you fully realize the expenses involved in this dream of yours. Don't get me wrong, I appreciate you emptying your trust fund for it, but—"

"There's such a thing as a *bank*, Blue. There's such a thing as *loans*."

"Yeah, and I've talked to them. Spoiler alert: they're not keen on the risk. Superheroes aren't exactly big money in Grand City these days, in case you hadn't noticed."

"We're not just publishing superheroes."

"You think a bank manager knows the difference?"

Jane locked the tablet's screen and put it down on the table in front of her. "Then it's your job to explain the difference. This is a solid investment for them. The company's going to turn a profit."

Blue pressed her lips together.

Jane knew Blue thought she was just being stubborn, and she couldn't really blame her for that. When Jane had decided to start her company, it had seemed so simple. The first few months in this parallel world had been a rough adjustment in a lot of ways, but one thing Jane hadn't ever struggled with here was money. The very thought of her *having* a trust fund was amazing enough, and the number of zeroes after her name had seemed endless. At first.

It was only once she started really putting together her business plan—looking at office real estate, the number of computers they'd need, base salaries, calculating staff numbers, researching taxes and health care packages—that those zeroes had dwindled more and more. They still weren't in danger of failing right out of the gate, no, but they had needed to scale back their plans. Hence the need for outside printers and distributors in the first place. Hence the negotiations with the Shapiro estate, the sole owners of the rights to a long-defunct comics company. Hence the blazer, the heeled boots, the splash of makeup.

And it was true, Mayor Maxwell could have easily forked over enough to make up the difference Jane was looking for.

She knew, in the way families knew this sort of thing, that she'd gotten way less in her fund than her "sister" did. But if Mayor Maxwell hadn't been willing to give his younger daughter the inheritance she was due when the other Jane was a respected art dealer, then he definitely wasn't going to help fund a comics publishing company. Jane didn't even need to ask to know the answer to that one.

Not that she was willing to ask in the first place.

Jane sighed. She checked her watch. The lawyer—a protégé of Mayor Maxwell himself—was still behind closed doors. "How much longer is this going to take?"

"Why are you so antsy? I know you can't have other plans— you're supposed to have been on your honeymoon right now, remember?" Blue shook her head. "Thank god you're not."

"I'm sorry, did you just imply you're *glad* my wedding burst into flames?"

"Of course not," Blue said. She looked at Jane. Her face was still and cold, as if sculpted out of marble. "Just, you know, you'd never have forgiven me if I'd Skyped you into this meeting."

Jane cut her a sidelong look. "Okay . . . ," she said, turning back to the tablet.

Thankfully, the lawyer saved them the burden of further talking. His door snapped open just as Blue took a breath, and Jane had never been so grateful to see a member of his profession walk into the room before. Jane stood up, screwing her professional smile in place. Stamping down on her feelings, putting on the show they wanted to see. She wasn't about to make the mistakes she'd made on her real Earth, the ones that led to her getting fired from her old comics company. As much as Jane might resent the changes coming over her, she knew they were necessary to succeed here.

So she extended her hand, all business, smile smile, look at how polite and nonthreatening she is, and she left her grip limp when he accepted the gesture. The way her mother always taught her.

"Mr. Simmons, so glad you could find time for us today. Shall we get started?"

∗ ∗ ∗

CLAIR HAD THE HEADQUARTERS TO HERSELF.

It was strange—six people don't exactly fill a high-rise, so you'd think there wouldn't be much difference between being alone in the building, and being alone in a room within it. You'd be wrong. With the others, they tended to cluster, an awareness running through the building of where everyone was and roughly what they were up to. Impromptu meetings and coffee breaks sprang up. Alone, the headquarters felt like an empty church: warm and slightly dusty, the sense of trespassing on sacred ground, echoes springing up where none seemed to exist before. Clair moved like the place would shatter at her touch. Everything familiar turned strange, as if Clair had never taken the time to notice the details before. Since when was there a storage closet *here*? How long had that book been sitting out *there*? Was that light fixture always trimmed with blue accents?

Even the command room; Clair had never realized how big it truly was. The conference table itself probably could have fit twenty people, easy. The screens loomed over everything like you were at the movies. Clair pulled a chair over, wincing at the faint squeak of the wheels, the wheeze of the leather as she sat down. She cleared her throat, and it seemed to boom through the room like she'd coughed into a microphone.

"Feeling guilty about something?"

Was it that Clair had gotten used to these sudden intrusions, that she managed not to jump out of her skin? Or, on some level, had she always expected Amy to appear?

"I don't know what you're talking about."

"You're snooping."

"I'm not *snooping*," Clair said. She keyed her access code into the computer station in front of her. "I have every right to be in whatever part of this building I want. I helped build it, after all."

"*I* helped build it."

"Yes, and then you gave it to me."

"It's not exactly like I had much *choice*," Amy said. "Become you, or die? What was I supposed to do?"

"I don't know. But I'm not the one who put you in that position. You want to blame someone, blame UltraViolet. Blame *your Jane*."

Amy's face soured, the hint of a flush creeping up her cheeks. The same look Clair would get whenever she knew she was being called out for something, but wasn't ready to admit it. Clair tossed her a shrug, then turned back to the computer.

"Bitch," Amy muttered. She stalked away, parking herself in one of the chairs around the conference table.

Clair took a breath. Tried to shake it off, tried to ignore the squeak as Amy spun lazily in her chair. She refocused on her work. She was going through the Heroes' old files, trying to find something that would confirm or deny Stacey's claim—that Electric Fury had been working with the Ruinator.

In theory, of course, Clair should have remembered without the help of the files. In theory, all of Amy's memories belonged to her now, inherited like the knickknack-crammed house of a dead aunt, and it was just a matter of figuring out how to dig through them all until she found the one she was looking for. In theory. In practice, some of the memories were buried deeper than others, and Clair could swear that Amy was clutching tightly to some of them, refusing to pass them over.

The Ruinator didn't feel like it should be one of those, but maybe she was wrong about that. Because nothing jostled the memories loose, no matter how many pages of reports she spilled through.

On the surface, his story was simple, like an issue of Jane's old comic books. A Big Bad who'd set his sights on constructing a device that would reopen the Rift, only larger and more unstable than ever before. The Heroes of Hope racing to track down where he'd be, trying to block him from acquiring any more of the tech he needed to complete the device. Several setbacks, several triumphs. Eventually, a breakthrough. In the end, they'd defeated him in an epic showdown. The fermion oscillator was taken, dismantled, the pieces destroyed.

It was this part of the file that gave Clair a sick feeling in her stomach, like something wasn't quite right. But she couldn't figure out what, or where the error might have occurred, and anyway, it's not like the Heroes would have purposefully falsified their own internal records of a supervillain attack. So, what, had they just been wrong, somehow? That didn't make sense, either.

Clair tapped through the documents. An arrest record from GCPD, when they'd handed him over; transfer files Marie had hacked later, to ensure that he went to the supermax prison he was supposed to; a list of each incineration site where the pieces of the fermion oscillator had been sent. It was certainly complete, and convincing. No reason to doubt.

So why did she turn, ready to grill Amy for details? And why was Amy suddenly gone, just as Clair was about to speak?

Clair let the air out in a huff, blowing the bangs off her forehead. She slumped back in her chair, and crossed her arms, and glared at the data still displayed on the screen, as if somehow it was at fault for whatever was happening to her.

Her phone chirruped in her pocket.

Clair drew it out, glancing at the screen. *Allison.* A jolt as Clair accepted the call. "Hey, what's wrong?"

"Hello to you, too," Allison said. "Is that any way to greet your sister-in-law?"

"Sorry." Clair leaned back in her chair, her feet on the control console, her face tipped toward the ceiling. "Hello, dear Allison, how are you doing today?"

"Ass," Allison said, and Clair laughed. "For real, though, I'm outside your headquarters. Can you tell your computer to let me in? I don't think it likes me much."

Clair sat up. Her feet stamped to the floor. "Outside?"

She leaned over, swiping the security camera's view to the main screen. Sure enough, there she was, in miniature. Leather jacket and jeans, hair in a high ponytail, phone to her ear. She glanced at the nearest camera, as if she knew Clair would be watching, and gave a quick wave.

"How did you even know I was here?"

Allison shrugged. "Educated guess. You weren't home, and you wouldn't be scheduled for work, since you weren't supposed to even be in town right now."

"Yeah, but . . . you didn't even ask, when you got here. It's like you just knew."

"I'm very smart," Allison said. "Look, are you going to let me in, or what?"

"Right, sorry. Hang on just a second."

Clair punched a sequence into the computer. On the screen, the front doors unlocked and slid open.

"Head to the elevator," Clair said. "I'll meet you."

"What level?" Allison asked as she walked in.

"From the lobby? There's only one."

"You guys are so weird."

Clair hung up. She dashed from the command room, shoes squeaking down the hall.

The elevator arrived just as Clair hurried up. The light turned green, a soft chime echoed through the halls. Then the doors slid open and, sure enough, there was Allison.

Allison gave Clair a look as she stepped out into the hall. "Why do you look so surprised to see me?"

"I don't know," Clair said. "Part of me figured this was all some kind of elaborate joke, I guess."

Allison huffed. "Please. You really think I would have been participating in something so juvenile?"

"It might not have really been you."

"I'm not even going to begin to unpack that." Allison breezed past Clair, letting herself into the hall. She pointed. "So, this way?"

Clair shook her head. "This way," she said, and began leading the way back to the command room. There were any number of other, more "appropriate" places to have this conversation, Clair supposed—the lounge, the kitchen, any one of several differently sized conference rooms—but somehow this felt right. Allison was family, after all, and moreover, highly trained in some kind of special ops. She was practically one of them, as far as Clair was concerned.

Clair entered her own credentials at the keypad: access code, retinal scan, voiceprint. Then she keyed in Allison's access. The Heroes had already set her up in the system as an ally. Clair motioned for Allison to input her own scans for the first time.

When they were done, the door swished open.

"Welcome, Clair. Welcome, AUTHORIZED GUEST."

Allison snorted under her breath as they entered. "Friendly place you got here."

"Jane did that, I'm afraid," Clair said, waving her hand in dismissal. "Her idea of a joke, or . . . something. Anyway, here it is. The heart of the operation."

She stepped aside, motioning broadly. At the curved sweep of screens that filled one half of the room, currently displaying (among other things) each of the Heroes' active trackers, a running scan of trending hashtags with geolocations inside of Grand City, and the muted face of GCN's afternoon anchor. At the conference table in the middle, and the projected map of Grand City hovering above it. Pale blue light filtered down from above, a stamp of the Heroes' emblem made of specialized fiberglass.

Allison turned in place, taking it all in. "Huh."

"What's wrong?"

"Nothing," Allison said quickly. "Nothing, it's just . . . I don't know. I expected the command room of a superhero lair to be a little more . . . I don't know, *commanding*."

"Headquarters," Clair said automatically.

"I'm sorry?"

"Super*villains* have lairs. Heroes have headquarters."

"What's the difference?"

Clair tucked her hair back, her cheeks burning. "I don't know. I don't make the rules."

Allison shrugged. "Okay, then." She took her phone out of her pocket, holding it toward the screens. Her finger poised over it, ready to swipe, and she looked at Clair expectantly. "May I?"

"Go for it."

"I got bored waiting for the rest of you to pick up the slack, so I did some digging on my own last night," Allison said. She flicked her finger, and a splash of data hit the main displays. "Cal's wife? Louisa Gaines-Goodman? Turns out, she's the *sister* of someone the Heroes put away eight years ago."

Clair walked over, taking in the spread of new information. A handful of mug shots stared back at her, as well as a rap sheet, and screen-caps of old news articles. Theodore "Teddy" Gaines. An angry, skinny kid in a basketball tank, arms covered in tattoos, a baseball cap over his dirty, white-boy dreads. The smirk in his mug shot conveyed the image of his middle finger perfectly, even if he wasn't technically allowed to hold it up for the photos.

He didn't look familiar, so Clair tapped into the Heroes' database. There wasn't much on him. A single entry, caught during what looked like Teddy's first criminal attempt to use his powers for personal gain.

"No offense, but he doesn't seem like much of a threat."

"I had a similar reaction," Allison said. She pinch-zoomed on her phone, dragging a document to the front of the screens. "Until I found out that Teddy Gaines was recently released from prison—*six years* earlier than the terms of his sentence."

Clair leaned in. A release order, signed and dated from only a month ago. "You think Cal had something to do with it?"

"I think if he *did*, he's now got someone with superpowers and a criminal history who owes him a huge debt." Allison shrugged. "Call me crazy, but I say it's too much to ignore."

"And you want the Heroes to find out?"

"God, no." Allison stepped back, looking genuinely *offended* for a second. She tucked her phone away. "Look, I admit you guys aren't entirely the clowns I used to think you were, but now that I'm invested, I'm still not handing over an investigation like this. I do, however, want *your* help."

Clair blinked. "Me."

"Hell yeah. Mind-reading with a single touch? You do realize you're basically the most valuable member of this team of yours, don't you?"

Did she? *Was* she? When Allison put it like that, Clair could see how the point felt self-evident, and yet. Mindsight had never exactly been the all-star player. Quite the contrary, in fact: if the Heroes of Hope were a kickball game at school, Clair was the scrawny kid that always got picked last. Not that they hadn't made extensive use of her skills before, but somehow it always paled in comparison to the others. They were more valuable in a straight-up fight, after all. But now, the idea that her powers might actually be considered *valuable*, that they were, in fact, sought after by someone who knew her shit, who'd assessed the team and said, "You know what? I want her," was . . . unsettling. Like the ground wasn't quite level anymore.

But maybe it shouldn't be. Clair's spine straightened, a flower brightening under the attention of the sun. Why shouldn't she be important to the team? Whoever said Mindsight wasn't a star player?

"All right," Clair said. She waved her hand over the main displays, tucking the information away for safekeeping. "Let's go."

ALLISON HITCHED HER BOOBS UP AS SHE PRESSED THE BUZZER. "FOLLOW MY LEAD."

"Follow—?" Clair started, a blush creeping up her neck, but a second later the screen in front of them snapped on, and a man peered out.

The blood dropped from Clair's face. She stole a fast glance at Allison's phone, held out of sight below the building's intercom camera. The mug shot she'd seen earlier peered back at her, the same as she remembered. The man looking at them through the intercom now, though . . . he was *similar*, sure, but also not, and it felt like more than just the age difference from the time the photo was taken. For one thing, there was not a single tattoo in sight, and prison wasn't exactly known for its tattoo *removal* services.

Then again, nothing about Teddy Gaines was proving to be what Clair expected. His new apartment was nestled in a sleek building in a hip corner of downtown, a place that just *screamed* "reward money." It was looking more and more like Allison was right.

Teddy stared out of the video feed for a moment, sizing the two of them up. Or at least, their chests. Clair crossed her arms as Teddy asked, "Can I help you ladies?"

"Theodore Gaines?" Allison said. There was something syrupy in her voice, the lure of a Venus fly trap. Sweet and enticing, perfectly benign, ignore the sharp spikes along the edges, look how nice and inviting she was.

His eyes slid right past Clair, settling on Allison. They ticked down. His mouth ticked up. "That depends on who's asking. You are . . . ?"

"Cameron Sweet, and this is Tiffany Straights," Allison said, and Clair nearly choked. What were they, strippers? "We're with Sweetline Magazine, and we're doing a story on the recent trend of hooking up with ex-cons among twentysomething women. I was wondering if we could get your thoughts?"

Clair stole a brief sidelong look at Allison. There was no way Teddy was stupid enough to fall for this. Right?

Teddy crossed his arms, leaning against something just out of sight of the video feed. "Huh. That's a thing?"

Allison giggled. Twirled the end of her ponytail. "Oh yeah. Apparently, that singer from Two-Sister Breakups went on Jillin' the Morning after she split with noted ex-con Malcolm Fitz? She spilled, like, *all* the deets. I think she has a book coming out!"

"Really." He turned his attention to Clair. To her surprise, his face was intrigued.

Dammit. Clair plastered a smile on her own face, quick as she could. She gave him a thumbs-up. "Um, yeah! You know how ladies love a, uh, bad boy."

Allison slapped Clair's hand down, disdain jolting up Clair's fingers. Clair folded her hands behind her back instead. Her cheeks were beginning to hurt from how far she was forcing her grin. God, was *this* what it was like to be straight? Clair had never longed more for the touch of a woman than she did right now.

Teddy raised an eyebrow.

"Did I mention," Allison said, "that anyone who agrees to an interview is going to be invited to an exclusive thank-you party, where they'll get a chance to meet the women we're *also* interviewing?"

Teddy grinned. "You should have led with that." He reached out, pressing a button just below the camera's line of sight, and the door in front of Clair and Allison buzzed as it clicked open. "Come on up."

The screen went black, the video feed snapping off.

Allison grabbed the door. "What the hell, Clair? You call that flirting?"

"Don't blame me!" Clair said, slipping in after her. "You can't spring something like that on a person without warning!"

"I didn't think I was 'springing' anything. How else did you expect to get up to his apartment?"

"Does your husband know what you do at work?"

Allison rolled her eyes. The elevator slid open for them, already at their level. "Don't try to change the subject. You almost botched our whole operation."

"Then maybe you shouldn't have asked the *open lesbian* to flirt with a man. I've never done that in my life!" Clair's stomach plunged in a way that had nothing to do with the elevator setting off. "Can't say I care to repeat the experience, either. How do you live like that?"

But Allison only shook her head, a half mutter beneath her breath.

They rode in silence. Walked down the hall in silence.

The door opened before they could even knock. Allison and Clair snapped their smiles back in place: one a perfectly alluring curve, one painfully stretched.

Teddy jerked his head. "Come on in."

The inside of Teddy Gaines's apartment was just as much of a sharp disconnect as Teddy Gaines himself. Tastefully appointed, bright windows letting the sun spill in, tidy enough. There were a few piles here and there, sure, but no pizza boxes covering the surfaces, no stacks of empty beer cans, no dead plants in the corner or dirty socks on the coffee table. For that matter, there actually *was* a coffee table. And . . . Clair tipped her head as she passed. It looked like there was an actual coffee-table *book* on the lower level, beneath the Xbox controller. Something artsy.

"Have a seat."

The couch was low-backed, sleek lines, muted blue fabric. There were probably supposed to be pillows in the corner, but that would have been a step too far, a sure sign they'd fallen into a trap. Allison kicked Clair's ankle, urging her forward.

She sat quickly. Her hands folded on her lap, careful not to touch the fabric. Her bright eyes and wide smile turned up toward Teddy.

Teddy held out two beers between his fingers, one for each of them. A third hung in his other hand.

Allison accepted hers easily, though Clair hesitated. Ignoring the fact that she didn't like beer, the idea of picking up any kind of read from Teddy was off-putting. But if Clair *didn't* take it, there'd be hell to pay with Allison later. Her displeasure was tangible even from here. Clair grabbed the bottle before she could talk herself out of it.

Only instead of the intense emotional stain Clair had been expecting, the glass bottle was oddly . . . cold. Like something important was missing. Clair stared at it, running her thumb over the label.

"So!" Allison said brightly. Teddy sat down beside her, and she held her phone out, voice memo recording between them. "How are you liking life on the outside?"

Teddy took a swig of beer, his mouth twisting bitterly as he swallowed. "Honestly? It sucks."

"Huh. I'm surprised to hear that."

Teddy shrugged. "Don't get me wrong, prison's a drag. But at least there I was my own man, you know? Like, what's so great about life out here? Shitty job, shitty apartment. Do this, do that. Follow the rules. Man, fuck the rules."

Shitty apartment? Clair raised an eyebrow. She glanced around, at the clean carpet, the nice TV, the photos on the walls . . .

One of the photos was missing.

There was, perhaps, no proof of this, but Clair had spent

enough time putting up photo murals in her and Jane's apartments over the years to recognize a gap when she saw one. The rest of the photos appeared to be old family shots, oddly dated. Some of the oldest were probably from the nineties, if the fashion choices were to be believed. A lot of them had Teddy when he was younger—a smiling boy, a surly teenager, his arm around his mom, his grandma . . . but no sign of Louisa Gaines anywhere.

Call it a hunch. Gingerly, Clair ran her fingers over the armrest of the sofa. Sisterly concern soaked through, as strong as bleach, but there was something else, too, something deeper. Something it was trying to cover up, like scrubbing bloodstains out of fabric. A layer of overlapping fears, too nuanced to separate at the moment. A layer of relief. A layer of guilt.

Clair breathed in deeply. *"Hate me for what I've done, fine,"* Louisa had said, right from this very cushion. *"I'll never apologize. You're going to be better off for it."*

And suddenly, Clair knew what was missing.

She looked up. Teddy was still talking, Allison was still listening intently, bobbing her head to the points he was making.

"You know I used to have tats? Great ink, yeah. This one piece, all up my arm here—"

"Tell us how you lost your superpowers, Teddy," Clair said, and the room went still. Clair took a swig of her beer. "That is what you're really angry about, isn't it?"

Allison turned sharply toward Clair. "Wait, are you serious?" and Clair gave a nod.

Teddy shifted in his seat. "Nah, man, I don't know what you're—"

But Allison leaped up, and her right hook silenced the rest.

Clair skittered sideways on the sofa. "What the—?"

"No superpowers," Allison said with a fast shrug. She pressed forward, yanking Teddy to his feet before he had the chance to get his bearings. He was already turning his head toward her, the words *fucking bitch* staining his lips along with the thin layer of blood.

Teddy yanked himself free, nearly ripping his shirt in the process. He ducked and lunged, clearly thinking he was about to gain the upper hand. He was fast, Clair would give him that, but

Allison was faster. She twisted and grabbed him by the scruff as he barreled toward her, letting his own speed carry him through. A spin, a flip—Teddy was splayed on the ground, the wind knocked from his lungs.

Allison towered over him, making sure he was really down. His arm was still in her grip, rising parallel to the leg that held him. She looked at Clair, then jerked her head toward Teddy.

"Go on, then," Allison said. "Do your thing."

"Um. This isn't exactly standard Heroes strategy."

Allison rolled her eyes. "Do you want results, or do you want to play things nice?"

Clair shrugged. But it's not like she could argue. She hurried over, crouching down beside Teddy.

"The fuck are you doing . . . ?" he mumbled, but Clair brushed off his forehead.

"Shh," she said as she pulled off her glove. "It's okay."

She took hold of his hand.

The ground sways beneath Clair—beneath Teddy. No, not the ground. A floor. It shudders and bounces beneath her, them. Him.

The taste of sweat and stale cotton fills Teddy's mouth. Why the fuck is he gagged? This isn't anywhere near as fun as he'd imagined it would be. Not that he has any illusion he was engaged in some tawdry sex act, but still—a guy can dream, can't he? Especially since he's been stuck in the back of a van for what must surely be an hour or more by now, and his shoulder is falling asleep beneath him.

They lurch to a stop. Teddy, lying on his side, slides just a fraction along the metal floor and bumps into something that's been poking at his back on and off. He can see enough light beneath the cloth over his eyes to know the door has opened, and then a pair of rough hands grabs him again, drags him out.

He should have stayed in prison. When they'd told him that morning he was being released, he'd actually laughed. *Nah, man, you expect me to believe that?* He still has six years to go. But they weren't joking, god, they weren't joking, and Teddy nearly laughed in their fucking faces.

Someone rips the blind off. Teddy flinches back, at the light or the motion or what, it don't matter. The gag comes out next, sticking to Teddy's tongue as he spits it into waiting hands. Woman's hands, and for a minute Teddy's hopes rise, until he spots his sister's familiar scar, just on the heel of her palm.

"Ah, shit," Teddy says by way of hello.

"Nice seein' you too, little brother."

There's already some snarky reply twisting up his mouth, but when he looks up, he's stunned into silence. For a minute he can't even think straight. Something about the situation is wrong, even more wrong than a couple of thugs hauling him into some rando warehouse and finding his sister waiting for them. Lou looks . . . different. Like she's gone all corporate. High heels and makeup and a short little business skirt, and it's not that she don't look good, he can't say she don't look good, but damn if he ever thought he'd see his sister cleaned up all right like that. She doesn't even look like herself. She's done . . . something . . . to her hair, though damn if Teddy knows enough about what women do to their hair to figure out what.

"Really?" a voice says, all snide and shit, and this is when Teddy realizes there's a man standing behind Lou. Also some kind of suit, done up like a fancy lawyer or a CEO or something just as bad. He's leaning against the wall, arms crossed, and he's looking at Teddy like Teddy's nothing but a bug on his shiny shoes. The man turns to Lou. "This is the man you want to save?"

"The fuck you talkin'—?" Teddy starts, but Lou cuts him off.

She turns to the man. "I don't expect someone like you to understand."

"At least we agree on something."

Lou steps away. She's not looking at Teddy no more. Her arms are crossed, and she says something to the man, too quiet for Teddy to hear.

He pushes himself off the wall. Does that shit where he threads his fingers and turns his palms out, cracking his knuckles. "Teddy Gaines," he says, like they're bros. "My man."

"I ain't your man," Teddy spits. He flexes against the binds that hold him. "Get me out of here."

"All in good time." He actually claps Teddy on the shoulder. Squeezes down, just a little too hard. "Listen, Teddy, here's the deal. For reasons I can't imagine, your sister here actually cares about you. She wants what's best for you. For you to become a proper, upstanding member of society."

"Fuck that."

The man laughs. Fucking laughs. His teeth are white like a movie star.

He lets go of Teddy's shoulder, and claps the side of Teddy's face as he turns away.

Teddy doesn't know what he's expecting. Something jumps in his stomach, like he's swallowed a damn squid. Something about the man puts him on edge. He's worse than the thugs Teddy dealt with in prison, worse than the crooked guards, the drug lords, the rapists and murderers. Teddy doesn't trust him, not for a hot second, and he can't imagine why Lou does.

She always has had terrible taste in men.

Now there's something in the man's hand as he steps over to Teddy again. The flash of metal—a knife? No, a needle, in a fancy-looking gun. Fuck, that's worse. Teddy strains against the binds again, but it don't do any good. "Stay the fuck away from me!"

But then Lou's arms are clamped around Teddy from behind, one across his chest and the other holding his head against her body, turning his head, and she's stronger than she has any right to be, fuck, she's so strong, and the man's coming closer, and Teddy's neck's exposed like a damn stripper laid out across the pole, and there's nothing he can do. He bucks, he swears. He spits at the man, but the man just gives him a look like, shit, really?, and it doesn't stop him. Something pierces Teddy's neck, and a burning floods his veins. He probably screams.

Teddy ripped Clair's grip away.

Clair blinked, refocusing. Reorienting. The world swam, just for a moment, as reality asserted itself across her senses. The pristine living room of Teddy's apartment, the slant of a sunbeam cutting in through the window. Allison, waiting impatiently at her elbow. Sometime while Clair was working, she'd released her hold of Teddy.

Teddy was staring at Clair. Eyes narrowed in suspicion. "Who the fuck are you people?"

"Nobody," Clair said. Her hand cradled the top of his buzzed head before she could think to question herself. "Forget we were even here."

JANE'S STOMACH RUMBLED AS SHE FINALLY STEPPED into the sunshine. She hadn't even realized how long they'd been in there, until they left and she found herself starving.

Blue laughed. "Wow. Someone's hungry."

"Hey, don't judge. We missed lunch for this."

"Come on, then," Blue said, smiling. "I know a great place. My treat."

Jane hesitated. On the one hand: getting something to eat was a fantastic idea, and probably where Jane was headed next anyway. And this was Blue, her Best Friend, on paper and in practice both. They'd eaten together a lot, especially over the past few months, as they'd begun to put the plans for their company into action. Plus, there was still plenty to discuss from their meeting. It could even be written off as a working lunch, a concept that was becoming second-nature to Jane.

But. On the other hand.

Jane did not entirely trust that smile.

It was hard to put a finger on exactly what was wrong with it. Something about the way it curled at the end, like it was a hook trying to snare Jane's chest. It reminded her of Clair, without actually being anything objectively like Clair.

Except that was silly, Jane told herself. She shook the thought off, and found that she was already following Blue down the street, as if the matter was settled. As if there'd never been a question in the first place.

A short walk later, they were settled in the rounded booths of a sunlit restaurant, menus unfolding between them. It was a nice place—upscale, but not so expensive as to be obnoxious. Modern and tasteful, but not pretentious. It was the kind of place Jane might have picked, if she knew about it, the kind she might have taken Clair to if she wanted to impress her.

At that thought, a chill settled over Jane. It was stupid to be worried over this, right? Right. After all, she had been friends with Blue for years—or at least, Blue had been friends with *Jane* for years—and there had never been any indication that Blue had ulterior motives toward Jane. Right? And even if there had, ever, in a time Jane wouldn't have any memory of, it wouldn't matter, because that would be the past, and this was now. And now, Blue was well aware of the fact that Jane was married. Almost married. Sort of married. Mostly married.

Shit. Jane bit her lip. She dug into the pocket of her blazer, retrieving her phone.

Before she'd left the lawyer's office, she'd sent a quick text to Clair. Just checking in. *Finally done,* Jane had written. *I'm starving. Where are you?*

Clair's reply had come in sometime during the walk. A single emoji of a closed umbrella. Their private signal: too busy to talk, but everything's fine.

Jane stared at it for longer than was probably necessary. *Everything's fine,* she told herself. *Everything's fine.*

"Jane," Blue said, her voice heavy with exasperation. "Are you even listening to me?"

Jane looked up. Forced a smile. "Sorry. I can't get a hold of Clair."

Blue's face went still. "Oh. Do you need to—?"

"No, it's fine." Jane locked the screen and set her phone, facedown, on the table. "She texted earlier that she'd be busy. I guess I'm just a little jumpy."

"Because of what happened at the wedding?"

The wedding. It's funny how easily Jane had forgotten about it. Not the attack—that part was vividly present throughout her day, lurking behind every thought, just waiting for an opportunity to pounce and send a panic down Jane's spine. The wedding itself, though, had slipped from Jane's mind like so much tulle falling through her fingers. Probably because they'd already been married for so long that this one didn't feel quite real. They'd already planned the day they'd wanted, already held their ceremony, already signed the paperwork, already said their vows. Till death do us part.

And beyond, Jane thought, because they'd already been parted by death once, and frankly Jane had no intention of ever returning to that state again. How did she even begin to explain to Blue why she was really worried? She couldn't. Not without telling her everything, and . . . she still wasn't ready for that. Not yet. Not here.

Still, the wedding was as good of an excuse as any. Jane nodded.

"I'm sorry Clair was attacked," Blue said. "But . . . maybe it's not such a bad thing that you need to reschedule the wedding. Gives you a chance to really consider this whole marriage thing."

Jane looked up sharply. "Excuse me?"

"I'm not saying it's necessarily a bad thing," Blue said with a shrug. "I know you love Clair and all, I love Clair, too, but . . . you have to admit, Jane, it was kind of fast. Hell, I'd call it a shotgun wedding, if you weren't both women. Unless . . ." Blue blinked. She laid her hand down flat on the table and leaned forward, lowering her voice. "Shit, is she trans? You're not pregnant, are you?"

Jane nearly choked. "What? *No*, I'm not—no."

"Okay, okay." Blue raised her hands defensively. "Look, I'm just asking. Can't assume."

"I am not having this conversation with you."

"Too bad, because *I'm* having this conversation with *you*. Someone has to, Jane. You don't even come out until recently, and now suddenly you're getting married? Have you thought about that? Are you sure you even want to tie yourself down to someone this soon? There's a whole world of women out there, and you're just, what, picking the first one you kissed?"

"I don't—" Jane started, but then the server swung by, two ice waters in his hands. He set them down between Blue and Jane, a blockade against their outrage.

"Afternoon, ladies. I'm John, I'll be your host today. Can I get either of you something more to drink?"

"Later," Jane snapped. She didn't even care that she was being rude, and she glared at him from behind her glasses until the tips of his ears turned pink.

"I'll be back in a few minutes," he mumbled, backing away from the table.

Blue opened her mouth, possibly to scold Jane, but Jane cut her off.

"I can't believe you. Where is this even coming from? You were my maid of honor, for fuck's sake."

"And I did my job," Blue said. Her lips pulled to the side, considering. "Okay, half of my job—but that wasn't my fault. The point is, yeah, you've known Clair since you were kids. That's different from being, well, *together*."

Jane's fist tightened around her napkin. "We *were* together. In secret. We told you that, when we first got engaged."

"Yeah . . . here's the thing, Jane: nobody believed you. Sorry."

Jane sat back, as suddenly all the indignation she'd been feeling rushed out of her, her confidence crumpling like a paper with a lousy sketch. What else didn't people believe? How much of Jane's story was in doubt? Okay, it's not like anyone was likely to guess they came from parallel worlds, as the existence of those wasn't exactly common knowledge. But there was still plenty to poke holes in.

Despite herself, Jane squirmed in her chair. Just a single wiggle, back and forth, as she picked at the edge of the napkin roll she'd been holding.

"If you really feel this way, why didn't you say something earlier?"

Blue glanced down. For a second, it looked like the top of her cheeks had tinted pink, but it was hard to say if it was a blush, or just a reflection of her hair off her sharp cheekbones. "I don't know. I just want you to be happy."

"I am happy. Clair makes me happy."

A fast shrug. "Okay." Blue picked up her straw, unsheathing it and stabbing it deep into the ice of her water. The cubes slushed together as she stirred, stabbed, stirred. "You can't blame me for asking."

"I don't," Jane said, and it wasn't until the words were spoken that she realized they were true. Despite the awkward situation this talk had put Jane in, despite the prodding, despite the annoyance, Jane knew that, from Blue's perspective, she was just being a good friend.

Blue glanced up. Her eyes searched Jane's.

Jane's phone buzzed on the table. "Oh, thank god," Jane said as she picked it up.

"Let me guess," Blue said, her face souring. "Clair?"

That was Jane's guess, too, though both of them were wrong. In fact it wasn't a text at all, but an alert on the app Marie had written to monitor breaking news in the city. A string of social media posts were coming in hot, like a rapid-fire set of panels, too tightly zoomed to make sense on their own, but together the picture became clear. An attack at a tech expo being held downtown. The convention center in chaos, clipped videos of explosions and jets of green acid. A billowing darkness, a giant fist. A flash of silver, sparking with electrical current.

"Shit." Jane stood up, already grabbing her blazer and purse off the back of her chair. "Um, listen, I've got to go. I'm sorry. I hate to bail on you like this, it's just—"

"Is everything okay?" Blue was rising from her own chair, a friend ready to jump in and help in a crisis.

Jane tried to wave her back down. "Yeah, no, it's fine, I'm fine, we're fine. It's, um . . ." Jane bit her cheek. She would say "work," but that obviously wasn't going to convince her business partner. Family stuff? Blue would see through that—unless someone had died, there was no way Jane was rushing off in this much of a hurry to deal with them. "It's just something. It's fine," she finished lamely.

She started to leave, but Blue reached out and snagged her. "Wait."

Jane looked down. Blue's fingers were looped around Jane's wrist, her thumb pressed against the beat of Jane's pulse. The motion had drawn them close, close enough for Jane to see the chip of Blue's nail polish and, when she looked up, the tiny pattern of stars she had tattooed beneath her ear, pink and blue and purple twinkling back at her.

Jane slid free.

This time, Blue's face definitely tinted pink, though she brushed her short hair back to cover for it. "Just . . . think about what I've said, okay? I'm worried about you." She wouldn't make eye contact.

"I will," Jane said, because agreeing was faster than arguing. She was already backing away.

It didn't mean she actually had to do it.

"THIS IS A BAD IDEA."

Allison shifted in the driver's seat. She hadn't said a word since they left Teddy's apartment building. She wouldn't stop throwing nervous glances in Clair's direction, and Clair couldn't exactly blame her.

Forget we were even here.

The words had come out of Clair like a whisper, like a prayer, like a spell. She felt her intention spilling from her fingers, gracing his head as a baptism. He'd been staring right at her as she spoke, and then suddenly he just . . . wasn't. She saw the moment of transformation, quick as blowing out a candle. The way his attention slid from her, unfocused. He blinked in confusion, as if he couldn't quite remember how he'd come to be lying on the floor. But then—and here's the part that really creeped her out—he'd stood up, brushed himself off, and walked right past the two of them as if they didn't even exist.

Went into his bedroom and shut the door behind him.

This is when Allison had turned to Clair, her expression utterly still.

Clair dipped her head as she slipped her fingerless glove back on. "It looks like you were half right. Cal seems to have gotten him out of prison, but . . . he's also the one who stole Teddy's powers. Some kind of injection. I don't know where he got it from."

Even as she said the words, Clair knew she should be reacting stronger than she was. She knew the threat Cal posed now was real and dangerous, possibly more than anything she'd faced since taking on Mindsight's mantle, but a sense of calm kept her panic at bay. Clair wasn't entirely sure why, but at the moment, she would take it.

Still, she expected a bigger response from Allison. For better or worse, this was big news. But when she looked up, Allison was texting. A chirrup signaled a reply, and Allison slid the phone into her back pocket. "We should go," Allison said, still not looking at Clair, and then she turned and led the way out of the apartment, down the hall, toward the elevator. Out the door. Into the car.

When Allison had started driving, Clair hadn't questioned it. It wasn't until they missed the turn for the Heroes' headquarters that Clair thought to ask where they were going, and that's when Allison had silently passed a phone over, the same phone she'd been texting from earlier. Clair had taken it without thinking. Resentment stained her fingers as soon as she touched it—Teddy's phone, smudged with a layer of smugness from when Allison had pickpocketed it. The screen was lit up with a text conversation labeled "Lou Bitch," only two messages appearing below. *Someone's after me can we meet?* said one "from" Teddy, and then his sister's reply:

Beef-Up Burgers, 37th and Brinkley. 30 minutes.

Clair handed the phone back. "This is a bad idea."

Allison shifted as she slid the phone into her jacket pocket. "She's the next link in the chain of investigation."

"But Cal's the one who used the injection."

"Yeah, well, we can't exactly get close to him, now can we? Besides, you really think he's smart enough to get his hands on a medical breakthrough like *that* on his own? No," Allison said, barreling on before Clair could answer, "odds are, she's the mind behind this. I'd bet you anything."

Clair's mouth twisted up. She didn't argue, though she wanted to. There was something about the way Allison said it, "a medical breakthrough," like they were curing cancer, while Clair could see it for what it really was: a weapon. And one currently in the hands of Cal, who had god only knows what kind of plans for it.

Wasn't that reason enough to see what else they could find out? Did she really need to agree with Allison's motivation?

A short while later, they pulled up in front of Beef-Up, and Allison cut the engine. Clair slipped out of the car, taking it in. She hadn't been in one of these since she was a kid, and the difference was staggering. In her memories, the place is loud and sticky, full of garish colors and posters of cartoon characters, a plastic display case at the register showing the latest kids' meal toys enshrined like holy relics. Little Clair would stand in line with Donna, her stomach jumping with excitement, mentally picking the best character from the display case. She never got the good ones, no matter how hard she crossed her fingers and wished.

What she stepped into now was an entirely different world. Gone were the plastic slides, the trash cans shaped like a talking milkshake, the hard purple benches designed for quick cleanup. Instead, the walls were paneled with reclaimed wood, the tables round and high, the ceiling dotted with frosted skylights that let in just enough sunshine to be cozy. In the middle of the room, a clutch of bamboo plants were surrounded by a circular work counter, electrical outlets and USB ports at the ready. There were no more shrieking children—instead, business people typed away on laptops, hipsters read dog-eared novels, and the line snaking up to the counter was spitting out more cups of coffee than burgers. Not a single chicken nugget was anywhere in sight.

"Wow," Clair whispered under her breath. "They've really rebranded, haven't they?"

Allison stepped to the side. "We should grab a seat."

"Aren't you going to order anything?"

"Clair. We're not here for that."

"Yeah, but we don't know how long it'll be before Lou shows up," Clair said. "And if we *don't* order something, we're just being dicks. Besides, you wanted to blend in, right?"

"Fine," Allison said with a sigh. "But don't go crazy with it."

Clair gave a haughty sniff. "I don't know what you're talking about." She flounced off to get in line.

When she was through, she carried her purchase across the restaurant. Allison had snared them a table, tucked into a corner. It was a good vantage point, with an excellent view of both the street and the interior, and Clair settled across from her in a way so as not to be an obstruction.

"Look!" Clair said with delight. She plopped a bright cardboard box on the table, decorated with cartoon characters and a word-search puzzle on the side. A Beefy Buddy Box. "They still make them."

Allison raised an eyebrow. "What did I say about not going crazy?"

"Oh, come on. Live a little." Clair popped the box open, and began to dig around inside. A tiny burger, a set of fries, a half-pint of milk and a straw. At last, drawn from the depths, Clair pulled out her treasure: a small figure seated in a pink plastic car.

Clair grinned. She didn't even recognize the character or the franchise it was part of, but there it was. Her finger trailed over the plastic wrapper surrounding it, reveling in the emotional emptiness it contained. The workers had worn gloves at every step of Clair's meal preparation, shielding her from both germs and unwanted memories. Clair set the toy beside her meal, not even caring about the raised eyebrows being thrown in her direction, or the huff of discontent Allison made as she buried herself in her phone and pretended not to know her.

"Now *this* is a trip to Beef-Up," Clair said as she began to unwrap her meal. Already, the stress of the day was melting off her like the fake cheese of her burger.

She lifted it to her nose, smelling deeply. Almost immediately, a blop of ketchup fell on the end of her fingers.

"Aw, man. Forgot napkins." She went to lick it off, but before she could, Allison pulled a tissue from her pocket. She waved it forward, a white flag in Clair's direction. Clair raised an eyebrow as she took it.

"What?" Allison asked. "I'm a mom. You think I *don't* have tissues on me constantly?"

"I guess I never thought about it." Clair wiped her fingers off—thankfully, it hadn't gotten onto the fabric of her gloves—then bunched the tissue and put it carefully on the edge of her wrapper for later.

"I've also got Purell, just for the record," Allison said. "And Band-Aids."

Clair bit the end off her fry. "No snacks?"

"What do you need snacks for? You've got a Beefy Buddy." Allison shrugged. "Also, I left the animal crackers in my purse."

Clair laughed.

A faint smile broke Allison's façade. She crossed her arms,

leaning back in her seat. "Oh, give me a damned fry," she said a moment later, waving for one.

Clair turned the box around, and moved the little cup of ketchup between them. "Help yourself."

She did; grabbing two fries at a time, and stabbing them recklessly into the ketchup. Clair shook her head, and Allison chewed in silence, swallowed them down, wiped her mouth with a fresh tissue from her pocket.

"You know," she said as she reached forward again, "I'm surprised the two of *you* never had kids. You and Jane, that is. Back in your world. You've been together a long time, haven't you?"

Clair spun the Beefy Buddy toy on the table between them. "Our whole lives." Not technically true, she supposed, but when you've been together since you were fifteen, best friends since kindergarten, the distinction between being a couple and not tended to lose its meaning. She shrugged. "We've just never felt it was necessary."

"I suppose that's just as well. You couldn't exactly have left them behind when you came here, and how would you explain something like *that*?"

"Probably would have been worse if it was the other way around, though," Clair said as she stabbed another fry into her ketchup. "Can you imagine? 'Hey there, we're your new moms—just like the old ones, but better!'"

Allison drew still, as if this had never occurred to her. Even now, after seeing Jane and Clair together for more than a year—did she honestly never stop to wonder, never pause to realize that her sister might be gay, as well? She cleared her throat. "You think . . . they might have gotten together, too, if things had been different? Amy and my Jane?"

"Without a doubt," Clair said. She was not going to hedge on this. She knew better. Her gaze drifted across the restaurant, looking for Amy. From the clusters of people who'd set up office at the tables, to the woman sitting by herself in the corner, to the impatient line leading up to the register. The line had grown since they'd arrived, a crush descending for their afternoon caffeine hit. Clair's attention slid across the patrons, taking note.

No Amy, and she was about to turn away, when her eyes snapped back.

There.

Not Amy, but Lou, stepping into place at the back of the line.

It was no surprise that Clair hadn't recognized her at first. The woman standing in front of her was Louisa Gaines-Goodman all right, but she was also a far cry from the wife who graced the campaign photos and news clips. In those, she was always done up to perfection, an image crafted by teams of political advisors and stylists and campaign managers. In those, she wore tailored pantsuits, designer miniskirts, four-inch pumps. In those, her whitened teeth gleamed alongside Cal's, her skin had been wiped clean, all flaws removed, her hair fell in cascading waves across her shoulders and upper arms.

But this Lou . . . this Lou wore no-name jeans that pooled over battered sneakers. A plain cotton T-shirt in heather blue, a green zip-up hoodie flapping open over it. Her navy baseball cap had the Grand City Public Library logo on the front. Mousy hair loose and straight, hanging as blinders on either side of her face. No makeup, or minimal at any rate. The transformation was incredible, and could only have been done on purpose.

Clair cleared her throat. Jerked her head, trying to divert Allison's attention without *drawing* attention. *That's her*, Clair mouthed.

Allison's eyebrow ticked up. She reached over the table, taking another one of Clair's french fries—and using the motion as an excuse to look in the direction Clair had indicated. A layer of steely determination congealed on the remainder of the fries as Clair picked up another; she dropped it, brushing her fingers off on the tissue-napkin Allison had given her earlier.

"What's the plan?" Clair asked low under her breath. "And don't you dare suggest flirting with her. I don't care if she is a woman, I'm not doing it."

Plans be damned. Before Clair could say another word, Allison sprang from her seat, and when Clair whirled around, she could see why: Lou must have spotted them, because she'd cut out of the line, and was making a fast track for the side door.

"Shit!" Clair said. She snagged the Beefy Buddy toy as she

scrambled from the table, stuffing it into her pocket. There was no way she was catching up to either of them in time, but that was fine. Allison was plenty fast enough for both of them.

Lou was almost to the door when Allison cut in front of her, rudely lurching forward as if hurrying to throw something in the trash can. Her arm stretched across Lou's path, blocking her like a toll booth. Lou skidded to a stop, Clair rushing up behind her.

Allison tipped her head. She looked Lou straight in the eyes. "Going somewhere?"

THE ISSUE BEGINS IN MEDIA RES.

A fight splashes across the first page, each of the Heroes engaged in combat: Granite Girl covered in green acid as she lands a punch against Acid Reign, her stony skin protecting her even as drops chew holes in her camo pants and black tank top; Pixie Beats running around the enormous head of Megacrush, attacking his eyes and getting him to stand there swatting at her like she's a whole swarm of colorful bees; Rip-Shift hidden in a cloud of darkness, only the slim shimmer of one of his tears lending any kind of identification, while Windforce attempts to sweep PitchBlack out of contention. The lines of action draw the eye in a lazy S-curve down the page, slaloming from one fight to the next to the next, until finally, in the lower right corner: Captain Lumen and Electric Fury.

On that first page, Jane is leaping out of the way as a lightning bolt streaks across the showroom floor of the tech expo. Turn to the next, and you're met with a close-up of her face as she lands on the ground, the determined grit of her teeth. She pushes herself to her feet, races forward and leaps onto one of the vendor tables, vaulting herself up to grab a colorful banner hanging down from the ceiling. She lands behind Electric Fury, gets in one fast blast of lasers at her back.

Jane ducked, avoiding a spray of acid that had escaped Granite Girl's portion of the fight. Her chest heaved, and sweat plastered hair to her forehead. Jane quickly swiped the worst of the sweat off her face with the back of her sleeve, before it could drip into her eyes. In the world of her comics, none of these real-life concerns are a factor, but the truth is, they'd been engaged in combat for a good five minutes now, and neither side was making much headway. She wondered how tired Electric Fury and the others were getting. She wondered if she'd stretched enough beforehand, as she'd hurried to get there. She wondered if Devin's back was still seizing up, like he'd been complaining about that morning when the team had made their plans for the day.

Another bolt of lightning streaked toward her, and Jane threw herself forward, curling her back to avoid it. Damn, that would hurt tomorrow. The lightning crackled just past the back of her ribs, close enough that a tingling sensation ran up Jane's spine, straight to her teeth. They needed *something* to shift the balance of this fight, and soon, or people were going to start getting hurt.

In the next instant, salvation came as if answering a prayer. Flashbangs went off without warning. Dozens of them, popping like fireworks throughout the main exhibition hall. The whole room paused—Acid Reign and Granite Girl, Rip-Shift and Windforce and PitchBlack, Megacrush and Pixie Beats—each of them frozen as if drawn flat on the page. Only Electric Fury reared back, her reflective catsuit flashing white as she threw her arm over her face to protect her vision.

The flashbangs swept the room clean, a purifying light that caressed Jane's skin like stepping through a crystal waterfall. She was the only person to see the SWAT team storm the building.

They arrived in full tactical gear. Storming in with riot shields, beneath helmets with thick visors to help them see through the lights. Padded body armor covered them head-to-toe. Faceless, nameless, they poured through and surrounded the scene as surely as if they were the panel borders themselves. Jane gave a fast whistle and a wave; their heads and guns snapped in her direction.

The SWAT team advanced, rushing toward them. Flashes were still popping all around, the room erupting into chaos as everyone else attempted to make a hasty retreat. Jane turned back to Electric Fury, ready to make her move, but Electric Fury was already glaring at Jane, squinting through the storm.

Jane thought Electric Fury was going to say something, but she didn't. Instead, as fast as the stroke of a pen, faster than Jane could even think—darkness swept the room, and Electric Fury collapsed into a bundle of lightning, bolting away.

"No!" Jane lunged, knowing it was useless, needing to do it anyway. Her fingers tightened on nothing but empty air. Static ran up her sleeve, the only trace of Electric Fury that was left. "Goddammit!"

The click of a machine gun sprang up from behind Jane as the darkness swept away, a jagged sound bubble that bristled against her skin. "Stand down!"

Slices of Jane's masked face. Just the hint of a silhouette at first, her back to the reader. A smudge highlights her cheekbones, the furrowed brow of confusion lending shadows to her face. In tiny fragments, she turns, her expression shifting through denial, to shock, to horror as she turns to face outward from the page.

Below her, a wide spread: a circle of rifles still pointed squarely in her direction, the barrels extra large as they vie for her attention like microphones waiting breathlessly for a statement.

"What the—?"

"Hands in the air!"

"What?" Jane whipped her head around, boggling at the crowd of officers in black body armor. They completely surrounded her, a tightening noose. "Guys, it's me. It's Captain Lumen. We're on the same side."

One of the officers jerked his gun at Jane. "Hands in the *air*!"

"Okay, okay!" Fear began to creep up Jane's shoulders. She shot her arms up, the bright red of her sleeves blocking her peripheral vision. Thankfully, the rest of the team seemed to have hightailed it out of there, or at least found cover elsewhere.

Still, that did nothing to help *her*. The flashbangs had finished by now, and a few members of the SWAT team had removed their protective eyewear. If Jane were to flood the room, how many did that leave for her to take down? More importantly, how trigger-happy were they? Jane's armor was good, sure, but even a bulletproof suit only did so much against an onslaught of machine gun fire. If they started shooting in earnest . . .

It didn't matter. She was going to have to find out.

But before she could, a jolt of electricity struck Jane from behind. Her back seized, collapsing her, as a rush of panic and anger swept across her chest—Electric Fury must have snuck back in, must have gotten in a parting shot at Jane. That was the idea, anyway, and it made sense, and it lasted right up until the crackling flash of a high-intensity taser caught the corner of her eye. Jane's knees hit the floor, and the SWAT team swarmed her like a football tackle. Then: a thick hood thrown over her face, the weight of bodies crushing her down, the smell of sweat and adrenaline making her gag. Scattered panels show Jane's arms wrenched back, cold cuffs finding her fists, heavy boots pounding near her head. Her powers welled within her, ready to burst, when something pricked her neck, and the issue slid from her fingers as the world winked out.

LOU'S ATTENTION DARTED TO THE DOOR BEHIND ALLISON. Her whole body tensed, ready to strike.

"If you're thinking of trying to rush me, I wouldn't," Allison said as she stepped more fully in front of the exit. "Wouldn't want to cause a scene, now would you? Imagine what it would do for the campaign."

Lou's fingers flexed. Like she wanted to throw a punch, or grab a weapon. It wasn't entirely clear, at first, if Allison's argument would work. Clair stole a fast look over her shoulder, but if anyone in the rest of Beef-Up Burgers had noticed their little formation, no one cared. Score one for self-absorption, she supposed.

"What do you want?" Lou asked, finally, spitting the question out like gristly meat.

Allison drew out a badge from her back pocket, flipping it open. "Agent Maxwell, ARRO. I have a few questions for you."

"Oh, please," Lou said. "ARRO? What's that even supposed to be?"

Allison gritted her teeth. "Abnormal Research and Reconnaissance Office."

"That can't be a real thing."

"Try something stupid, and you'll find out just how real it is," Allison snapped. "Now. Like I said, I have questions."

Lou snorted. "I'm not telling you anything."

"Oh, that's okay." Allison jerked her chin. "My friend here doesn't need you to speak."

Slowly, as if there was a knife to her throat, Lou turned around. Her eyes widened. "Mindsight."

It came out as barely a whisper, but it coursed straight to Clair's heart. It wasn't so much that she was surprised Lou knew who she was, since Cal would have told his wife the Heroes' identities. There was something in the way Lou said it, the way she was looking at Clair now. A bit of surprise, a dash of awe. More than anything, though, it was said with *fear*. And for the first time, Clair wondered if perhaps that reputation had been earned somehow.

But before Clair could do anything, Lou's face iced over. She tugged her baseball cap down, shook her mousy hair into her face. "I've got nothing to say to you."

Then, faster than either of them could react, Lou plunged through the door.

If Clair hadn't been standing right there when it happened, she probably wouldn't have believed it. Not that the power itself was so remarkable, compared to everything Amy and Clair had seen since gaining their powers. More the shock of the moment. One second, Lou stood in front of Allison, trapped between her and Clair. The next, Lou had gone fuzzy around the edges, racing forward as if Allison, and the door, simply didn't exist. Allison lurched, starting to react, but Lou plunged straight into her, straight *through* her. She flickered like a projection and then, in an instant, had reappeared on the other side of Allison, whole and solid once again.

Allison glanced down, clutching at her chest in alarm, as Lou bolted up the street behind them.

Clair jumped forward, grabbing Allison by the arm. "Are you okay?" she asked, but Allison shook her off. She was already turning, slamming the door open with her shoulder. Clair caught it behind her, the glass smudged with annoyance.

They chased Lou down the street, past a bagel shop and a bookstore, into a side alley. "Stop!" Allison shouted as she drew a gun out from a side holster hidden beneath her leather jacket.

Lou didn't stop. The alley filled with the crack of a gun, the ping of a bullet off a dumpster. A warning shot, one Lou didn't heed. She dodged to the left and then, without a word, phased straight through the wall of the building.

"Dammit!" Allison ran up to the spot where Lou had disappeared. She slammed her palm against the brickwork. "Goddammit!"

Clair came to a stop, puffing, behind her. She put her hand to her stomach; she definitely should not have eaten so much of her Beefy Buddy meal. "Now what?"

"I don't know," Allison snapped. "Check the front of the building—maybe we can get inside, search the place."

Clair nodded. She turned around, looking out onto the street, and that's when she spotted it.

Across the way, a familiar building. Nothing particularly noteworthy on its own, yet the sight of it snared her. Electricity seemed to hang in the air, a crackle that raised the hairs all along the back of Clair's arms. She found her eyes trailing up, up, up the building, until she was staring at the lip of the roof, until her senses blocked out and her memory overtook her. Leaning over the edge, wondering how to get down. Her head spinning at what had just happened.

This was it.

This was the building where Electric Fury had taken her

the very first time they'd met. When they'd been fleeing the oncoming police, when she'd grabbed Mindsight's wrist and used her powers to hurtle them as electrical current across the city. And maybe there were other things Clair should have been caring about, more "pressing" issues, but she knew, she *knew*, that untangling the mystery of the Amy visions meant untangling the mystery of her past with Electric Fury. And she couldn't bring herself to look away, to move. To care about anything else.

"Clair! Are you even listening to me?"

Not really. Allison's voice drifted through Clair's perception like a dream. Barely touched, only half real.

She found herself turning around. Not so much to reply to Allison, but simply to take in the whole of this area, to put a greater context to the place. To see if there was anything she might have missed that first night when she climbed down the building as best as she could. Her eyes shifted past where Allison stood. Then they snapped back. Widened.

"Allison, look out!"

Too late. Lou appeared through the wall, arms outstretched, a ghost coming to seek its revenge. She grabbed Allison from behind, hooking her into a headlock.

Allison staggered, dragged backward. Her gun clattered to the pavement as her arms flew up to claw at her attacker. Lou kicked it aside, and Clair raced after it. If she could get her hands on it, throw it back to Allison . . .

Of course, Lou may well be able to phase through bullets as easily as walls and people, but it was better than leaving Allison defenseless. And if the gun was truly no threat to Lou, then why had she bothered to disarm Allison in the first place?

Clair hung along the edges of the fight, looking for an opening. Allison had used her momentum to knock Lou back into the wall behind them. Lou phased into it, unharmed, and Allison's solid back slammed against the brick instead—but at least the motion had allowed Allison to slip free of Lou's misty arms. Allison whirled, ready to strike, as Lou came back out of the wall. They fell down in a tumble, Allison attempting to catch Lou in a chokehold, but Lou just rose to her feet, smooth as a ballerina, slipping right through Allison.

It was the exact opening Clair had been waiting for, and she took it.

She thought Lou would be too busy with Allison to notice. Thought she'd be able to get her own hit in. But her fist connected with nothing, Lou's body as insubstantial as a projection. The momentum of her punch threw Clair off balance. She fell, straight through the ghost of Lou.

A rush of memories sucked down into Clair's lungs, like breathing in frozen mist.

Lou lying on her back, neck craned to look upside-down at the TV towering over her, mashing buttons as her brother jumps around the living room, shouting out instructions. *Jump, jump! Watch out! Stomp it!* A, B, A, A. Lou's mouth twitches into a smile. One by one, the goombas fall.

Now Lou is standing in her bedroom, smoothing out the dress she's going to wear to prom, not that she has a date. The tag is still on it, she's not allowed to take it off because they'll be returning it the morning after. The door springs open behind her and Lou jumps, terrified—if she tears the dress!—but that's the least of her worries. A spray of silly string, and her brother's riotous laughter. *Teddy!* The scream rips itself from her throat, so hard it's a wonder she will be able to speak at all.

A spread of news articles. Lou printed them out from a library computer, cutting away the ads and pressing them between the soft-worn pages of her copy of *This Lullaby*. Her brother's trial isn't enough to warrant extensive coverage, so she makes do with what she has, what she can infer between these vague black lines. Lou won't dare attend, won't dare set foot into a courthouse. What if her powers fritz out on her? They've barely started to manifest, and any little thing sets them off these days.

Clair came back to herself just as Allison grabbed the gun from Clair's fingers. The alleyway snapped into sharp focus in an instant, the smallest brush of skin passing between them. Barely anything, but enough for a bullet of determination to pierce Clair's stomach.

She knew what Allison was about to do.

"Allison, no!"

Clair rolled fast, grabbing at Allison's arm as it was still raising into position. The two of them toppled, falling against the pavement. Clair wrestled forward, trying to keep Allison down, even as Allison attempted to throw her off.

"Run!" Clair shouted, twisting around to look at Lou.

For a flicker of a second, it looked like Lou wasn't sure. In that hesitation, Clair knew she'd made the right call. Lou and Teddy had the same eyes, the same flinch whenever they heard a loud noise. Looking at her, Clair saw shades of a hundred more days like the ones she'd seen in Lou's memory—games and fights, meals and bedtimes and homework, a video game cartridge slid toward you when you were sad. Clair had grown up with four younger brothers. She recognized a sister's protective gaze when she saw one.

Go, Clair mouthed.

Lou turned, the back of her jacket flashing like a rabbit's tail as she phased into the nearest wall.

Allison's strength surged, and in the next second, Clair found her ass hitting the pavement. The gun was ripped from Clair's hands as Allison pushed herself, hard, to her feet. She was already shouting, accusations whipping freely from her mouth. "You idiot! What did you do that for?"

Sitting there, hands still stinging from the wrestling match, the question felt absurd. What did she do that for? There was only one answer:

"We don't kill," Clair said. Evenly and deliberately, as if daring Allison to question her.

Allison snorted. "You mean you don't. You and your team, and your holier-than-thou morals. Get it through your thick head, *Mindsight*. This is the real world, and that woman was a clear and present danger."

"No." Clair drew herself to her feet. "She wasn't. She was *scared*. We attacked *her*, remember?"

"Don't you dare pull that shit on me. This wasn't unjustified. I saw the situation—I made the call. Period. You had no right to interfere. And now, because of *your* stupidity, we'll never get a second chance at her. The investigation may as well be at a dead stop."

"Some things are more important than an investigation."

Allison shook her head. "My soul doesn't need saving, Clair."

"I know it doesn't. You're a good person, Allison. And somewhere, deep down, you know I'm right."

Allison stepped back, blinking in surprise. Her whole body stilled. For a second, it even looked like maybe Clair had gotten through to her. But then Allison's face twisted up.

"I was wrong about you," she said as she stuffed her gun back into its holster. "I shouldn't have asked you to come."

"Allison—"

"No. Go home, Clair. Go back to your team, and your rules, and the training wheels they keep you in. You'll never be the hero this city really needs."

IN THE EARLY DAYS, THE NEWLY FORMED HEROES TOOK up residence in the halls of the Maxwells' mansion at Charlotte's Landing like a fleet of feral cats. They spread themselves through the house, claiming rooms at random. The rest of the Maxwells— Mr. and Mrs., Allison, the household cleaners and the new Latina cook—were packed up and living in a brick Victorian in an elite corner of Grand City. Rumor was that Mr. Maxwell was turning his aspirations toward the public sector, and anyone running for mayor needed to have a residency within city limits. So maybe it was that. It was as good an explanation as any, she supposed, for the empty halls, the plastic-covered furniture, the disconnected fridge. No one else needed to know about the resentment leaching through the walls, the fights that hung like ghosts in the dining room and master suite. Amy did her best not to pry, carving out a space for herself in the rooms that hadn't been splashed with emotion. It was a big house, after all.

In theory, training started at 6:30 sharp. Cal was on leave from the Marines, training the rest of them in the time he had, but he refused to get up quite as early as he did on active duty. He'd wanted to bump the start even later, but . . . well, Jane had spoken. Certainly she was always ready that early, in black Nike spandex, her hair contained in a french braid, a towel slung around her neck. She was usually already stretching by the time Amy showed up, 6:28, 6:29, 6:25. Jane greeted her with a curt nod, barely breaking stride. Her body was already toned from years of 5Ks and half-marathons and yoga, ab muscles flexing as she held her arms high, as she leaned one direction and then another. Amy always averted her eyes, but somehow it never felt quite fast enough.

Cal was usually the next to arrive. 6:35, 6:40, always claiming to be right on time. By this point, Jane had usually worked her way to a warmup routine, often jumping jacks to start. Cal's ogling was overt, his neck twisting as he passed her, a low whistle here or there. His excuses rotated whenever Jane yelled at him for it—he was paying her a compliment, he was admiring her form, she was overreacting, he was only human—and one day, Amy knew, Jane would simply get tired of trying.

So because of their early start, breakfasts were everyone-for-themselves, and lunches tended to be fast and cheap in the gap between training sessions. But dinners, now . . . dinners were another story altogether.

In the kitchen, Marie reigned supreme. Her parents were ultra-conservative, and had raised Marie under a strict world-view that it was a woman's duty to handle the cooking with a skill of a master caterer. She may have resented every moment of it while she was growing up, but her talents couldn't be denied, and even she wasn't willing to subside on the takeout, boxed mac and cheese, and plain buttered noodles the rest of them could provide. Instead, she directed the Heroes as she saw fit. She'd quickly sorted them into skill sets on that first weekend—those who could chop, those who could sauté, those who were only useful for setting the table—and now they each were pieces of a program she would run each night, assigning tasks and deallocating them again once their usefulness had finished.

Which is how Amy ended up sitting beside Cal on the couch most evenings, watching the proceedings. Him with a beer bottle, her with a glass of lemon water. They'd already set the table, Cal laying out the dishes, practically throwing them down like frisbees, and Amy spending the next five minutes fixing their position and adding flatware, glasses, and rolled-up napkins. Now they were pretty much useless.

Which was fine by Cal, so fine that Amy often suspected him

of practiced incompetence. He settled easily into the couch, one leg thrown wide across the opposite knee, a beer bottle held loosely in his fingers. Amy's designated spot was beside him, a full cushion of space between them. The differences could not have been more noticeable: Cal sprawled proudly, one arm thrown over the back of the couch, at ease in his surroundings, his skin; Amy trying to keep herself as small and quiet as possible. She clutched her glass, taking tiny sips. In Charlotte's Landing, Amy wore full gloves, the better to avoid accidentally reading the other members of the team. She listened more than she spoke. Cal's voice, by contrast, projected across the whole room, commanding attention no matter what he said. "Nice one!" he'd call, after Tony accidentally dropped a spoon. "Keep it up!" he offered as Devin got through chopping what looked like a whole pound of carrots. "Smells great!" as Keisha added the seasonings. "Ha, that was a close one!", or "You're not going to use *that*, are you?" as Marie juggled what seemed like five tasks at once.

To Jane: "You know, if you like hot sausage . . ."

Amy looked up. Jane cut him a glare as she moved the cast-iron pan from the stove into the oven. But she didn't say anything, turning to Marie next, and there it was, that was the moment: the first slip of resignation.

Amy's hand tightened around her water glass. She took a breath, gathering her strength as she turned sideways on the couch. Scooted a little nearer. They used to be close, after all. Her and Cal. Maybe, if anyone could get through to him . . . ?

Anyway, she had to try.

"Cal. Listen, I know you don't think you're doing anything wrong, but you've got to stop talking to Jane like that."

Cal rolled his eyes, dragging them away from Jane as he turned his attention toward Amy. "Not you, too."

"Me, too," Amy said. She fought hard to keep her voice from wavering. "You realize how inappropriate it is, don't you?"

"Jane doesn't mind."

"*Yes*, she does. She's told you so herself."

"Nah." Cal waved her comment off. "She's just playing hard to get. You watch—if I stopped, she'd miss it."

Amy hesitated, just a second, to steel her rattled nerves. She set her glass down on the nearby coffee table, hoping this made her seem determined. "I'll take that bet."

"Ames. Seriously, let it go. I've got this. You know, you think you know everything about everyone, because of your powers, but—"

"I don't *need* my empathic powers to know she wants you to stop. Just empathy. You should try it sometime."

"Hey," Cal said, eyes narrowing. "Just because you're too chickenshit to make a move with her, don't expect me to cower in the corner with you. *Some* of us have balls."

Here he paused, reaching down to cup his for emphasis, but Amy barely even noticed. A ringing had flooded her head, as if his words had physically slammed her to the ground. *Just because you're too chickenshit.*

Amy shifted away from him on the couch. "I don't know what you're talking about."

Cal snorted. He took another swig of his beer. "Sure. Because I'm too stupid to notice something like that."

"Cal—"

"Look, I don't care that you're a lezzie. Truth is, it's kinda hot," he said, his leer raking quickly up and down her body like a pair of wandering hands. He smirked. "But you and me, Samey Amy, we used to be tight. I know how upset you were when she moved away. I know what happened at that party."

Jane's twisted face filled Amy's mind. Her words were as fresh as they'd been the day it happened. Amy winced. She glanced at the rest of the Heroes, tucked off in the kitchen. Nobody seemed to be paying them any attention, but Amy lowered her voice just the same. "It's . . . it's not what you think."

Cal laughed. "Yeah, okay."

"I'm serious. I'm not . . . She doesn't—"

"Oh, I know *she* doesn't," Cal said. He held his beer bottle lightly by the neck as he gazed with longing across the room. His eyes traced every one of Jane's movements, missing nothing.

A tight feeling billowed up in Amy's chest as she watched him. Because of course, she was watching *him*, and not *her*. Because of course, Amy could never watch *her*. Amy could never openly stare at Jane, her googly-eyed crush on display for all the world to see. Amy could never gawk, or leer, or whistle. Amy could never make unwanted passes, or throw flirts around like dollar bills at a strip club. Cal's sexuality dripped from his pores, leaving a thin sheen behind on every surface he touched. It was always *there*, looming in the room like a giant, invisible grizzly bear. And it's not that Amy wanted to behave like him, not *really*—she knew his behavior was obnoxious at best, and borderline harassment at worst—but just once, *just once*, she'd like to walk into the room and have the *option*. She'd like her attraction to be acknowledged by those around her, a brief nod in greeting before it was allowed to drift into the background of their lives as accepted fact.

She didn't want his life, but she wanted his freedom. The freedom to move about the world as he was, as it suited him. The freedom for his identity to be not only allowed, but *encouraged*.

Was that really so much to ask?

"... just saying, a smaller target is a reasonable first run," Devin was saying as Amy forced her attention back to the rest of the room. He'd finished the carrots, chopping fat chunks of juicy tomatoes instead.

Thankfully, it seemed Cal had moved on. He raised his beer now, gesturing toward the rest of the Heroes. "I'm with Tony. What's the point of being superheroes if we're not going to tackle the big problems?"

"*Thank* you!" Tony said. "See? Someone gets it."

"We all get it," Keisha said as she capped the oregano. "We all signed up to fix the 'big problems.' What Devin's saying is we need to start smaller. We're not ready."

Marie raised a spoon in agreement, sauce dripping down the handle. "Right. Let me taste that," she said, standing on her toes as she bumped Jane aside.

Tony sighed. He reached up, massaging his bicep. Tony had started even scrawnier than the rest of them, and as a result, was working twice as hard these days to catch up. "Yeah, sure, and that's great and all," he said. "But if we keep using training wheels, we'll never learn how to ride."

"We've never even been out in the *field* before," Jane said as she wiped her hands off on a towel. "I think we'll graduate soon enough, thanks."

"Yeah, but in the *meantime*, King Sting is out there terrorizing people. Whereas one strike from us, *bam*—we lure him into one of my rips, I seal it as he's halfway through, his prickly ass is two pieces of toast on the side of the road."

The kitchen fell into silence, like hard-boiled eggs plunged into an ice bath. The chopping stopped, the stirring, the tasting. Amy glanced at Jane, whose face pinched inward like she'd tasted something spoiled. Amy let out a tiny breath.

Marie set her spoon down on the counter, sauce pooling beneath the ladle. "You're saying we should *kill* him?"

Tony raised a thick eyebrow. He'd been working with a half-glass of scotch near him on the counter, and now he paused with it halfway to his lips. "Uh, yeah? What, you think we're supposed to let him go?"

"I did *not* sign up to hurt people," Keisha said.

"Nor I," Devin added, his mouth twisting up.

"He's not a *person*," Tony said. "He's . . . I mean, he's—"

"No different from us," Jane said. "He's got weird powers no one understands."

"But he's a *bad guy*! We're the heroes. That's our *job*."

Jane shook her head. "Not like that. We have to be better."

"I agree. We're not heroes of vengeance," Keisha said.

"We're heroes of virtue," Devin said.

"Heroes of strength," added Marie.

"Of hope," Amy said.

The team glanced over. Keisha smiled. "I like that."

Marie nodded. "Me, too."

"It's good," Devin said.

"So it's settled, then?" Jane asked. "We don't kill. There will always be another way."

One by one, the team nodded. Tony shrugged. "Fine. Another way."

Jane beamed. She reached over, raising her own glass. Her eyes settled on Amy. Was it just her imagination, or was there the smallest sparkle in them? "To the Heroes of Hope!"

"The Heroes of Hope!"

Amy blushed. She looked away, hoping no one had noticed, knowing there was nothing in particular *to* notice. It was only once she turned her head that she realized Cal had been watching her the whole time.

His beer bottle sat on the coffee table in front of them. He hadn't joined the toast.

TURNS OUT, BEING ARRESTED WASN'T ANYWHERE NEAR
as cool as the teenage version of Jane would have imagined.

In the comics of her youth, she'd have handled it so differently. Jane's drawings weren't anywhere near as refined at that point— flat colors, uniform lines, rounded cartoon noses and eyes—but Jane could still see it just as clearly now. A colored pencil sketch of an imposing prison, locked in the middle of a sea like Alcatraz. Crude bolts of lightning split the sky, beneath a heavy overlay of navy blue and lashing gray rain. Our hero chained, spread-eagle, to a cell wall as if in an old-timey torture dungeon. Overdramatic speech bubbles, "I'll never talk!", and a villain with a pointed face and steepled fingers, "Oh, we'll just see about *that*, dear Captain!" There would, you could guarantee, be at least one "mwa ha ha" before it was over.

Instead, in the real world, Jane's foot jittered nervously against the concrete floor, *tap-tap-tapping* like the wild beating of her heart. She was stuck in a random interrogation room in a random precinct in the middle of the city, her wrist handcuffed to a cold metal table. As if she was a petty criminal—a shoplifter, a mugger, a carjacker—and not the dangerous fugitive that Cal and his ilk painted the Heroes as these days.

At least they hadn't taken away her mask. That was some small mercy, though perhaps the only one. Jane still didn't know what had become of the rest of her team. If they'd made it out without being captured, or, if they *were* captured, where they'd been taken, and what was happening to them now. For that matter, she didn't even know what was really happening to *her*. Arrested, sure, yes, but—weren't there procedures for this sort of thing? Jane didn't know, exactly, what "booking" someone meant, but she was pretty sure they'd missed a few steps in the process. No one had asked her name, taken fingerprints, read her rights. That couldn't be a good sign. Instead, she'd been taken directly here, cuffed to the table, left to wait. A clock on the wall behind her ticked loudly, relentlessly, and dammit, she'd needed to pee for a while now.

Finally, the door clicked open. Jane sat up straight, bracing herself—but nothing could have prepared her for what happened next.

Her father walked in.

Okay, Mayor Maxwell, but still. For the smallest moment, he'd actually *been* her father, the idealized one who used to live in her fantasy world, coming to bail her out of trouble. But then the truth of the situation caught up with Jane. She ducked her face, fast. She didn't trust her mask to do the job completely, not up close, not under a bright light like this. And that did nothing for her voice, which, shit, Jane was only just realizing she didn't have access to the voice changer in her suit. Why hadn't she ever asked Marie to make that thing wifi-enabled?

All of these thoughts crashed in and pulled out as a wave, as Mayor Maxwell crossed the small expanse to the chair opposite Jane. She glanced at the door, trying to see who else she'd have to face, but it turns out he'd come alone. That . . . didn't seem right, either, the mayor down here all by himself, but Jane couldn't decide if this was a blessing or a curse, so she wasn't going to breathe a sigh of relief yet.

His chair scraped against the floor as he pulled it back. Creaked under his weight as he sat down.

He put his hands on the table between them, fingers interlaced.

"So."

Jane kept her gaze down. She focused on the class ring he wore, the red gem pooling like an enormous drop of blood.

He spread his hands. "Well? You're not going to say anything? I'll have you know, I went through a *lot* of effort to protect your identity here." His fist curled up, and he ticked off on his fingers, one by one. "No cameras. No two-way mirror. No prints taken, no mug shot, and oh, no one's touched your mask. You're welcome."

His hands stilled. Then flattened against the table.

"Really, Janie? You're just going to sit there?"

Jane's head snapped up, jolted from her careful nonchalance.

A satisfied smirk crossed Mayor Maxwell's face. "Well, well. I guess your old man finally managed to surprise you."

Surprise wasn't really the right word. What Jane felt now went far beyond surprise. It was shock so deep it turned her stomach. It was cold fear freezing her heart. It was panic heating her skin. She was lucky her arms were already up on the table, thanks to being cuffed and all, because this gave her stability she would not otherwise have. It wasn't so much the loss of her secret identity, though that was certainly disaster enough. If he knew about this, what else did he know? How much more did he suspect? Was any of it—the parallel worlds, the other Jane, Clair's rebirth— safe from him?

Worse still: what did he want to *do* with this information? Because one thing was sure: in either world, Paul Maxwell always collected on his debts.

Jane stared across the table. A choice opened up before her, spread as if on two opposing pages of a comic book. Jane watched the scripts play out. In one of them: she denies everything. There's a panel of Captain Lumen in the chair, looking oh-so-innocent, hand at her chest and eyes sparkling like a Disney princess as, aghast, she spins an elaborate story to explain away the situation.

Rainbows and unicorns dot the edges of the text block. But even from here, Jane could see the side-by-side panels, the speech bubble spilling over, Captain Lumen's words hanging like a storm cloud above the glowering face of the mayor. Where her panel is bright, his panel is blocked off, shadowed, his mouth a firm line above the hard edge of his jaw, and the words at the end of Captain Lumen's speech bubble sputter out as they get swallowed by the darkness of his disbelief. Beneath that, wide and pooled in shadow, the captain's shoulders slump in defeat.

In the other . . .

Jane swallowed, but all that was left in her throat was sandpaper. Her voice creaked as she spoke. "How . . . how long have you known?"

"About all this?" He waved at her costume, as red as the ring on his finger. "Long enough. You're really not as good of a liar as you think you are. I would have thought you'd realize that, after the last time you and your mother tried to keep something from me."

Jane frowned. *Last time?* Jane made a mental note to ask Mrs. Maxwell about it later, because she certainly wasn't about to ask Mayor Maxwell to clarify.

Mayor Maxwell continued. "Look, I've held back the tide as long as I could, but I'm afraid Cal's right. As much as you and your friends like to think you're doing good, the days of superheroes in this city are over. It's time you accept it."

"You can't honestly believe that."

"What I believe isn't important. I'm the mayor; I have to act in the best interests of my city—and you're not in their best interests anymore. If you ever were in the first place. I'm sorry if that hurts."

A flash of memory crossed Jane's vision: her father's retreating back, suitcase hanging by his side. Jane's fists tightened. "No you're not. You've never cared about hurting me."

"Sure." Mayor Maxwell tugged at the cuffs of his thousand-dollar suit. "Because I've never done a *single thing* to protect you. Because I didn't fight my hardest to keep the police force off your back for as long as I could. Because I didn't pull strings last year when the city council wanted to revoke the permit for that headquarters you love so much. Because I've never changed appointments to make sure the house at Charlotte's Landing stays empty when you need it. Hell, Jane—it's not even like I provided you with the best possible quality housing and schools your whole life, and never asked for a single thing in return, even when you were at your least grateful. No." Mayor Maxwell jabbed his finger against the table. "It's much easier to paint me as the bad guy than to admit you wouldn't have *anything* if it wasn't for me."

Jane's mouth soured. Oh, it was a good speech—but such bullshit. The perfect politician. The perfect liar. If Jane didn't have proof, she might have even believed it. But she did. Her other life, her real life . . . he hadn't been there for her. And maybe things had been hard at times, and maybe she'd struggled to pay the bills, and maybe everything had turned dark and tragic at the end, but it had been a *good life*. For a long time—up until Clair's death—it had been the best life. She wouldn't let him sully and dismiss it like that.

Jane narrowed her eyes. "I didn't need any of those things. I could have made it on my own."

Mayor Maxwell pinched the bridge of his nose for a moment, before spreading his hand in defeat. "Fine. You know what, fine. You want to hate me, you go right ahead. I'm used to it. I'm *also* used to doing what's best for you, even while you kick and scream about it, so here's what's going to happen: I'm going to walk out that door, and I'm going to give a statement to the press praising the efforts of the GCPD and condemning the Heroes of Hope for blatantly disregarding the rules of society."

"This is supposed to *help* me?" Jane asked.

"I'm not finished. Meanwhile, the police are going to get a call from the city's DA. She's found a technicality, and they're going to have to release you. I suggest you use the back exit—less media attention. I trust you can make your own way from there."

Mayor Maxwell stood up. He was halfway to the door when Jane turned in her chair, as far as the cuffs would allow her.

"Wait! Why are you doing this for me?"

Mayor Maxwell stilled. He half turned, his profile caught in silhouette. "You know, it's funny," he said, his voice shockingly soft, "I thought I was used to your hatred. But the fact that you even have to ask? That hurts, Janie. More than you'll ever know."

THE APARTMENT WAS DARK WHEN JANE GOT HOME.

Clair left it that way on purpose. When midnight hit and there still wasn't any sign of her, she'd gone around and bitterly snapped off each light switch, brushed her teeth, thrown on a pair of pajamas. The shades were drawn, the front door deadbolted, the alarm system armed. Let Jane find the place bundled down for the night. Let her have to make a commotion coming in— throwing switches, punching codes, jangling keys. There would be no slipping in silently, no creeping through the living room like a teen breaking curfew.

Ordinarily, it's not like Clair would have made a big deal out of it. Even outside of being superheroes, the two of them had complicated lives that sometimes kept them out later than expected. For Jane, this usually involved project deadlines and coffee cups littered across her office; for Clair, fundraisers and schmoozy business dinners hoping to pluck extra coins from the purse strings of museum benefactors. Or, of course, either of them could have gotten invited to a friend's birthday party that ran long, a bridal shower or bachelorette event, a family emergency. Jane and Clair kept each other updated with occasional texts as a courtesy—and sure, Jane needed more frequent communication from Clair ever since her rebirth, as a way to keep her anxiety at bay, but that was understandable. Clair, however, didn't need much. Didn't tend to worry if Jane forgot to message her.

Usually.

But that was *before* the flurry of messages Clair had found from the rest of the team, begging Clair to call them as soon as possible. Clair had just started off for home, her cheeks still stinging from everything Allison had said to her in the alleyway. She'd pulled her phone out to unmute it, and that's when she'd spotted them.

Everything else fell away. All thought of Cal and the memory of the cure he'd used, every lingering fear that Clair had made the wrong judgment call about Lou, even the very street she was walking down disappeared, folding away in an instant. Familiar walls and countertops sprang up in its place, and Clair found herself standing in the depths of a moment long since gone. Jane, sketching as her phone rang. The cramp of her hand around the pencil, the blissful unconcern as she swiped the call. Later, the fact that she hadn't even wondered if something was wrong would haunt her for more than a year. Clair had absorbed that memory early on, still kissing Jane as they clung to each other in the first moments of Clair's rebirth, and it had never really left her. She always wondered.

Never mind that the news the team had for Clair now wasn't anywhere near that serious. The heart is a fragile thing, and that moment between realizing something terrible had happened and the next, where you learn that your worst fears *haven't* yet come true, is vast and dark and monstrous.

It didn't help when, maybe an hour later, as Clair and the rest of the team stood pacing in the command room trying to figure out what to do, they didn't even learn of Jane's release from her. A news alert popped up on Tony's phone, *Captain Lumen Released on Technicality*. Jane's text came in ten minutes later, and all it said was, *I'm fine*.

When the sounds of Jane's arrival finally did break the night, Clair wasn't even pretending to sleep. She lay like someone had tucked a doll into bed: flat on her back, the sheets creaseless beneath her, blanket pulled to her armpits, hands neatly by her sides. She lay there so still and so quiet for so long that eventually she swore she could hear the whispers of the apartment; the achy joints of the floorboards, the grumble of the walls, the gossip zipping through the power lines.

Jane didn't turn the light on when she came into the bedroom. She didn't need to—her infrared vision would show her where things were clearly enough. She stopped in the doorway. She didn't say anything, no *You-shouldn't-have-waited-up*s, no *Sorry-I'm-late*s. No explanation, no surprise, no guilt.

Carefully, Clair sat up. The blanket slipped, slumping down toward her waist. The liquid anger had been sitting in her chest for so long that it had cooled and hardened into a raw blade. All she had to do was open her mouth, reach down, and grab the hilt.

She wasn't used to being angry at Jane. Not *really* angry at Jane. Annoyed, sure. Frustrated, yes. Bitter, sometimes. When a stretch of time is shared between two people for as long as they had, passing moments back and forth until life is as soft and broken-in as the blanket a teenager still won't give up in secret, there's going to be plenty of opportunity for broken feelings. This was different, and Clair found she wasn't quite sure what to do with it.

"Where were you? The team said you'd been *arrested*."

She tried to keep her voice level, but a sharp edge slipped out at the last second, a flash of steel.

At first, Jane shrugged off her jacket as if Clair hadn't said a thing. Her lack of a sigh echoed through the bedroom, weary and spent. "I'm fine. It wasn't a big thing."

"Not a big thing." Clair nodded. "Right, sorry. My mistake. See, I assumed this meant the police had finally turned on us, thus endangering not only our team's mission, but our very lives and livelihoods and identities, but if you say it's *not a big thing*, then I guess—"

"Jesus, Clair. Can we just *not*, right now?"

"No," Clair said. She threw the covers aside, launching to her feet. "No, we can't 'just not.' You don't get to block me out! I'm your *wife*. That means you *talk* to me."

"Right, like how you talk to me?"

Clair's anger slammed to a halt, and panic leaped in to take its place. She could *feel* the ghost of Amy hovering over them, even though no mirror of Clair's pajamas stood anywhere in the room. Clair's eyes searched Jane's, desperately. How did she know? What tipped her off? Her fingers twitched with the urge to find some excuse to run her hand over Jane's hair, or cup her chin, or plant a soft kiss. To steal her secrets. To find out where Clair had slipped up.

But she didn't. She said nothing, did nothing. She could not even begin to.

Jane smirked in victory. She put her hands on her hips, in

full Captain Lumen mode. "I reached out to Stacey earlier. When were you going to tell me she'd been investigating Electric Fury?"

"Oh." Relief fell from Clair's shoulders. "That."

"What *else* would I have meant?"

"Nothing. Look, I wasn't keeping things from you." Not that, at any rate. "Stacey started the investigation on her own, and anyway, she didn't find out anything useful. Not really."

Jane threw her arms up. "How can you be so unconcerned about this?"

"Because there are bigger issues at stake right now," Clair said. And then, more as a distraction than anything else, she added, "Cal has a cure for superpowers."

Jane laughed. Once, and not kindly. "What are you even talking about? No, he doesn't."

"*Yes*, he does," Clair said. "I saw it. Well . . . I saw a memory of it. He's already used it once, Jane, and given the kind of rhetoric he's been spouting, it stands to reason he plans to use it again. Maybe even against one of us."

Now, finally, Clair knew she'd gotten through. Jane rocked back, as if physically distancing herself from Clair would shield her from the information she'd just heard.

Suddenly, a sliver of guilt wedged itself into Clair's ribs, just enough to pinch her breath. All the anger she'd felt earlier broke up and drifted off, collapsing under the naked fear now pouring off of Jane in waves. True, Jane needed to know this, but there were probably better ways to have handled it.

Clair took a shaky step forward, her bare fingers reaching out. "Jane. I'm sorry. I didn't mean to just throw that at you."

Jane sidestepped, shaking her head. "No—I'm fine, it's just a lot, and . . . I need some time to think."

"You'll think better in the morning," Clair said. She dropped her hand, useless, at her side. "It's late. Come to bed."

"No . . ." Jane crossed her arms, hugging herself. She would not look at Clair, toeing at the deep pile of the carpet instead. "I'm going to sleep in the guest room."

And with that she turned, slipping from the bedroom with barely a whisper. Clair shut her eyes, cursing herself under her breath.

A slow-clap from the corner. The smack of palms together, one . . . two . . . three, like the clap of a hammer driving nails into a coffin. Clair did not open her eyes, did not dare give her the satisfaction of looking over, but the sound of Amy's sarcasm chased her through the darkness just the same.

"Good going, genius."

IN THE MORNING, JANE LEFT A NOTE ON THE BEDROOM door—*Heading to HQ. Everything's fine. Text me when you get up. xo, Jane*—and yeah, it wasn't exactly poetry, but it would do.

She stepped outside. The sky was stained gray-blue, and the watercolor wash bled down to the streets, turning the pages of her walk monochrome. Loosely painted buildings, more blurs than shapes, replace the crisp, colorful illustrations that normally fill this stretch of the city. Even Jane isn't entirely realized: hands deep in her pockets, head ducked as if it's raining, black ink splashing beside her footsteps like she's trudging through puddles.

Her fight with Clair comes back to her, wedging itself rudely between one frame of sidewalk and the next. A close-up of Clair, in greater detail than the surrounding images. The soft slope of her nose, and the angry shadow that cut her face in half. Her speech bubbles, heavily jagged and shaded along the bottom, spill over the panel borders, disconnected fragments that scrape and claw their way out until roots of what she has to say have spread across the entire page.

When was the last time she'd fought with Clair? Really *fought* with her? Their misunderstanding in the wake of their ruined wedding notwithstanding, Jane was hard-pressed to come up with a single recent example. Had it even happened since Clair had come back? Jane's mind flailed, her life since then spreading out in front of her, a thousand little moments frozen in comic pages. She flipped through the back issues of their life, but didn't find anything.

By the time she arrived at the headquarters, Jane still didn't have the answers she was seeking. She looked up at the building, watching all the sketch-lines and watercolors falling away from the world, revealing the hard, cold reality bristling underneath.

She let herself inside.

The rest of the Heroes were scattered throughout, each caught in their own task like stacked montage panels. Jane found them in turn, checking in, saying hi. Nobody mentioned the arrest, though it was clear they were all still worrying about it, and Jane couldn't blame them. Just because the mayor had managed to get Jane released this time, that didn't mean the police wouldn't turn on any of them again. Who knew what would happen the next time they donned their uniforms and sprang into action? Would they all still even want to risk it?

It wasn't a question worth asking, not out loud, not yet, though it colored the corridors of the building just the same. Jane could practically see it, the color palette shifting just enough to put the reader on edge.

She found Marie in her lab.

"I thought you had a whole company devoted to this," Jane said as she entered, the soft *Welcome, Jane* trailing after her. "Why do your experiments here?"

Marie waved her off. She didn't even turn around. She was hunched at one of her workbenches, blond hair pulled back into a tight bun, goggles on, microtorch blowing as she welded two pieces of impossibly tiny tech.

One of the things that had been hardest to adjust to, upon moving to this version of reality, was the differences in the lives of her friends. When Jane had made her comics, she'd changed everyone's names and professions, some of their family lives. She was basing her characters off of real people, after all, and the superhero personas they'd all invented as teenagers, but that didn't mean her friends would appreciate becoming illustrated celebrities. Like many details, Clair had helped Jane brainstorm. It wasn't until the discovery of parallel worlds, and this real-life team of heroes, that Jane realized the details had been *real*. Pulled from the mind of Amy, connected to Clair via her dreams. Clair hadn't even realized she was doing it, but over the years she'd fed Jane so much information about this world that in some ways it didn't even feel real anymore. Marie's tech company, Tony's job as a police officer—these were nothing but storylines, as far as Jane had ever known.

"Hey. You doing okay?"

The question jolted Jane out of her own head. She adjusted her glasses, trying to reorient herself. "Huh? Of course I'm okay. Why wouldn't I be okay? Nothing's wrong."

Was that too much denial? It felt like too much denial. Jane's mouth slid into a slash.

Marie raised an eyebrow as she went back to her work. "Okay, then."

Jane sighed. Her phone chimed, and she glanced down. Mrs. Maxwell: *Don't forget debate prep, 8pm. The mayor would really appreciate you being there.*

"Yeah, like that's going to happen," Jane muttered. She slid the phone back into her pocket, and crossed her arms awkwardly over her chest. "So, listen, I need a favor."

"Yeah, I assumed as much," Marie said.

"I need you to look into the possibility that Cal has a cure for superpowers."

Marie set down her microtorch. Turned, slowly and deliberately, toward Jane. Her goggles ballooned her eyes to cartoon proportions, and so Jane saw every nuance as Marie asked, "Are you fucking kidding me?"

"No." Jane's cheeks were heating underneath Marie's scrutinizing gaze, and Jane turned away, pretending to be interested in a weird little device on the table. "Clair apparently found out yesterday."

"And she didn't think to tell the rest of us *immediately*?"

"Look, I *know*. I'm not any happier about this than you are, but if it's true, then we need to know, and we need to know now. I'm not risking us going up against him if he's got something like that up his sleeve."

Jane fiddled with the edge of the device. A dial on top, two prongs coming out the end. Marie's notes lay spread out beneath, technical diagrams from her diagnostics. It was easier to focus on this, and suddenly Jane found herself envious of Marie's technical abilities. When something was broken, there were clear reasons, and clear solutions. Fix a circuit, replace a worn-out part.

Take something apart and put it back together again. Give it a polish. Good as new.

When Marie did finally speak, her words intruded over the edges of Jane's view, a speech bubble breaking through Jane's control:

"I thought you two told each other everything."

Jane snorted. "Yeah. I did, too."

"Don't tell me you're having trouble."

"No, we're not," Jane said quickly. She shrugged, still not looking up from the weird little device. "It's nothing, really. It's silly. I guess I just never thought it would be like this. You know? I used to dream about this. If you'd told me, back when she was dead, that I would get her back, but it still wouldn't be quite *right*, I'd have laughed in your face. How is it *not* right? She's *Clair*. She's *back*."

"Is she, though?"

Jane set the device down. She cut Marie a sharp look. "What are you talking about?"

"Okay." Marie pulled her goggles off, the band snapping up as the tension was released. She laid them carefully on her workbench. "I didn't want to say anything, because it's none of my business, really. If the two of you are happy, then shit, who am I to argue? But . . . I've been studying the data we've gathered on Mindsight's powers over the years. We've always assumed a flare would result in Amy absorbing a personality to the point where the original is overwritten."

"Because the team saw it happen," Jane said. Slowly, like speaking to a child. "Visions of a future—"

"Where she was overtaken by Dark Atom, I know. I'm not stupid, Jane." Marie reached up, rubbing at the back of her neck. "Thing is, there was never anything in her brain scans to indicate something like that would work. And yes, we got the vision from SecondSight, and their powers are pretty reliable. But Amy's . . ."

Jane crossed her arms. "What *about* Amy's?"

Marie shrugged. "I don't know. There are a lot of things about her powers I didn't understand. Our Jane was never willing to explore them, always too worried about causing a flare, so Amy never ended up growing hers with the same control the rest of us did. I didn't argue with it at the time because, well, Jane was our captain. It's only recently I've started to wonder if maybe that was a mistake. What if Amy's powers were growing this whole time, but in a way we couldn't track or understand? Looking at it now, going over the data again . . . I'm thinking it wouldn't have been impossible for Amy to have implanted the vision for us to find."

"Yeah, but why would she do that?"

"As an escape?" Marie said. "A way to start over? Amy put on a convincing face, but she wasn't a happy person, Jane. Sometimes I wonder if we ever really knew her at all."

Jane turned away. Her arms were still crossed, and she gripped her elbows in a kind of frantic hug.

She would not listen to what Marie was saying. It wasn't possible. It *wasn't*. Clair was *back*, Jane had seen it for herself. This was some kind of sick game. Jane didn't know why Marie was playing it, what she hoped to gain from it, but there was no other explanation. None.

"Jane—"

Jane spun back around. She kept her voice bold as she said, "This is nuts."

"I'm sorry," Marie said. "I know it seems like a lot, but—"

"A *lot*? You're saying my wife has been lying to me—that she's not even really my wife! What, you think I wouldn't have *noticed* something like that? Why should I even listen to you, anyway? What proof do you have?"

Marie held herself still. She did not shy away from Jane's accusing glare. "I don't have proof."

"Exactly!" Jane said, throwing her arms wide. "You're just making shit up now."

"Hey, *you're* the one who came to *me*, remember? I wasn't going to say anything, but you told me yourself, it doesn't feel right. I'm just saying, tread cautiously. If your gut is telling you there's something wrong, you should listen to it. Maybe it's nothing—maybe your wife really is back, and this is just simple adjustment pains. But if it's not, then you need to think long and hard about what you actually want, Jane Maxwell. Because I don't think you've done that."

Jane scowled. Fine, so she had expressed *mild* concerns. That was a big leap away from being willing to entertain the idea that Clair wasn't really Clair.

After all, hadn't Jane known it was her? Hadn't she looked into Clair's eyes, the minute they'd opened, and seen the change for herself? The spark of recognition only a wife would have? And all that time, all those private jokes and hidden meanings, all the memories they'd rehashed in the months since? There was no way Amy could have been *that* convincing, for *that* long. Just no way.

No way.

She took a breath, ready to speak, at the exact moment that a tablet on Marie's desk began to flash an angry red. Jane snapped her mouth shut, swallowing down her argument.

"Shit," Marie said.

Jane forced herself to assume a professional air. "What's wrong?"

Before the question was even out, Marie was already on her feet, already halfway to the door. The tablet was gripped tightly in both hands, held fast in front of her chest. Like a child clutching a notebook against themselves, but there was nothing innocent or cherubic in Marie's face.

"I know what Electric Fury has really been up to."

"ALL RIGHT, WHAT'S SO IMPORTANT?"

All eyes snapped to Clair as she marched into the lounge. She didn't blame them. It was a much more bossy, demanding stance than she would normally take—much more Captain Lumen, much less Mindsight—but Clair didn't care. She had barely slept the night before, and when she did, it was impossible to tell whether she was dreaming, or just picking up impressions from the sheets. Visions of yesterday still swirled, unfettered, in her mind. Teddy's memories, Lou's attack, Jane's bitter face.

So when a message had come in on her phone, jerking Clair awake, she hadn't exactly taken kindly to it. Even though it had saved her from an otherwise restless, crappy sleep, she would take that over what faced her now.

What *didn't* face her. Jane was sitting on the edge of the couch that snaked through the room, elbow on the armrest and head in her hand, gazing into the fish tank as if it held the answers to life's mysteries. She must have snuck back into their bedroom at one point for a shower and clean clothes, because she was wearing a fresh T-shirt and crisp blazer, dark slacks, and her hair had been washed and thrown into a ponytail before it could dry. A different pair of glasses than yesterday, the ones with thinner metal frames that she wore when she wanted to feel in control.

Clair found herself ensnared. Despite everything, the sight of Jane had always been enough to stop Clair in her tracks. She remembered the agonizing months between when she'd figured out that her feelings toward Jane weren't solely based in friendship, and the night she finally broke down and confessed. She hadn't been planning on it. The night had started just like so many others, the two of them following their same familiar patterns. Clair remembered the rush, squeezing her heart so hard it would surely burst. She was almost certain by then that Jane was like her, even if she didn't return the feelings exactly, but there was a vast chasm between "almost certain" and "certain," and Clair hadn't been entirely sure she had the courage to make the jump.

What would it have been like, to hold all of those feelings inside of her for years longer? To know you had to keep things to yourself, keep your head down, try not to let your eyes linger? In some ways, Clair mused, it was a wonder Amy had managed to keep her shit together as well as she had.

Clair perched along a hard bench that sat beside the elevator.

A soft weight settled in beside her. The same teal dress she'd put on that morning, a wide skirt with a white belt and scalloped edging. White patent-leather gloves. The same lingering smell of shampoo and hairspray. The same yellow-painted nails. Amy crossed one leg over the other, and hooked her hands around her knee.

"Isolating yourself?" she asked. "That doesn't sound very smart, Clair."

"Shut up," Clair muttered. "I don't need your help."

She turned back to the rest of the team, pointedly ignoring the figure beside her. Devin and Marie held center stage, his 'fro and her blond locks each backlit by the fish tank as the rest of the team looked on from the curving couch.

Devin took a breath. "Okay, so. We've been running an analysis on everything that was reported stolen from the tech expo," he said. "We thought, maybe if we could identify what Electric Fury and her cohorts want with the equipment, we might be able to figure out their next move. Now, this stuff was cutting-edge, the very latest that dozens of tech companies had on offer. And that's just the public showroom. It's an open secret that the real show at the expo happens . . . unofficially."

"How unofficially are we talking?" Jane asked, cutting in. "Like, backroom corporate deals unofficial, or black-market arms deals unofficial?"

"Both," Marie said.

Jane sat back in the couch. "Charming. I'm sorry I asked."

Devin picked up a tablet from the coffee table. He swiped at the screen, and a projection flew up to hover in the middle of the room. "This is a list of everything the police know about, plus a few things Marie was able to find out through some, uh, careful monitoring of the tech companies' internal emails."

"Hold up." Keisha turned toward Marie, braids sliding down her arm. "Aren't those companies rivals to your own?"

Marie shrugged. "Some."

"Okay, but doesn't that make it kind of, I don't know, illegal to go snooping through the emails? Also unethical?"

"If you think they're not doing their damnedest to hack into my own company, you're nuts," Marie said. "My honeypot server has been broken into fifteen times in the last month alone. It's just how this game is played."

"And that makes it okay?"

"That makes it okay."

An icy silence fell in the lounge. Neither Marie nor Keisha was willing to yield the argument, but neither were they prepared to debate it here, now. No doubt it would come up again, but for now, Devin cleared his throat.

"Uh, so, there's any number of uses this stuff could be put to, of course," he continued. "Hence the analysis. We designed an algorithm to look at every known way these components can interact, and—"

"Okay, we get it, there's a lot of science going on here," Jane said. "Cut to the chase."

Devin slid his hands into the thick of his curls. He wouldn't look at anyone, not directly. "We think they're building a new kind of superweapon. Possibly nuclear in nature."

Waves of shock rippled through the room. You could tell who was in the know on this, and who was hearing it for the first time. Clair looked over, but Amy was gone.

Amy was always gone whenever truths came to light.

She turned back to the rest of the room. Clair didn't even need her powers to see the way Jane was wrestling in her mind. She knew, on some level, that this had to take priority over the potential of Cal possessing a cure for superpowers, but how long would it take Jane to accept it? Betrayal and the need for revenge were bitter tastes to swallow down and ignore, even if only for a little while.

But Jane was a Hero, and ultimately, no matter how tough, a Hero did the right thing. Clair's heart ached a little as Jane took a breath and said, "That would fit with Electric Fury's previously established patterns. Stacey Hutchinson found out that she was involved with the Ruinator's efforts to build the fermion oscillator," she added, for the others' benefit.

Tony's head snapped up. "Holy shit, seriously?"

"Why are we only just *now* hearing about this?" Marie asked.

"Yeah," Keisha added, "I thought we were supposed to—"

"That doesn't matter," Jane said, her voice cutting over everyone else's. "The point is, we know now. We stopped the Ruinator; we can stop her, too."

The team glanced at each other, processing this. No one pointed out that there was no "we" last time, not involving Jane at any rate.

"The plus side," Marie said, "is that in order to build this, they'd need to ionize the binding agent—and once they do, that'll trigger a spike in radiation levels we can track."

"So we'll know where they're hiding?" Clair asked.

"Exactly." Marie snapped her fingers. "We get that signal, we mobilize."

"And that all sounds great, except things didn't go all that well against them in the bank," Jane said. "Or the tech expo, for that matter. I'd rather we found a way to reduce their numbers before we go charging straight into the heart of their operation."

Keisha shrugged. "We could try to lure some of them away somehow."

"Yeah, but to do that, we'd kind of have to know what they want," Tony said. "Which is sort of the whole problem. Building a superweapon is one thing, but we've got no data on what, exactly, they plan to do with it once it's done."

Clair cleared her throat. "There is one thing."

Jane's attention snapped up. Her eyes met Clair's for the first time since Clair had arrived.

"No," Jane said. "Absolutely not."

"It makes sense, Jane. You want to get Electric Fury's attention, you offer her what she really wants." Clair took a breath. She looked at the rest of the members of the Heroes of Hope, because they would know she was right, even if Jane wouldn't. "You offer me."

AFTER THEIR FIRST MEETING—THAT SHARED RESCUE OF a mugging victim, that single jolt away from danger—Amy had told herself she wasn't looking for her. Every time she went out heroing, every time she scouted rooftops and rubbed elbows in seedy nightclubs. Every street corner, every subway stop. She wasn't looking for her when she went to get her groceries, and she wasn't looking when she stopped at the post office to mail a package to her cousin, and she wasn't looking when she stood in line for coffee.

What was she even looking for, anyway? It's not as if Amy knew the woman's name, and Amy doubted she went around in a shining silver catsuit when she ran to the bank. Would Amy even recognize her if she saw her? Maybe they'd already passed a dozen times on the street. She should just give up.

She didn't. Because it wasn't pessimism that had driven her into the bar that night, as much as she tried to tell herself otherwise. Amy's moods sometimes led to drowning her sorrows, sure, but she'd always made a habit of drinking alone, where she could cover her shame. The bar she entered now was quiet, sure, largely unpopulated at this early hour. But it wasn't private. It wasn't *Amy*.

But it might have been *her*.

Amy couldn't say what gave her this sense. Low-grade hopelessness hung throughout the room, staining the wood paneling and the crappy dive-bar photographs that were blown up and framed, crooked, on the walls. If Amy was angry, she'd want to be somewhere like this. Somewhere she could pick fights.

So she bought a drink, and she took it over to an empty table in the corner. She positioned herself to see the room with ease, though she kept her head low so as to avoid spooking anyone. There was no sign of the woman—there was never any sign of the woman—but that was fine, Amy told herself. She had time.

A few drinks later, Amy wasn't paying much attention to the rest of the bar anymore. She sat slumped onto her table, chin propped on one hand, the other spinning her empty glass in front of her. It was getting harder to deny the truth to herself: that she was waiting, watching. Hoping. The longer the night went on, the more she drank and the more she admitted, the more she also had to admit her disappointment. The more she had to admit it wasn't working.

Amy sighed. She turned carefully in her chair, looking out over the sea of patrons. The bar had gotten crowded over the last couple of hours, bodies slipping in while she wasn't looking. Someone had turned on music, which thumped underfoot, the words lost in the crowd. Amy blinked, squinting against the neon lights as she searched for the clock. She was sure there was a clock on the wall here. Somewhere.

Maybe not. Amy was just giving up, resigning herself to a wasted night. She reached into her back pocket, hunting for spare cash.

That's when *she* looked over.

It started as just a quick glance, not even in Amy's direction. *She* was just turning her head—checking, perhaps, for the same clock Amy had sought. Her eyes slid by where Amy sat, unknowing, indifferent. *She* looked behind her, the length of her neck exposed, her lips slightly parted. The shine of her lipstick caught the light over the bar, neon green reflected on the deeper, seductive pink. The color of places yet to be explored, the promise of more. When *she* went to turn back, her eyes passed over Amy a second time, and the lack of recognition slayed across Amy's chest like a katana.

But then she stopped.

Then she turned again.

Then she *smiled*.

She slid from her barstool, drink held loosely by her side. She was not in her glittering silver catsuit, but her maroon leather pants were just as tight. Amy's cheeks flushed as *she* runway-strode the length of the bar, one foot in front of the other.

Her glass clinked down on the table. Her chair slid out, her chair slid in. Amy watched these motions. *She* was flirting before she even opened her mouth. Each shift of her muscles was a striptease, one Amy couldn't look away from if she tried.

She didn't try.

"Fancy running into you here."

Amy's attention shifted: up, up, up to her face. The crackle of her eyes, the hook of her smile. Her hair hung loose past her shoulders, straightened, smoothed down, the white reflecting the neon lights of the bar as if sprinkled with confetti. Amy found herself leaning forward, elbows on the table, hands clasped loosely in front of her like a sloppy prayer. "It wasn't a coincidence."

Had Amy ever been so bold with a woman? She doubted it. As the words left her mouth, perhaps there was the smallest moment of doubt—or not so much doubt, but an undercurrent of danger, not recognizing the waters around her, not recognizing herself—but her instincts were rewarded. *She* smiled, even more broadly. *She* ran her finger around the lip of the glass she'd carried over, and Amy shivered just to watch it.

In this moment, things could have gone two ways. Amy saw her choice, clear as vodka, in front of her. The path Amy should take: to walk away, forget this ever happened. No harm in trying, she supposed, but she'd had her fun, and now it was time to be reasonable. And Amy was always reasonable. That was her role in life—in friendships and at work, with her family, in the ranks of the Heroes. Everyone else was free to have their whimsies, their outbursts; or to repress them, the model of control, like Jane, each emotion locked so deep that even Amy couldn't access them. But not Amy, no. Amy talked sense into people. Amy presented good arguments, nudged you toward your better self.

Her better self was already standing by the door. Amy felt her hovering, a ghost of what she could do, and maybe, maybe she almost listened. After all, it was reasonable.

So that was one choice. Down the other . . .

Look at her. *She* was everything Amy shouldn't want. She was chaos, she was rage, she was darkness. She was the sharp edge of a broken glass.

How to explain the appeal of a woman like this?

To understand, you need to go all the way back to high school. Junior year. Jane was gone, and with it, her group of friends had drifted apart, like removing the thread that bound their separate pieces together. Even Cal . . . they still saw each other, sometimes. In the hall at school. At Easter services, Christmas Eve candlelights. They were friendly, but what was there to say, anymore? Jane was gone, and Amy was alone.

It was a year of terrible decisions. Amy threw out all her old clothes, buying nothing but black in their place. She dyed her hair. Wore thick boots. Tried smoking, but the taste made her gag. Her powers were growing, the darkness of the world never more than a touch away. This was the year she started wearing fingerless gloves, just to cut down on the amount of contact she was forced to have with the world. She wore long sleeves and long pants, year round, tugging her cuffs down so hard that her parents once forced her to bare her arms and prove she wasn't harming herself.

In the midst of this, she met Rachel.

It didn't take a genius to figure out how they became friends. Two depressive girls, skirting against goth but neither committed enough to go full-on with the accessories. Rachel was in Amy's pre-calculus class, assigned to the desk in front of Amy's. Amy had barely noticed her, at first; in the past year, Amy had taken to bending her head over her desk during classes, forehead leaning on her fist, hair a curtain to block out the rest of the students. When papers were passed back, then forward again, she did her best to grip them with her knuckles, the pages tucked between the knitted half-fingers of her gloves.

But then, one day, the worksheets slid from her grasp. Just as Rachel was handing them back. The pages fluttered, and Rachel reacted. She grabbed them so fast, they'd barely started to fall. Her hand was clamped around Amy's before Amy even realized what was happening, and in that instant—oh, such torment. The contact was so brief that Amy only got a fraction of it, but even that, even that, the anguish of Rachel's life was exquisite. Cultured and cultivated, brewed into the finest bitter shot. It was everything Amy's angst and roiling hormones were telling her she *should* feel, but were diluted out of her life by the warm embrace of her good suburban home and her loving, supportive family. Just the smallest taste, and already Amy knew she wanted more.

Their friendship, then, was not a good thing. For either of them, but mainly for Rachel. Looking back, even two years later, Amy would feel a remorse so deep it would drive her to a college halfway across the country, but right then, right there, junior year pre-calculus—it was all she could think about. How to befriend her, how to get close to her, how to find excuses to brush against her hand, carry her backpack, hold her coffee, pull her hair back out of her face as she puked up in the bushes and a dozen different bathroom stalls. It wasn't a crush, and it wasn't lust—not entirely. It never went anywhere, at any rate. It was the emotions Amy craved most, the delicious torment. The long-suffering anguish.

Amy wasn't proud of the way she let Rachel's life implode, the role she played in the subsequent months. When they broke apart, and Amy moved away, she thought she'd put all that behind her. No more bad decisions. She threw herself at college, at studying, at getting her shit together. Then Jane reappeared in her life, begging Amy to join the Heroes, and that felt like the cap this story needed, the final note that closed the book on self-destructive tendencies.

But now, oh.

Did this woman know what Mindsight's powers were? Even without it, she clearly understood the sway she held, the raw urgency coursing through Amy's veins with each track *she* took as she reached over and ran her finger up and down the length of Amy's thumb. It was a lie, earlier—there was no choice. Amy was gone. Already drowning in the bottom of the woman's glass. Her body was betraying her, the shocking urgency of the ache between her thighs at a level rarely felt, barely remembered.

It did not matter, then, how terrible of a decision this was. It did not matter, then, what would come to pass between them. *She* was already standing up, already hooking her fingers through Amy's, already drawing her from the table, from the bar, from the safety of Amy's life. Amy knew it wouldn't end well, even then, but she didn't care. *She* drew Amy along, and Amy let her, because she couldn't imagine saying no. In that moment, *she* was everything. A song Amy couldn't get out of her head, an addiction she couldn't shake. She was the flame dancing at the edge of the firepit, waiting to get out. She was the feeling in your stomach when you looked over the edge of an abyss, whispering for you to jump. She was freedom, she was danger, she was bliss. She was drinking to forget; she was who you drank *to* forget.

She was Fury.

LIBBY WAS ASLEEP AGAINST ALEX'S SHOULDER WHEN HE ANSWERED THE DOOR.

Jane's eyes widened. "Oh!" Her voice lowered, automatically, into a whisper. "I'm sorry, I didn't mean to disturb you."

"It's fine," Alex said softly. He patted Libby's back as they swayed together in the doorway. "She's out like a light. You here to see Allie?"

"Yeah. I, um . . . I should have texted first, but—"

"Let me guess," Alex whispered, "you were worried she'd tell you to stuff it?"

Jane blushed. She shrugged, sheepish. "Probably something with a few more expletives, but yeah. Or just not answer."

Alex chuckled. "That does sound like her. Come on in."

Jane followed Alex inside. Jane had found out from Mrs.

Maxwell that Allison and her family were staying at one of the Maxwells' houses in Grand City—as if it was nothing, as if every family owned several houses in prestigious locations. This was the one most favored by Allison, whenever she was in town, to the point where Jane got the impression that it belonged to her in all but name. Which shouldn't have surprised Jane, and certainly shouldn't have hurt, and yet as she'd walked up to the door, Jane had mentally cataloged the house, looking for anything that might be perceived as a flaw.

To her dismay, she hadn't found any. The place was amazing. A sprawling townhouse in the heart of downtown, just beyond the area UltraViolet had decimated with her doomsday device. That probably wasn't a coincidence.

Inside, the place was just as fantastic. Reclaimed wood floors, high ceilings, expensive art on the walls. Alex moved through the halls with ease, leading the way.

He wasn't anything like what she thought Allison's husband would be. Not that Jane had given it too much thought, but still. It's funny how sometimes you don't even realize you *have* an expectation, until suddenly you're faced with something that defies it. Alex was soft and kind, unassuming, bearing the brunt of the childrearing and what society classify as "mothering." And while Jane had certainly learned to see the kinder, more family-oriented side of Allison on occasion, she was still a hardened government agent, full of sass and refusing to take anyone's shit. It was hard to imagine these two together. Yet somehow, here they were. Making it work, by all accounts.

Alex led Jane through the house, until they reached a well-worn living room. Soft couches lined the walls, and toys covered the floor. Gracie was asleep on one of the couches, buried underneath a blanket patterned in cartoon cat heads.

"She's just down the hall," Alex said as he gently set Libby down beside her sister. "Door on the end, can't miss it. Go ahead."

"Thanks."

Alex was right, Jane couldn't miss it. Fresh light filtered through frosted double-doors, and when Jane pushed them open, they revealed a massive home gym, way more expansive than anything Jane had seen outside of the Heroes' headquarters. A full bank of exercise equipment took up one wall, while a boxing ring stood in the middle, and beyond that, a rock-climbing wall loomed over everything.

It was there she spotted Allison.

She hadn't gotten started yet—not on the climb, at any rate, though her shirt was already soaked through with sweat. Instead, she was attaching her harness and safety gear. She glanced up as Jane approached.

Jane was expecting something snide. But all Allison did was jerk her chin toward the racks of equipment along the wall. "Care to join me?"

"Ah, no," Jane said. She gave a nervous laugh. "I don't climb."

Instinctively, her hand went to her collarbone. Her fingers worried over the subtle knot where the bone had never quite healed properly. Jane had broken it on a family camping trip when she was nine, stupidly trying to climb a rockface.

Allison spotted the motion. Raised an eyebrow. But before Jane could open her mouth to explain, Allison said, "Jane did the same thing." She hooked her safety straps in place, giving them an angry yank to make sure they were secure. "She never listened to anyone."

"I'm not sure that's a fair assessment."

Allison huffed. She stepped up to the rockface and grabbed the first handhold. "You didn't know her."

"Yeah, fair enough," Jane said. She didn't know why she felt inclined to try to defend that other Jane, anyway. Jane tried to push it out of her mind. She took a breath, but before she could get to the point of her visit, a circular little speaker trilled from a nearby bench.

"Allison: Thomas moves Bishop to H3."

Allison barked a laugh. "Oh, he would—the bastard."

"What the hell is that?" Jane asked.

Allison glanced over her shoulder. "What, the myMind? Don't tell me your world is too primitive for virtual assistants."

"No, I'm not talking about the *myMind*." In fact, Jane's mom had gotten an Echo Dot this past Christmas, and had spent the whole visit asking it useless questions and telling it commands, just for the thrill of it. A myMind was basically the same thing, except they were manufactured by a company that didn't exist on Jane's original world. In truth, all these kinds of gadgets vaguely creeped Jane out, but that wasn't the point. Jane looked at it, then to her sister. "Are you . . . I'm sorry, but are you seriously playing chess right now?"

"Yeah?"

"But . . . you're rock climbing."

"Which requires my hands, not my brain—not much of it, at any rate."

"Jesus," Jane muttered. "It's no wonder you gave your sister such a complex."

Allison glanced down, eyes narrowed. "I never gave her a *complex.*"

Jane raised an eyebrow as she gestured around her. At the gym, the myMind. The absurdity of it was obvious to her. "Seriously? How are you supposed to even see the board?"

"In here." Allison let go of her handhold, just long enough to tap the side of her head.

"You can picture an entire chessboard. Every piece."

"Actually, at the moment I can picture . . . five? That's how many the myMind is relaying for me, anyway. I'm still waiting on a letter from this girl from my old chess club—she's hella old school, and refuses to play digitally. Shame, really. What?"

Jane gave a strangled laugh. "Five. Five games of chess. At the same time. And you still don't see it."

"Honestly, Jane, it's not that hard. You'd have learned how, too, if you'd only practiced enough as a kid. Or . . . Jane would have. Sorry. I don't know, did you ever learn how to play chess in your world?"

She had, though only in the most rudimentary way. What the basic rules were, how the game ended. Marie had been in the chess club with Devin, and once or twice they'd tried to bring the rest of the friends up to speed, but no one else had ever gotten into it the way they did.

"Look, I didn't come here to talk about chess," Jane said. "I need your help. I'm putting together a mission, and . . . I'd like you to come."

Allison paused her climb. "I'm surprised you'd ask me that," she said. "After yesterday."

"What about yesterday?"

Allison sighed. She reached up, grabbing the next handhold. "Maybe you should ask your wife. Suffice to say, my working style doesn't jive well with your team."

Jane rocked back. Clair had clearly done some investigating on her own, to have found out that Cal had a cure for superpowers, but Jane had no idea it had involved Allison. At first a flash of annoyance coursed through Jane, that Clair hadn't said anything, but shame quickly replaced it. If Jane hadn't been so caught up in her own self-pity, she would have asked. She should have. An ache lodged itself in Jane's chest. It was up to her, to set things back together after whatever subtle shift had occurred between them, and she would—soon. For now, though, she needed to stay on-mission. There was a plan to complete, after all, and it would work a lot better if Jane had Allison at her side. Regardless of whether Allison believed that or not, *Jane* believed it.

She looked around the gym. There was plenty of safety equipment left along the racks, and Jane shrugged out of her blazer, then went over to them and helped herself. After the disaster of her broken collarbone, she thought she'd be banned from ever so much as attempting to climb anything more than a staircase ever again, but to her surprise, her dad had taken her down to a climbing gym much like this, as soon as she'd finished healing. *You want to be an idiot, you're going to learn how to do it properly,* he'd told her. *I won't have a daughter of mine plunging into danger headfirst.*

The lessons had thankfully only lasted a few weeks. Until Jane had burst into tears enough times that her mom finally put her foot down, and her dad had backed off. Jane hadn't been back up on one of these things since, but she was certainly fit enough to handle it these days; and despite her annoyance, she did remember the safety rules.

A few minutes later, she was working her way up the fake rockface. One hand at a time, one foot at a time. She didn't think about what she was doing. She tried to focus only on the motions themselves, the pull of her muscles. If she actually took the time to consider the circumstances, she would have surely freaked out.

It was kind of like heroing, in that regard.

Finally, sweating and about ready to puke from the effort, Jane pulled herself up over the edge. Allison was already sitting there, waiting for her, legs dangling. She stared at Jane, as Jane crawled up, as she turned around. As she sat and caught her breath beside her.

Allison handed Jane a water bottle. "You climbed up."

Jane wiped the thin layer of sweat from her forehead. "Damn right, I did."

"But you hate climbing."

"Yeah," Jane said with a laugh. She unscrewed the cap of the water bottle. "I do."

Neither of them said anything for a minute. Jane guzzled water, and dabbed the sweat up with the hem of her shirt. She was grateful that her slacks were stretchier than they looked, more legging than pants. She took her glasses off, folding them carefully beside her, as she mopped at her face.

"Jane wanted me to go with her," Allison said finally. "At the campground? All the older kids were climbing it, even though no one was supposed to . . . I think she wanted to prove herself. Or, I don't know, maybe it was just her idea of fun. I never could figure her out. I told her it was too dangerous. I told her to forget about it."

"I take it she didn't?"

Allison frowned. "No. One day Dad was out fishing, and Mom was taking a nap in the tent. I was supposed to watch you—watch her. She begged me to take her to the cliffs, and I just kept saying no. So she snuck off while I went to the camp toilets. I mean, I knew where she'd gone. As soon as I got back, I woke up Mom, and we raced off to stop her."

Allison fell silent. She reached beside her, where a small stack of towels lay waiting. For a moment, she just patted the sweat off her face, her neck, staring unfocused at the gym spread out below them.

Jane cleared her throat. "And . . . ?"

Allison tossed the towel aside. "We were too late. Jane had

already tried to climb it, and she'd already fallen. Mom carried her back and took the car to drive Jane to the hospital. I had to wait for Dad to get back. I had to tell him what happened."

"It's not your fault," Jane said, and Allison gave a strangled laugh.

"Actually, it's entirely my fault."

"Okay, but at least you came for her."

"It's not a big sister's job to rescue you *after* the fact," Allison said. "I was supposed to keep her from getting in trouble in the first place."

"In an ideal world, sure. But listen to me," Jane said, talking over the beginning of Allison's argument. "In my version of this story, no one knew where I'd gone. I laid there for ages—I was in so much pain, I thought I was going to throw up. I kept waiting for someone to come get me, but . . . they didn't. Eventually I had to haul *myself* up, and find my way back to camp."

Allison frowned. "What's your point?"

"I would have given *anything* to have someone looking out for me, right then. When I first hit, I was just screaming and screaming, wishing someone would hear me. I didn't know what the damage was. I didn't know if I would be able to stand up. I thought maybe I'd bleed out in the woods and get eaten by wolves. I kept imagining someone coming to find me, but deep down . . . I knew they weren't. Believe me, Jane was enormously grateful that you came for her. She didn't even care that you hadn't 'stopped' her from going in the first place."

"You can't know that," Allison said, though Jane thought she heard a chip of doubt in her voice.

Jane shrugged. "Maybe not with absolute certainty, no. But anything less? Totally. Remember, I lived through the alternative."

Allison didn't say anything. She looked down at the gym, or at her hands. She adjusted her safety harness. Checked the snugness of her climbing gloves and shoes. Jane gave her the space, the silence, for a while, letting this sit amiably between them. It felt almost like the kind of silence that might even fall between sisters. If there was such a thing.

"I still maintain that you can't be as sure of that as you are,"

Allison said finally. "But . . . thank you, for trying to make me feel better about it."

Jane bumped her shoulder against Allison. "You're welcome."

"You really think it would help to have me on the mission with you?"

She'd asked the question quickly. As if she had worked up to it, as if she wasn't sure she should ask it in the first place.

"I know it would."

Allison took a deep breath. "Okay," she said. She reached over, hesitating for just a second before finally patting Jane's knee. "Okay. If you need me, Jane, then . . . your big sister will be there for you."

THE HEROES DECIDED IT WOULD MAKE A MORE TEMPTING
target if Clair went to ground for a while beforehand. Clair didn't
argue. A break from her own life actually sounded like a great
idea, and so she descended upon her parents' house with an
overnight bag and a tight fist of optimism in her chest. Maybe
this would be exactly what she needed. Some time to clear her
head, to return to her roots. What better place to figure out who
she really was, than the house she'd learned to define herself in?
And what better way to approach it, than to delve deep into her
past?

Which is how Clair found herself setting up a workspace in
the basement. A creaky folding chair, a rusted card table no one
had used in years, and a stack of boxes that had been sitting in
her parents' house since she'd emptied her childhood bedroom
and moved out to college. Or . . . well, that Amy had packed,

technically. Still, a lot of the stuff should be familiar. The decision felt right. Perfect, actually.

Donna, however, didn't seem convinced. She hovered over Clair's shoulder, shifting from foot to foot. "You sure you wouldn't be more comfortable in the living room? We can easily just lug this stuff up there."

Clair laughed under her breath. "Oh, I'm sure. It's a little too crowded up there for me right now."

As if to illustrate her point, a loud *bang!* shook the floor above them. Clair and Donna exchanged a smirk. Even from here, they could hear the sounds of Mike's video game, the hum of the humidifier in the guest room for Nicole. Between Clair staying off the grid, and Kevin and Nicole crashing to save money until after the baby was born, the house was fuller than it had been in years.

"I guess it's good we didn't downgrade last year after all," Donna said.

"You don't honestly expect you'll ever be able to do that, do you?"

"I can always dream," Donna said. She fist-bumped Clair's shoulder. "Besides, it would be a lot easier if my kids ever got around to taking their crap out of my basement."

Clair rolled her eyes. "Yes, Mother." She slid a box from the nearest shelf and set it down. The corners of the box were tucked under each other, overlapping. Donna taught Clair how to fold lids like that when she was only five, during one of their many, many moves between crappy apartments. *Like a hug,* she'd said as the flaps snugged tightly against each other.

Donna reached over, ruffling Clair's head. "I'm kidding. You know you'll always have a place with us, Bug."

"I know," Clair said. It was hard for Clair to tell if this was a lie, but at the very least, it was a truth-shaped wish, and that had to count for something.

Donna left Clair alone a few minutes later. After Clair had settled into the creaky old chair, after she'd taken her phone out and started up a playlist to keep her company. "Holler if you need anything," Donna said from the stairs, and Clair thanked her, and then she was alone.

Probably. Clair stole a quick look around the basement, but there was nothing except for shelves and boxes, the extra freezer and the old folding treadmill.

Clair took a deep breath as she slid open the first box. The truth is, she didn't know what to expect from these. Not just what she would find inside, but how would it feel to sort through them? Would it be a fond venture into nostalgia, smiling at old memories? Or would it be more like going through the belongings of a dead relative, bittersweet but slightly invasive?

There was only one way to find out.

In the end, both feelings were a little right. The first box was mostly school papers, fifth grade through eighth. A few of the assignments Clair remembered from her own years, a few were only familiar through Amy.

The second and third boxes were more interesting, but also less organized. Old Beefy Buddy toys mingled with abandoned embroidery projects; a stack of letters from a school-assigned pen pal from Tokyo lay beneath a small box that held Amy's collection of trackballs from various computer mice and old laptops Simon would disassemble. There was a diary with a picture of an old English fairy garden on the front and a busted, useless plastic lock ostensibly holding it together, the pages only a quarter filled. Three different Little Mermaid Barbie dolls, their hair a tangled poof, half-dressed in an assortment of neon, eighties fashion chic. Clair dug through. A hot-pink-and-black Koosh ball, an envelope of photos from a school trip to a re-created colonial village, bear-shaped playing pieces to a board game long since lost. Most of it was wholly unnecessary at this point, if not obvious junk—sure, she might have thought the joke written on her candy wrapper was funny when she was ten, but had she *really* needed to keep it in a box for twenty years? Clair set aside what she wanted, but threw most of it into either the *Trash* or *Donate* bags at her feet.

By the time she got to the fourth box, she felt like an old pro. She sifted through it quickly. Toss, toss, keep. Toss, keep, toss. Ribbons and old drawings and paper dolls made by cutting figures out of magazines and gluing them to pieces of cardboard.

But then, at the bottom of the box, there was a slim blue envelope. *Amy Sinclair,* it read, and beneath that, this address. The postmark was from September 2000.

Clair drew a card out. The front was filled with cheerful bubble letters, *You're Invited!,* along with cartoon balloons and a smattering of glittering confetti. Inside . . .

Inside were the date and time of Jane's going-away party. Clair's heart ached. For Amy, knowing she'd be losing this opportunity forever, but also for this other version of Jane. Straightaway, Clair recognized Jane's handwriting. She could already see Jane sitting at the kitchen table, head bent over her work, as her mom made her sign each of the invitations she was sending out. *Looking forward to seeing you!* The exclamation point was dotted with a heart, but Clair could see the way Jane's pen had dug into the paper, the shaky curve of the *O*s. Had Jane just signed a stack of them, stuffing them into blank envelopes, or had she known this was the one Amy would get? Clair ran her finger across the letters, but the invitation was so old by now, the emotion long since faded. Still, Clair shut her eyes, remembering. The knot of hope that had twisted Amy's stomach as she'd gotten dressed. The care she'd taken in wrapping Jane's present. The way it had all fallen apart.

How easily it could have held together.

But it didn't. Not here, not for Amy and Jane. Clair sat back, the chair creaking beneath her, a sorrow that wasn't her own filling her heart. She didn't know why Amy had chosen to keep the invitation. Why she'd ever *want* to remember. Because she did remember. Looking at the invitation now, it all rose to the surface. Every look, every word, stamped with perfect clarity into this mind Clair had inherited. A lot of Amy's life was still fuzzy to her, gaps in the most inconvenient places. But not this.

Never this.

JANE'S GOING-AWAY PARTY WAS BREAKING UP BY THE TIME Amy ventured back down the stairs.

She had used the commotion of the pizzas' arrival to cover her escape in the first place. The upstairs bathroom wasn't exactly the most comfortable spot to wait out the next few hours, but at least the chances of anyone finding her there were slim. Mr. Maxwell and Allison were out of the house, and Mrs. Maxwell was too busy playing hostess to bother coming up the stairs. Any guests would be shown to the guest bathroom, off the main hall. It felt as safe as anything, right now. Amy sat on the fuzzy toilet seat cover, face in her hands, listening to the sounds of the party below.

It was only once she started hearing the front door that she edged her way back out into the hall. Car horns beeped outside as parents and older siblings came to pick up the girls who lived farther away. Amy creeped to the top of the stairs. She kept to the shadows, watching the guests depart. Timing on this escape would be everything—she had to make sure to slip downstairs at a moment when the hall was empty, so no one would know where she'd gone, but not *so* isolated that it looked weird when she reappeared in their midst.

She watched Jane shut the door behind Brittany. Jane turned away, retreating out of sight down the hall, and this was probably as good as it was going to get. Amy darted down the first few steps, her shoes in her hands to muffle her footsteps. But at the landing, she slid to a halt: Jane hadn't, in fact, gone all the way back into the kitchen like Amy had expected. Instead, she was standing by the coat closet, her back turned against the remains of the party. She had the closet door open, pretending like she was looking for something, and probably from any other angle it might have been convincing. Only Amy, hidden above, could see that Jane had taken the necklace Amy had given her out of her pocket, and was running her thumb over the comic-strip pendant.

Amy's heart leaped into her throat, so fast it felt like she might vomit. Was this her moment? She tried to will herself down the stairs. Unlock her knees. Peel her fingers from the banister. Something. *Anything.*

She opened her mouth. She meant to say Jane's name, but a creaky sound escaped her throat instead.

Jane whirled, her head snapping up to where Amy stood on the landing. Her eyes narrowed, an arrow straight to Amy's heart. "What are you doing up there? You weren't supposed to go upstairs."

The heat in Amy's chest burned the words from her throat. Her mouth flopped open, useless. "Uh . . . I . . ." Her cheeks were warming now, her ears roasting pink. She shut her mouth.

Jane just glared up at her, waiting for an answer. The necklace was gripped tightly in her fist, only the loop of the chain hanging free to catch the light.

Laughter spilled into the hall. Two girls clomped in from the kitchen—popular kids, Trish and Amber. They'd never bothered with Jane and Amy before. "Jane!" they said and then came to a stop, spotting Amy. Trish's eyes went wide, and Amber smirked.

"Oh! Sorry," Amber said, delight lending singsong to her voice. "I didn't mean to *interrupt* anything."

"You're not," Jane snapped. She stuffed the fistful of necklace deep into her pockets. Trish giggled.

"It's okay," Amber said. "If you want a minute alone with your *girlfriend*—"

"Shut up! She's *not* my girlfriend, do you hear me? I wouldn't date her even if I *did* like girls—which I *don't*, don't be disgusting, okay?"

Amber put her hands up. "Okay, okay, whatever. It was a joke?"

"It wasn't funny," Jane said. "Just . . . just get out. Go home."

"Jane—"

"Leave me alone!"

"Hey!" Mrs. Maxwell's voice cut into the room, followed quickly by her stern face. She put one hand on her hip, glowering at each of the girls in turn—Jane, Trish and Amber, even Amy still up on the stairs. "What's going on here?"

"Nothing," Jane snapped. Nobody else said a word.

Mrs. Maxwell raised one perfectly groomed eyebrow. "It didn't *sound* like 'nothing.' It sounded like you were being very rude to your guests, Janie, and I won't tolerate—"

But she didn't get to finish. That was all Jane could take. Before Mrs. Maxwell could stop her, she'd turned and burst out of the hall, heading through the kitchen. The sound of the back door slamming shut echoed into the foyer, and Mrs. Maxwell did call after Jane, telling her to stop—but she made no actual move to follow her, chase her down, find out what was wrong.

So Amy did.

Mrs. Maxwell was already turning back, already beginning to offer apologies to Trish and Amber for her daughter's behavior, when Amy ran down the last of the stairs and tore past her. Amy's shoes slipped from her fingers, landing hard on the kitchen tiles as Amy pushed the back door open.

At the time, she couldn't have told you why she was doing it. It didn't make any sense. Amy's heart was a pile of shredded ribbons flopping uselessly in her chest. She did not expect anything, not now, not anymore. Jane's words were playing on repeat through Amy's mind, a screaming loop that made it hard to listen to anything Amber or Mrs. Maxwell said. *Not my girlfriend. Wouldn't date her even if I did like girls. Don't be disgusting.* They thundered in time with the pounding of Amy's stocking feet against the dead grass.

"Jane!"

Jane had reached the oak tree by the river when Amy caught up with her. From a distance, she was nothing but a smudge against the dark trunk, hidden in the shadow of the tree's boughs. She leaned against it, her forehead pressed to the bark. Storm clouds had started to build on the horizon, blotting out the clear skies that had graced the party earlier. Amy didn't even need to get close to see Jane's shoulders shake.

This is why she'd followed. Because underneath it all, Jane still needed someone; and underneath it all, Amy was still her friend. Her best friend. That still meant something.

"Jane?"

Jane turned. The glower on her face was as dark as the sky, her cheeks streaked like windowpanes during a rainstorm. She lunged, and the shove hit Amy's chest like a thunderclap.

"Get away from me!"

Amy stumbled back. Her foot caught on a root, and she went down hard, ass and hands stinging against the cold ground. Humiliation and bitterness cracked open, pouring down on her as a deluge. Amy shut her eyes against it. Flashes of Jane's memory bolted across her vision, too quickly to make sense of it all:

lifting the camera in the vast, empty rooms of the new house, the *click* of the shutter; crying into her sheets at night, the blankets layered thickly over her head to muffle the sounds; the feel of her contacts as Jane leaned over her vanity, telling Amy about the move; the folded stacks of Jane's new school uniforms; the extra twenties now suddenly appearing in her wallet; the promise of a car hanging over her.

Jane's voice crashed through them, cracking the memories in half like an old oak dying in a storm.

"This is all your fault! You and your stupid gifts, and your stupid sneaking around, and your stupid face! Why did you have to even come today? Why can't you just leave me alone?"

Amy bit down on a sob. The truth sat lodged in her throat, choking her into silence. Even her excuses—*I'm your friend, I'm sorry, I was worried about you*—clogged up her tangled chest, unable to escape.

A strangled cry of frustration escaped Jane. "You ruin *every-thing*! I hate you! Just—just take your stupid necklace and get the hell out of my life!"

The chain of the necklace caught Amy's cheek as Jane flung it at her, hard enough to leave a scratch. Still, Amy barely felt it. Jane's rage was drowning her. Even as Jane stormed away, the emotions remained, a hurricane above Amy's head. They battered her from every direction. Anger—humiliation—fear—longing—anxiety—panic—hatred. One pummel, and then another, and then another. It was all Amy could do to drag herself back to her knees, to breathe in gulps. She snatched the necklace from the dirt, knowing what she needed to do.

Her nails bit against the ground.

IT WAS AN EASY ENOUGH WALK, FROM CLAIR'S PARENTS' house to what used to be Jane's. Across a couple of backyards, along a line of trees that butted against the far side of the ballpark. Once, the grass had softened into a familiar path, but now its sharp edges jutted up against Clair's shoes, soldiers resisting the weight upon them. Clair trampled them down, just the same.

At the yard that was once the Maxwells', Clair turned left.

She kept to the edges, hoping not to be seen, hoping she wasn't disturbing anyone. There was still a path going down toward the river—apparently, the tree and the water held some appeal to the newer residents. Clair's feet hit dirt, and she followed the line until she stood, once more, below the tree where everything changed. Twice. Clair reached out, her fingers running against the bark. *Two roads diverged in a yellow wood . . .*

It took only a moment for Clair to pluck the right image from Amy's memory. She crouched down, drawing the spade from her pocket. Last time, Amy didn't even have that much to work with, so it shouldn't take much effort for Clair to find it. Assuming it was still here at all, but something told Clair it would be. Call it faith. Call it a hunch. Call it fate.

Clair dug. As the smell of dirt hit her face, it carried her back to when she'd done this the last time. Amy's hands clawing at the ground—it would take her days to get all the dirt out from under her nails. Part of Amy had wondered if she should look around for a sharp rock, or even a broken twig, a branch, anything, but that would mean stopping, and stopping meant thinking, and thinking meant feeling. The sobs racking her chest were already hard enough to stop. She needed to do this fast, outrun the pain. The anger of the chain burned against Amy's palm as she worked, so hot that she'd be surprised, later, to find it hadn't left a mark.

The spade hit something tough. Clair set the spade on the grass, pushing through the soil with her fingers. She pried the necklace out, carefully, like unearthing a root. Dirt fell from the chain, sprinkling back to earth.

"What are you doing?" Amy asked. She was already crouching beside Clair, as if she'd been there this whole time.

Clair brushed dirt from the metal, tinting her fingers dark. "You never came back for it."

"Of course not. I never wanted to see that thing again." She shifted, just a little away from Clair. "I still don't."

"You weren't curious?" Clair asked. "Not once? Not even a little?"

Amy scowled. "You weren't there. There was nothing to be curious about."

"She was fifteen," Clair said. "She was scared."

Amy pushed herself to her feet. "No," she said, squinting toward the horizon.

"Look"—Clair stood up—"I'm not saying what she did was okay, but you don't think the situation was hard on her, too?"

"She's not your Jane," Amy said. "She never was."

Clair looked down at the pendant in her fingers. "I know that."

Did she, though? Lately, it was getting harder to tell. Living in this skin, looking around and having the world tinted distinctly Amy-colored from the memories that swirled loose in the back of Clair's mind . . . When Clair had finally loosened this one, finally seen what happened, she couldn't help but see the situation from Jane's perspective. Jane, her Jane, had been *terrified* to come out to her parents. It took years of being with Clair before Clair was finally able to convince her it was for the best. What if she'd been backed into a corner instead, what if she'd felt exposed? What if that happened on top of the loss of Clair as a safety net, without the history of their relationship to ground herself against? Would she have lashed out, the way this Jane had? At the moment when Clair had fetched the spade from her parents' garage, it felt impossible to know.

Clair ran her fingers across the necklace. The tiny comic strip, a flower of hope blooming by the end. It had felt so *right*, when Amy purchased it. Her young hands had shaken as she'd handed over her money, and the bag was sweaty from her grip by the time she got home. Everything she wanted, everything she wished for, all the potential she'd poured into this gift. Amy had blamed herself for it, later. For her foolishness, for her optimism, for buying the necklace. These were the feelings that still clung to the metal, all these years later, Jane's anger and embarrassment long since gone. But Clair knew the gift had been the right call. Because Clair knew everything Amy had stood to gain, if it had gone differently.

And that . . . that was worth every heartache, every risk.

That was worth *everything*.

A FEW NIGHTS LATER, A SINGLE TRAIL OF LIGHTNING CREEPS ACROSS GRAND CITY.

On some pages, it's subtle. But it's always there. Darting along the track of the elevated train downtown. Dancing along a string of twinkle lights above an outdoor café, unnoticed by the happy diners chatting beneath. Leaping between the stoplights, right across the pedestrians in the intersection below. Now it's just the faintest crackle, the line barely on the page, as it disappears down a storm drain. On the top of one page, the lightning hugs a lamp-post in the park. The lamp is right beside a bench, empty now. First it looks fairly normal, a pool of yellow against the deeper dark, but then the lamp flares brightly, glass exploding out as the bulb overloads. In the next panel, it's plunged into darkness. A stray dog noses the bits of shattered glass that litter the sidewalk, a low growl drawn in wavy lines like a ghost emerging from his throat.

In Grand City's seedier districts, the lightning passes innocuously over drug deals and hooker-issued blowjobs. It slinks across the neon sign of a strip club. Hovers over basement card games, the lights above the table flickering just enough to annoy one of the bouncers by the door. "Fold," one of the players says. His speech bubble is jagged and shaded along the bottom to convey his annoyance. A laughing face opposes him, bald and tattooed.

"What's the matter, Marty?" another speech bubble says, the speaker off-panel for the moment. "Bringin' too much debt home to the missus?"

The lightning zips from the lamp to a light switch in the corner. The bouncer is glancing down, as if something about the movement has caught his eye, but it's not enough for him to raise the alarm. He probably doesn't even realize what he's seen, because in the next panel his attention is back on the game. But before the lightning can disappear completely, another speech bubble breaks the room, highlighted in blue:

"You could always take a potshot at the Heroes."

Electricity sparks, briefly, around the light switch. Waiting.

The panels cut back to the poker game. Marty is standing up by now, stuffing the scant remains of his money into the pocket of his low-slung jeans. Most of the players, including him, are drawn in shadows, just a few lines to represent nose, ears, chin.

Marty pauses. Just long enough for a thin slice of panel, between the one of him gathering his money, and the one where he shakes his head. You see it from the back, his shoulders bristled at the idea. "Nah. Got enough trouble without tangling with the likes of them."

"Might want to reconsider," another player says. He's the youngest, feet up on the edge of the table.

The panel centers on him, his smiling face rendered in detail: hair slicked back, toothpick clamped in his teeth, wife-beater shirt and jeans with holes in the knees as he tips his chair onto its back legs. There is something vaguely weaselly in his appearance, like he'd sell you his dead mother's shoes with her feet still in 'em.

"I hear the target's good, if you can get it," he goes on. "Shipment from some fancy lab downtown, headin' out. Heroes are protecting it, but if you're tough enough to handle them . . ."

The light switch sparks, drawing the players' attention.

Outside, the crackle of lightning picks up energy. Gone is the subtlety, the muted colors as it moves languidly across city blocks. The next pages are nothing but speed, a trail of popped bulbs and overblown circuits, of people yelping as they look up, annoyed, at the power going out above their heads.

It continues on like this, along the harbor, across the bridge. Outside the main city limits, the lightning leaps freely to the electrical wires that reappear along the side of the country roads. Sparks trail above taillights, leaving them as long streaks of red and white.

Two miles out, it finds what it's looking for.

"What are you doing?"

Jane jumped. Her marker flew across the page, a lightning bolt cutting across the picture of the open road. She slapped her hands down on the paper and hunched over, like a kid caught looking at naughty pictures, but it was too late. Allison was already standing over her, had probably already seen.

Still. "Nothing," Jane said, even as Allison bent to pick up a page that had fluttered down by Jane's feet.

Jane winced. The page in question was from earlier in the sequence, the Heroes getting ready. Allison's own form was rendered in miniature, dressed in Captain Lumen's red suit. It was all part of the lure: Allison posing as a stand-in Captain Lumen while Jane sat there in a wig and a trench coat. In the page of the comic Allison held now, they were both in a locker room at the headquarters, clean white tiles and polished benches and smooth lockers. The page was framed from above and to the side, like peering in over the lip of a scale model; Jane and Allison drawn small and distant at first, then cutting back and forth between close shots of their faces. Mirror versions of each other, so similar that people often had difficulty telling them apart. What would it have been like, Jane wondered, to grow up with that? Never your own person, always someone else's smaller shadow.

"Sorry," Jane said. She reached up, adjusting the short brown wig on her head. "Old habits. It . . . it helps me unwind."

She reached for the page, but Allison turned just enough to keep it for herself. It would have normally been too dark to see Allison's face, but a simple shift in perception solved that problem for Jane. Allison studied the page as well as she could in the dark. The two of them were on top of a transport van, the one Allison had arranged to borrow from ARRO so their mission would look genuine. It was stopped in the middle of the road. Nothing but a blanket of pine trees to either side of them, and a single slice of empty pavement stretching out beneath. Their van sat in the wash of a street lamp, X marks the spot.

"Damn, Jane," Allison said after a moment. "This is really good."

Jane flushed, grateful for the relative dark. "Thanks."

Allison paused. The drawing was still in her hand, though she was looking at Jane now. She took a breath.

But Jane would never find out what Allison was going to say. Lightning split the sky. The rumble shook the ground, and Jane and Allison hit the top of the van. Jane's drawings scattered to the wind.

A weight slammed onto the roof of the van, someone landing behind them. A voice broke the night.

"Hello, Mindsight."

"A WAREHOUSE," GRANITE GIRL SAID WITH A SIGH. "I should've known. Why is it always an abandoned warehouse?"

Clair shrugged the hood of her jacket up over her head. She'd forgone her usual Mindsight outfit in favor of something that would obscure her identity, and Clair found herself feeling oddly naked without her trench coat and fedora. She rubbed her palm, taking comfort in the familiar leather of her maroon gloves, at least. "Could be worse," Clair said, talking to distract herself. "Could be a chemical plant."

"Do you ever get the feeling like we really *are* just running around in Jane's old comic books?"

"Occupational hazard," Clair said. "When art imitates life, it's easy to feel like life is imitating art."

Granite Girl made a noncommittal *hmm* as she tapped at the data on her tablet. A display of the warehouse took up most of the screen, a crude green map of the interior. While the rest of the Heroes were out with Jane, making a convincing target for Electric Fury and her band of villains to draw them away, Granite Girl and Clair had gone to the location where the readings had spiked earlier that night. Clair had argued that she should go alone—wouldn't it look suspicious to have Granite Girl *and* the real Mindsight missing from the action?—but the whole team had overruled her on this one. *"It's not just that you're being targeted,"* Tony had said at the meeting, when the plan was being finalized. *"We'd never send anyone into a situation like this alone. You know that."*

She did know that, but that didn't mean she had to like it. She zipped her hoodie up to her neck. "Ready?"

Granite Girl nodded.

They left the safety of the shadows.

It was a quick jaunt across the empty parking lot. No lights overhead, no working cameras left. Nothing but moonlight and broken pavement, rats and the distant bark of a dog. There wasn't even a lock at the door, not even a chain looped through with a padlock. Granite Girl dragged it open, her mottled gray arms gleaming in the moonlight. The metal groaned and screamed, breaking the peace of the empty parking lot. Clair winced, but Granite Girl assured her that she'd done an infrared scan, and there were no other heat signatures around.

Inside, they were met by empty shelves. Rusted metal, strung with cobwebs, stacked two stories up. Some boxes and crates and barrels remained, but most of it had been emptied out, either by the company when it was abandoned, or by squatters in the long years since.

"Straight ahead," Granite Girl whispered. Light from the tablet shone up onto her face, a child telling a ghost story at camp.

The warehouse was certainly creepy enough to qualify for one. Even with moonlight spilling in from high windows and skylights, Clair could barely see the room. She pulled her phone out, turning on the flashlight. Dust covered everything: the shelves, the few remaining crates and barrels. The floor beneath their feet was covered in trailing lines, dirt kicked aside by either many pairs of shoes, or else the same few shoes many times. That was a good sign—not only did it confirm that someone had been here recently, but Clair and Granite Girl's footprints should go unnoticed.

They followed the trail. After a moment, the shelves that had crowded the entrance space disappeared, and in their place . . .

Clair stopped walking. Granite Girl stopped walking.

"What the hell?" Granite Girl asked.

Clair held her phone high, the beam of her flashlight sweeping the open room. A few dozen folding army cots huddled in the darkness, half-made. Nothing else.

"I thought this was supposed to be where they were building some big superweapon," Clair said.

"It *was*." Granite Girl turned away. Her tablet lit the harsh silhouette of her shoulders as she jabbed at the screen.

Clair moved closer. The blankets were scratchy, patched and unwashed. Clair's mouth twisted up. Ordinarily, she wouldn't dare touch it, but part of being a Hero was doing the dirty work, and so she made herself pick up the corner of one. Made herself brush the fabric between her fingers.

Pain flared in her head. A rush of impressions shouted at her, like suddenly finding herself in a mosh pit. The deadly drumming of guns—voices screaming at each other—the thump of bass turned up so loud it was impossible to hear yourself think—the rush of something hard hitting your veins—the crack of a jaw as it lands against a cell floor—pain bursting through nerves, heads and hands and hips—the buzz of a tattoo artist's needle and the cat-scratch of it against your skin. Clair dropped the blanket, clutching at her head.

She stepped back, and something *shushed* beneath her shoe.

Clair lifted her foot. A glossy brochure for Sutton University. She frowned as she bent to pick it up.

It did not give her the same headache, but like the beds, the brochure had been passed between so many individuals that the impressions were a jumbled mess, too mixed to sort out any kind of coherent narrative from it. Clair opened it up. Pictures of happy students mingled with traces of boredom beneath her fingers. Whoever had slept in these beds, whoever had handled this brochure . . . they were doing a job, nothing more. She flipped the brochure over, and a simplistic map of Sutton's main campus greeted her.

Granite Girl came up behind her. "It's not here," she said, unnecessarily.

"Maybe not," Clair said, "but I think I know where we'll find it." She held the brochure up for Granite Girl to see, the map facing out.

"What's this?" Granite Girl snatched the map away, studying it against the light of her tablet. "You think they're going to attack the debate?"

"I mean, if you were a supervillain hellbent on destruction, wouldn't attacking the democratic process be a good place to start?"

"I suppose . . . It's the most we have to go on, at any rate. We should report this to the captain. She'll want to know what's—"

"Shh," Clair snapped. "Did you hear that?"

Granite Girl fell silent. The two of them listened, waiting. For a moment, everything was still, but then—a heavy set of footsteps, echoing through the room.

Clair grabbed Granite Girl's arm. "I thought you said the place was empty."

"It *was*," Granite Girl said. "I thought it was."

A figure stepped out of the darkness. Just a silhouette at first, vague and indeterminate, but it did not stay that way. Clair and Granite Girl stared, their heads tipping back, as the figure's head rose up, up, up toward the ceiling. His shoulders expanding, his neck thickening, his flat-top buzz nearly brushing the lights. The crash of thunder broke through the warehouse as he slammed one fist into his opposite palm.

Clair gulped. She pawed at Granite Girl's shoulder, even as the skin turned to stone beneath her touch.

"It's not empty anymore. We should get out of—" Clair said, but Granite Girl was already charging forward. Clair grabbed for her, too late. "Granite Girl!"

It was no use. Granite Girl cannonballed across the room, literally tucking her small frame into a roll as she slammed hard against him. She uncurled, springing to her feet. Megacrush reached down, but by the time his hand swept the air, she was already gone. In the next instant, before Clair could even react, Granite Girl leaped at Megacrush, scrambling up him. He plucked her free and tossed her aside. She landed hard against the ground, several cots *crunching* beneath her.

Clair jumped back. "Oh, goddammit," she muttered. Granite Girl was already back to her feet, already jumping back into the fray. Clair started to reach for her gun, but then she remembered the report from the others. How bullets had just pinged off of Megacrush, not even phasing him. She stuffed the gun back into its holster. It's not like Clair had superior marksmanship anyway, not like she'd be able to aim for the soft spot of the eyes or something—if that would even work. Clair ducked as another cot went flying over her head, crashing onto a metal girder behind her.

Maybe . . . maybe it was better if Clair left this one in Granite Girl's capable hands.

And in other circumstances, that may have been a good idea. But no sooner had Clair thought this than Megacrush scooped Granite Girl up like she was nothing. Clair could only stare, transfixed. He held Granite Girl in front of his face, leering down at her with a wicked grin. For a split second, Clair had the horrible thought that he was going to *eat* her—just chomp her head off, blood spurting from the stump of her neck—but he didn't.

Instead, he started to squeeze. Or, well. *Crush.*

Granite Girl ground her stone teeth, obviously biting down on a scream.

Here's the thing a lot of people misunderstood about her powers: yes, there were lots of things that couldn't hurt her in this form. She wasn't susceptible to cuts, or being stabbed, or even most bullets. She was mostly protected against acid and other corrosive elements. She could take a beating like nobody's business. But she was not *invulnerable*. Granite conducted electricity, due to the elements inside of it. If she fell from a great enough height, at the wrong angle, she could shatter. She couldn't swim, so unless she was able to snap back, she'd drown underwater.

And, of course, even a stone can crack under enough pressure.

Megacrush's fist tightened, and the scream that Granite Girl had been holding back broke free.

Clair ran forward. Blankets and pieces of broken cot lay scattered underfoot, and Clair hopped from point to point to avoid tripping over them. She had no plan. She ran on blind faith, on impulse, on the hope that maybe somehow something from Jane's comics would bleed over into reality, and she'd find herself suddenly knowing exactly what to do, just as she needed to do it.

Unfortunately, nothing occurred to her by the time she reached Megacrush. "Hey!" she shouted. She pounded her fists against his leg, but one quick jerk of his foot sent her flying. Clair stumbled backwards, tripping over debris from the smashed cots. She landed hard, one of the splintered poles that used to hold a cot together nearly impaling her in the process.

That would do. Clair grabbed one of the broken poles, scrambling back to her feet. She reared back, jabbing the cot pole hard into Megacrush's calf.

A *snap* split the room.

The force of her attack sent her staggering forward, slamming into him. Wood scraped against her cheek as she bounced back, righting herself into a defensive stance as she assessed the attempt.

It had done nothing, the wood splintering against Megacrush's toughened skin like a toothpick. It was hard to say whether he'd even noticed, though he did step back, readjusting his stance. Clair sprang back at the last second as his foot crashed down beside her. Both of his legs towered over her, pinning her in place like she was a cat twisting between his ankles. She was close enough now to see the thick forest of wiry black leg hairs poking out beneath his shorts, to see the thin layer of sweat clinging to the skin, and the smell—Clair clapped her hand over her face, gagging into her palm. Instinctively, she glanced up.

Well. She *was* looking for a vulnerable opening . . .

Clair darted forward, just long enough to grab another piece of broken cot off the floor.

She gripped the pole tightly in her hands, and bounced from foot to foot to psych herself up. She looked back up, wincing. "Sorry!" she said, and then she thrust upward with all her might.

The roar that followed shook the entire warehouse. Clair raced out from underfoot, narrowly avoiding the wild stamping of Megacrush's legs. Her attack had done the trick, all right—Megacrush flailed, twisting hard as he attempted to reach behind him. Granite Girl flew from his hand. Clair watched in horror as she struck the wall, her skin fading instantly to pale peach as she crashed to the ground.

"Shit!" Clair ran forward, fearing the worst.

But Granite Girl was already groaning, already pushing herself up onto her knees. A bruise marked the skin below her mask, a cut ran down her arm. Nothing a quick hop in a rejuve pod wouldn't fix, and Clair's chest loosened as she ducked down and offered her hand.

"*Now* can we go?" Clair asked, dragging Granite Girl to her feet.

Granite Girl clutched her head. She squinted back as Megacrush let out a triumphant wail, finally plucking the offending post free. "Did you seriously just stick him in the—?"

"Let's not talk about that," Clair said hurriedly. "Ever." She leaned over, clutching Granite Girl's shoulders. "Come on!"

JANE STRAIGHTENED UP.

Mindsight's coat from the back, the cut of her bob and the tilt of her hat visible over her shoulder. She's caught in the streetlight, the only bright spot in a panel filled with darkness. Each color is shaded by a series of tightly packed lines, cutting angled across the page like rain. She looks over her shoulder, and her face is caught in shadow. Unknowable.

Caught out like this, trapped beneath the street lamp, Jane is purposefully vulnerable, and the feeling of it raced up her legs.

Run, her instincts whispered to her, but there is no running, not here, not now. Instead, she stands tall.

"What's the matter, Mindsight?" Electric Fury called out. "Afraid to face me directly?"

Jane turned. She watched the transition—a panel where Electric Fury didn't know, another one where she did. It was too much to hope that their simple costumes would be enough to keep the truth from Electric Fury forever, and in fact, they weren't really meant to. The whole point had been to lure her here. Jane would have to take care of the rest for herself.

Electric Fury sparked. Her hands clamped tight into fists. "Where is she?"

Jane spread her arms. "Right here."

Lightning coiled up Electric Fury's arm. She reared it back, ready to strike. "Wrong answer."

"Stop!" Allison shouted. She leaped in front of Jane, a splash of stolen red blocking Jane's vision. As if she was a real Hero, as if Jane was someone to be protected.

"Allison! What are you—?"

She never got to finish. A flash cracked across the top of the van like a whip. It struck Allison in the chest, lifting her off her feet, and sent her crashing into the woods by the side of the road.

A strangled cry escaped Jane. She ran forward, teetering on the edge of the van. There was nothing to be seen, not in normal lighting, though when Jane blinked, a blurry outline of Allison's heat signature huddled somewhere in the undergrowth. Jane whirled back, enraged, just as Electric Fury flicked a lazy hand in her direction.

A rope of electricity lashed out, wrapping around Jane like a lasso. Current stuck pins into every muscle of Jane's body at once, seizing her up. Jane's mind blanked, washed clean by the pain. Her powers abandoned her, running like scared rabbits. She staggered forward, and Electric Fury pulled her close. Her face appeared as if through a haze, her voice washing in dreamlike waves over Jane.

"I'm going to make this easy for you," Electric Fury said, whispering into her hair. "Give me want I want, and I promise I'll kill you before you have the chance to watch her die."

Jane flinched against the electricity jolting across her skin. Electric Fury tightened her grip, and a surge coursed through Jane, so hard that she felt she could see her own skeleton. A wordless gasp escaped her, and a flash of Clair's laughing face splashed itself across the back of Jane's eyelids. Jane's fists clenched even harder than they already were. Her jaw resisted, her muscles bound tight, as she forced out, "I'll never . . . tell you . . . where Mindsight is."

"What, because you were supposed to marry her?" Electric Fury laughed under her breath, the heat of it warming Jane's forehead. "Oh, Captain. Let me give you a piece of advice, dear, from someone who *knows*. If you're smart, you'll get as far away from that woman as possible. Oh, she's a good lay, don't get me wrong—but it's not worth it. In the end . . . she *will* betray you."

Jane forced her neck to work, shaking her head. "You're delusional."

Electric Fury's fingers ran through Jane's wig, trailing sparks. "I'm many things, my dear, but delusional is not one of them. Not anymore. Your girlfriend saw to that. Now. Tell me where I can find her, and this will all be over."

Current arced harder across Jane, pressing the point home. Jane squeezed her eyes tight, ground her teeth together. Her heart skipped, shuddering underneath the strain. How much more of this would she be able to take? And where was the rest of the team? They should have been here by now.

Stall, her powers whispered to her. They stirred, restless, beneath her skin, shaking off their earlier fear.

Jane forced her eyes open. She looked Electric Fury square in the face. Such a smug façade, such a collected exterior. She was presenting exactly the image she wanted Jane to see, but Jane was used to looking beyond the surface of a drawing. Used to deconstructing every image, reading context into each line, each shadow. And while Electric Fury's eyes, dancing with the spark of her electricity, were the perfect image of hate, there was also a deeper pain buried down in there. She'd been hurt, badly, and the hurt had forked across her body like scar tissue.

Your girlfriend saw to that.

Except Clair wasn't Jane's girlfriend.

Jane took a breath. Gathering her powers, gathering her strength. Her heart fluttered again. She would only have one shot at this. She glared at Electric Fury, allowing her own hate to pool into Jane and bounce back at her.

"She's . . . my . . . *wife!*"

A burst of light escaped Jane, flaring from every pore at once. Bright as the sun, and pure as rage. Electric Fury flinched back. Her lasso loosened, just a little, as space opened up between them, and Jane didn't waste any time; she wrenched her arms up as far as she could manage, and seized the rope of lightning running from her to Electric Fury.

It was enough to topple Electric Fury, but unfortunately, not enough to free herself. That's all right. Jane dragged Electric Fury toward her, the silver catsuit sliding easily across the top of the van. She had visions of getting the upper hand, maybe finding some way of entangling Electric Fury in her own lightning, but . . . it was not meant to be.

Jane should have seen it coming, but she didn't. As soon as Electric Fury was close enough, she grabbed the lightning herself. Her foot shot out; it hooked Jane in the gut, flipping her over, across the roof, to land hard on the other side of Electric Fury. A single panel of the silver heeled boot, driving hard against Jane's stomach, and then Jane's mind blanked as she became weightless, coming back to her only as pain flared upon impact.

For a second, Jane could only lay there, struggling for breath. Electric Fury drew herself to her feet, energy sparking even harder around her. The lasso was still around Jane, and Electric Fury tugged it, cinching it harder around Jane's chest.

And then, finally: shimmering light split the air. Reality parted like a curtain as Devin stepped onto the roof of the van.

He didn't come as Windforce this time—not really, anyway. With the lightning rod collector strapped to his back, his normal wingsuit would have only gotten in the way, so he'd opted for all black like some kind of special-ops agent. A basic ski mask obscured his face as he advanced toward them. Though the wind still picked up around them, a sudden storm descending over the road.

"Last chance, Electric Fury," he called across the roof. "Let her go."

Jane gritted her teeth as Electric Fury's lasso sent a jolt across her skin. "Less talking—more zapping!"

"Right, sorry," Devin said. He reached over, flipping a switch on the base of the lightning rod.

A warm glow emanated from the end of the device. He raised it up, pointing it squarely for Electric Fury. A flash broke across the van, sweeping everything clear.

White pages, nothing but square speech bubbles breaking the emptiness:

It's working!

Ha ha! Take that, bitch!

Wait. Shit, that's not—

No, no, it's hurting her, too, I don't understand, it shouldn't—

Turn it off, dammit! Turn it off!

—it won't—!

. . .

Is she . . . ?

. . .

A page of black.

WATERCOLOR SKIES. THIN STROKES OF GRASS TICKLE
the bottom of Jane's feet. The ripple of a river flows in front of
her, the surface of the water broken up by ribbons of ink that
highlight the tip of each silent wave. She sits against the papery
bark of her old oak tree. Waiting.

It's not such a bad place to spend her time. Certainly, her
imagination contains worse. Here, at least, is pretty and peaceful.
The field spreads out behind her, the worn-down path that leads
back to her childhood home. The grass is a brilliant collection
of three separate shades of green, the colors bleeding together
as the blades swish in an invisible breeze. The air is clear, and
the sun . . . well, it's not *warm*, since nothing is really *real*, exactly,
but she's so well versed at imagining other senses that if she tips
her head back, she can just about feel it on her cheeks.

How much time has passed? Jane cannot say. She stares at her
own hands. She's rendered so well that it's almost impossible

to tell it's all a painting. It feels like she just got here, but, at the same time, she knows every inch of the canvas around her. When she turns her head, it looks endless. It's not.

Jane pushes herself to her feet, and it happens in an instant. One second she is against the tree, just leaning forward to shift her weight. The next she has already risen. The act was an illusion, motion implied between two separate images. Jane's brain fills in the rest: the feeling of her muscles constricting, the rise against gravity. The memory blends, like mixing paint colors, until it's hard to tell the difference.

Jane.

Jane stops. Her name isn't so much a sound as simply *there*, as much a part of the world around her as the painted skies and the soft brushstrokes of grass and the subtle cotton canvas beneath her fingers. But her heart speeds up just the same, because even without a voice, Jane will recognize Clair anywhere. She turns; one painting, and then another. One view, and then another. The river, and then the open field. A scratch of black ink spreads its wings, taking flight in silence, and Jane is alone.

The words roll in. Rippling the canvas. *Jane, look at me. Open your eyes.*

Open her eyes? Jane looks over her shoulder, but of course no one is there. She turns back, stares at her hand. Her eyes feel open, but she sends commands to her muscles anyway, trying to stretch them wider.

Nothing happens. Her face feels exactly the same, her view looks exactly the same. When she reaches up, she touches lashes, lids—she does not try to poke at her eyeball, but she does attempt to blink, only to find her body ignoring her. She cannot close her eyes, she cannot open them. They are painted still, and the image resolutely refuses to change.

Oddly, this realization does not panic her. Nothing in this place is cause for distress. Is she even capable? If she's nothing but pigments on a canvas, can she feel fear? Even the question itself is detached, more academic than personal.

But then:

Come on, I know you can do it. Just open your eyes, please. Come back.

And the desperation in the words seizes Jane, stopping her cold. Again, there is no sound to it, not exactly, but Jane would recognize that feeling in any context, through any sense. And maybe she cannot feel it, but she can remember it.

She remembers what it was like to close her eyes as she felt it. Retreating into the darkness. Every time, she'd hoped to leave the hospital behind, and every time, she'd failed. The sounds had chased her, the smells, the feeling. Reality wouldn't leave her behind then, but maybe it could leave her behind now. Jane focuses on the memory, drawing it nearer. Conjuring up the darkness, the terror, the uncertainty. The black fog that hung over the question of what happens next. Once, Jane had thought that knowing *anything, any* decided outcome, would be better than this Schrödinger's cat future sitting in front of her; until she realized, with horror, that in some small way she'd kind of wished for Clair's death.

She'd never been afraid of the dark unknowing again.

By the time Jane looks back up now, heavy brushstrokes have covered the world with smears of black. Jane reaches out. Her drawing hand passes across the canvas, and a faint line appears on the horizon. Light shimmers in, catching each heavy brushstroke. Jane runs her hand back and forth, strokes that widen the gap.

Glimpses of the outside world poke through. The healing glow of a rejuve pod. Clair's hands, worried together in an empty prayer. The sights are fleeting, disappearing before Jane can grab hold of them, but they're *here*. More importantly, they're real—tangible in a way that Jane's painted world is not. The darkness slams back, the painted back of her eyelids, but if Jane could open them once, she can open them again.

She reaches out, one more time. Swipes her hand, as if painting a line across the empty world. A scraping sound, like canvas tearing, sweeps through the blackened landscape. Jane's fingers search. She can almost feel it, the frayed edge of something not quite real. The beep of a heart monitor breaks through, and Jane hears it speed up as she grabs hold of that sound, that feeling, that idea. *Jane?* Clair's voice, stirring with anticipation. *Yes,* Jane wants to tell her, as she swipes her hand faster, frantically now, light and sound just beginning to slip their way into her perception. Black paint swirls around her, blotting it out, but Jane keeps stretching, keeps drawing her way toward the sound of Clair's breath. She cannot speak, not really, but she holds the words inside of her. *It's me, I'm here, I'm here, I'm here, I'm—*

Jane sat up with a gasp, gulping down lungfuls of air. Real air, in real lungs. A real room surrounded her, the glare of harsh overhead lights illuminating every rough texture, every layer of dust, every corner of grit. Every detail that usually gets glossed over and ignored. Even without her glasses, Jane felt the imperfections of the room surrounding her, and she clung to them as tightly as the arms that snared her now. Clair's arms, holding fast. They shook even as they clutched her, salty relief dripping into Jane's hair. Jane held on, returning the embrace, as a stream of *It's okay, it's okay, you're okay, I've got you, I love you, it's okay* blessed the top of her head. Clair's breath warmed Jane's skin as the whispered frenzy continued.

Who was she reassuring, though: Jane, or herself? Certainly Jane did not need it, and now, realizing this, she did not *want* it. Clair's relief crawled over Jane's skin like ants, and Jane snaked away from it, wrenching herself free of the embrace.

"What happened?" she asked instead. Memories of Clair's death washed in and out, threatening to drag Jane down, and she had to fight against them. She knew it was stupid to be angry —hadn't she fought to return? Hadn't those same memories spurred her to save Clair from the very fate that Jane herself remembered? But the fact that Jane had woken up, and could *be* angry, was a sting against her heart. The joy that dripped off Clair, even now, as she rubbed a soothing hand over Jane's shoulder, was the dream Jane had never gotten. Not for years, anyway. Not until long after she'd given up on it.

"You were trying to lure Electric Fury out," Clair said to her. She was trying to keep her voice steady, but it was uneven with breathless relief. "Remember? You and Allison and the team, you took a van out—"

"Yeah, I remember *that* part." Jane let the pieces slot themselves into her mind: prepping with Allison, and sketching on top of the van, and the stale taste of fear as Electric Fury had appeared at last. And then . . .

Jane reached up, instinctively touching the part of her arm where Electric Fury's "lasso" had snared her. She brushed up the loose sleeve of the pajamas they'd put her in. Feathery pink lines branched across her skin, though Jane could see they were already fading. Jane traced them with her finger. "She got away, didn't she?"

Clair bit her lip. She nodded. "You were trapped in her electrical current," Clair said. She looked down. Her fingers twitched, twisting up a piece of the blanket on Jane's bed, as if the lightning was coursing through *her* instead. "The team had to turn off the lightning rod, when they realized that it was . . . that you were . . ."

Jane's fingers found Clair's, settling them. Reassurance passed like sparks between their skin. "It's okay. I get it."

She did. Even if she didn't want to, even if part of her wanted to be bitter. Jane sucked in her annoyance and let it out in a long breath. The team had done what they were supposed to do—they'd valued lives, even if it meant letting a criminal run free. Even if it made their jobs harder. How could Jane fault them for that? It was the core of who they were.

Clair shut her eyes, nodding. "I'm sorry," she said, her breath shaking around a forced laugh. "It's just, I thought—I didn't know if you were going to—"

"Shh," Jane said. She kissed the top of Clair's head, pressed her cheek against Clair's cheek. *Come back.* The memory of the fear in Clair's voice mingled with the longer, dustier memory of Jane's own grief, and Jane let the certainty of what she was going to say seep into Clair's skin like the tears between them. "It's okay. I understand, you know I understand. But I'm here, and I promise, Clair . . . I will always come back to you."

AFTER THE DISASTER OF THE GOING-AWAY PARTY, AMY didn't see Jane again for six years. It was just easier. It's not like Jane was around much, anyway—her private school in Charlotte's Landing kept her busy, and her visits back with the rest of their friends were limited, and easy for Amy to avoid. The rest of high school slipped by, a blur of black clothes and poor choices and hundreds of entries in Amy's anonymous online journal. The internet was the only place where Amy could truly be herself. Safely hidden by pseudonyms and a handful of false details about her life, her website became her lifeline. She spent *hours* at the computer, tinkering with graphics and hand-coding HTML into Notepad. Briefly, at the beginning, she'd even considered going by "Clair," the nickname she'd attempted to pick up back in sixth grade, but the memory of Jane's snide reaction still stung, and Amy didn't want to think about it every time she logged online.

For college, she moved a thousand miles away.

It was good for Amy: a fresh start, far away from everyone who'd known her, a chance to reinvent herself, to *be* herself. In college, she flourished, shedding her old skin, growing into something new. Experimenting with her life, with her opinions, seeing what stuck. She changed majors three times in two years, moved from one dorm to another, then into an apartment.

By the time she saw Jane again, she was twenty-one. She still wouldn't exactly call herself an *open* lesbian, not yet, but: she had, at least, gone to her first lesbian bar on her birthday. She'd dated a woman in secret for a couple of months in sophomore year, and then another for most of junior. Slowly, slowly, she was coming into her own. Slowly, slowly, she was moving out of the shadow of her love for Jane.

If only the dreams would stop.

Sometimes Amy thought maybe they finally had. Sometimes she'd go a week, maybe even almost a month, with nothing more than the vaguest hint of this other life, the one her secret self lived out in parallel to Amy's own. Once, while she was just starting to date this girl, Isabelle, Amy had thought they'd finally left her life for good.

It never lasted.

Amy had never told anyone about them, because how could she? What would she even *say*? During the day, she lived her life as normal, but at night . . .

At night, she lived her life over again.

With Jane.

They'd started when Amy was sixteen. More than a year since Jane moved away, more than a year since Amy had allowed herself to think about her as more than a passing thought.

At first, Amy didn't know what to make of them. There was no reason for it—one day they were just *there*, constant background noise to her life. The first week, they'd seemed like a curse, but by the time a month had gone by, she'd begun to enjoy them. By a year, she was lost.

It had to stop. Amy knew this. She tried everything, over the next few years. Meditation and medication. Ignoring them. Obsessing on them. Staying up all night, hoping to exhaust herself into a dreamless void. Going to bed early, hoping to beat them to the punch. Eating before bed. Not eating before bed. Amy read endless websites about dream interpretation, checked out library books, consulted medical texts that were way too dense to even begin to understand. Once, she snuck a bottle of wine out of her parents' supply, hoping that if she passed out drunk, maybe *then* they would stop. Instead, she had one of the most intense dreams she'd ever remembered, one where she and Jane first started exploring beneath their clothes, and in the morning she had her first hangover, and ended up grounded for a month.

Nothing helped.

By now, she'd almost given up trying. Senior year of college, the future once again hazy on Amy's horizon. She was mentally composing a new entry for her online journal as she returned to her apartment on a rainy spring morning that would change everything. Amy's headphones pumped the restless notes of The Decemberists. A cold drizzle misted through the warm air, hitting her skin with refreshing clarity as she stomped through puddles in her heavy Doc Martens.

There was no indication that this was different from any other day. Amy crossed the campus, went a few blocks through downtown. Climbed the stairs of her apartment building. She threw the door open, her mind already spilling ahead of her.

Then she froze, her hand still on her keys in the doorknob.

Was she dreaming? That seemed the only immediate explanation—and certainly her dreams about Jane took on a wholly realistic quality that none of Amy's other dreams ever had, so it's not like she could rule out the possibility. Amy's heart thundered in her chest, remembering the one she'd had that morning, when she'd fallen asleep in class. Her and Jane, at the start of junior year. Together, the way they always were in the stolen moments of sleep; they'd just moved into an apartment in Grand City, boxes filling every inch of their closet-sized space.

It didn't explain this vision. Jane, in black slacks and a green silk blouse, her hair twisted into a knot on the back of her head. She looked like a board member of a Fortune 500 company. She looked like she belonged on Wall Street or Capitol Hill. She did not look like she belonged in Amy's apartment, the sun catching her from behind so that when she turned, smiling, at the sound of the door, she looked like a literal angel.

Amy yanked her keys free. "How the hell did you get in here?"

"I let her in," Stacey said. She was just coming out of the kitchen, a plate of nachos steaming in her hand. Stacey glanced at Jane, then at Amy, as she came to a halt. You didn't need to be an empath to read the tension in the room. "She said she was your friend . . . ?"

"I am," Jane said while Amy's voice spoke over her: "She's *not*."

Amy's fist tightened around her keys, the metal digging into her skin. It was just like Jane to decide to ignore the years of silence that had passed between them, to just up and declare them friends without the slightest care of what Amy thought.

"Shit," Stacey said, her voice unusually low for her. "Ames, I'm sorry, I didn't—"

"It's okay," Amy found herself saying. "You didn't know."

Stacey shifted the nacho plate in her hands, raising it up to her broad shoulders in an automatic waitress impulse. "Okay, well, I'm sorry, but—Jane, was it? You're going to have to leave." She motioned toward the door with her free hand.

"No—wait!" Jane took a step forward, her hand outstretched. "Please, Amy . . . give me a chance. I just want to talk."

It was the vulnerability that made Amy turn away. Jane's voice, so much more like the one from Amy's dreams than her memories. Amy closed her eyes, hearing it whisper in her ear: *I love you to pieces.*

In her dream from that morning, they'd laid tangled together on a folded-down futon, the afternoon heat pouring in through the open window. Their bodies were sweaty from moving, the baby hairs around Jane's forehead plastered to her skin. Clair had propped herself up onto her elbows, kissing a line that had started at those sweaty tendrils, leading down past Jane's ear, along the soft arch of her neck.

Amy shook the image away as she yanked her keys free from the lock. The discordance of their jangle satisfied her as she threw them into the bowl by the door.

"I want you to leave." She was surprised by her own strength, though she knew it wouldn't last. Already, curiosity softened the edges of her anger. If Jane stayed, if she begged hard enough, Amy knew she would crumble. She didn't dare even *look* at Jane right now, the better to avoid those sad, familiar eyes. Instead, she shrugged out of her messenger bag, her back turned.

So she didn't see as Jane approached, and she didn't see, until she'd glanced behind her, Jane's hand reaching for the exposed skin beneath the cuff of Amy's short sleeves. And even though Amy jerked out of the way at the last possible second, even though Jane's fingers did nothing more than brush against her, it was enough. The smallest touch, a breathy kiss of skin-on-skin. It was barely anything.

It was enough.

It was always enough.

Amy was drowning before she even realized she'd plunged. Desperation chokes her, like a lungful of ash. A lick of flame against her skin. When she looks up, the building is crumbling around her. There's a heavy panic in her chest, a vice around her heart, but as she looks down at her hand . . . her hand . . .

Her fingers are still glowing, the remnants of the burst of light that brought the ceiling down in front of her, and this is when she *knows*. Deep in her soul, all of her doubts erased.

"—seriously, if you don't leave now, I swear I'm calling the cops," Stacey was saying as Amy ripped herself free of Jane's stolen memory. She'd moved forward, until she was wedged between Jane and Amy. The nachos sat on the end table, right beside the bowl of keys. Jane was arguing, their voices rising rapidly. It was just like Jane, to underestimate the strength of a woman like Stacey. Did she think all of that weight was purely fat?

"Hey—*hey!*" Amy shouted. She grabbed Stacey's shoulder, careful to stay on Stacey's shirt and to keep the fingerless gloves between them. "Stacey. I appreciate it, but . . . I'll listen to what she has to say."

Stacey raised an eyebrow at her. "Are you *sure*?"

Amy nodded. "I'm sure. It's been a long time. I should at least hear her out."

"Okay . . ." Stacey hesitated for just a moment, cutting Jane a look, before she stepped aside, grabbing her nacho plate as she did so. She pointed at the pile of chips and cheese sauce. "But I'm keeping these in the kitchen, until you decide if she's worthy of them."

The beginnings of a smile tugged at Amy's cheeks. "Sounds like a plan."

Stacey gave one last *hrpmh* as she turned away, clearly not convinced. Her red ponytail swung over her shoulder, wagging at Amy like a disapproving finger as she retreated back to the kitchen.

And then it was just the two of them. Alone, and in the flesh, for the first time since the going-away party. It was a moment Amy had imagined a thousand times, a thousand different variations. Running into her by accident, reunited at a graduation party or a wedding, seeking her out to tell her off or to confess her longstanding love, rushing to her bedside after a tragic accident. Amy had longed for, and dreaded, this moment for six years, because of course it was going to happen. She had never imagined an outcome where it didn't happen, where their paths just never crossed again. Amy and Jane. There were days when their reunion seemed fated, as she dreamed of everything they could be, as she tried to picture how things could possibly lead from their doomed reality to that happy ending she knew so well.

In none of them did the beginning of it look like this.

Maybe Amy should have taken that as a sign, but she didn't. Instead, despite her anger, despite the unforgivable words that had passed between them the last time they'd spoken, a flicker of hope began to burn in Amy's chest. Because she knew, now, what Jane had gone through—the fear of discovering her powers, the uncertainty of what it meant for her life—and she was *here*. In this moment when everything was murky and shifting, when life felt overwhelming and impossible, when she didn't know where to turn next, she was *here*. She had turned to Amy.

"So . . . listen," Jane said. She glanced at the open kitchen doorway. Took a step forward, lowered her voice. She was so close now that the smell of her perfume, real and unfamiliar, ensnared Amy's senses. "I'm just going to cut to the chase. This is going to sound crazy, I know, but—"

"You have superpowers," Amy cut in. "And you're wondering if I do, too."

Jane's eyes widened. "How did . . . ?"

"Because," Amy said with a shrug, "the answer is yes."

JANE FOUND CAL OUTSIDE HIS CAMPAIGN BUS, IN A PARKING lot behind the elementary school he was visiting. Him and a handful of . . . aides? Volunteers? It was hard to say, and some of them were so thuggish they might as well have been fulfilling community hours, so who knows, really? All of them were in the shade of a nearby tree, sitting on top of a picnic table. Papers and tablets and phones were spread out across their laps as they drew up battle plans.

It had taken Jane half a day to drive out here. Cal was campaigning in the upper corner of the state today, shaking hands and punching up his stump speech with an audience that didn't really matter. Chasing after him wasn't exactly Jane's first choice, but the debate was tomorrow night, and Allison had rightly pointed out that Jane wouldn't be the best person to talk to Mayor Maxwell about what they'd learned. Part of Jane had wanted to argue, because if they could get through to Mayor Maxwell the kind of dangers the debate presented, then what did they need to talk to Cal for? But Allison had only raised an eyebrow, seeming to read this thought off Jane's mind, and they both knew the odds of reaching either man individually wasn't great.

So here she was.

Jane took a breath. She pushed her glasses up, tugged down the hem of the flannel shirt that she wore as a jacket over her T-shirt, and strode across the open parking lot.

Cal himself was the first to look up. For a second—just a second—it was easy to forget they were enemies. He'd been saying something to his team as he raised his head, a crinkle of laughter beside his eyes. His attention landed on Jane and he smiled, genuinely smiled, not the practiced grin for the camera or the wolfish hunger as he locked eyes with his target. Despite everything, they'd been friends for a long time before UltraViolet had managed to corrupt him. Jane hated to admit it, but a part of her missed having him around. When he wasn't being crass or overly flirty, at any rate, he was enthusiastic and helpful, funny, even kind in his own way, and the dynamic of the Heroes was . . . oddly *off* without him.

"Well, well," Cal said, still smiling. "This is an unexpected surprise."

Unfortunately, he was the *only* one happy to see her.

Before Jane had a chance to respond, one of the aides looked up and narrowed her eyes. She had a sharp gaze, hardened and deadly, and when she craned her neck, getting a better look at Jane, a slip of tattoo peeked out from the collar of her shirt. "What are *you* doing here?" the aide asked.

Jane drew back, momentarily startled. How much had he told his team? But then Cal reached over, putting his hand on the aide's knee and squeezing his fingers down, just a little, and Jane realized that the aide was only reacting to the political rivalry between Jane's "father" and Cal.

"Now, now," Cal said. "This is a friendly campaign, Still Jill. Besides, Jane and I go way back. Don't we, Jane?"

"All the way back," Jane agreed. She dragged at a piece of hair that had escaped her low ponytail and snaked across her face in the breeze. "We were together at the beginning, and we'll be there until the bitter end."

Cal's mouth quirked up into a smirk, but Jill only looked on in confusion, switching back and forth between the two of them like she wasn't sure she entirely understood this conversation.

Cal stood up, brushing the wrinkles from his pants. "Would you care for a tour of the campaign bus?"

Jane smiled. Cold and deadly. "I'd love one."

They set off together. Cal led Jane along, one hand resting lightly in the space between her shoulder blades. For just a second, she was worried that he was attacking her, even attempting to use the cure—but no, he wouldn't try something so brazen, not here. Not in front of his staff, and not in such a middle-of-nowhere town where no one would witness Jane's downfall. No, this was a calculated move, one Jane didn't appreciate in the least. She couldn't shake it off, couldn't even protest, not without breaking the illusion that she herself had helped to craft. A reminder of the power Cal held in this situation, of the power he perceived himself to have in *all* situations. A photo of Cal's grinning face was plastered on the side of the campaign bus, blessing the scene.

"Hey guys," Cal said as they climbed up the steps into the bus. "This is my good friend, Main Jane. Can we have the room, please?"

Jane cut Cal a fast glare. The rest of Cal's aides and staff got to their feet, smirking to themselves and to each other as they passed, forcing Jane to wonder exactly how many "good friends" Cal brought in here through the course of his campaign, and exactly how much—if any—sanitizer was used on the furniture afterward.

Still, inside was nicer than it had any right to be. Jane had been expecting something akin to an old RV: stuffed with built-in furniture, secondhand and vaguely sad. Instead, she was met with pristine white walls and carpeting, plenty of light from the windows, and an inviting circular couch along the back that hugged a round conference table. Jane was impressed, despite herself.

Cal strode over to the circular couch. He made himself at home. "That was a bold move, coming here. I have to admit, I wasn't expecting it from you."

"You're saying I'm not bold?"

Cal smirked. He motioned for Jane to join him. "Not as much as my Jane, no. No offense."

Jane shuddered. *My Jane.* It's not that the phrasing was wrong, exactly, and certainly others had used similar expressions before, to distinguish UltraViolet from Jane herself. There was something in the way he said it, though. Some level of possession, like he was rubbing his musk all over the memory of her.

Jane did not sit down. Instead, she leaned against the wall, arms crossed. Keeping her distance. "Cal, you understand that she never *actually* had feelings for you, right? That she was just using you? Manipulating you?"

"Relationships are complicated," Cal said. "I don't expect you to understand."

"Excuse me? You realize I've been with the same woman since I was *fifteen*, don't you? And that she was once dead for a year and a half? You want to talk to me about complicated?"

A patient smile. "Yeah, okay. I'm sure."

Jane bristled. Arguments rose up in her throat, but Jane bit them back before they escaped.

Barely.

She was here on business, she told herself. Here on business. It was the only thing keeping her from walking across the bus right here, right now, and clocking that self-satisfied look off Cal's movie-star face.

So instead of anything she *wanted* to do, Jane took a deep breath instead. Counted to five. Let it out. "I want you to call off the debate. Or at least find a way to postpone it."

Cal laughed. "Now, why would I do that?"

"There's reason to believe it's going to be attacked. By a group of Enhanced, led by a woman called El—"

"Electric Fury?" Cal cut in. He waved his hand in dismissal. "Jane, Jane, Jane. This is *Grand City*. High-profile events are always targets for attacks, the vast majority of which never pan out. Doesn't mean we cower in our beds each night, pretending it will all go away. If I'm going to be representing the good people of this city, I need to show them I'm not afraid of what plagues us. I can't do that by backing down."

"So you'd rather let innocent people be put at risk, than chance tarnishing your reputation slightly?" Jane asked, her voice sick with exasperation. "Cal . . . you used to be *good*. There's got to be a part of you that remembers."

Cal sat back on the couch, one arm stretched out along the headrest. His wedding ring caught the light. He'd undergone so many changes over the last few years, but surely a part of him had to be the friend she used to know . . . right? Okay, Cal may have always been a bit insufferable, even kind of an ass at times. That didn't make him inherently *evil*, did it? All those years the Heroes had been together, all the scrapes they'd been through. If he had the propensity toward villainy all along, why did it take UltraViolet to bring it out of him?

And for a moment, it did seem like perhaps Cal was experiencing a rare moment of self-reflection. He wasn't looking at Jane anymore. He'd drawn out a silver business-card case from his shirt pocket—shit, how much monogrammed crap did he have these days, anyway?—and flicked it open with his thumb. He fanned a stack of them out, obnoxious metal slips with his profile etched onto the front. But maybe that was the point— maybe they were a reminder of everything he'd allowed himself to become.

Jane took a breath. "Cal—"

"If you're so worried, why don't you just ask your daddy?" Cal looked up, and whatever softness might have been there a moment ago, it wasn't there anymore. He lifted one of the business cards, tapping it against the table in front of him. "Surely if the threat is as credible as you say, he has the power to cancel the event."

Jane's face set into a hard scowl. "I'm . . . trying," she managed to say through her teeth.

Cal smirked. "Let me guess. He doesn't want to damage his poll numbers. So you come here on your own, because you want *me* to be the sacrificial lamb. Maybe the two of you are even hoping that if I panic at the last minute, he'll come out looking stronger when nothing happens?"

Jane said nothing. There was nothing to say. That was, probably, exactly what Mayor Maxwell had told Allison, though

Allison had conveniently not given Jane details of their conversation when she'd texted. Just that it was "too late" to cancel.

"It's a clever play, Main Jane, I'll give you that," Cal said as he stood up. The business cards were whisked back into the case, the case back into his pocket. Cal tugged his sleeves straight as he came around the table, making sure the cuffs were rolled just enough to convey his humility. He walked across the small expanse of the campaign bus, until he'd almost passed by Jane. Standing beside her, but not looking down. Cal combed his hair back, using the reflection of the windows. He gave himself a winning smile, then tapped Jane on the shoulder. "But you tell the mayor I'll be on that stage tomorrow night. And if he doesn't want to show, well . . . I guess all eyes will just be on me, then."

CLAIR WAS ALREADY AWAKE WHEN THE ALARM WENT OFF.
Lying on her back in her childhood bedroom, her eyes tracing
the glow-in-the-dark stars she'd stuck to the ceiling when she
was ten. The screen of Jane's phone lit up, chasing out the soft
light of dawn, as the familiar notes of 4 Non Blondes filled the
room. Jane's head stirred against Clair's shoulder. Traces of a
weird, hilarious dream slipped between Clair's fingers as she ran
Jane's hair through them.

"It's okay, go back to sleep," Clair whispered to her. She nosed
against Jane's scalp as the song continued to drift around them,
softly singing the "hey-ey-eyes" into her hair.

Jane sleepy-sighed, burrowing back down. But it wasn't a
return to her dreams that filled her mind. She slipped a hand
beneath the cuff of Clair's sleep shirt. Warm fingers skated over
Clair's skin, sending a shiver of enticing images up Clair's spine.

What's going on, indeed.

An hour later, Jane was in the shower, and Clair was in the kitchen, staring at her phone. Ostensibly, she'd come down to make coffee, and so she had—grounds in the filter, water in the reservoir, light on. Donna and Simon had never felt it necessary to upgrade to a Keurig. Clair leaned on her elbows on the counter, waiting impatiently as the sputters and gurgles filled the kitchen.

Stacey's contact information was lit up beneath Clair's hovering thumb.

Clair shouldn't do it. Alerting the press was one of the things she and Jane had discussed last night, and they'd both agreed: nobody would take the warning seriously enough to get the debate canceled, and in the meantime, all they'd be doing was adding to Cal's narrative about the dangers of superpowers. It's possible *some* of the audience might decide to stay home, which was the biggest pull in favor of doing it anyway . . . but in their place, others might come in protest. Short of calling the whole thing off, there was no way to control the numbers.

And that was a perfectly fine argument. A perfectly fine decision. The Heroes were going to spend the whole day combing the building beforehand, searching for the superweapon. Tony would head to his precinct first, see if he couldn't convince Captain Daniels to send out a few more officers for security. And of course, they'd all be on site that evening.

Almost all.

Was Clair just feeling jilted? Yes, Electric Fury tended to go after her, especially if she went out as Mindsight, which posed both a risk to herself and created a danger for others if anyone got caught in the crossfire. There was logic in her sitting this one out. She hadn't even bothered arguing against it, when Jane laid out her thoughts on the matter, just nodded, said, "Yeah, that makes sense," and moved on.

The patio door slid open as Clair lifted the phone to her ear. The line between that moment and the one before it was so thin that it couldn't even be called a decision. Cold bit at Clair's bare toes as she stepped onto the back deck.

Stacey's phone barely had the chance to ring. "Hey," she said. Her breath came in heavy across the speaker. "I was just going to call you."

"You were?" Clair's stomach did a funny little jump. She turned away from the house.

"Yeah. Hang on, let me . . ." Stacey's high voice faded out, the sounds of movement taking her place. Background voices drifted louder and softer as Stacey walked, as well as the occasional ringtone or even the trilling of a landline phone.

Finally, the click of a door. The sound of the office cut off. Stacey took a breath, then let it out again as a sigh.

"Okay. Listen, you know that safe deposit box you asked me to look into?" Stacey said. "Turns out, it belongs to a guy named Peter Romanov. *Officially*, he's an investment broker with Struss and Wiles, but I did some digging, and apparently this guy is a huge player in the underground post-crime collection scene."

"Right . . . Want to try explaining that as if I *don't* know what any of those words mean?"

A soft laugh came over the line. "It's a bunch of rich ass-holes who like to buy up weird debris from the scene of any major Enhanced attack," Stacey said. "Twisted hubcaps, chunks of cement —yeah, most of it's pure junk, but once in a while they'll turn up something like a spent dart or a broken computer circuit the police missed. Rumor was that someone even found a torn scrap of Captain Lumen's suit once, remember from that time when she experimented with a cape?"

In fact Clair didn't, not really, but she wasn't going to share the gap in her memory with Stacey. All she knew was that it started shortly before the team went up against Dark Atom, and Amy's powers were forced into a flare as he attempted to superimpose his personality over her own. They'd seen it coming, so they'd been able to foil his plans, but the attempt still hurt like hell, and she'd spent a full week in a rejuve pod. Amy's memories of her recovery after that were patchy, coming to Clair only in bits and pieces. The healing process dragged on, her powers dampened from overuse. It was on the heels of this, as Amy began to toe back into working with the Heroes, that she'd met Electric Fury.

Clair shook her head, shooing the memories away. "Why would anybody want that shit?"

"Aside from fetishists? There's a serious contingent that

believes if they can scrape together enough of this stuff, eventually they'll find something that contains a piece of what makes Enhanced so special. Something that lets them recreate the magic, if you will. But listen, you're not letting me get to the most important part."

"I'm glad something about this is important."

"For a while now," Stacey said, ignoring that, "there's been a rumor that someone's managed to get their hands on the collector's holy grail—an actual piece of a superweapon."

Clair's throat went dry. "That's . . . not possible. We would have secured anything of value."

"I'm sure we'd all like to believe that's true one hundred percent of the time, Mindsight, but let's be honest: at the end of the day, you and your team are only human. Now, before you argue with that, I have to tell you, I don't care if you don't believe me. As a journalist, it's my job to keep an open mind, and follow any lead that comes to me with a reasonable source or sufficient credibility. I'm sorry to say, this had both."

Stacey's words landed hard enough to make Clair flinch. Still, she couldn't exactly argue with them. As much as Clair wanted to believe the Heroes would never make such a mistake, it . . . wasn't *impossible*.

At the very least, she needed to find out what Stacey thought had happened. Even if it was nothing. Even if she was wrong.

"What did he have?"

A weighted silence fell over the line. Just the sound of Stacey's steady breathing.

Clair swallowed down a lump in her throat. "Stacey? What did he have?"

"An axion core."

The world slipped out from beneath Clair. She staggered forward, catching herself on the railing of the back deck. Her phone slipped from her fingers, and Clair just barely caught it, pressing it against her chest. Could Stacey hear the wild beating of Clair's heart? The way it had staggered, tripping over itself, and now raced to catch up with what she'd heard? Clair hastily put the phone back to her ear.

"Mindsight? Are you still—?"

"You're *certain*?"

"I saw surveillance footage. When he dropped it off in the safe deposit box."

Clair shut her eyes. It was impossible for her to actually be absorbing Stacey's memory of the footage through the phone, but she could imagine it so well it felt as if she had. Peter Romanov. Clair saw him clear as day: expensive suit, expensive hair, expensive teeth. In her mind, he stands in a small room made of marble, a single box sitting on a table in front of him. He checks over his shoulder, making sure, before he lifts the messenger bag he's been carrying. It's still slung around his neck, but he doesn't need to take it off. He rests it on the table and draws open the flap. His hand plunges into the fabric, but he doesn't spend long feeling for his target—probably, it's the only thing in the bag. It's certainly not something he normally carries around. He starts to draw it out, but before Clair can actually see it, real or imagined, a headache shoots behind her eyes. Clair clutched at her forehead. The memory fell from her thoughts, clattering to the cold slats of the back deck.

She opened her eyes. Nothing but the stretch of an empty backyard—dying grass, and a swing set that hasn't been used in years.

Clair rubbed at her forehead. "They're not supposed to record that kind of thing."

It was easier to focus on this small offense than to consider the broader implications. If the axion core had actually fallen into this investment broker's hands, if it had actually been stolen from the safe deposit box . . . The core had been at the very heart of the Ruinator's fermion oscillator, the only thing that would trigger the reaction to reopen the Rift. The idea that the Heroes could have missed something like that felt laughable, and yet . . . Clair couldn't remember how it had all gone down, in the end. All she knew was they'd won.

"Yeah," Stacey said, "the bank is way in the wrong, and the fact that I'm not breaking *that* story is the only reason we're getting this intel. Don't let the sacrifice of my journalistic integrity be for nothing. You need to stop Electric Fury before she can hurt anyone else."

Clair winced. "You can't really think Electric Fury is planning to use it."

"Why not? She used to work for the Ruinator."

"Exactly. She *worked for* him. A hired goon. You know how it goes in their gig. There's nothing to suggest she was ever actually invested in his beliefs."

"There's nothing to suggest she wasn't, either. Look, I'm . . . not going to pretend to understand why you've been trying to protect her, but as your friend—"

"I'm not protecting her!"

"—*as your friend*, I'm saying you need to be more objective about this. Ever since she showed up, you've been weird, but I'm trusting you, because you've never given me reason to doubt your judgment."

Clair didn't say anything. It was hard to argue, because it's not like Stacey was entirely wrong.

"Mindsight?"

"I'll take care of this," Clair said. Then, because she felt she needed to, she added, "I promise."

A skeptical silence hung on the line for a moment, and Clair didn't blame Stacey for that, not really. What else was Stacey supposed to think about the situation? Even Clair could not articulate exactly why she knew it wasn't true. It was more a sense than a rational decision. Maybe something from Amy's memories, lending her an instinct. But somehow, for reasons Clair didn't want to think about, she knew that, whatever Electric Fury's plan was . . . this wasn't it.

That's what she told herself, anyway. As she hung up the call, as she padded back across the deck. Clair ran her hands over her arms, hoping to bring some warmth back.

Jane had come down by the time Clair let herself inside. The smell of shampoo filled the kitchen, mingling with the coffee. Jane turned, a steaming cup fogging up her glasses as she lifted it toward her face. "Everything good?"

Clair nodded. "Yeah." She waved her phone dismissively, and set it down on the counter like it didn't even matter. "It was nothing."

* * *

THE DEBATE WOULDN'T START FOR ANOTHER HOUR, BUT the auditorium at Sutton University was already packed by the time Jane arrived. Reporters, spectators, political advisors. They filled the building itself and spilled out across the sidewalk and Sutton's lawns, gathering in packs like it was a keg party. Half of them didn't even appear to be interested in the political process, grizzled jawlines and full-sleeve tattoos, so who knows, maybe Cal *was* bribing people with the promise of free beer.

"Christ," Jane muttered as they passed through the doors. "You'd think there were actually people of importance here tonight."

Allison cut Jane a heavy look. She was dressed in a crisp black pantsuit and white shirt, half political daughter and half superspy, and it was hard not to shrink under her gaze. "Look, I know you don't much like him, but can you please try not to disrespect Dad tonight? Regardless of your feelings, this is a real election, and even you have to agree that he's a far better choice than Cal."

"Now there's a campaign slogan for you. Vote Maxwell: He's Better Than a Complete Tool."

Allison's voice dipped low into warning. "Jane . . ."

"I just don't know why you keep siding with him. He cheats on Olivia. You know he does."

"Jane!" Allison stole a fast look around, before yanking Jane angrily off to the side. "Please. Even you should be able to see this is neither the time nor the place."

"It never is."

Allison heaved a sigh. Her already quiet voice shrank to an angry whisper. "Oh, for Pete's sake, fine. You really want to do this? Really? Then here it is: I'm not going to stand here and defend everything Dad's ever done. I admit he's made some mistakes in his life, but—"

"*Mistakes?* How can you—?"

"But a family *forgives* each other, Jane. That's the whole point. Something you'd know, if you ever bothered being part of one."

Jane took a step back. "Wow. Just . . . wow." So much for her sister being there for her, then.

Perhaps Allison realized she'd taken it too far. Her cheeks

tinted red, just a little. But if she was going to apologize, she never got the chance.

"Heeeey, look who it is!"

Allison shut her mouth, her lips twisting in distaste for just a moment before she wiped her expression clean. She and Jane turned in time to see Cal striding forward, Lou tucked beneath his arm. The two of them wore matching patriotic blue, both Cal's suit and Lou's skirt pressed sharp as a knife.

And just when Jane thought they'd hit the bottom of the evening.

"Main Jane! Allie! Allow me to present my beautiful wife, Louisa. Louisa, these are my good friends, Jane and Allison Maxwell."

Jane looked quickly between Lou and Allison. Clair had finally told her all about the trip to Beef-Up Burgers—their attempts to apprehend Lou, the powers she possessed, the way Allison had nearly killed her. She knew Allison had the sense to keep that encounter hidden from view—if there was one thing Allison excelled at, it was repressing her feelings for the sake of appearances—but what about Lou?

Allison gave the world her most dazzling smile. "Such a pleasure to finally meet you." She extended her hand as the flashes of several cameras went off nearby.

To her credit, Lou didn't even react to Allison. If she was bothered by what had happened in the alleyway behind Beef-Up—if she even recognized Allison, even remembered what happened —she did not show it. She took Allison's hand without hesitation, returning her smile point for point. "The pleasure is all mine, Ms. Maxwell."

Cal tugged at his collar. "Goodness, all these gorgeous ladies here this evening. I'd never forgive myself if I didn't stop to get a picture."

"Oh, I don't—" Jane started, but Cal had already taken out his phone. Before she could stop him, he'd slid beside her; Allison on Jane's other side, Lou roped in next to Cal. One big happy group.

Cal's arm extended out for a selfie, his other snaking around Jane's shoulders.

"Are we really doing this?"

Cal squeezed Jane's shoulder. "Smile, Jane. The press is watching."

Jane's lips drew back tautly. "I swear to god, Cal, when this is over, I'm going to take you down," she said through her forced smile. "You know that, right?"

Cal laughed. "Oh, Jane. That's what I've always liked about you—you're such a kidder."

Click.

"Perfect!" Cal said as he examined the photo. He fist-bumped her arm. "Thanks for being such a pal."

Oh, to hell with the press. "I am *not* your pal!" Jane said as Cal strode off toward the stage doors. Jane sighed. "Goddammit."

Allison shrugged. "Keep it together, Jane. It's just a selfie."

"It's never just a selfie," Jane said. "Not with him." She set off, following the path Cal had taken.

A few moments later, she found Cal alone on the stage. He had a stack of index cards in his hands, old school, and appeared to be practicing arguments and rebuttals as Jane approached.

"Hey," Jane said when she drew nearer. "I just wanted to see if there was any chance you'd changed your mind about this whole thing."

Cal didn't even glance up from his cards. "Which whole thing? My anti-superhero stance? The debate? Our friendship?" He looked over, just long enough to leer in her direction. "Us?"

Jane crossed her arms. "The debate. Though your whole political career would also be acceptable."

"Shame," Cal said. "That's one of the few things I won't reconsider."

"I don't understand—how can you be like this? Have you really changed *that* much? Or did we just never notice what an insufferable asshole you are?"

Cal laughed. He lifted his hand, tipping it back and forth like a scale. "Probably a little of both."

"So you're really going through with this? Even knowing the risks. Even knowing that people are going to get hurt."

Cal shrugged. "Not my fault. I'm not the one organizing the attack. Or the debate, for that matter."

He turned away before Jane could say anything. Not that she had anything else to say. This was clearly a waste of her time. She'd kind of known that, going in, but . . . she'd had to *try*.

She was about to turn away when Cal withdrew a stapler from his jacket pocket. He snapped it a few times, mock stapling, and then set it down on the podium in front of him and adjusted its position.

Jane jerked her chin toward the stapler. "What's the deal with that?"

"What, this?" Cal held it up. His face went deadly serious. "This is my supersecret weapon. A few quick clicks, and I can transform this into a handgun, ready for action."

Jane rolled her eyes. "Honestly, Cal."

"I'm kidding, Jane. It's a stapler."

"I can see it's a stapler. I'm asking why you have it."

Cal shrugged. He snapped the stapler again, *snap snap snap*. "To staple things?"

"Ugh," Jane said, throwing up her hands. "Never mind."

"No, wait!" Cal said. "You're leaving before the best part! Would you like to guess what my pens are for?"

But Jane had already turned away. She flipped him the bird over her shoulder, his laughter trailing behind her as she moved off the stage.

THE SINCLAIR-COOPER HOUSEHOLD TURNED ON THE TV.

"I don't know why we have to watch this," Mike said, grumbling, as he slumped down deep in the couch beside Simon.

Simon put on his wire-frame TV glasses. "Because one of these men is going to be elected to represent us in the Senate."

Mike snorted. "And?"

"And you're going to learn about the political process whether you like it or not," Simon said. "One day it's going to be important to you, and I will not let a son of mine be ignorant about the power he has to enact change."

"Besides," Donna said. She settled in on the other side of Mike, wedging him uncomfortably between his two parents like sullen peanut butter in a family sandwich. She pointed at the screen, just as the debate logo faded away and the headshots of the candidates appeared. "You *know* one of these people. It's like knowing a celebrity!"

"The lamest celebrity ever, maybe," Mike said under his breath. Donna ruffled his hair.

Clair watched the process from the corner of the living room. She'd been keeping to herself all day, glued to her phone as she and Jane texted occasional non-update updates back and forth. The rest of the family was gathered in the middle, Simon and Donna and Mike on the couch, Kevin perched on the oversized ottoman. Even Nicole had been carried in and propped in the big red recliner, surrounded by blankets and pillows. A tray table sat at Nicole's elbow, a spread of snacks and drinks ready for her. Clair supposed it was nice that they wanted to support the Maxwells so much, but something about it made her uncomfortable. A kitchen chair, pulled in from around the corner, was fine for her, despite Donna's occasional prompting to come closer.

Perimeter's still secure, Jane texted. It was the third time in the last hour she'd checked, but Clair wasn't about to chide her for being overly thorough.

"I still don't get why we have to support him, just because Clair's marrying his daughter," Mike said, and something about the tone of his voice made Clair look up. Mike was gesturing at the TV, muted and showing photos of the two candidates side by side. Cal, bright and youthful as a movie star. Mayor Maxwell, stately and steady as iron. "It seems like a shitty reason to vote for a guy."

Simon adjusted his glasses, and put on his Dad Voice. "That's not why I'm voting for him. You're right, we don't *have* to support him for that. We're supporting him because he best represents our values as a family."

Now the shot on the TV switched again, panning along backstage as staffers and camera operators and lighting techs moved from place to place. Clair spotted a slice of black pants, a gray jacket, a brown ponytail. She smiled as she looked down at her phone. *Just saw you! Or your back, at any rate.*

Three bouncing dots as Jane typed her reply.

Dammit. I thought I was being so careful to avoid them.

You should purposefully jump in front of one, Clair texted back. *Flash a peace sign.*

An emoji popped up, someone shrugging. *I would, but I left my Be Gay Do Crimes shirt at home.*

A laugh burst out of Clair. Donna glanced over the back of the couch.

"Sorry," Clair said. She held her phone up, indicating the source of her amusement, and Donna turned away.

Donna wrapped her arm around her youngest son. "But also, that's part of why we're watching," she said. "So you can see for yourself. Maybe you'll decide you like him, too. Maybe you'll think we're crazy for not voting for Cal instead. That's what debates are for."

Nicole cleared her throat. "I'm voting for Goodman."

Clair's fingers stilled over her onscreen keyboard. Half a message sat in the box, but she couldn't remember what she was going to say.

She looked up.

She wasn't the only one to have this reaction. Donna and Simon boggled at Nicole. Mike was smirking, as if this proved a point. Kevin, at least, was supportive, one hand reached out to rest across Nicole's blanketed knee.

"What?" Nicole said. She shivered as if the chill in the air was real. "I like him, okay? He has conviction."

"If by 'conviction' you mean—"

"Honey, it's starting," Donna said, cutting Simon off. She reached across both him and Mike, grabbing the remote from the armrest by Simon's elbow.

The sounds of the debate drowned out the room. Music faded, along with the murmur of the audience. The camera cut to the grinning face of the moderator, Jill Jones already holding up her pen for quiet. *"Ladies and gentlemen of Grand City, thank you, and welcome to the first senatorial debate between Cal Goodman and Mayor Paul Maxwell . . ."*

"... I'M YOUR MODERATOR, JILL JONES. THE FORMAT FOR
tonight's debate will be as follows."

Jane turned away. Cal and Mayor Maxwell were behind their
respective podiums, and so now, thankfully, Jane's part of the
process was on pause until the debate was over. She gave Mrs.
Maxwell's a hand a squeeze, for luck and to let her know she
was moving off, and then she met Allison's eye and the two of
them slipped from the room.

The hallway outside the auditorium was just as busy.
Reporters and bloggers and camera crews were already cap-
turing the sound bites that representatives from each campaign
had started to spin. Bright lights and linoleum flooring bounced
the lies and half-truths against each other, the voices overlapping
to a dull roar. They had to cut down three different hallways
before they finally found any peace.

"Fuck, the political process is a nightmare," Jane said as the heavy door to a locker room thunked shut behind them.

Allison choked on a laugh. "You think that's bad? Try getting funding approval from a boardroom of oversight staffers and a three-star general."

"You know, there *are* organizations where—"

"Stop." Allison held her hand up. "I'm not joining the Heroes."

Jane let this sit for a moment. She went over to a locker on the end, where they'd stuffed a duffel bag earlier that evening. It wasn't the first time she'd floated the idea, and probably wouldn't be the last. She just couldn't understand why someone like Allison, with her skills and desire to do good, would want to work in a place ruled by red tape and regulations. Especially when the alternative was so readily available, so easy to seize.

"Yeah, but just think of all the good you could do with us," Jane said as she came back, bag in hand. She unzipped the outside pocket and withdrew an extra earpiece, which she held out to Allison.

Allison hesitated, just a second, before she took it. She turned it over in her hands. "It wouldn't work, though." She shrugged, reaching up to tuck her comm into place. "I'm too Lawful Good."

Jane nearly dropped her bag. "You . . . you know about alignment charts?"

"Hey, I'm not a complete government drone. I played in some of your D&D games when we were kids." A frown crossed her face. "Jane's games. Sorry."

"*You* joined us for Dungeons and Dragons?" Jane asked, ignoring the correction. "You?"

Allison shrugged. "They were fun. Kind of."

"Wow." Jane clutched the bag to her chest. "Wow, I am going to have to rethink *everything* about you."

"Let's not make too big a deal of it." Allison moved to the door, but just before she got there, she paused. Looked back over her shoulder. "But for the record, I make a fantastic paladin—I kill at working within the restrictions. Just . . . if you ever decide to pick it up again."

She was gone before Jane could pick her jaw back up off the floor.

A few minutes later, Jane had finished changing. She'd redesigned parts of her suit over the last year-and-change, removing the corset-like lacing, making the whole thing easier to slip into and out of. She tossed her bag back in the empty locker, and then paused in front of a mirror to adjust the fit of her red mask and cinch her hair into a high ponytail.

By the time she slipped into the hall, she was transformed. Gone was the sight of the daughter of Mayor Maxwell, here to support her father—Captain Lumen had taken her place. Jane tapped her earpiece, turning it on.

"—telling you, it's no contest," Allison was saying. "Superspeed wins out against almost any other power on the line. Period."

"Excuse me, but I've actually *fought* against a speedster," Marie said, "and they're nowhere near the top five hardest superpowers to deal with."

Jane cleared her throat. "Hate to interrupt such important scientific discourse, but can I get a status report, please? Some of us are actually trying to work here."

"Sorry, Captain," Marie muttered while Allison huffed, "There's nothing wrong with a little friendly discourse."

Jane said nothing. Marie took a breath. "Right, so . . ."

"MAYOR MAXWELL, THIS NEXT QUESTION IS FOR YOU."

Clair stood up, slipping out of the room. Jane still hadn't replied to her last text, but that was fine, Clair told herself. That was fine. Obviously nothing was wrong—she could still hear the debate from the kitchen, and, well, if something truly dire was happening, surely it would have been interrupted? So everything was fine. Good. Fine.

She flicked the lights on and crossed the room. A glass from the overhead cabinet, water from the tap. Clair filled it right to the very top, the surface bulging along the rim. She lifted it carefully, slurping it up. She could see her reflection in the darkened window over the sink, the bright cherry pattern of the scarf that held her bobbed hair back as a headband. The kitchen shone, dated but spotless, in the background.

The TV droned on from the living room. *". . . to protect our children,"* Cal's voice was saying. *"That's the most important thing."*

Outside, a flash of lightning. Clair's skin went cold. She leaned over the sink, peering up toward the night's sky. Clouds obscured the moon, veiled the stars from view. There *was* a chance of rain later, she remembered that now. Clair let out a breath. "You're getting too jumpy," she whispered to herself.

"No you're not," Amy said.

Clair jumped, barely biting down on a shriek. She put her free hand to her heart as she turned around, the other still clutching her water. Her gloves were wet from where it had spilled over the lip of the glass.

"Jesus, Amy. A little warning, maybe?"

Amy's eyes narrowed. "I *am* your warning. She's coming, Clair. I can feel it."

"That's not possible," Clair said as a roll of thunder crossed the field outside. She motioned at the window. "See? It's just weather. The debate—"

"She doesn't care about the *debate*! You're her only real target. And if you think you're safe just because you're with Mommy and Daddy, you're an even bigger fool than I imagined."

Clair frowned into her water glass. "We never called them that."

"Yeah, I was being snide, dumbass."

A bolt of lightning flashed outside—too close. A *crack!* shuddered the house.

The lights snapped off.

Clair's glass slipped from her fingers, shattering against the linoleum.

The only things left were the voices from the living room—Clair's family, reacting to the power loss—and the TV, still somehow booming out Cal's rebuttal. *"Mark my words: a reckoning is coming."*

"I told you," Amy's voice said in the darkness. "She's here."

But Clair didn't need to be told that. She leaped across

the broken glass, carrying the feeling of shards lodged in her throat.

JANE MADE HER WAY THROUGH THE UNIVERSITY'S HALLS. Looking for signs of anything amiss, in both visual light and infrared. She moved slowly, keeping a reflective bubble of light around her so that the milling crowd wouldn't see her. Most of them were involved in their own work at this point, but there was no sense in being careless. Jane slipped by reporters tapping furiously on laptops, tech crews adjusting levels and switching camera angles, aides anxiously biting their fingers as their candidate took the mic. Clair's friend Stacey was there, too, tapping away at her phone as she peered through the open door to the auditorium.

Jane had almost finished circling the room when something snagged at her attention. A faint sound, almost beyond the range of her hearing, like a tea kettle in the distance. Jane looked around, but if anyone else heard it, they were brushing it off as unimportant. They remained fixed on their individual work, as a cheer erupted from the crowd in response to something Cal had just said.

That couldn't be good.

Despite herself, Jane edged a little closer to the stage door. Mrs. Maxwell was backstage, hands clasped neatly in front of her as she waited. She was the perfect model of patience, as if she didn't have a care in the world. As if this debate, this election, wasn't going to potentially change the course of her and her husband's lives forever.

Jane shook herself off. It wasn't her business, she told herself. If this world's Mrs. Maxwell wanted to stand by that sleazebag, then Jane wasn't going to bother arguing anymore. She'd already presented her case more than enough times, and been shut down on each instance.

Besides, there was still the matter of that whistle.

It started and stopped in spurts, so it was hard to figure out exactly which direction it was coming from. Still, Jane did her best to follow it. Toeing through the crowds, out into an empty hall. Jane followed the noise, pausing and tipping her head once in a while, just trying to grab hold of it. She tracked it, past a trophy case, and into an empty lecture hall.

The sound was much louder in here. More of a whine than a whistle, really, now that she was closer. It filled the lecture hall, raising the hairs on Jane's arms. A part of her knew, even as she let the door fall shut behind her, even as she toed down the steps between seats, that she should alert the rest of the team. But she didn't. Instead, she followed the sound to the front of the hall, up onto the teacher's stage. Over to a table.

Something small and shimmery lay in the middle of the table. Between the stacks of books, the model of a DNA strand, the microscope.

Okay, that was enough of being brave on her own. Jane tapped her earpiece. "Hey, I think I found something," Jane said. "It's . . . I'm not sure what it is, but . . ." She leaned over, and as she did so, the whine grew suddenly louder. The device clicked open, the surface peeling back like flower petals. Jane sucked in a breath. "Shit. Guys? We've got—"

But an electric squeal cut her off, the comm in her ear going dead. Jane winced, grabbing at it, as the lights snapped off, the lecture hall plunging into darkness.

"RELAX, IT'S FINE," SIMON SAID AS CLAIR BARRELED INTO the living room. He had just stood up, and was motioning for the rest of them to stay put. "I'll just check the breakers. I'm sure it's nothing."

Mike pointed, his voice cracking as he said, "Yeah, but Dad, the TV's still on." Though at least Donna had muted it, as they sorted out the situation.

Simon nodded. "Right. Separate breaker. Give me two seconds, and we'll be back to normal."

"No!" Clair said. Everybody jumped at her outburst, but Clair didn't care, didn't dare stop. "We need to get out of here. Right now."

"What are you *talking* about?" Kevin said, a sneer marring his face. "It's just a power outage."

Clair shook her head fiercely. "No. I'm sorry, but it's not. Please, just . . . just trust me. It's not safe here."

In the flickering light of the TV, Clair met each of her parents' eyes. Simon, studious and cozy in his dad-polo and wire-frame glasses; Donna, turned around to look over the back of the couch, her fingers already tightening on the back cushion. They were the only two who would fully understand the gravity of the situation, and Clair did not think, she just felt her powers open up inside her, the wash of memory flooding the room. The sight of Electric Fury standing over her in the train. The way Clair's hairs had stood on end, just being that close to her. The rage crackling in her eyes. Amy's voice: *She's here.*

"What . . . what the fuck was *that*?" Kevin snapped.

Donna sprang to her feet. "Later. Everybody up. Kevin, lift Nicole. Mike, help clear a path for them." She looked around, at the confused faces still staring up at her. "Did nobody hear me? I said *now!*"

It was clear the rest of them still had plenty of questions—and didn't even necessarily believe there to be a danger—but when Donna spoke in that voice, nobody argued. Donna oversaw the process as she gathered blankets and pillows up from the couch and the compartment beneath the ottoman. Simon, meanwhile, went over to the hall closet, loading down his arms with the emergency flashlights, a first-aid kit, a baseball bat.

"Where are we going?" Mike asked, but Donna shushed him with a look.

They were almost to the door when a flash of lightning burst through the room.

Clair threw her hand up, shielding her eyes. The negative of her bones splashed across her vision.

Electricity popped and crackled in the doorway. Blocking the exit. Electric Fury stretched, her neck popping. Then she grinned at them, the white of her teeth catching the light of the TV so they practically glowed.

"Hi, Fam," Electric Fury said. She opened her arms as if for a hug. Lightning leaped the distance from shoulders to fingers and back again. "It's so nice to finally meet you."

* * *

THE TRAP CLICKED OPEN. A SPRAY OF ACID LEAPED FOR JANE'S FACE.

If she was anyone else, the darkness would have hidden the danger from view, but Jane saw it happen. The trap coming alive, the nozzle revealed. She jerked aside, throwing herself across the lecture stage. A searing burn caught her cheek, part of her ear—she smelled burnt hair, but she could live with that. She ducked, sliding beneath a smaller side table as the spray widened its scope. An umbrella of acid shot from the device now, like a jet in the middle of a fountain.

"Shit!" Jane scrambled in the pockets of her suit. Before they'd left, Granite Girl had passed out prewrapped acid-neutralizing packs, just as a precaution, and Jane slapped one against the side of her face now. Her burning skin flashed cold as ice, before calming to a numb ache.

Still, all the packs in the world wouldn't do her any good if she left the disintegrating safety of her side table. She leaned over, trying to peer through the spray. The acid pod didn't seem to have any kind of wifi connections pouring off it, so it had likely been triggered from a low-tech switch Jane must have inadvertently set off. But if she could get a clear shot at it, she could at least knock it aside, maybe far enough that it would clear a path to the door.

Jane squinted. Through the green mist, she could just see the edge of the microscope, glinting in a slice of moonlight spilling in from the windows. It might not be the perfect solution, but Jane would take it. Tentatively, she reached a hand out. She leaned far to the side, the better to avoid the spray of acid raining down in front of her. There were no perfect angles in this equation, but screw it. Jane took her best aim, and shot a laser beam at the microscope as quickly as she could.

It hit the metal base, melting a piece of the microscope, which collapsed against the spray pod, knocking it off-center. Not very far, and not exactly where Jane would have wanted it, but the reach of its spray was now farther from the table where Jane was hiding, so . . . it would have to do.

Jane took a breath, bracing herself, and then she ran, dodging the acid as best as she could. When she reached the back of the room, her palms slammed against the door, throwing it open, and she spilled out of the lecture hall.

Unfortunately, she was not alone.

PitchBlack stood at the end of the corridor, a dark slash against the tan walls.

"Ah, Captain," he said, his thick Russian accent echoing down to Jane. "So glad you could come."

CLAIR SHOVED HERSELF IN FRONT OF HER FAMILY. "YOU STAY AWAY FROM THEM!"

"Aw, Amy," Electric Fury said. Her bottom lip pouted out. "If that's a request, you're supposed to say 'please.'"

"It's not."

Electric Fury shrugged. "Good, then I don't need to listen to it."

A flash of Electric Fury's intention crossed Clair's sight.

Clair's body reacted without conscious will. As Electric Fury flung her hands out, so did Clair. There was no way Clair's powers could stop an electrical bolt, but that was fine.

She wasn't trying to stop it.

It struck Clair in the hand, cutting straight through the fabric of her gloves, but it did not stay there. Pain shot through Clair as every muscle contracted at once. Her heart seized. Her breath shot from her lungs.

Dimly, she thought she heard something, shouts maybe—her mother's voice, her father's, her name called out in terror. It was hard to say. All Clair felt was the clench of her muscles, the strain of her teeth pressed together, the flutter of her heart, the fibers of the rug like daggers beneath her forehead. She did not remember collapsing, but it was not a surprise to find herself on the floor.

"Get. Up."

Amy's voice. It cut through the pain, through the confusion, through the blur.

"That's right. Listen to me. You are not going to let us die today, you got it? You're going to get the fuck off this floor, and you're going to keep fighting, and you're going to protect my family, or so help me god, I will kill you myself." She grabbed Clair by the shoulders. Tugged hard. "Come on. Up. Up!"

But it wasn't Amy's grip that finally yanked Clair back to her feet. Electric Fury's fist latched down tight on Clair's throat. It was the only thing keeping her upright, even as Clair jerked her arms in a feeble effort to claw the fingers off her.

"You're going to pay for your sins, Amy. Slowly."

She threw Clair across the room. Clair tumbled over the back of the couch, her foot hooking a lamp as she crashed to the floor.

A flash of lightning threw everything into black and white.

Donna screamed. Her pain and terror flooded the room, finding Clair even in the dark. Not fear for herself, but the thought of her children, of Kevin and Nicole and the baby that had been struggling to grow between them. Memories of Clair's birth, tangled up with each of her brothers' years later. Their scrunched faces as Donna cradled each of them in her arms for the first time, the feel of her lips against their tiny heads as she blessed them into the world. *My babies.*

It was Donna's fierceness that surged through Clair now. Donna's strength that unlocked Clair's muscles. Clair grabbed the edge of the couch, drawing herself up with every ounce of determination her mother had to give.

By the time Clair stood, Electric Fury had Donna in her grasp. One hand clamped tightly in Donna's dark hair, the other poised and ready, sparks popping between her fingertips. Donna was on her knees, her eyes wet and latched on to Clair. Pleading.

It's okay, Clair thought, looking straight at her mother. As if she could transmit this promise, as if she could seal their fate with sheer force of will. *It's okay.* To her shock, it looked as if Donna's muscles relaxed, just slightly. Like she knew.

Electric Fury nodded at Clair approvingly. "Very good. I was hoping you'd be strong enough to see this."

Clair blinked. She did not call her powers—her powers were not something to be summoned, turned on and off at will like Jane's or the others'. They were a part of her, entrenched as deeply as her eye color or the ticklish parts of her skin. This was something Amy had always viewed as a character flaw, and it was a sentiment Clair had inherited without question, but she rejected it now. Rather than trying to distance herself from them, Clair let her powers fill her up, head to toe, and they sprang to the surface, eager puppies ready to prove themselves. The walls of the physical world dissolved. What was touch, anyway?—she did not need it, did not want it. She felt the connection she had to each person in the room: her brothers, angry and bewildered at the sharp turn of events; Nicole, isolated even in their shared terror, even from the baby inside her; the embarrassment lodged hard in Simon's throat; the peace of Donna's faith in her. In the center of it all, the storm of rage that had invaded their home— Electric Fury, breathing hard. The pounding of her heart felt like it would break Clair's own chest.

Clair took a breath, steadying herself. All she had to do was dive.

Hotel sheets, smooth and cool, beneath them. Low music playing out of someone's phone. The stretch of Electric Fury's toes became Clair's own, the luxuriant pull of her muscles as she stretched out across the top of the mattress. Cool night air brushes over them.

Morning, technically, she supposed. Clair latched on tight, and in the memory she found, Electric Fury looks at the watch on her wrist, the soft white numbers confirming what she already knows. Their time is running short. Still, she puts it out of her mind as a mumble sounds beside her.

Mindsight's shoulders turn. A smooth expanse of back is replaced by the shift of bare breasts, their weight settling against themselves as Mindsight rolls over. Electric Fury pulls herself up, nuzzling against her, the kiss of a breath against Mindsight's neck.

"Hey," Electric Fury whispers.

Mindsight's fingers trace lines up Electric Fury's back. Sparks dance along her skin, a gentle current running between them. "Hey yourself."

"Stop it!"

A sharp jolt snapped reality back, all of Clair's muscles seizing as Electric Fury passed through her in lightning form. Clair stumbled as the memory ripped from her mind. All at once, her powers seemed to shatter on the floor.

But it had gotten Electric Fury away from Clair's family, and that was all that mattered. "Run!" Clair shouted to them as her knees buckled beneath her. She caught herself on a lamp, her head spinning.

Her family didn't need to be told twice. They scrambled over each other in their haste—Kevin, staggering slightly as he carried Nicole, Simon sweeping Donna into the tuck of his arm, Mike fleeing faster than any of them. At the door, Donna turned, reaching desperately back. "Clair!"

"Go!" Clair lurched aside as Electric Fury collapsed back into lightning, hurtling herself toward Clair once more. Clair whirled, tracking her as she crackled back into solid form.

Electric Fury's hands snapped open, lightning balls springing to life above her palms. "You're going to regret that."

"No, please," Clair said quickly. "Wait—I don't want to hurt you. You don't have to do this."

Electric Fury threw her head back, a single sharp *ha* cracking through the room. "Like hell I don't. I spent a long time figuring out my revenge for you, sweetie. It was all planned. But now I think I might just take my pleasure in watching you die slowly."

She lunged forward. Her hand clutched down, yanking Clair up by the collar. Fingers on Clair's throat, nails against skin. Nothing but the whisper of rage in Clair's ears, like the roar of the ocean. Clair clawed at the grip, desperation pouring off her. "No, stop!"

"Goodbye, Amy."

"*I'm not Amy!*"

ELECTRIC FURY'S HESITATION CRACKLED THROUGH THE room. It would not last long, so Clair grabbed hold of it while she still could.

"Please, wait, I promise, I—I know how this looks, but if you truly want revenge on Amy Sinclair, you've got the wrong woman. Please."

A sneer towered over her. "Impossible."

Clair gave a frantic shake of her head. "No. You know her powers—my powers? When they're flaring badly enough, there's a moment where another person's essence can be absorbed so deeply that it overwrites the original. That's what happened. I swear to you. I came from this."

She ripped her glove off. Held her hand up. Her wedding ring, polished like new, caught the light from the still-muted TV.

"The person who hurt you, she's not even here anymore. If you kill me, all you'll be doing is taking an innocent life."

Never mind the visions she'd been having of Amy—Electric Fury didn't need to know about that. Clair glanced to the side, just for a second, just to see, but the room was empty save for the two of them. Electric Fury's hand stayed locked tight on Clair's throat as she raised the other, glowing brighter than fire. The light of it threw Electric Fury into sharp relief, a film noir version of herself.

She didn't believe Clair.

She believed Clair.

She didn't believe Clair.

Clair watched the war play out across her face, neither side willing to yield. But then, the smallest crinkle bent Electric Fury's forehead. A chink in her armor.

"Who the hell *are* you supposed to be, then?"

"I'm—"

Clair choked. That was the question, wasn't it? All this time since she'd been back, the gnawing insecurities that had plagued her dreams. Maybe the visions of Amy weren't even real, maybe they were nothing but a manifestation of doubt. Who was she? Was she really real, really "back"? Every piece of evidence suggested the answer was "yes," but suddenly Clair realized she'd never entirely believed that. A part of her had always been sitting back, waiting for the other shoe to drop. For her to be revealed for the fraud that she was.

"Now you're getting it," whispered a voice in her ear. Her own voice, Amy's voice. It wasn't even coming from a body anymore— but was it ever, had it ever really needed to? Amy had said it herself, she would get her body back. Maybe that process was nothing more than Clair admitting the truth to herself. That she didn't even really exist.

That she was nothing but a memory.

But then the bubble of a laugh rose up through Clair's mind; Jane's laugh, Jane's smile. *No.* The answer billowed up inside of Clair, drowning her with its certainty. No, she would not accept that. She would not play second-fiddle to herself, not anymore. She would not allow herself to be sidelined in her own life. Her thumb found her ring, grounding herself as her fingers tightened into a fist around it. She met Electric Fury's gaze dead-on.

"My name is Clair."

* * *

"WAIT!" JANE LIFTED HER HANDS, SHOWING THEM EMPTY. "Stand down. I don't want to fight you. I'm not your enemy."

PitchBlack made a noise low in his throat, halfway between a chuckle and a growl. "This where you're wrong." He reached into a pair of holsters at his hips, the barrels of twin guns flashing into view. "Also where you die."

Well. Jane supposed that made things simpler, at any rate.

He was the first to lash out. A bullet flew down the hall, narrowly missing Jane's head as she veered to the side. She twisted back, firing a laser beam in an effort to disarm him, but he took off running. Darkness shrouded the hall, though Jane could see the outline of him as he hightailed it back toward the auditorium.

"Oh, hell no," Jane said. "You're not getting away that easily."

She set off after him. Damn, but he was fast. Jane tapped into her comm, testing to see if she could get any kind of signal now that she was away from whatever had shorted it out in the lab, but it sat dead in her ear like a lump of dried wax. She was on her own.

Fine, then. Jane hurtled around the corner, and there he was, in the distance. For a moment, it looked like he wasn't sure quite where to go. But then he swung left, pushing through a door.

By the time Jane plunged in after him, he'd already sucked the light out of the room. They were in the wings of the auditorium, just offstage. Squinting, Jane could see the lights blaring on the other side of the darkness, the candidates carrying on as if nothing was wrong. Perhaps they didn't even know.

For everyone else in the wings, though, there was nothing but black. Whispers darted through the room, as aides and campaign managers scrambled to figure out what happened.

"Did a breaker go?"

"Where's the light switch?"

"Does anybody have a flashlight?"

"Keep your voice down!"

"There's one on your phone."

"I can't even *see* my phone!"

"The debate's still going, though, right? I think I can hear them."

"It's definitely still going. Maybe the problem is backstage?"

"That's something, at least."

Thankfully, they seemed to be chalking the experience up to a power outage—however odd this particular one was—and Jane would take it. So long as they were convinced the situation was easily explained, they wouldn't suspect it was actually an Enhanced attack. They wouldn't panic.

This blissful ignorance wouldn't last long, though, and so Jane picked her way through the crowd as quickly as she could. Around people groping their way through the dark, around flailing elbows, around people standing there shaking their phones as if somehow the screens would blink back on by magic. There was nothing Jane could do for them, not without making things worse. Nothing, save for taking PitchBlack out before he could cause any more trouble.

He was easy enough to find. In the wash of wifi and radio waves that lend shape to everyone else, the darkness seemed to morph around him. Jane slipped past a small crowd, clustered together, and then she hesitated. Had PitchBlack actually *waited* for her? That didn't feel right, but now that she was here, Jane couldn't worry about it. Before she'd even broken from the rest of the people caught backstage, PitchBlack was attacking.

Jane dove to the side, hoping to draw him away from the crowd, and sure enough: PitchBlack landed in a roll, and as soon as he sprang back to his feet, he turned his sights on her. He shot forward, clearly intending to plow straight through Jane.

She held her ground, even as every impulse told her to dodge. Held it, even as he drew closer, even as an impact became more and more apparent, even as her legs ached to leap aside. Held it, until, at the last possible second, she spun out of the way. PitchBlack barreled past her, so close that their elbows knocked together, so close that he could not block her as Jane slid one of his guns from its place at his side.

PitchBlack whirled. He patted down his holsters, his fingers dipping into the empty space where one of his guns should have been. Jane did not need to see details to know he was glowering at her. His voice caught low in his throat as he said, "That was mistake, Captain."

Someone near Jane jumped. "Who said that?" they asked, still shaking their phone as if trying to jerk life back into it.

PitchBlack drew his other gun. Jane's muscles tensed, ready to leap—but it wasn't Jane he was aiming toward next. It was the random bystander, the one who'd startled at the sound of PitchBlack's voice. He was turning on innocent civilians, when they couldn't even see it coming. PitchBlack raised his weapon, taking aim in the dark.

Hero training kicked in. Jane leaped at PitchBlack, throwing herself in his path.

But it was not a bullet that found her. Instead, PitchBlack dove forward, grabbing Jane. Her momentum carried her, bolstered by his own strength, and soon her feet left the ground completely, her body turned weightless. Jane's mind blanked, panicked. Her vision flared white, PitchBlack's darkness switching off as he hurtled her into the spotlight.

"CLAIR." THE NAME DRIPPED AS IT CAME OUT OF ELECTRIC Fury's mouth, like pulling hair from the depths of a drain. "You really expect me to believe that?"

"I swear, it's true. Look at me," Clair said. "Really stop and _look_. I don't know you. I don't know what was done to you, but whatever it was . . . I'm sorry."

"Liar!"

"Stop!" Clair shouted as Electric Fury collapsed into a bolt of lightning.

The energy of her rushed at Clair. Compressed and furious, as if the god of thunder himself were hurtling Electric Fury toward Clair's body. There was no avoiding it. There was no dodging. There was no shielding to hide behind, no lightning rod to ground her. Clair was an exposed circuit, and Electric Fury poured into her, current arcing across every nerve, every muscle. Clair tried to brace herself, but it was impossible. Her body convulsed, energy filling her up, Electric Fury's rage filling her up, until she was saturated in it, electrified by it, subsumed by it.

A flash of memory.

Just a taste.

This same feeling, but welcomed. Lavished, even. A darkened bedroom, and the collapse as Electric Fury's energy overpowered Amy, as her muscle control subsided to the current flowing through her. *"People are controlled by energy,"* Electric Fury had told her once, as she'd trailed her kisses, sparking, across Amy's skin. *"Sometimes . . . it doesn't have to be their own."*

So you do remember me.

"No!"

The word ripped itself from Clair's throat with such force it left it raw. Her consciousness snapped back into place. She looked down, and the current still crackled across her skin, but Clair could feel the hold of it now, fighting for purchase within her. Clair's own powers roared back, bitter at being suppressed.

With a burst of light, the electrical current leaped from Clair. It struck the wall, a scorch mark against the paint as a burst of silver and white expanded, and Electric Fury fell to the ground. Clair's head spun, memories washing at her before she could stop them.

The trail of a finger running up her spine. A soft face nuzzling against her shoulder blade.

"What's wrong?"

"Nothing."

Electric Fury props herself onto an elbow, and Clair feels the pillow beneath her as if it was her own. "Really? I may not be a mindreader, but I can tell when you're upset."

She's rewarded with one of Mindsight's giggles, bright as a summer breeze. "Ugh, be grateful you're not." Mindsight sighs. She runs her hands through her hair, the dark strands threading between slender fingers.

Electric Fury leans over. The spark of a kiss lands on Mindsight's ribs, the empty stretch of skin that Electric Fury likes so much. "You can tell me," she whispers.

"I can't, though." Mindsight's voice is small as she reaches down to run a hand over Electric Fury's head. "It's work . . . Sort of."

No real names. No talk about work. No emotional attachments.

Those were the rules she and Mindsight laid out between them, after their first night together. They'd worked so far, and it's not like Electric Fury *wanted* to break something that worked. Especially after her last experience—it wasn't worth it.

Still . . .

Electric Fury bites her lip. "Well . . . if it's only 'sort of' work, then you can 'sort of' talk about it. Come on. Be as vague as you like. Or, I don't know, use code names. I don't care. Just . . . talk to me. I want to help."

Mindsight smiles. Her thumb runs down Electric Fury's cheek, unconsciously tracing the path of a tear. "I know you do."

"So . . . ?"

A sigh. Mindsight's head falls back, loose waves spilling across the pillow. "It's just . . . it's complicated."

"Shocker, that."

"Shut up," Mindsight says, laughing. But then her face turns serious, a curtain falling across the scene. Her finger traces the shape of her own navel, a sight Electric Fury is fighting desperately not to get distracted by. She almost doesn't notice when Mindsight finally says in a rush, "I'm in love with one of my teammates."

A crackle of electricity shoots to the pit of Electric Fury's stomach. Whatever she expected Mindsight to say, this wasn't it. Her mouth sours, the taste of burned metal scorching her tongue.

No real names. No talk about work. No emotional attachments.

Mindsight's hand slips toward Electric Fury's, and Electric Fury holds herself still, like there's a snake in the room as their fingers lace together. Her rage has always served her well, but she does not trust it to shield her now. Indifference is the best game she can play.

Electric Fury rolls away, onto her own back. Their hands slip apart naturally.

"So what's the problem?" she asks. She does not want to ask. She has to ask. "She doesn't return your feelings?"

Mindsight's breasts rise and fall in tune with her obvious heartbreak as she sighs. "No. I don't even know if she likes women, though it's hard to get a read on her. Even for me. She keeps herself so distant, and, we used to be close? Not like *that*, obviously, but as children. But now . . . Sometimes I get the sense that she's afraid of me. Or, not even *me*, but my powers. Like she's trying to hold me back somehow."

A crackle of energy, stronger than memory. Strong enough to rip the world in half, for Clair to spill forward in her parents' living room. She caught herself against the plush carpet, staggering onto her elbows and knees.

"Stay the *fuck* away from that," Electric Fury snarled. She towered over Clair, stabbing one heeled boot down hard against Clair's back. "Those are *mine*."

"I'm—I'm sorry," Clair said. "I didn't . . . I didn't mean to—"

"Save it, bitch. I'm not some peep show for you to paw at to get your jollies. You want to claim you're not really her? Then prove it."

Electric Fury's boot hooked itself beneath Clair's shoulder. It jerked up, flipping Clair onto her back on the carpet. Electric Fury held her hand out, lightning spinning a tight circle around her fingers. It danced between her digits, coiled and waiting, ready to lash out.

"What's the last thing you said to me?" Electric Fury asked.

Clair's eyes widened. "I . . . I don't . . ."

And maybe it was something on Clair's face, some blankness, some hesitation that went beyond merely not wanting to answer. Whatever it was, Electric Fury saw it.

Whatever it was, Electric Fury *knew*.

The lightning between her fingers snuffed out. A spark disappeared from her bitter features. She took a step back, pulling her boot off of Clair's chest.

"Oh my god. You really don't know, do you?"

Clair shook her head. The answer—the truth—shouldn't have stung as much as it did.

"Fury . . . ," Clair said. She raised herself up onto her elbows. "Whatever it is you're looking for, I—"

She never got to finish. Before the words were even out, Electric Fury's brow had narrowed, cutting the answer from Clair's tongue. With a spark that split the darkened living room, Electric Fury collapsed into lightning once more . . . and was gone.

Clair dropped back onto the floor, her heart pounding. Outside, she could feel the lingering presence of her family, hidden away somewhere, a thousand questions waiting to be answered. Clair would get to it, she owed them that much, but for now . . .

A flicker of light caught her attention. Clair jerked her head, suddenly terrified that Electric Fury had changed her mind, that she'd come back for round two, but it wasn't lightning that had drawn her eye. Somehow, against all odds, the TV still flickered behind her, muted but present, and Clair's eyes widened as she took in the image on the screen.

"Shit, the debate!" she shouted as she flipped herself and scrambled to her feet.

JANE HIT THE POLISHED FLOOR OF THE STAGE. SHE SLID along her back, past the legs of Mayor Maxwell, coming to rest as a tangled heap right between the candidates.

"What the—?" the mayor started. His eyes widened as he spotted the bright red uniform of his daughter at his feet. "What's—?"

Jane did not have time to offer a rebuttal. She pointed behind him. "Duck!"

To her shock, Mayor Maxwell had half-decent reflexes. A bullet flew overhead as the mayor dipped behind his podium, his hands gripping the sides as if it was the only thing left he had to cling to in life.

Security rushed the stage as Jane scrambled to her feet, a wave of black suits and dark sunglasses. They parted around Jane, breaking half for Cal, half for the mayor.

PitchBlack, however, only had eyes for Cal.

He'd leaped onto the stage just before firing off his shot, but he did not stay there, and in this moment, Jane had a choice: she could stop him, or . . . not.

Not very heroic, perhaps, but could anyone blame her? After everything Cal had done to the team, not just in terms of his original betrayal when he sided with UltraViolet, but everything he'd done since his return to sway public opinion against them. Of course, the spiteful part of Jane wanted to turn away, let

PitchBlack attack him. The devil she'd draw on her shoulder was even whispering that it wasn't as if he didn't have training—he'd served in the *Marines*, after all, and then spent the better part of a decade fighting as part of an elite superhero team, surely he could handle himself?

The problem was, that's exactly the image Cal would have loved everyone to see. Jane did not even need to turn to feel the cameras pressed to her back like wet noses of hungry dogs. The air was alive with wifi activity, tweets and posts and pictures and videos streaming not just through the official airwaves, but all the phones held aloft in the dark seats beyond the stage.

She ripped the mental drawing from her shoulder, crumpled it into a ball. Let it ride in her fist as she sprang to her feet and aimed it for PitchBlack's jaw.

The *crack* of her punch was the thunder that precedes the storm. A familiar gust of wind teased at her ponytail, and Jane smiled as the rest of her team swept in. Rip-Shift and Granite Girl, leaping down from a shimmering line above PitchBlack; Pixie Beats blooming to life in a colorful whirl; Windforce, riding in on the current.

Jane leaped aside, letting them do their thing. She quickly checked on the candidates. The mayor had been escorted offstage, and Jane turned, just in time to see the university's bodyguards rush Cal.

"What? No!" Cal shouted as he was lifted from his feet. "Not *me*, you idiots! Attack them! Can't you see they're dangerous?"

His protests did no good. Cal grabbed his stapler from the podium as they passed, clutching it to his chest as if he'd developed some kind of office supply fetish in his time off the grid, which—oh, who knows, weirder things had happened. Or maybe he just wanted something to hold as he shook his fist and threw a tantrum like a toddler. Shouts of "No, put me down!" and "I will not yield to these people!" echoed out into the auditorium as they carried him off, stage left.

By the time she turned back, the rest of the Heroes had already apprehended PitchBlack, and were in the process of handing him over to campus security. All around them, cameras flashed and snapped, videos sucked down the moment, and every move the

Heroes made was carried out over the wifi like a flock of pigeons released to the sky. Not all of the coverage would be good, Jane knew, and not everyone would take their actions in a positive light. Still, it made her feel better to know they'd done something solid, something *good*. Even if it meant saving Cal. Jane went to join her team, flush with pride at everything they stood for.

And then a handful of police officers appeared on the outskirts of the stage.

Jane spun away, grabbing Pixie Beats's and Rip-Shift's hands. "Time to go!"

CLAIR WHIPPED THE HEAVY DROP CLOTH AWAY. GLEAMING black paint and shining silver chrome winked hello from the sleek lines of Mindsight's old vintage motorcycle.

As soon as she spotted it, she knew she'd made the right choice. A tingle raced up Clair's arm as she ran her fingers across the surface. "Hello, old friend," she whispered.

"Please tell me you're not thinking what I know you're thinking," Amy said from behind her. "Clair, this is nuts. We have to make it all the way across the city!"

"Exactly. What better means?"

"Anything! Literally any other option is a better choice than this."

Clair swung her leg over the bike, ignoring Amy.

"Do you even know how to ride one of these?"

"Nope." Clair turned, cutting a level gaze at Amy. "But you do. I'm going to bet muscle memory will take care of the rest."

A nervous laugh escaped Amy. "And if you're wrong? You could get us both killed, Clair. You realize that, right?"

Clair shook her head. "Not this time." She hoisted the helmet up from where it hung off the handlebars, snapped and adjusted the strap beneath her chin. She glanced back. "Well? Are you coming, or not?"

"CAPTAIN! CAN I HAVE A WORD, PLEASE?"

Jane stumbled. The question choked her, as if the tail of her father's speech bubble had lashed out and wrapped itself as a python around her neck. For a moment, a flash of panic—was he trying to stall them long enough for the police to arrive? Jane wouldn't have put it past him. She hesitated, just a panel too long.

When she turned the page, Mayor Maxwell was in front of her, filling the entire frame.

He held his hand out.

Jane blinked, staring at the gesture. In her mind, the close-up of his hand was rendered in such fine detail it may as well have been a nature drawing, far at odds with the cartoony world surrounding him.

She did not want to take his hand.

Not as a daughter, no, but not as Captain Lumen, either. They stood in the wings of the stage, aides and reporters suddenly gone quiet as they all noticed this moment.

Everyone was watching. Mrs. Maxwell and Allison, campus security, event organizers, the rest of the team. All of them waiting. Cameras and news crews and phones pointed openly in her direction. She knew that the longer she put this off, the worse it was going to look for all of them. That was the point. That was the problem.

Jane gritted her teeth as she slapped her palm against her father's. Mayor Maxwell squeezed down, holding on to Jane as if she might slip through his fingers and disappear at any second. He pulled her closer, pumping her hand, dragging on the moment as shutters snapped around them.

"What about the needs of the city?" Jane asked. She made sure to keep her voice low, so as not to be overheard.

Mayor Maxwell let out a tiny sigh. Not enough to be seen by the crowds. "I was wrong."

He said it so softly that if they'd been any farther apart, Jane never would have heard. Even now, she wasn't sure she'd heard correctly. Paul Maxwell, admitting he was wrong? Jane stared at him, dumbstruck. She was just about the same height, if not a fraction of an inch taller, but he had never looked small to her before now. Was it just her imagination, or did he even cower for a moment underneath the steely gaze of Captain Lumen?

"I thought that by going with popular opinion, I'd be helping people," Mayor Maxwell continued when Jane said nothing. "That was a mistake. What I should have been doing is taking a stand. I see that now. I hope to do better. For all of us."

Jane turned toward the cameras. Mayor Maxwell followed suit, never one to ruin a photo-op. Together they grinned at the press as Jane whispered out of the side of her mouth, "Why are you really doing this?"

Mayor Maxwell flinched. "Does there need to be a deeper reason, Jane? You can't just take the win?"

Jane slid her hand free. "Not from you."

A wrinkle appeared on Mayor Maxwell's forehead. A well-worn line, straight down his brows. Jane had been on the receiving end of that look across two lifetimes by now. When she was a child, it used to slay her. Now she just straightened her spine, rising up to meet it.

Jane strode away. She waved away the reporters—*no questions*—as she joined the rest of her team.

"What was that all about?" Rip-Shift asked. The Heroes folded Jane into their ranks, a blockade against the attention.

Jane shrugged. "Who even knows, with him?"

"Does this mean he's going to back off the anti-superhero initiatives?" Windforce asked.

"Guys, *I don't know*. He's not exactly the most open person."

Granite Girl shrugged. "At the very least, it sends a positive message to the media. If at least one of the candidates is on our side, that should help public opinion."

"Hang on," Pixie Beats said. "Speaking of the candidates . . . Where's Cal?"

Jane stopped. She looked around. Though it had seemed crowded backstage a moment ago as everyone watched her and Mayor Maxwell, she realized with a sickening twist that Pixie Beats was right. Cal should have been there, involving himself in some way, obnoxiously sticking his nose where it least belonged. And even if he'd been out in the hall when Mayor Maxwell had first approached Jane, *someone* should have found him by now, to make sure he knew what was going on. One of the major photo moments of the night had just occurred, and . . . he'd *missed* it.

"Split up," Jane said. She grabbed the replacement earpiece that Granite Girl tossed to her, powering it up as she tucked it quickly into place.

The rest of them scattered, and Jane returned to the empty hallways. She did not have it in her to be in the spotlight anymore tonight. Besides, what were the odds that *Cal* would allow himself to blend into a crowd unnoticed? No—wherever he'd gone, whatever was so important he'd allowed himself to miss the spectacle, Cal was doing it in private. Jane would bet money on that.

She could only hope it wasn't something tawdry.

It didn't take Jane long. A couple of turns, a quick dash down the hallways. Maybe she was always meant to find it, because it seemed as if fate had nudged her along. Like this was just one more sequence in the issue's storyline.

Jane saw the feet before anything else. Sticking out from around the corner, the shine of their shoes caught in a perfect square of moonlight. Framed for her to find.

"Oh, no no no." Jane swept up, crouching between a pair of downed bodyguards. Her stomach seized. She did not even need to check for a pulse to know they were dead. Blood pooled beneath their twisted necks, and the sliced flesh kissed the ground beneath each of them.

Only that wasn't the worst part. Bloody boot prints, enormously sized, led away down the hall, along with a slick red trail like they'd been dragging something.

Or someone.

Jane drew herself to her feet. "Guys?" she said, tapping her earpiece. "We've got a problem. I think they took Cal."

"I'M NOT SURE I'D EXACTLY CALL THAT A PROBLEM . . . ,"
Rip-Shift said over the comm.

Jane ignored this comment, even as part of her kind of agreed
with it. She was too busy following the trail of blood, too busy
worrying over what-ifs. Issues of possible futures crowded her
mind, vying for attention. They shouted at her like hungry
reporters—Jane! Jane! Jane!—and Jane elbowed through them,
ripping pages down as she passed.

The trail led her outside. Down a sloped path, sidewalk cutting through pristine grass. Out here, the campus grew thin,
buildings few and farther between. Just open spaces, rolling
lawns, smooth paths. Up ahead, an empty parking lot stretched
out, an endless sea of pavement. It didn't make sense. There was
nothing down here, except—

The stadium.

Jane set off at a run.

She had been to the stadium plenty of times on her own Earth. Her dad brought her to football games every autumn. It was Mr. Maxwell's alma mater, after all, and he'd bundle the two of them in red-and-silver Sutton scarves and hats, carrying her on his shoulders down this same hill, under this same moon. At the end of the night, they'd spill out with the rest of the crowd, cheering, her dad belting out the school's anthem regardless of who had won or lost, raising his voice at anyone that dared to cut him a dirty look. He'd drive her to Beef-Up Burgers, no matter how late, and he'd buy two milkshakes, and Jane would swing her feet beneath the greasy table, grinning, still humming her father's song.

There was no music left now. No sounds at all. Jane had never seen the place so quiet. Emptied out like this, it felt somehow even larger than when she was a child.

Jane passed through the main entrance. Banners fluttered overhead, announcing the next game. She ran down the cement hall. Past the concession stands and the restrooms, past the turn she used to take with her dad for his favorite seats. There was only one time she'd gone onto the field, an alumni donor drive Mr. Maxwell had attended. There'd been a picnic smack dab in between the goalposts. Jane wasn't sure if she'd remember the way, but now that she was closer, she didn't need to.

Voices echoed inside the stadium. Jane slowed her approach, toeing through the empty hallway that led up to the field. Too quiet to make them out at first, though they were obviously angry, and Jane was sure the deeper one belonged to Cal. Sure enough, his was the first to resolve into clarity, its booming pitch solidifying the closer Jane got.

"—thanks to *you*, the whole plan goes off the rails, and for what? So you could settle a personal score?"

"It's deeper than that."

Jane drew still, as if the voice had seized her heart. Goddammit, she'd been *right*—Electric Fury was working with Cal, all this time. Yet somehow, vindication didn't seem to bring her the satisfaction she'd hoped. Jane toed a little closer, just enough to peer around the corner. The field stretched out, bathed in moonlight. To anyone else, perhaps, it would be hard to see the two figures standing a short distance away, but Jane recognized them in an instant. Electric Fury's catsuit, glinting in the moonlight. Cal's crisp white shirt. There wasn't a single stain on him, not a mark, not a scratch. His clothes were barely even rumpled.

"Oh, I'm sure it is," Cal spat. "But don't forget who found you, after what she'd done. Don't forget who pieced you back together. Face it: you *owe* me. Even if I *wasn't* paying you to stir up fear in the city, your ass would *still* belong to me!"

Jane tapped her earpiece. "Are you guys getting this?" she whispered, nearly breathless.

"Loud and clear," Rip-Shift said.

"That bastard," Pixie Beats added.

Electric Fury glared at Cal. "Look, I did my job."

"Oh, *did* you? My mistake. See, I thought *you* were supposed to goad the Heroes into attacking, so that *you* could be the one to take me hostage. Instead, I've got fucking PitchBlack entering from the wrong fucking side of the stage, allowing the guards time to fucking *rescue me*. Am I missing something here?"

"I told him what to do," Electric Fury said. "It's not my fault if I'm the only competent person you hired."

"No, but it's your fault you didn't stay on task! Now I've got to try to piece together some other spectacle, when all eyes were *already on me*. I hope it was worth it."

"Shit," Jane whispered. She supposed that explained why Acid Reign had planted bombs in the university, why PitchBlack was at the debate. Though it still didn't answer the question of where the doomsday device they'd been tracking was, or what all those empty cots had been doing in the warehouse instead. Or why Clair was being targeted, specifically, but did it really matter? She'd *gotten* them.

Now it was just a matter of proving it.

Out on the field, Electric Fury raised her head. Her gaze leveled with Cal's.

"Did you know?" Electric Fury asked.

"Know." Cal sneered. "Know *what*? Stop being coy, woman, and just say what you fucking mean for once."

"That Amy is gone. That the woman running around as Mindsight is some kind of duplicate, living in her skin."

Cal rolled his eyes. "*That.* Of course I knew—it makes no difference."

"No *difference*? You promised me revenge!"

"Against Mindsight. She's still Mindsight. It's not as if—"

The stadium lights snapped on. The jumbotron roared to life. Cal's face, caught midshout, snapped into an instant frown. He pointed to someone, off camera.

"Not *yet*, you idiot!" he shouted, his voice booming through the speaker system. "Cut the damn feed before—"

The squeal of a mic cut him off. Silence hummed as the power shut back down. Only Electric Fury's voice was left, to drift across the field like the mournful coo of a dove.

"You know what she did to me. *She's* the one who's supposed to pay for it. Not some would-be version of her. Her."

Cal's face went soft. He leaned in, brushing Electric Fury's white bangs aside.

"She will. I promise you, she will."

Electric Fury batted his hand away. "Were you even listening to me? She's *gone*."

"And you believed that?"

Jane's attention flicked to the jumbotron. The massive screens were still and silent, towering over the edge of the field, but a moment ago they'd been activated, automatically honing in on Cal. Which meant that somewhere, probably all over this stadium, cameras were just waiting to watch and record every move . . . every *word* . . .

Cal leaned in, whispering something in Electric Fury's ear.

Jane balled her fists. "I'm going in."

"What?" Pixie Beats said.

"No, Captain," Rip-Shift said, "don't be stupid, wait for the team!"

"It's all right." Jane took a breath, steadying herself. "I've got this."

"Captain!"

Jane ignored the voices in her ear. "I trust you," she said, and then she tapped her earpiece, switching off the comm.

She charged through the open doorway, bursting out onto the stadium grass just as Electric Fury bundled into a ball of energy and jolted away. A surge of annoyance coursed through Jane—she'd wanted to snare the both of them at once, but . . . she supposed this would have to do. They'd find Electric Fury later, of course, but she'd been a Hero long enough to know that Cal had to be the priority right now. Especially if he was the mind and money behind all this mess in the first place. And so:

"Cal!"

Cal whirled on his heel. "Captain Lumen! Oh, thank god. Have you come to rescue me? Those vicious people, they—"

"Oh, give it up. I heard every word."

"Ah." Cal nodded. He slid his hands into his pants pockets, his mouth cocking up into a smirk. "And you think that makes a difference, do you?"

"I think once the people find out what you've really been up to, it will."

Cal heaved a weary sigh. "Really. And how, exactly, are you going to prove your outrageous claims? The people are already suspicious of your motives, Jane. Throwing mud at your opponents isn't exactly going to help your cause. It might make you seem desperate. Hysterical, even."

"Well, you know, they say a picture is worth a thousand words," Jane said. She let her lips pull back into her own smirk, taunting him. "I wonder how much more punch a video carries?"

Cal's attention flicked toward the stands, the cameras silently watching the field. "You didn't."

Jane shrugged, her hands thrown in the air for exaggerated effect. "It was your idea. All I did was flip the script."

He didn't need to know that nothing was actually transmitting. Jane was too cautious to release the raw footage—who knows what kind of secrets Cal might have accidentally revealed about the Heroes? Still, she felt her tether to the cameras as they saved every word, every motion. There were so many, sprinkled all across the field so as not to miss a single moment of action.

Cal ground his teeth together, and the cameras captured that, too. Jane could practically see the gears of his brain churning: frozen frames of his thought process overlaid across the top of his head, like a cutaway straight to his brain. Should he run? Should he fight? Should he fall into a vicious pit of denial, lies spitting from his mouth like venom? Would anyone believe him? Would any of that work?

He never got the chance to decide.

A tear split the field as the Heroes poured through. Granite Girl, Pixie Beats, Windforce, Rip-Shift. Even Allison, a tactical vest strapped over her suit jacket. They raced into formation, surrounding Cal, and Cal watched them take their places, one by one. He'd been on the other side of this maneuver enough that he had to know the odds.

"It's over, Cal." Jane jerked her chin toward the team. "Take him."

Allison strode forward. "With pleasure."

"Wait!" Cal said. He reached into the breast pocket of his suit—Allison stopped and raised her gun, ready in case, but all Cal was retrieving was his stupid silver comb. He flashed them a grin as he raised it up, smoothing back his hair. "If I'm going down, I've got to look good for the cameras."

"Oh, for god's sake," Allison muttered. She crossed the last of the distance between them with a single step, grabbed his arm. Wrenched his hands behind his back as she clapped cuffs around his wrists.

A dusting of blond hairs sprinkled across the shoulder of his suit jacket.

It was so small that Jane shouldn't have even noticed it, except it was the kind of detail she would have made sure to include in a comic. A single, smaller panel, inset inside the larger scene of Allison arresting Cal. Across the bulk of the page, everything is normal: Allison's stern face, half snarling as she leans in to read Cal's rights in his ear; Cal's usual smug smirk, like he's in total control, even as the whole of his scheme falls to pieces around him; the rest of the Heroes standing by, ready, though really there's nothing for them to do by this point, and in the background, Rip-Shift is already reaching into his coat for his phone. Then this smaller detail, seemingly incongruous, zoomed-in and isolated from the rest. It was hard to even make sense of. The hairs are tiny, flecks like he'd just finished shaving, and they fell, fresh, against the jacket just as his hand was wrenched away from his head. As if they were just cut.

The next page is split in half, a line dividing Captain Lumen's face. At first, shadows highlight her terrified expression as her eyes widen, as her mouth gaps open. A tiny speech bubble, barely a whisper, slips out—"Shit"—and then beside it, across the divide, a jagged bubble tramples the rest of the page as she shouts, *"He's got a knife!"*

Allison barely had a chance to look up.

The cuffs fell to the ground. Cal was already whirling. The flash of his blade led the way as he plunged the knife deep into Allison's side.

"Allison!"

Jane was running before Allison hit the ground. The rest of the team was advancing, too, but Cal's bloodied knife slashed with military precision, keeping them at bay. Before anyone could get close, Cal pulled the stapler from the inner pocket of his suit jacket, popped it open. He held it up toward Jane, as if it was any kind of threat. "Stay back!"

The sight was so absurd that it stumbled Jane to a halt. Like her whole brain had fritzed out and needed a reboot. Her feet caught against the grass, digging in. But if she was thrown by the appearance of it, it was nothing compared to what happened next.

Piece by piece, the stapler transformed. Jane couldn't help but stare as the metal shifted: one piece elongating, another shrinking, the shape of it continually molding to fit Cal's hand. By the time Jane realized what was happening, she was staring down the barrel of a gun.

This is my supersecret weapon . . .

It had never been the stapler itself.

"Since when do you have *superpowers*?"

Cal's mouth pulled into a smirk. "Since the night you abandoned me."

Jane remembered. In the factory where they'd held her hostage, when UltraViolet wanted to steal Jane's powers for herself, Cal had crashed into a rack filled with chemical beakers. Then, later, he'd gotten zapped by a burst of UltraViolet's powers and knocked unconscious. Either one of those, or both, could have triggered the emergence. No one had really paid attention to it at the time—too busy preventing, you know, the end of the world and all—but when they'd looked back to gather him up at the end, he was just gone. Who knows what he'd been up to since then. What kind of experimentation he'd tried, what his abilities were now.

Jane hung on the edge of the moment, as time seemed to solidify around her. Lines sprang up, sharpening every edge, scribbling shading along the barrel of Cal's gun. Colors smudged into marker strokes. This couldn't be real. Jane fell into her denial like spreading open a familiar issue of your favorite superhero story, swaddling herself from the hurt of every betrayal that had led them here. Look, everything was going to be fine—see how neat everything is, trapped in clean borders, white gutters forcing all the pieces into their proper shape? A nine-panel grid, orderly and true. Cal's white teeth, as his lips pull back into a sneer befitting a supervillain. The moonlight pools over them in the perfect dramatic setup.

Then the comic slipped from her fingers, reality crashing back down around her as the crack of Cal's gun brought everything speeding toward Jane all at once.

THE DISTRACTION OF IT ALL WAS ENOUGH FOR CAL TO GET IN A SINGLE SHOT.

Just one.

Jane jerked, leaping aside. Her toe caught on the grass as the bullet grazed her shoulder. Heat flared across her skin as Jane hit the ground. Music and smoke and swirling lights snapped on all at once. An explosion of glitter burst from a tube buried under the dirt, as a series of wireless signals bounced from a control room in the stands to preprogrammed smoke machines and halftime lighting rigs.

The field pounded beneath her, churning with chaos. Jane rolled over in time to see Cal racing off, though it was entirely possible that she was the only one who could track his movements in the strobe lighting. She dragged herself to her feet as the rest of her team swarmed to her. Her red uniform probably made her an easy enough target, even in this storm of a light show.

Rip-Shift was the first to reach her. He raised an arm, catching her as she stumbled to get her bearing. "Captain—!"

"I'm fine," Jane said, shouting to be heard over the music. "Don't worry about me, just get Allison to safety."

Rip-Shift nodded, and hastily gathered Allison up in his arms. A shimmering line already waited in front of him, the far edge of the field visible through the rippling curtain. He plunged through, the tear sealing up behind them.

"What's the plan?" Windforce called as the rest of them caught up.

"First things first: we need Granite Girl to find the control room and shut this light show down. None of the rest of you are going to have much luck until then."

Windforce frowned. "You can't just block it?"

Jane shook her head. "I don't know where it's coming from, and it's too broad to just shield the whole stadium."

"Don't worry about it," Granite Girl said. Her stony face set with determination. "I'll shut it down."

"What about Cal?" Pixie Beats asked.

"I've got Cal. Besides," Jane said, her attention slipping toward the far side of the field, "it looks like you all are going to have your hands full."

Her team turned, each of the Heroes of Hope taking in the new arrivals as best they could through the artificial smoke and pounding lights. Even Jane couldn't make out many details from this distance, but she didn't need to. A towering shadow. A slip of green hair, the spike of a crown nestled on top. A figure that phased straight through the others as she pounded across the open grass. Jane's mouth twisted up, because of *course* Lou would be working with the others now, given that Cal's association was no longer a secret.

"New plan!" Jane shouted. "The rest of you—that! Go!"

The team sprinted off, jumping into action. They barely even needed to be told. Jane looked away, surveying the rest of the stadium. Cal couldn't have gone far. Or, okay, he probably *could* have, but somehow she knew he wouldn't. All she had to do was find him.

She took a step, and something crunched underfoot.

Handcuffs. What used to be handcuffs, though the actual cuff portion now lay in a crumpled heap, thin and flexible as aluminum foil. Her footprint bent them in half, the flimsy metal pounded into the dirt. Jane breathed out a sigh. If Cal could change the nature of objects, it only stood to reason that a pair of handcuffs wouldn't hold him. They were going to have to find another way—knock him out, somehow, so that his powers would switch off long enough to isolate him somewhere.

Where was another problem, but not one Jane had to deal with yet.

A stray burst of acid flew over Jane's head. She ducked as the blue blur of Windforce raced by, sweeping the spray up and hurtling it toward where Megacrush clashed with Granite Girl. It careened across the field, loose droplets hissing against the grass, and along the racks of equipment laid out for practice. A shout came from the distance, Cal's familiar voice as he swore at Windforce. Jane shifted her vision, and his heat signature flared brightly behind one of the giant dummies of a blocking shield.

Jane tore across the grass. Artificial smoke cloaked the turf as she drew closer to Cal's hiding place. Flashes of red laser beams skittered through the haze like hyperactive fireflies, but with Granite Girl distracted, it would be a while before anyone was able to shut down the show.

Almost there. Jane was just beginning to form her plan of attack when Cal leaned out and fired off three quick shots. Jane dove to the side. Cal's arm was covered in body armor, a muscled sleeve replacing the slick fabric of his suit coat. Rather, transformed into: Jane could see a portion of his chest as he ducked back behind the equipment, the cut of his jacket closing over his shirt, bulking out, the weave growing sturdier before her very eyes. Soon he would be as well-protected as he was when he was still working alongside the Heroes of Hope.

She had to find a way to flush him out—*before* that could happen.

"What's the matter, Cal?" Jane called over the bursts of music still pummeling the open field. "Don't want to fight a woman?"

A cheap tactic, perhaps, but if Cal wanted a good, old-fashioned superhero showdown, Jane could give him one.

She didn't expect it to take much to goad him into fighting her head-on.

Sure enough. Cal stepped back into view, glowering at Jane in what he must have thought was a very intimidating pose. She had to give him some credit: he was, at least, selling the look these days. Gone was his black tactical suit, the armor that made him look like he was wearing a knock-off Batman costume.

His uniform now was midnight blue, the same shade as the business suit he'd been wearing. The weave of it shone like battle armor. His belt had thickened, the buckle spreading out to coat most of the front with silver plating. Polished shoes had turned into heavy boots. The smartwatch he'd worn earlier had morphed into a slimmed down version of the wrist-mounted dart gun he always used to wear. He fished a fancy metal pen out of his pocket, fed it into the mount, and the deadly tip of a dart shot out the other end.

So that's what the pens were for.

Jane leaped aside as a dart whizzed past her. She straightened up, and jutted her chin in Cal's direction. "I like the look. What are you calling yourself these days?"

"I don't need a playground nickname," Cal said. He drew out one of his obnoxious metal business cards, and by the time it flicked away from his fingers, it had already reshaped, its edges tucking and sharpening into a fine point. A throwing star struck the board behind Jane.

"You sure? You have enough toys for the playground."

"If you think I'm going to stand here bantering with you," Cal said as he reloaded his gun, "you're wrong."

He struck fast. Faster than Jane was expecting. In the flick of a page he'd advanced, jumping from a distance shot to a close-up with nothing in between. Jane twisted aside at the last second. Across the field, the jumbotron captured their movements, as if Jane was the protagonist of a summer blockbuster, and Cal the masked nemesis she'd been stalking for the whole movie. The flare of her lasers, the crack of his gun. The swing of fists. Light flashed across the field, blue and neon yellow and purple, a psychedelic dance party brought to the halftime of their battle. Cal's arm was already in an upswing when a burst of confetti broke the gap between him and Jane like a landmine going off. They both stumbled back, and the shrapnel of glitter caught Jane's ponytail as she ran for a row of practice blockers.

A bullet whizzed past Jane's shoulder. She ducked, grabbing hold of a rack full of padding and swinging herself around behind it. A quick slice from her lasers and the whole thing was toppling forward, toward Cal's advancing form. Jane gave the rack a good kick, speeding it along, but Cal had already sidestepped as it crashed to the ground. He ducked, his leg swinging wide as his foot hooked Jane's.

She should have seen it coming—she was already off balance from the kick—but she didn't. Her world upended, lines sliding free of their colors, everything jumbling at the corners of the pages like a kaleidoscope. Jane hit the ground so hard that stars flashed. Her breath escaped her like a ghostly snake slipping from her lips.

Jane blinked, the world washing in and out around her. The darkened field, stained with confetti. The imposing silhouette of Cal's heavy boots, drawing closer. Jane's hand pushing against the field, her skin stained with blood and dirt, as she rolled herself onto her back. The glaring screen of the jumbotron, Cal's enormous face haloing the dark shadow of his head as he towered over her.

In the grass, Jane's fingers twitched. The glow of the screen was the only thing she could hold on to—brighter and more vibrant than life, saturated with color. She did not even need to look at it. She felt the light, spilling out from the pixels, spilling across the field. Spilling toward her, answering her call.

Cal's boot found Jane's chest, slamming down like an anvil. Jane winced as he pointed his gun, the line of sight aimed straight for the middle of Jane's forehead. "So much for being a hero."

"That's what you think," Jane wheezed. Could he even hear her? It didn't matter. Her fingers snapped closed, like dragging a tablecloth down, and the field plunged into a temporary darkness.

A burst of light tore from Jane, flushing most of the page white. Only faint outlines in pale yellow remain. Jane, her face screwed up in concentration, her head pressed down against the barely seen grass; Cal, staggered back, grabbing his face. The gun is captured in an inset panel, mid-drop, motion blurs and lines drawing it to land at his feet. On the next page, color begins to seep back in, watered-down paint spilling over its outlines. Jane, in a stacked sequence from her crouched feet, up her straightening legs, to the upward swing of her arm as she decks Cal across the jaw. The jagged *POW!* is a vibrant contrast, solid black and angry red.

"Should have made yourself some sunglasses," she said, all but spitting the speech bubble at Cal's feet.

The jumbotron flickered back to life, the light returning to its pixels. The image shifted, autozooming from Jane to Cal and back again, as if the camera wasn't quite sure where to settle. It showed, in patches: the mirthful shake of Cal's chest as he pushed himself up onto his elbows; the nervous twitch of Jane's fingers as her hands snapped into readied fists; Cal's hand, dragged across his mouth. A smear of red painted out from his lips in a single brushstroke. He pulled his hand away, looking at the matching streak across the back of his knuckles. Cal spat a mouthful of crimson, staining the verdant green field.

"Bad move, Main Jane."

He reached for his wrist-cuff. Jane raised her arms, her legs springing into a defensive stance beneath her, but Cal was not going for his darts, or his throwing-star business cards, or any other weapon that he might have hiding up his sleeve. Instead, all he did was push a button.

Immediately, the preprogrammed halftime show clicked off, the jumbotron whirring down to black. Stadium lights flared in their place, whole banks of them snapping on at once. Even Jane, not needing to, instinctively held her arm up to shield her face. By the time she lowered it, twin doors had sprung open on opposing sides of the stadium, and clusters of people were pouring onto the field in waves.

"Look at that," Cal said, drawing himself to his feet as smoothly as a cape unfurling. "My fans have arrived."

"WHERE DID *THEY* COME FROM?"

Though even as she asked it, a sense of understanding began to creep up on her. They poured into the stadium, two or three dozen, it was hard to say. Scars and tightly wound muscles. Tattoos. Sneers and scowls. Their polo shirts and khakis were at odds with their swagger, like an ill-fitted suit. Like Mormons, they all matched. Their outfits may as well have been bought in bulk, one size fits all.

And all in a row, every single one of them had buttons pinned to their shirts. *A Goodman for Senate.*

Jane's stomach plunged. She'd seen those faces before—just not in such great numbers, and never without other crowds surrounding them. But they'd been there, wherever Cal had appeared in public. Faces slipped into the crowds, bulking out his numbers, making him appear more instantly popular than he really was. And just like that, Jane knew what all the empty cots were for.

His own private army of henchmen, ready and waiting to do his bidding. For a while, it had meant cheering at speeches and drinking cheap beer at rallies. Now, it meant putting all those weighty fists to good use.

Cal's mouth hooked upward. "Prison is such a good recruitment ground." He leaped back as the crowd began to crush ever closer to where he and Jane were standing. "You'll never be able to take them all."

Jane turned away, swinging a punch as one of them broke for her direction. Cal was half right: the Heroes couldn't kill them, but they *could* incapacitate them, and they could certainly round them up and trap them somewhere out of harm's way. Assuming they could handle a crowd that big, which—Jane wasn't going to worry about that. Not right now.

She looked around, ready to find the rest of her team, only to discover that they were distracted down the far end of the field. Clustered around Megacrush, chasing him like confused puppies, and . . . Jane squinted. It was hard to tell at this distance, but it looked like Pixie Beats and Granite Girl were attempting to shove some sort of pole up his—okay, so that was something Jane really didn't want to consider, even as Megacrush ran around the edge of the field, barely keeping ahead of them. Acid Reign was with the whole clusterfuck, trying to get a shot in wherever she could, but Windforce was mostly holding her off. Lou had broken from the pack, racing toward the same point as Cal, probably called back.

Jane tapped her earpiece as she leaped to avoid an incoming cluster of Cal's new goon army. "Guys, what the hell? We already know how to handle Megacrush—just hit him *really hard*."

"With what?" Granite Girl snapped through the comms. Her breath came through as a grunt as she lunged, unsuccessfully, toward Megacrush's backside. "Rip isn't back yet, and even if he was, I am *not* doing another Portal-punch."

"Oh, for—" Jane sighed. She dove beneath an oncoming wave of attacks, and sprang up on the other side. "Pixie—come give me a lift. I'll handle this."

"Captain," Granite Girl said, "I don't know if that's—"

"She's not doing anything for you," Jane said as she bobbed to the side. A flash of light from her palm distracted the next two thugs, allowing her to slip away. Her feet pounded the grass as she started running for her team. "You can skewer him well enough on your own, if you get the opening. Now *move*."

There was no more debate. Pixie Beats broke from the group, shrinking down and propelling herself across the field as she leaped in miniature from one piece of practice equipment to the next. She landed next to Jane a moment later, blooming to full size.

"Okay, so what's the plan?"

"I need you to shrink me, and pitch me across the field," Jane said.

Pixie Beats's eyes widened behind the glamour of her masquerade mask. "You're serious?" she asked, and when Jane nodded she said, "But without me holding on to you, you'll billow back up to full size before you ever reach them."

"I don't need to reach them," Jane said. She held her hand out, waiting for Pixie Beats to take it. "I just need a better view."

It was clear that Pixie Beats wasn't entirely convinced this was a good idea, but she was too well-trained to ignore a direct order from her captain like that. She shook her head as she took hold of Jane's shoulders. "Try not to barf."

"No promises."

An instant later, Jane was collapsing. The world *whooshed* as the field expanded around her, everything ripped from its normal sense of scale. Jane's head spun, her stomach churning. She barely had time to think before she found herself cupped in Pixie Beats's warm brown hands. Jane tried to hold herself steady as Pixie Beats reared back, but it was impossible.

Jane was flung through the air.

She tried not to scream, or to vomit. The world turned head over heels over head, a camera spinning endlessly, as everything began to shrink back down to size. Jane could barely make sense of it, barely keep herself oriented. This wasn't going to be the best aim by any stretch of the imagination, but it would have to do. Luckily, her target glared in front of her, easy to spot.

Before she even landed, she shot two laser beams at the stands that held up a massive rig of lights. Metal screamed as the weight shifted, the whole thing rattling over the field.

"Windforce, now!"

Jane hit the ground in a roll. She sprang back to her feet as a stiff gust kicked up across the stadium, strong enough to slide Jane down the grass. Jane staggered forward, keeping low as she raced through the localized hurricane. The rest of her team was also scattering, clearing the area, as the lighting rig groaned and wobbled under the barrage of wind.

Megacrush, meanwhile, was swatting at his face while a colorful flutter of punk-rock ballerina bounced from point to point, distracting him. Pixie Beats must have ridden in on the storm. And so Megacrush did not see what was coming—just let out a wordless roar as the lights toppled, crashing down over his head. A flutter of color burst upward as Pixie Beats's miniature form deftly slipped through the beams of the lighting rig.

Windforce whooped, but Jane did not have time to revel in their victory.

"Captain!" Pixie Beats shouted, pointing behind Jane.

Jane turned, just barely in time to lean back and twist out of the way as a spray of slime-green acid crossed over her. The maneuver sent her falling backward, nearly twisting her ankle as she hit the ground, but she didn't dare stay there. Her hands and feet slipped against the grass as she scrambled up, running in a duck to avoid the acid spray. Windforce was already doing what he could, attempting to redirect it up and away, but there was nowhere safe to dump it. Property damage aside, between Megacrush's smaller, unconscious form trapped beneath the stadium lights, and the Heroes springing either for cover or into action, and the oncoming wave of Cal's goons . . . there really weren't a lot of options.

And now Acid Reign rounded back, her attention fixing squarely on Windforce. He raised his arms, the wind abruptly shifting and lifting him out of harm's way. Acid began to rain across the field, and suddenly everyone scrambled, Heroes and goons alike. Jane winced at the smell of burning flesh, the scream coming from a handful of Cal's minions.

Jane ripped one of the training dummies from its post, throwing it over her shoulders like a backpack. "We've got to do something about Acid Reign before she hurts someone!"

"Yeah, I'm sure we'd all love to, but how?" Granite Girl shouted. She was the only one not cowering, her stony skin steaming and hissing as pelts of acid tried and failed to dissolve into her.

"I don't know!" Jane shouted, flinching as another spray landed across the training dummy on her back. "Neutralize her powers or something! You guys are the science freaks—figure it out!"

"With *what*? We don't have anything to counteract acid. I mean, if we could get our hands on a base, or some baking soda or something, I guess, but—"

Granite Girl leaped aside, cutting herself off. Windforce had swept a clutch of Cal's goons into the air. They landed hard, ripping up a swath of dirt and grass in his wake. Damn, but this place was going to be a mess tomorrow.

The slow prickle of an idea worked its way up Jane's spine. She knew she'd gotten it, before she actually knew what it was. Jane's attention slid toward the grass. Trampled now, of course, but normally this field was kept pristine. Teams went out and tended to it not just every morning and every night, but after every game, every practice. Jane's dad, in the heyday of his youth, had been part of the student volunteer team tasked with keeping each blade in order—and far from being a punishment, Mr. Maxwell had been honored to do his work. Sutton took a weird sort of pride in their football field. *Over a hundred years, and not a single season played on anything other than real grass*, is how her dad used to put it. Jane could never understand what the big deal was, why it was such a point of elitist pride, but at the moment that didn't matter. What *did* matter is that Mr. Maxwell liked to talk about the things that were important to him; and so, years later, Jane looked down at one of the white lines dividing the field like gutters on a comic spread, and remembered something her dad had told her once.

"Windforce!" Jane waved her arm, flashing the tips of her fingers to get his attention. He looked down, a gust billowing up to hold him steady, and Jane pointed at the line running down the field. "Chalk!"

She didn't need to say anything more. Even with his face hidden behind the spandex of his mask, Jane knew he'd gotten the idea. He tossed her a quick thumbs-up as he spiraled to the side, a spray of acid arching through the air, and then he was off. Zooming over the field, a narrow stack of panels running behind the length of his body as the background shuffled rapidly by.

It would probably take him some time to track down where Sutton kept their field supplies, and to locate the chalk they used to line the grass. The university didn't use paint, like you'd find on modern, artificial turf, oh no. Jane's dad had been very clear about that. It may cost more, and be a boatload of extra work to re-line the field each time lines got smudged in play, but that was just part of the authenticity, he'd said. And even though Jane had never done the best job in chemistry class, she remembered enough to know this: chalk was a base. Enough of it, and it should neutralize Acid Reign's powers.

In the meantime, though, the Heroes were one more man down in the fight. Not that they were doing much fighting, with the rain of acid chewing up the field. Still, now that Cal's army had followed in the Heroes' footsteps and found some semblance of protection beneath the practice equipment, however temporary, they were done wasting time.

The goons charged forward, surrounding the Heroes.

Jane drew herself up tall, lines and ink straightening her spine, drawing back her shoulders. Her arms raised, light filtering between the lines of her fist.

But it wasn't *her* light that broke the moment.

A blinding glare spilled across the darkening field, sharp shadows cutting off the attack. Everyone else flinched, throwing their arms across their faces, cursing—and so it was only Jane who looked up, only Jane who saw the tear rip itself across the skin of reality. Rip-Shift leaped through, the glare of the remaining stadium light streaming out behind him, his long leather coat flowing like a cape in his wake.

"Show-off," Jane said through the comms as Rip-Shift landed smack in the middle of a cluster of Cal's goons.

Rip-Shift laughed, landing hard and then using his momentum to bounce into a backflip, his boot connecting with three separate goons. "Always."

The chaos of his arrival wouldn't last long. Jane threw herself forward, sliding beneath the tangle of two more goons and slicing laser beams across their legs. They toppled, screaming, as Jane came up on the other side.

"How's Allison?"

"Recovering," Rip-Shift said quickly. He whipped around, landing a solid punch. "She's tucked into a rejuve pod. The scans indicate she'll heal up."

"Oh, thank god."

"Behind you!"

Jane ducked as one of the goons swung a punch over her head.

"Took you long enough," Windforce said. He landed neatly in the grass as a gust of wind immediately swept the area clean of the shower of acid. A bag of powdered chalk was laid heavily across his shoulder as he exchanged a neat fist-bump with Rip-Shift.

"Wouldn't miss it," Rip-Shift said. He sliced two tears in the fabric of reality, sending one goon crashing into another. He nodded at the bag. "Where we going with that?"

Windforce shifted the bag into his arms. "I thought you'd never ask."

Another goon came rushing at Jane, and she leaped away, leaving Windforce and Rip-Shift to it. Acid pitted against her protective dummy once more as Windforce swept up and over the field.

Jane craned her neck, watching an arch form overhead as a flurry of chalk fell softly across the grass, the light from the stadium rigs catching the particles like a rainbow. Acid Reign was already running, racing for cover, but Windforce had her surrounded. Jane looked away as a scream cut over the field— she had to trust that her team knew what they were doing, that the chalk wouldn't cause too much harm to Acid Reign as it counteracted her.

Besides, Jane had bigger targets. In the distraction, the goons had allowed an opening to appear, and now Jane spotted Cal at the far end of the stadium, head tipped low in conversation with Lou. Somewhere, she'd found the time to change, ditching her heels and miniskirt for jeans and a loose hoodie. The two of them were a narrow panel wedged between the larger shots of fighting and chaos, so crowded that it almost blended into the background shadows. Jane reached out, shoving the larger panels aside in her mind like parting a curtain.

Two down. Two to go.

A direct assault would never work, much as Jane might wish to. In her mind, she was already racing ahead: the streak of her character blurred into a red battering ram, slamming through the panel borders and clusters of goons as if they were nothing. Flares of light knocking enemies aside, collisions at high speed felling the rest like bowling pins. Jane allowed herself this fantasy for just a moment, her lip ticking upward, but no, she had to be practical about this.

She threw the protective shield of her training dummy aside.

Did her powers know, somehow, what she wanted from them? Before she could even summon them, Jane felt her body shifting. Light raced toward her, bending around her—sidling up against her like a second suit. Colors shifted, the red leather on her arms growing mottled, then muddy, then reflecting back not its own light, but the grassy green of the field beneath her. When Jane looked down, even she could barely see herself. Just the faintest ripple, moving across the grass like the wind.

She started cutting across the field. Jane slipped around and behind the scattered pieces of practice equipment, now strewn about the grass. Her heart sped up. This could work. Cal was just standing there, watching the chaos. So smug, so sure that everything would turn out in his favor.

She was almost to him, when something made her pause.

Jane wasn't sure what. A sound, perhaps, or maybe just some sense, picked up from more than a year spent training and heroing. It didn't matter. She turned around, looking over her shoulder, and that's when she spotted it. Her fatal mistake.

A string of footprints, left behind in the chalk like it was fresh snow. Leading right to her.

It happened so quickly.

One second, Jane was frozen in place, and then the next, the panel was ripped from Jane's mind as a cold mist cut straight through her neck. For the smallest fraction of a heartbeat, she thought someone had cut her head clean off, that any moment now it would topple from her shoulders, that the last thing she'd ever see was her body collapsing behind it.

But no. The thing that had sliced through her was not a blade. Lou's arm re-formed on the other side of Jane's neck, her hand clamping down hard enough to cut off Jane's forming breath. The shock of it all—the cold, the fear, the realization of what was happening—weakened Jane's legs, and she collapsed to her knees on the churned-up ground.

In just a second, she would regain her senses. In just a second, she would come back up swinging, a defense at the ready. But she did not have a second. A cold blade at her neck, a real one this time. A hot breath in her ear.

"Don't even think about it," Lou said. She glanced at the rest of Jane's team, scattered on other parts of the field as they knocked out or rounded up the last of Cal's goons. "Call them off."

Jane hesitated. Just long enough to weigh her options, just long enough for Lou to press the tip of her knife harder against Jane's neck, drawing the first drop of blood. Jane winced as she reached up and tapped her earpiece. "Stand down. Everyone, stand down *right now*."

The team looked over, uncertainty clearly visible in their postures. They were holding the very last of Cal's goons, and Granite Girl leaped up and clocked him, knocking him out, and then shrugged at Jane in a *sorry-not-sorry* sort of way.

Cal stepped forward, brushing flecks of grass and powdered chalk from his suit. "Thanks, honeybunch," he said, grinning. He undid the band of his wrist-mounted dart gun, cupping it gently in his hands. Immediately, the metal began to twist and re-form, molding itself to suit his next needs. Jane didn't even want to know, but she would, soon enough.

It took only a moment. Cal turned his hand, showing her the results. A small gun of some sort, almost like a water pistol.

Cal reached into his suit, drawing out a vial of blue liquid, and fear shot straight to Jane's veins.

The cure.

The one that he'd used on Lou's brother, Teddy. The one that had stripped him of his superpowers.

The one that would strip *Jane* of her superpowers. Cal bit off the cap, spitting it into the grass. He popped the vial into the back of the injection gun, clicking it into place.

"Cal, stop," Jane said. "Listen to me. You don't have to do this. Whatever beef you've got with the team, we . . . we can work it out. We used to be friends. Please, you have to remember that."

Cal scoffed. "Did we? Because what *I* remember is a woman who never gave me the time of day. What *I* remember is a Jane who did once love me . . . until you took her away from me."

"She really didn't, though. Cal. Listen to me."

"No. I'm done listening to you." Cal took a step closer. "Good-bye, Captain Lumen."

But before he could reach her, before he could do anything, a set of doors along the stadium wall crashed open, panels bursting free of their pages.

It was all the distraction Jane needed.

She jerked back, away from the blade at her neck, and brought her hand up to clock Lou in the sternum. Lou staggered back, caught too unaware to phase in time. Jane leaped away, scrambling on her hands and knees across the grass. In the chaos, Cal had dropped the injection gun, and if she could get to it first, then she would be safe. Maybe, perhaps, she could even use it against Lou and Cal, though the thought left a weird squirm in Jane's stomach.

It didn't matter. All she had to do was grab it—she could worry about the rest later.

A hand phased through her, cold as ice. It seized the injection gun before Jane could, then whipped back upward, pressing the point of it to her neck. Jane froze, as if she'd been pinned in place.

"Don't think I won't pull this trigger," Lou said, and Jane believed her. Jane raised her hands in surrender as Lou nudged Jane up, to crouch on her knees.

Jane glanced over, trying to see what had caught Cal so off guard that he'd dropped the injection gun.

A shadow fell over the grass. Slim gray pants. Polished shoes. Trench coat flowing like a cape around her legs. The sharp angle of a fedora. Mindsight's arm was raised, pointing straight as an arrow as she glared down the sightline. Straight over her sleeve. Straight over the gun in her hand.

Straight to Cal's face.

Jane had never seen this side of Clair before, and the sight of it stopped her heart. The moment hung around them, time slowing to a crawl.

Clair pulled the hammer back as Jane watched, breathless. When she spoke, her voice was level, commanding. Deadly.

"Get away from her."

CAL STARED AT CLAIR, INCREDULOUS.

"Really? You're pointing the gun at *me*?" He motioned toward Lou, toward Jane, as if there was any chance that Clair hadn't seen them. "You do realize that she's the one holding your wife hostage, don't you? One wrong move, and she'll use the cure."

"That's fine," Clair said with a shrug. "She can go ahead and try it, for all I care. We both know it doesn't do shit."

"What? How can you say that?" Lou asked. "You *saw* it work—we know you stole the memory from my brother."

Clair nodded. "That's right, I did. My powers let me see that, and they absolutely showed me Teddy losing his powers. But you know what else they did?"

Here she made sure to look Cal straight in the eyes. She motioned to the gun in her bare hand. Just for a moment, she held it out so that Cal could see the model she was holding, and not just the end of the barrel pointed for his head. Cal's own gun, which Clair had scooped up from the field. The grip was saturated with his secrets.

This time, it was Clair's turn to smirk. "You dropped something."

Cal's face twisted in a snarl. He started to lunge forward. "You *bitch*—!"

"Oh, no no." Clair wrapped her hand around the gun, snapping it back into position. Cal stilled in his tracks. "None of that talk, now," Clair said. "Not unless you want me to tell your better half here what the cure *really* is."

Lou looked over, from Clair to her husband. "Cal? What's she talking about?"

"Nothing," Cal snapped. "She's trying to divide us. You can't trust anything she says."

"You ever wonder why *he* was the one who needed to first use the cure on Teddy?" Clair said, raising her voice. "Why he didn't just give it to you, and let you handle it in private?"

"Shut up!"

"Tell her to let Jane go," Clair said, "and I will."

"You know I can't do that."

"There is no cure," Clair said, speaking quickly. She kept her eyes on Cal, but her voice was pointed straight at Lou, and Clair felt the tension in the air as Lou processed this. Clair barreled on. "It's just his powers, transforming Enhanced back into ordinary people."

Cal snarled at her. "That was a mistake, Clair."

"But . . . ," Lou said. "No, that doesn't make sense. The vials—"

"She's *lying*," Cal said.

"Placebos!" Clair shouted over him. "To make you think you needed his supply. To keep you under his control."

Lou turned. "You lied to me." The words were soft, almost a question.

Cal rolled his eyes. "You're really surprised?"

Maybe she was. A ripple of disbelief seemed to cross the field, brushing over Clair. Lou hovered on the edge of the realization—not fully on Cal's side anymore, but not yet ready to let Jane go, either. The injection gun was still clutched in her grip, as if she couldn't quite let go of the idea of a cure in her hands. If Clair could just have a moment or two longer, if she could tip the scales just a little further—

But she wasn't about to get that chance. Cal laughed, just once, a gruff half-snort of superiority. "You're right. I don't need the vials—I can take her powers away anytime I want."

He lunged toward Jane.

Clair fired off a shot. It cut across his path, biting into the grass of the stadium. "Stay away from her!"

"Or what?" Cal said, even as he reared back. He raised his hands. "We both know you're not going to kill me, Clair. It's not the Heroes' *style*."

Clair pulled the hammer back. "You really want to take that bet?"

"Oh, *please*. Don't try to play the badass with me. Let's not forget, I was *there*. We made a pact, back in the beginning."

"Wouldn't be the first time one of us has broken our word."

Cal's face flushed. "I was loyal to the captain! To Jane!"

"So am I." Clair shifted her gun, making sure her line of sight was true. "Now stay *back*."

Cal straightened his spine. His hands fell. "No."

"You'd rather die?"

"You'd rather kill me?" Cal said. When Clair's gun didn't move, he tipped his head to the side, as if seeing her in a new light. "Maybe you would. But what would sweet Jane here think of you then? Hmm? She'd never look at you the same way. All that sweet, bristling, unconditional love. Well—they *say* it's unconditional, don't they? Let me tell you a secret, Clair: there are always limits. Even for the two of you. Now . . . put the gun down. You're not a killer."

"PLEASE," AMY BEGGED, FOUR YEARS AGO. "YOU'RE NOT A KILLER."

Electric Fury laughed. "You have no idea what I really am, Mindsight."

Amy stepped back. Her skin tingled, as if the words had zapped her. "How can you say that?"

After all the time they'd spent together, all the hours in each other's arms. All the careful mapping they'd done of the topography of each other's bodies. Their rules rang through Amy's mind—*no real names, no talking about work, no emotional attachments*—and for the first time, Amy realized how hollow they sounded. How little they'd mattered.

But maybe they'd mattered to Electric Fury. She wasn't even looking at Amy anymore. Her foot was up on the coffee table as she zipped up the side of her boot. Amy had interrupted her while she was getting dressed, in her signature silver catsuit. It was the first time Amy had been to Electric Fury's apartment, but somehow Electric Fury hadn't been surprised that Amy knew the address. That she's shown up at her door.

"See, that's your basic problem," Electric Fury said. She straightened up, tossing the waves of her white hair over her shoulder. "You were always so obsessed with yourself. With this teammate you're so desperate to be with. You wanted to see her in me, but the truth is, I'm never going to be a hero. This?" She twirled her finger around, indicating the high-class apartment, the costume, the inherent truth of her work, laid bare for Amy to see. There was no way Electric Fury had managed this level of success through legitimate means. "This *is me*. It's all I really am."

"I don't believe that," Amy said. Electric Fury started to laugh again, and so Amy rushed forward. "*No.* You can try to convince me all you want, but there's goodness in you, Effie. I know there is. Please, just . . . let me help you. Whatever your boss has on you, whatever you're afraid of happening—"

"You really don't get it, do you?" Electric Fury said. "I'm not *afraid*. I'm not being coerced. I want to do this. I *like* my work. Face it, Mindsight. You fell in love with a supervillain."

In love with a supervillain. Amy's cheeks plunged cold, then hot. She could only imagine the splotches that were blooming across them now, like she'd been crying. *No real names. No attachments. No talking about work.* Those were the rules, and if there was one thing Amy had always been good at, it was following the rules. She shook her head. "I'm not—"

"Then stop me."

Amy rocked back. "What?"

"You tracked me down in my apartment. I'm as unarmed as I ever get." Electric Fury shrugged. "I won't fight you. But if you don't stop me, I am going to walk out that door, and I am going to do the job I set out to do. So it's your choice, Hero. What'll it be?"

Amy could only stare.

Suddenly, she knew this is what she'd been avoiding. The reason for all their rules. They hadn't talked about what they were doing in their relationship. Mindsight and Electric Fury. A superhero, and . . . someone who wasn't. Amy wasn't stupid. She knew how it would look, if word ever got out. She knew what it meant, if they ever broke their silence.

So they ignored it. For months, they'd ignored it.

It had seemed so simple. At the time. In all that time. If one of them wanted "company," they'd head to the bar where they'd met. When the other showed up, they didn't need to say a word. A drink or two, perhaps, for courage, and then one or the other would stand, and then it was hooked fingers, cash left on the table, a slow walk to the door, a taxi hailed at the corner. The warm assurance of breath on a neck, the warmer slip of a tongue on an earlobe. Hands sliding into places they really shouldn't in public. They drove to an apartment above a bagel shop just before the edges of South Shits, and usually had to kick the door open as the tangle of their bodies spilled through. Amy asked no questions, and Electric Fury offered no answers.

And her skin? Her skin told Amy nothing. The anger Amy had felt that first night, as they'd escaped, rushed at her again, like a dozen shots taken at once. The power of it filled her up, lifted her out of her daily life. While she was there, in bed, she could forget about the Heroes and the danger they faced. While she was there, in bed, she could forget about her problems at work. While she was there, in bed, she could even forget about Jane—Jane's smile, Jane's face, the smell of Jane's hair. It all fell away. Nothing but the bliss of unfettered rage remained. Amy ravaged in it, hungered for it. Licked it clean off Electric Fury's skin, until her tongue went numb from the electricity of it all.

Amy went numb again now, standing in Electric Fury's living room, though it wasn't the same. It wasn't at all the same.

She looked away.

"That's what I thought," Electric Fury whispered. She stepped up and kissed Amy's cheek, right by her ear, a tingle of electricity and anger cutting straight to Amy's spine. An involuntary shiver ran to the tips of Amy's fingers and toes, and she closed her eyes against it. Shit, but she loved that feeling.

The click of a door sounded behind her. When Amy opened her eyes again, the apartment was empty.

She'd let her go.

CLAIR BLINKED, DRAGGING HERSELF BACK TO THE present. The hilt of the gun was warm from being gripped in her hand.

You're not a killer.

Was she? If someone had posed this question to Clair even a few hours ago, she'd have said the very idea was absurd. Of course she wasn't. Despite the surge of bravado which had propelled her here, straightening her spine as she leveled her threats, who was she kidding, really? As much as she hated to admit it, Cal was right. Jane would never look at her the same way again. Clair, her Clair, wouldn't have ever considered such a thing. Clair, who'd always rushed in with a glass, scooping the spiders up so Jane didn't crush them, carrying them over to the window, tossing them onto the street. Clair, who took pity on city pigeons, whistling to them and talking to them and leaving a bird feeder stuck in the dirt of her window box. Clair, who'd been killed once before. Who knew what it was like. The depth and the cold and the stillness. The silence. She still had nightmares, sometimes, about slipping back into that silence. There was *no way* she ever would, ever could, condemn someone to that void.

So why was the gun still in her hand?

Clair swallowed. Down the barrel, she still had a perfect target in the middle of Cal's forehead. One shot. The muscles in her finger twitched. The urge to contract them bubbled in the pit of Clair's stomach, a sick thrill that made her head spin. Could she do it? Could she? Would she?

She would never find out. In the heartbeat it had taken her to make up her mind, two things happened at once: Amy threw herself against Clair's arm, yanking down with the weight of her whole body . . . and Lou rounded on Cal.

JANE'S HANDS HIT THE GRASS AS LOU THREW HER
forward. By the time Jane's senses caught up with her body
and she sprang to her feet, Lou had already phased through Cal.
She came up behind him and grabbed his neck.

"You asshole!" Lou shouted, her fingers sinking hard into
flesh. "I want a divorce!"

Cal's only immediate response was a gurgle. Jane started to
lurch forward, but before she could even take a step, Clair had
run up and thrown her arms around her. A wash of relief that
may not have belonged to Jane dumped over her head, the rush of
it leaving her dizzy as she peeled herself back from the embrace.

"I'm fine, I'm fine, I promise," Jane said, landing a fast kiss
on Clair's cheek. She hoped it would carry with it both that she
understood Clair's need to be reassured, and the pressing weight
of time on Jane's shoulders. The quick squeeze of Clair's hand
that met Jane in reply, nudging her on, certainly made it seem

like the kiss had done its job. She would just need to have faith that she was right.

"Uh," Windforce said, pointing to where Lou was whaling on Cal, "should we maybe help?"

"Looks like she's got this," Granite Girl said with a shrug.

It was hard to argue with that assessment. Lou had Cal pinned, his arms wrenched up behind his back so that he couldn't touch anything, couldn't transform anything. Any time he tried to lash out, Lou would phase out of the way. Her fists pummeled him, all of the rage she'd been holding back finally set loose.

"Guys, seriously?" Jane said, tossing the words back over her shoulder. She charged forward, throwing herself into the fight just as Rip-Shift elbowed Windforce.

"At least we're here to *see* this one. Remember the last time the girls took down Cal? We missed the whole thing."

"All right, that's enough!" Jane shouted at Lou. She threw herself at the two of them, wrenching Cal from Lou's grasp.

Cal stumbled back, landing on his ass in the torn-up field. His bloody lips curled into a smirk. "I knew you cared."

"Oh, shut the fuck up," Jane said. She opened her palm, a flash of light straight to Cal's face. In his weakened state, it was enough to knock him out, and he landed hard on the grass, a dead weight that Jane happily let fall from her grip.

Lou shoved herself forward, until she was right in Jane's face.

"Get out of my way, Captain," Lou said. "My fight isn't with you."

"It is, if you're going to continue to commit assault."

"*Assault?* He's the one who—"

"I know. I know, but Louisa, listen to me. This isn't how you do it. Let me take him in. He needs to face justice for what he's done."

Lou gave a strangled laugh. She ran her hands through her loose hair, the careful smoothing long since worn out. "How? You've seen what he can do. No prison can hold him. Even if it could, he'd just sleaze and charm his way out of it. The public loves him. You'll never convince him to stop."

"We can. We're superheroes, and I'm telling you, we'll take care of it. I have a plan."

"Like I'd trust you to handle this."

"You're going to have to," Jane said. She rushed on, "Look, from what I've heard, you're not a *bad* person. Do you really want to have that kind of blood on your hands? Do you really want *Cal* to be the person who made you into a killer?"

Was this going to work? Jane honestly had no idea. It's not like she knew Lou, after all, not really. All she'd ever known of her was what Clair had told her, and what she'd seen for herself—Lou being handled, dragged around like a dog, sicced on Cal's enemies. Jane couldn't say for sure, but their alliance had never looked like it had been born out of respect or loyalty, and now Jane stood, holding her breath, waiting.

"Please," Jane said. "He's not worth it. Now, I'm offering you the chance to leave, peacefully. I suggest you take it."

Lou ground her teeth together, chewing on the possibility. "Fine," she snapped. She raised a finger, pointing so close it nearly grazed Jane's nose. "But mark my words, Captain—if he *ever* comes near me or my brother again . . . I will murder him with my bare hands."

"He won't," Jane said. "I promise. We've got this."

Lou spat at Cal's feet. "You'd better."

And with that, she flipped the hood of her sweatshirt up, turning away.

"Captain . . . ," Rip-Shift said warily, but Jane raised her hand, holding his thought. She waited until Lou had jogged across the grass. Waited until she disappeared, phasing straight through the stadium wall rather than bothering to find a door, before Jane finally whirled back toward the rest of the team.

"Guys, we don't even remotely got this," Jane said, her voice tinged with panic. "What are we going to do?"

A matched set of blank faces met her eye. Granite Girl's was stony in more ways than one, Rip-Shift's presented a perfectly cool slate. Even Windforce, hidden away behind blue spandex and goggles, was silent. Pixie Beats reached up, shifting the glittery masquerade mask as she itched at the skin underneath.

No one said anything. No one wanted to be the first to admit it—that they were out of options, out of ideas. That they were completely screwed. Jane looked at them, her team, and knew in that moment that they had lost. Cal would wake back up, eventually, and then . . . what were they supposed to do with him then?

It was in this pause that Clair cleared her throat. She was standing behind Jane, and her words drifted over Jane's shoulder, a speech bubble slipping in from out of frame.

"I can fix it."

A RIPPLE OF SUSPICION CROSSED THE TORN-UP PLAYING field, sending a shiver down Clair's back.

Jane turned, her masked gaze settling on Clair as if she'd forgotten she was even here. But that was Mindsight's role in the group, wasn't it? Come in when we need you, stay silent when we don't. Amy had gone along with it, had allowed her Jane to boss her around, to diminish her. To ignore her. And look where it had gotten them.

No more.

"What are you talking about?" Jane asked while Granite Girl cut across her with the much more succinct, "How?"

Clair squared her shoulders. Moment of truth. She glanced over, but Amy was nowhere to be found, and so it was Clair alone who stood with her head tall and her back straight, her feet planted wide like the Hero she was. Clair alone who said, "I can wipe part of his memory. He can't continue his plan if he doesn't know he wants to."

She paused, giving the team a second to absorb this. Reactions came fast and strong, pinging at Clair without the courtesy of her physically reaching for them. Shock, apprehension, concern, annoyance. More than a little fear. Clair tried to brush them off, to block them out, but they hung thick in the air like smoke, stinging her eyes.

"Wait, so . . . you can *do* that?" Rip-Shift asked finally, though the question may as well have come from all of them.

"What else haven't you told us?" Granite Girl asked.

Clair shrugged. "I really don't know. This is all new to me, and I'm not even sure if Amy realized the extent of her powers.

But I'm telling you, I can do this. We wipe out parts of his memory, he forgets that he was ever evil. Problem solved."

Jane held up her hands, cutting off the group's budding arguments. "Okay, okay, but . . . it can't be that simple. Cal, he—I mean, this isn't exactly a recent problem."

"I know. I'll have to go deep, probably all the way back to when UltraViolet first started corrupting him. But if I can block that, he should go back to being the person he was before. And he was *decent*, once. Even if he was a bit of an ass, his heart was in the right place. You all know this."

"And when he realizes that he's forgotten the last, what, five years of his life?" Windforce asked. "Then what?"

"We tell him he's suffered memory loss. We were just in an epic battle here, guys. It won't be hard to convince him that he fought alongside us rather than against us. As for the campaign," she continued, already feeling their next objection bubbling to the surface, "we tell him an Enhanced was using his identity to try to dismantle the Heroes. A shapeshifter, or mind-control powers, or whatever, anything will work. The point is, he never has to know."

"He'd still have his powers," Rip-Shift said.

"Technically, yes. And we can either tell him, or not. It's possible that if he doesn't realize he has them, he just . . . won't use them. Much like how we all were, before the Rift."

Rip-Shift tipped his head, Clair's reflection mirrored back to her in his sunglasses. "It's a bit different."

"A bit, yeah. But you'd be surprised how much not knowing what you can do can control you."

The team fell silent. Clair felt each of them turning this over in their minds. Weighing their options. Their opinions were important, yes, but in the end, it wasn't everyone else that Clair had to convince. She fixed her attention squarely where it mattered.

On Jane.

Would she agree to it? It was hard to say, even for Clair. Certainly, Jane would be able to see Clair's point of view on the matter—a good wife always could—but would it be enough to sway her? It was a risky move, to be sure, though no more than handing Cal over to the authorities and hoping they could contain him. Less, probably. Jane had to see that, in the end. If nothing else, Jane had to understand that point.

For a moment, they just stood there, looking at each other. A whole conversation seemed to shift back and forth between them, conveyed in subtle movements and ticks of their faces. *Are you sure you can do this? Is there really no other way? / Yes, I am. You have to know I'm right.*

"He's one of us," Clair said, out loud this time, and now she knew that she'd won. "Regardless of what he's done, at the end of the day, we protect our own."

Finally, Jane sighed. "It . . . could work."

"Wait," Granite Girl said. She stepped forward, into the middle of their impromptu huddle, and held her hand out, as if offering up her objections on a platter. "We're not *actually* considering this, are we? Whatever happened to him facing justice?"

"Lou was right, though," Jane said. "No prison's going to be able to hold him, not if he can manipulate the world into whatever he wants it to be. And we can't exactly keep him knocked out forever. So what does that leave?"

Granite Girl scowled up at her. "What, so because it's complicated, we just . . . let him take the easy way out, instead? How is that fair?"

"Forgetting who you are isn't 'the easy way out,'" Clair snapped. "Trust me, this is a just punishment."

"For him, or for us?" Pixie Beats said. "Look, I'll say it. If we do this, he's gonna need to be watched. We'd be bringing him back into the family. Are we really ready to do that?"

"I think we have to," Jane said, and this time no one argued. Everyone could recognize when the captain had made up her mind. She turned to Clair, her face set. "Do it."

Clair didn't need to be told twice. She crouched in front of Cal. He looked so small, suddenly, his face bruised, his short hair tousled. Like he was nothing more than a sleeping child. A wave of something almost like pity washed over Clair, a chill that made her question—just for a second—what she was about to do to him.

She brushed her bare hand over the top of his head, before she could talk herself out of it. That was all it took.

In an instant, she was surrounded by impressions of him. Everything he'd said, everything he'd done. Everything he'd felt. Clair shut her eyes, and rode out the assault. The first wave was always the hardest, the memories sudden and jumbled and over-whelming. But if she stayed with it, if she calmed her thoughts, if she took a deep breath and let her mind focus . . . she could find what she was looking for.

Sure enough. Clair swept through his memories, snipping out any time where he was *overtly* evil, any time where he managed to silence the better angels of his mind. She scrubbed out the filth of his betrayal, the scheming he'd been up to in the meantime. The anger that burned beneath the surface, charring the edges of his older memories. When she got to UltraViolet, Clair hurried through the process, not wanting to see too much. She ripped patches out with abandon, leaving only the good feelings and impressions behind.

Only time would tell if her efforts were successful, but for now they would have to trust that Clair had managed to do her job. Clair opened her eyes. Pulled her hand away. She sat back on her heels, a fine layer of sweat across her forehead. She looked up at Jane, at the rest of the team. They'd crowded around her as she'd worked, as if there was something to see.

Clair shrugged. "It's done."

The reactions to this were mixed. Some sighed with silent relief. Some looked understandably wary. Granite Girl's face was a mask of solid stone, impossible to read.

Jane shrugged. "Well. I guess . . . I guess we're done, then."

"Wait, that's just—that's *it*?" Windforce asked.

"You wanted something more?"

Windforce pulled his mask off, his brown face flushed from the heat of being trapped beneath spandex. "I don't know. Just . . . Call me paranoid or whatever, but that felt too easy. Like there's something else still coming."

"He's right," Pixie Beats said. "It's never that simple."

"Simple?" Jane said. "Were you guys even in the same battle I was?"

Windforce shook his head. "Look, no offense, Captain, but you haven't been in nearly as many of these situations as we have. I'm telling you, something about this isn't sitting right."

Jane sighed. She opened her mouth, but something cut her off before she could begin. A voice, crashing across the open field.

"You should listen to them, Captain."

Lightning broke the stadium in half and thunder boomed, so loudly it shook the ground. A flash cut across the field, blinding everyone except for Jane—but Clair didn't need to see, to realize what was happening. She'd be able to see Electric Fury anywhere, anytime. The voice that she knew as well as her own trailed like cold fingers down Clair's spine.

"Ugh, so glad I'm finally rid of that idiot," Electric Fury said as she rolled her shoulders. "You know, as much as I hate you, I really should be thanking you. You've made my plan much simpler."

"No, but," Clair said, "but you were working for Cal. I don't—"

Electric Fury scoffed. "Please. He may have been paying me to stir up fear, but I had my own agenda."

Clair shook her head. "No, but that's not . . . that's not possible, I . . . I was your biggest target."

"Oh, you'll still suffer at my hand, trust me," Electric Fury said. "But there are bigger things at stake tonight than just you and me. And now, thanks to your little distraction here, I have everything I need."

Clair frowned. That wasn't right, she knew that wasn't right, but before she could wrap her head around exactly what wasn't right about it, Jane stepped forward, cutting Clair off as she wedged herself between them. "Which is what?"

Electric Fury smiled. "Like I'd tell you. Let's just say, Cal thought he had what it takes to be a supervillain, but really, he had no idea. The city will be mine soon enough." A smirk curled up the edges of her lips. Electric Fury stepped back, spreading her arms as if she'd already won. Her silver catsuit glinted in the faltering light of the stadium. "Goodbye, Mindsight. If you want to finish this . . . you know where to find me."

The first sparks of transformation crossed her skin.

"Oh no you don't!" Jane shouted. She leaped at Electric Fury, a shockwave of determination bursting out of her and pummeling across the field. It struck Clair with the taste of sweat. There was no way Jane was letting her go, not after all this, but—

Electric Fury was already collapsing, her body breaking down to electrical currents. And if Jane was touching her when she disappeared, she'd be dragged off right along with her.

Clair lunged, reaching forward. "*Jane!*"

It didn't matter. Clair's fingers closed on nothing but the faint crackle of disappearing electricity, raising the hairs all up the back of Clair's arm . . . and both Jane and Electric Fury were gone. Clair's head swam, her stomach roiled. "No . . . no, no, please," she whispered, but there was nothing to be done. She turned in place, as if somehow it was that simple, that she'd just misplaced them. But the field was empty, nothing but the shocked faces of her teammates reflecting back at her, and the whisper of Electric Fury's final taunt, twisting through Clair's mind. Her hands clenched tight, remembering.

You know where to find me.

THE NIGHT THE HEROES OF HOPE CAPTURED THE RUINATOR, THEY CELEBRATED IN STYLE.

Champagne popped in the command room. They were forgoing their usual victory drink on the rooftop—tonight, they wanted to really let loose, and it wouldn't do to celebrate in public. After all, they'd just captured a Big Bad who'd been eluding them for the better part of a year, always slipping through their fingers at the last second. Who'd caused millions in property damage, who'd threatened the lives of everyone inside of Grand City more than once. It had taken the entirety of the Heroes' resources, and more than one favor from an old friend, but in the end . . . they'd done it. The Ruinator sat in custody in the Vault below their headquarters, awaiting transfer to a supermax prison in the morning.

The battle had been epic. The Ruinator had been setting up his fermion oscillator in an empty tent at Grand City's annual summer carnival. The Heroes got an anonymous tip, someone working on the fairgrounds who'd spotted something odd going on. When they arrived, it was just in time—the Ruinator was about to take to the airwaves, the fermion oscillator primed and ready at his back. But then the Ruinator's henchbots swarmed in just as the Heroes did, as if they'd been waiting for this moment. Buzzing, annoying little machines, half chainsaw and half drone. Neither Captain Lumen's wifi powers nor Granite Girl's hacking skills had ever been enough to take them down. The fight spilled out across the fairgrounds, straight down to the wharf. The Ruinator's powers came from a talisman that gave him connections to the natural elements, and the water of the harbor had swept up, a towering wall that threatened to wipe out several city blocks.

Still, finally, they'd done it. With the clock down to the wire, with the air full of rain and wind and the hiss and spark of whizzing buzzsaws crashing into each other, they'd managed to wrestle the talisman away from him, and to slap a pair of cuffs on his wrists.

Now it was time to revel in their hard-won victory.

Even Jane was in a good mood. She'd taken off her jacket, but left the body armor on over her tank top. Tight laces ran up and down her sides, and Jane kept tracing them with her finger as she danced, her hips swishing in time to the music. Once, she'd even turned to Amy, their eyes locking across the crowd of the command room. Jane's cheeks were flushed, sweat glittering on her skin. She'd reached out, hooking her finger as she beckoned Amy toward her.

Amy looked away. She pushed herself to her feet so fast that her chair spun empty in her wake.

In the hall the lights were brighter, the air cooler. Amy plunged in, letting the shock of it slap some of the heat from her cheeks. She turned to go, nearly slamming into a small figure huddled beside the door.

Marie. She'd slipped from the party early; Amy had seen her tinkering with her smartwatch, her brow constricted, and then the next time she'd gone to look, Marie was nowhere to be seen. Now here she was, leaning against a wall in the corridor outside, nose buried in the glow of a tablet screen.

The taste in Amy's mouth soured. She took a drink from the champagne glass that she'd carried out with her.

"I thought you loved parties," Amy said. She jerked her head back toward the door, the pounding of the music audible even out here. Then, just out of spite, she added, "Tony seems to be enjoying himself."

Marie looked up from her tablet, her eyes narrowing in on Amy. "What are you implying?"

Amy shrugged. "Nothing." She frowned toward the tablet in Marie's hands. "What are you doing, anyway?"

Marie didn't answer at first. She studied Amy, probably trying to decide if she was willing to let the Tony thing drop. In truth, it was more a hunch than anything to do with Amy's powers, but it was good to know that her instincts were still sharp. Amy took another drink, trying to play it off as unintentional. Casual. Nothing to see here.

Maybe it worked. Or maybe Marie just didn't care enough. Either way.

"Doesn't this victory strike you as a little convenient?" Marie said finally.

Amy's laugh clapped through the hall. "You call that convenient? Did you forget how many henchbots we were up against back there?"

"Of course not. But there were so many things that could have gone wrong. We could have gotten there too late, we might not have been able to steal his talisman, his henchbots could have already—"

"Okay, I get it," Amy said. She shook her head. "That doesn't prove anything. Sometimes we get lucky. You shouldn't question every victory, Marie. It'll make you paranoid."

"I'm not questioning *every* victory. I'm questioning *this* victory. If it even is a victory."

Irritation bristled across Amy's skin like champagne bubbles. She couldn't even quite say why, but she *needed* Marie to let this go. "Why would you even think that? The Ruinator is locked up—his fermion oscillator is dismantled. There's nothing left to question."

"I've had the computer running an analysis on the axion core ever since we got back," Marie said, ignoring this. "There's something *off* about it—I can feel it."

"If something was wrong, Jane would have picked up on it," Amy said, her tone snipped. "She's the one who can tap into wifi signals, remember?"

Marie waved this off. "There's a big difference between being physically connected to technology and *understanding* technology."

"Now you're just being elitist."

"Call it what you will." Marie held her tablet up. "We'll know soon enough."

Amy gave an exaggerated sigh, like she was humoring Marie just by having this conversation.

The problem was . . . as hard as Amy was fighting to dismiss it, a bigger voice inside of her was telling her Marie was right. Hadn't Amy felt it, the whole time the team was out there? Hadn't she been primed, looking for Electric Fury during every moment of the battle, waiting for the moment when she'd sweep in and join her boss? Amy had seen for herself, as Electric Fury got ready to leave that morning. She'd let her go.

A tingle of electricity ran up Amy's spine. *Face it, Mindsight. You fell in love with a supervillain.*

That's when it hit her. She had been so caught up in the word "love" that she hadn't stopped to consider the rest of the sentence. Not *henchman*, or *goon*, or even plain-old *villain*. Because that's not what Electric Fury *was*. Her allegiance to the Ruinator had never been that of a stooge to her boss. It was a *partnership*. They had never intended the Ruinator's attempt to succeed. He was merely the distraction—and the Heroes had fallen for it.

Amy had fallen for it.

Marie's tablet chimed, jerking Amy out of her thoughts. The buttery-smooth voice of the headquarters's computer system purred from the speaker. *"Analysis complete."*

Amy knew what the results were before Marie even spoke.

"Holy shit," Marie breathed. "It's . . . it's a fake."

"What?"

The confusion was more for Marie's benefit than anything else. A flair for theatrics that Amy had developed after several months of slinking around behind the rest of the Heroes' backs.

"The Ruinator was never building the real fermion oscillator. I don't know how, but . . . there's got to be another one somewhere. We need to get the others," Marie said. "Shit, I hope they're not too drunk."

"No!" Amy reached out, stopping herself just short of grabbing Marie's shoulder. The Heroes' code, that they would never use their powers against each other, seized Amy's arm midreach. She clenched her fingers shut, instead, holding herself back. "That is . . . What proof do we really have?"

"You mean *besides* a fake axion core?"

Amy's nails dug into the palms of her leather gloves. "Right. Which . . . let's be honest, do any of us really understand the technology? Maybe you're just misreading the—"

"What is your problem?" Marie stepped back, eying Amy's hand as if wary of her touch.

Heat rushed to Amy's cheeks. "I don't know what you're talking about."

"Yes, you do. You don't want us to go after the truth. In fact, this whole time . . . you've been trying to hold the investigation back, haven't you? What are you hiding, Amy? Are you working for them?"

A nervous laugh escaped Amy's chest. "Don't be ridiculous," she said, but Marie's face didn't change. Amy's stomach soured. "Marie. Honestly. It's *me*."

"You say that like it's supposed to mean something."

Amy took a step back, as if she'd been slapped. The glass shook in her hand. "Whatever happened to team loyalty?"

"I could ask you the same thing," Marie said. "I've been trying to ignore it, trying to give you the benefit of the doubt, I swear I have, but you've been acting weird for *months*, and even before that . . ."

Amy paused, waiting. For the first time, she was genuinely curious. The time during Electric Fury's influence, Amy could understand, but what else did Marie think she picked up on? What more did she suspect?

"Go on," Amy said. "Before that?"

"I don't know," Marie said. "But sometimes, I wonder if we really know you at all."

Silence fell between them. Amy opened her mouth, a rebuttal at the ready, but none of the words made it out of her throat. She closed it again, her face twisting into a frown.

"I'm going to get the others," Marie said. Was it just Amy's imagination, or was her voice a dare?

She started to step forward.

Anger surged through Amy's veins. It tasted almost electrical, a familiar tingle on her tongue. "No, wait!" She lurched forward again. Stopped herself short, again. Always, that wall between her and the rest of the people in her life. Even those she was closest to—especially those she was closest to.

Everyone but Electric Fury, that is.

All at once, Amy knew what she had to do.

"You're right," Amy said. "You really *don't* know me at all."

She lunged. Her fingers closed the gap around Marie's wrist—closing a circuit. It was the easiest thing in the world, as if her powers were always meant to do this. She did not need to ask. Already, Marie's recent memories were opening themselves up to her. Amy rifled through them, like flicking through a filing cabinet, and just as easily, she found the ones she was looking for. Marie's suspicions. The way she'd noted Amy's hesitation, her unexplained absences from team meetings. The moment Marie first held the axion core in her hand for herself, the subtle sense of *wrong* that had come out of the device with it. Running her analysis, leaving the party. This conversation. Amy found them all, plucking them free and setting them in the trash.

Marie's eyes were locked on to Amy's. Something like fear sparked in the depths. "Amy . . . what . . . ?"

"Relax, it's fine," Amy whispered to her. Her words slipped, simultaneously, into Marie's ears and her mind. "You've just had too much to drink, that's all."

Marie fell asleep with nothing more than a whimper. A child up past her bedtime, she collapsed into Amy's waiting arms. She was so small, it was easy to catch her. To settle her against the wall, to dishevel her blond hair. Amy plucked the tablet from her grip, and replaced it with her own champagne glass, settling it angled in Marie's lap. She dipped her fingers in the remaining drink, splashing the smell of it across Marie's shirt.

Amy straightened up. She looked up, over her shoulder. A security camera stared back at her, its black eye wide and accusing. "You'll be the first to go," she whispered. She raised the tablet, still saturated with Marie's technical expertise. She pulled up the footage, watching herself stride away. The screen winked black. By the time the elevator arrived, she'd already gotten through about half the files she needed to either delete or modify. As far as the rest of the Heroes would ever know, their victory over the Ruinator was a true success. All that was left was to handle Electric Fury, and that was something Amy would take care of herself.

She already knew where to find her.

"FURY! I'M HERE!"

Clair's voice echoed through the open level of the parking garage. The place was completely deserted. Darkness stretched out, seemingly endless, around her. Only a string of emergency lights in the ceiling, and the meager contribution of her phone's flashlight, provided any sort of context to the pillars and speed bumps. Clair swept the beam across the vastness.

"You might as well come out! I know you're here somewhere!"

The scuff of a shoe made Clair turn. A figure slipped from the shadows, but not the one Clair had wanted.

"We shouldn't be here," Amy said as she came up to stand beside Clair.

"Tough," Clair said. She took another breath. "Fury!"

At first, nothing but silence. Clair's heart thundered in her chest. Dammit, if she wasn't actually here, if Clair had been wrong—

But then, with a crack to split the night in half, Electric Fury zapped into form. Clair flinched, shielding her eyes until the flash had passed. When she lowered it, there she was, exactly on schedule. Lightning sparked and danced across Electric Fury's silver catsuit, as she stretched her newly re-formed muscles, cracked her joints. Her grin lit the darkness of the parking garage, flashing electric in the night.

"So you found me," she said. "Still want to claim ignorance about your past?"

Before Clair could answer, Electric Fury snapped her fingers.

Lightning jumped from the point of contact, flickering a lamp to life. A pool of light spilled down from above. A bright, futuristic device of some sort towered behind Electric Fury, humming and crackling with energy. It seemed to have been constructed here: heavy bolts mounted it to the floor, and spokes drilled into the ceiling far above. Wires hung in a complicated net above it, feeding liquid into the main chamber of the device, which bubbled and spat as angrily as Electric Fury's glower. Clair could only stare, uncertain.

"It took a while to rebuild, but I managed," Electric Fury said. She ran her finger across the glass. "If you don't want to admit to recognizing it, let me jog your memory. This is the fermion oscillator the Ruinator and I were building. The one your team *thought* it had secured—what they didn't know is that I had been crafting the real one in secret. Remember, Mindsight? Only you figured out the one your team dismantled wasn't real. Imagine that. All those supposed geniuses, and you were the only one to see through it."

Clair remembered. The sick lurch as she realized what was missing, what it meant. The deep-seated understanding that it was up to her, and her alone, to put things right. Never mind that Electric Fury's assessment of events wasn't entirely true— Clair was not here to correct her misconceptions.

"Do you remember what happened next?"

"Don't answer that," Amy said, but an impression was already rushing at Clair. Vague and fuzzy at this point, but there. Clair frowned.

"I . . . I tracked you down."

"That's right! *You.* Without the help of any kind of tech, any scan. You intuited it. Your powers led you straight to me. Straight here, in fact. Level 5."

A flash of memory pierced Clair's mind: Electric Fury, lightning throwing harsh shadows across her anguished face. Clair clutched her head, as pain shot from temple to temple.

"Clair? Clair!" Amy's hands found her shoulders. "Clair, listen to me. You can't remember this. She's trying to trick you, but you can't let her. You have to stop. If you keep this up, it's going to kill you."

"Why?"

Amy sighed in frustration. "I can't tell you that. Just *trust* me for once, all right? Please. Your life depends on it."

"'Why'?" Electric Fury repeated, clearly thinking the question had been for her. She snorted. "To stop me, of course. As if that would do any good. But you never could give up your white-knight complex, could you, Amy? Oh, no. All that Hero training, all that pathetic do-goodery. That was always going to matter the most to you. Wasn't it?"

"Don't listen to her," Amy said. "She's trying to distract you."

"But that was then," Electric Fury continued. "It might not be what matters now."

She stepped aside.

Clair's heart lurched up into her mouth. There was Jane—unconscious, slumped against the side of the fermion oscillator. At least she did not appear hurt, that was one small consolation prize. Still. There was a lot of space between them, and who knew how complicated it would be to get past Electric Fury to reach her?

As if sensing this thought, Electric Fury made sure to move closer to Jane's huddled form.

"I admit, I planned to have *you* be the one to ultimately throw the switch," Electric Fury said. "But then this brash little superhero threw herself into my path, and—well, who am I to turn down such a lovely present?"

A bitter laugh broke out of Clair. "You can't honestly believe she's going to go along with your plan."

"Oh, I think you'll find that people are willing to do just about anything," Electric Fury said as she rested her hand on Jane's back. "All you really need, is to give them the right . . . push."

It started with a spark. Then a surge of electricity, tendrils lashing out to ensnare Jane's body. It jolted her upright, her head snapping to attention, her eyes popping open. Energy crackled across Jane's skin, her uniform. It danced circles around the balls of her eyes, staring hollow and unseeing through the sparks. Electric Fury's energy, powering Jane's movements, as she made her stand. Made her rest her hand on the side of the oscillator.

"Jane!" Clair was running before she realized she was running.

Electric Fury's free hand snapped up, index finger popping. *Stop. Naughty, naughty.* An electrical spark flared brightly at the tip as she tick-tocked it back and forth. "No, no. Make a move, and I swear I'll fry her heart."

Clair skidded to a halt, her heart lurching into her throat. Her skin crawled, as if she was the one being jerked around like a puppet. Her hands balled into fists. "You bitch! Let her go!"

Electric Fury laughed. "Now where would be the fun in *that*? Honestly. It's like you're not even trying."

Clair stormed in a circle. She raked her hand through her hair, practically tearing it out in her haste. "Goddammit, Fury!" she said as she rounded back to face her. "You have a problem with me, fine—take me on! I'll fight you anytime, anywhere. Kill me, if you really want to. But she's innocent in all of this. You have to see that!"

"All *I* see is a woman who's unwilling to accept the consequences of her own choices," Electric Fury snapped. "You did this, Amy. Not me. Do you understand? Not. Me. *You're* the one who couldn't leave well enough alone. *You're* the one who had to track me down, to interfere where you weren't needed. *You're* the one who's so blinded by loyalty to your so-called Heroes that you were willing to cross any line, just to follow their dogma."

"Don't listen to her," Amy repeated. The same tired mantra. *Don't ask questions, don't listen, don't try to understand.* Clair turned, just long enough to cut a sharp glare in her direction. Couldn't she tell how tired Clair was of hearing that? How much she bristled against the ignorance, the darkness nestled inside her? She needed to shine a light in, see what was going on in there.

Or maybe Amy *could* see.

Maybe that's what she was afraid of.

"Well," Electric Fury said, drawing Clair's attention back. "I guess now we're going to find out just how committed to your principles you really are."

With that, Electric Fury turned. She plucked something from the side of the fermion oscillator, and threw it over. It landed with a clatter by Clair's feet.

"Pick it up," Electric Fury said.

"Don't pick it up," Amy said. "Don't play this game with her."

"Like I'm going to listen to you," Clair muttered.

She picked it up before Amy could stop her.

Clair turned it over in her hands.

"You know what it is," Electric Fury said.

Clair frowned. She *did* . . . and she didn't. A small device, with a dial on top, two prongs coming out the end. Clair couldn't even begin to understand the significance of it, though she knew it was significant. Her senses told her nothing, though, the metal oddly dead in her hands.

Amy rounded in front of Clair. Planted herself straight between her and Electric Fury. "Clair. For fuck's sake, for once in your life, *listen to me*. You need to walk away from this. There is no version of this that ends well for you, do you understand? *None.*"

Clair shook her head. "I don't . . . I don't know. I can't just—"

"Did you ever think about me, at all?" Electric Fury asked. "After what you did? Did you even *care*?"

Clair opened her mouth, but it was Amy who spoke. Amy who turned, her face twisting in anguish as she looked backward over her shoulder.

"Of course I cared," Amy said.

"Then how could you do it?" Electric Fury said. "How could you—"

"*No!*"

Amy rushed at Clair.

It's cliché to say an experience was like being hit by a truck, but in Clair's case, she'd actually picked up that sensation once, from accidentally brushing against Marie after a particularly difficult mission with the team. So she knew what it felt like: the jar and crunch of metal against something so solid, the force as it knocked you clear off your feet. The odd peace as you hang suspended in the air for a moment, shock and trauma freezing time until your brain caught up with the reality of what was happening. The impact, a split second later, as everything suddenly sped up again, faster than before.

Clair could only lay there for a moment. The world had grown quiet and fuzzy around her, her chest burning while she struggled to grab hold of the present. She dragged herself onto her hands and knees, her muscles buckling as she tried to catch herself.

"I didn't want it to come to this," Amy said. She was a short distance away, prowling a tight line back and forth. But it wasn't *her* that really drew Clair's attention, so much as what she was protecting.

Clair had seen a lot of weird shit in her day. Even without Amy's memories of being Mindsight, her time with the Heroes had already been full of enough strange sights that she thought she was numb to it. But nothing prepared her for this: the image of herself, again, frozen in the moment Amy had struck her. Standing there, the weird little device in her hands. Everything about the moment was preserved. The slight parting of Clair's lips, the swing of her bob as she raised her head. The frozen shine of electricity, still running down Electric Fury's arm and twisting like pythons around Jane's body.

Weirder still: ribbons of memory floated through the room, swirling between Clair and Amy, between Amy and the frozen version of Clair, threading the three of them together as it twisted and shimmered. Clair saw snatches of her childhood flash by, then high school, then college, then their lives as adults. Two versions of it all, one Amy's and one her own. They were mixed up together, shifting back and forth until it was impossible to tell where one ended and the other began.

It didn't make sense. None of it. Mindsight's powers had nothing to do with time, and so . . . what? Was this even real?

Clair looked down, quickly assessing—yup, she still appeared whole, two arms, two legs, and clearly she was solid enough that she could slowly push herself to her shaky feet. She didn't want to make any sudden movements. The look in Amy's eyes was downright *feral*.

"Amy . . . what did you *do*?"

Though even as Clair asked it, a sense of understanding began to settle in her. Her heart ached, or no—her chest, just between the ribs. The space where a flare came from. Clair pressed her fingers to the bone, trying to hold on.

Amy's lips curled back in distaste. "What I had to. I tried to be kind to you, Clair. I *wanted* it to work out, with you keeping control of my body. I've enjoyed being you. But that isn't going to work if you continue to pursue this. I'll take my body back before I let that happen."

"Let *what* happen? Amy, what are you trying to keep from me? What did we do to her?"

"I can't *tell* you, you idiot!"

For a second, the memories flashed brighter at the outburst. Some skipped forward, others back. Clair's chest ached harder, as if her soul was being siphoned out—and, hell, maybe it was. She didn't know how this was supposed to work.

All she knew was she couldn't let it.

There—in the corner of the room, a glimmer of silver. Electric Fury's catsuit, half remembered.

Clair ran for it. The ache in her chest burned hot, threatening to rip her apart, but she didn't care. If she did nothing, she was dead anyway.

"What are you *doing*?" Amy shouted.

Clair didn't answer. She ran at the memory, leaping the last several feet. Amy scrambled after her, her fingers brushing Clair's ankles and Clair toppled forward.

She landed on smooth concrete.

They both did.

Amy was the first to her feet. "No!" she shouted. She looked around, panic skittering in her eyes. "No, you can't be here! Get out of here!"

"No." Clair pushed herself up to her elbows. "I won't."

At first, it was hard to even tell that anything had changed. The parking garage stretched out around them, the same as it had a few moments ago. The same buzzing lights flickered overhead, the same empty rows stretched out in all directions. The same painted letters on the wall behind the same fermion oscillator, *Level 5* stamped in fading white. Only in this version, Jane was gone. In this version, Electric Fury's voice cut across the open floor of the parking garage, as cold as the night.

"I wondered when you would show up."

Clair whirled, her heart in her throat. Electric Fury stood several yards away. Clair opened her mouth, but it wasn't her, or even Amy, that Electric Fury was talking to.

The memory of Mindsight stepped out of the shadows.

She was dressed in full uniform. Her hat low over her eyes, the edges of her coat shifting as she approached. Deep maroon gloves, full-fingered this time, raised in supplication before her, like taming a tiger. Standing there now, at the height of her status as a Hero, it was impossible to think of her as anything else but Mindsight. Here, in this stolen moment from the past, she was not even Amy. And maybe Amy saw that, too, because she stilled beside Clair, as if snared by the sight of her former self.

"Last warning," Mindsight said, and even her voice sounded the part. Gone was the usual reserve, the tiniest hesitation she normally wore like a second skin as she waited for Captain Lumen to tell her what to do. Mindsight shook her head. "Don't do this."

Electric Fury sighed. "Look, we both know you're not going to hurt me, so let's stop pretending, all right? Face it, Mindsight. I've *won*."

It was certainly hard to argue with that assessment. The fermion oscillator was nearly complete; even as they stood there, it began to purr to life. Sparks snapped from it like angry snakes, lashing out at anyone who dared step too close. The liquid in the center had reached a full boil, blue bubbles raging furiously inside the glass enclosure. And Electric Fury . . . Electric Fury kept her hand on it, feeding energy into the system as innocently as a battery.

Except there was nothing innocent about this situation. Clair felt the urgency here. Whether from context, or instinct, or a trace of memory rising up to the surface, it didn't matter. Electric Fury was about to do something terrible.

Amy's hand gripped Clair's elbow, pinching down hard. "Clair. Listen to me. Get us out of here."

"Please don't do this, Effie," Mindsight said, drawing Clair's attention. "The Ruinator is locked up. They've taken away his talisman—he's got nothing left anymore. You don't owe him anything."

Electric Fury scoffed. "And *again*, you think this is about a man! What kind of lesbian are you? Did it really never occur to you that maybe I *want* to carry out his vision? That maybe I helped build this in the first place because I believed in it? In what we were doing together?"

"Innocent people are going to die!"

"Nobody's innocent," Electric Fury spat. "Not really."

"Clair!" Amy said. "We need to go *now*."

The tug on her arm became stronger, insistent—and yet, the strength of it was hindered, somehow, by the nature of this place. Clair shook her off. She stepped forward, backward into her own past. Amy's past. For once, it felt one and the same. All three versions of them—Clair, Amy, Mindsight—were linked in a way Clair couldn't explain, but felt deep in the recesses of her heart.

Mindsight raced forward, but a burst of electricity sparked across the ground in front of her. It billowed out from Electric Fury, sweeping and protective, and Mindsight was toppled back, landing in a slide on her butt. The fermion oscillator whirred, whining, beside Electric Fury. Almost at critical. It didn't take a genius to work out what would happen next.

"You can't stop me, Mindsight. You can't even touch me."

"Effie, *please*!" Mindsight shouted. She scrambled back to her feet. "You've got to stop! I can't let you do this!"

"You don't have a choice."

Mindsight whirled. Her attention flew around the parking lot, straight over and through Clair and Amy. Desperation crackled off her, an energy all its own. "There's always another way," she whispered as she spotted something and raced past Clair.

A toolbox lay off to the side, probably left there by Electric

Fury's own hasty assembly of the fermion oscillator. Spare parts littered the inside, wiring and cables, plugs and sockets . . . and a weird little device, two prongs out the front, buried underneath a pile of circuit boards.

Clair recognized it with a jolt. The same device Electric Fury had tossed to her, just before Amy had attacked, just before they'd stepped into this moment of the past. Clair looked down, shocked to find she was still holding it.

Mindsight raced back. She stood in front of Electric Fury, as close as she could get without being zapped. "Stand down."

Electric Fury's laugh arced across the parking garage. "That won't help you."

"Don't be so sure." Mindsight cranked the dial on the device up to the very top, until the air around her hand seemed to buzz, until even the hairs on Clair's own arm were raising in response. "If I'm not mistaken, this thing's been supercharged by the same force that went into the axion core. One jolt from this," Mindsight said, raising it in Electric Fury's direction, "and the whole system shorts out. No more threat."

"One jolt from that," Electric Fury said, "and you'd overload more than just the fermion oscillator. I'd die."

Mindsight nodded. She held the device steady. Straight for Electric Fury's heart. "Like I said. No more threat."

Electric Fury's lips curled into a smirk. "You'd never."

"You sure about that?"

"I am," Electric Fury snapped, though her voice was tainted with more anger than certainty. "You couldn't hurt me. You wouldn't."

"To save the people of this city? Hell yes, I would."

Clair sucked in a breath. She didn't know if it was her connection to Amy, or Mindsight, or both, or just the tension saturating the air, but she could feel the choice in front of all of them, the weight of it as it teetered on the edge of a tipping point.

Amy's hand found Clair's sleeve. "Clair," she whispered. Clair didn't look back, couldn't tear herself away. Amy's voice slipped into her ear, pawing at her, begging. "Stop. Take us out of here. Please, please, don't make me do this, I don't want to watch this again, I can't, I—"

Electric Fury narrowed her eyes. "Do it, then." She lunged for the final switch.

The weight fell over. The choice collapsed, and there was only one path forward.

Mindsight activated the device.

Lightning reflected in Clair's widening eyes, sharper than any other bolt that had coursed through the evening. The crash as it struck its mark was almost loud enough to cover up the wail that raised the hairs on the back of Clair's arms.

It didn't take long.

Barely an instant.

A flash and jolt of fury swept across the three versions of them, sizzling through the air, raising the hairs on their arms. A scream, boring into Clair's soul as it dissolved into nothing. Air burst outward, hot and bitter. Haze stung Clair's eyes, the metallic smell of electrical fire and burnt flesh. It coated the inside of her mouth, until it felt like she would gag.

A strangled scream burst out of Amy, so high-pitched it was almost silent. Clair watched her fall to her knees, then her hands, then vomit straight onto the smooth floor. It was an understandable reaction, one Clair felt in her own bones.

But Mindsight . . .

Mindsight wasn't moving. The device was still clutched in her grip—her chest heaving, but her face dry. Stoic. Scorch marks stained the concrete where Electric Fury had been a moment ago, and Mindsight just stared at them, just . . . stood there.

Her fingers jerked. The device clattered down by her feet.

A low moan made Clair turn around. Amy, crumpled in a heap on the ground. Her head was twisted around just enough to stare with deadened eyes, tracking as Mindsight began to disassemble the fermion oscillator in silence.

"I killed her," Amy mumbled, her lips kissing the cold concrete as she spoke. "Oh my god, Clair. I loved her, and I . . . I killed her."

"Oh, Amy," Clair said. "No. You didn't. She survived. You know she survived."

She went to reach out to her, but Amy scrambled back, clawing at the floor. Her laugh was manic.

"Don't you get it at all? It doesn't *matter* if she survived. *I* pulled that trigger! *I* made that choice! I thought she was dead, and no matter what really happened afterward, *I chose that*. I made that happen!" She turned to look at Clair, her face falling slack. "I'm a fraud. All this talk about being noble, about taking the higher road. We made a vow, Clair, way back. A promise. The Heroes don't kill. I broke that. And I thought . . . I thought, if I let you take over, I could escape it. I could be reborn, pure, and it would be like it never happened. That I'd have a second chance. To be better. But now it's ruined."

"How do you figure that?"

Amy frowned. "You *know*. You're tainted."

"Is *that* what you've been doing? Trying to protect me?"

"You can't be a Hero, knowing what you've done," Amy said, deadly grave. "Believe me, I tried. I tried so hard. For a while, when your Jane showed up, I thought . . ." She frowned. "But it wasn't enough. You'll never be able to live with it."

"Hey, now. Don't go writing me off before I've even had the chance."

Amy shook her head. "It doesn't matter. You don't know what it was like. I—"

"Made a horrible choice. One none of us would have handled well. You chose to save the city, not just over the woman you loved, but over the purity of your own soul."

"Don't you dare try to make this sound noble."

"I'm not," Clair said. "What you did was wrong, regardless of why. But listen to me. Amy: I know you think I'm 'tainted' now, but I'm telling you, *I* didn't do that. Now, if you want to take your body back, I'm . . . I'm not going to stop you. You can have it. But don't insult me by pretending like I can't handle this knowledge. I'm stronger than that. I can live with this."

"You'll never be the same."

Clair nodded. "I know. Believe me, I know. This is a lot. I'm not going to pretend like I'll wake up tomorrow and magically be okay with everything. It's going to take time to adjust to this knowledge, but I'm going to manage. I'm going to survive. Because I have something you never did."

"What's that?"

A soft smile tugged at Clair's lips. "I have Jane."

Amy shut her eyes. For a moment, it looked like Clair had given her what she'd needed, the promise of some kind of peace from the guilt of what she'd done. But then, like flicking a switch, her eyes snapped open in horror. "Shit," Amy said, grabbing Clair's sleeve. "Not for long, you don't!"

"GO ON, THEN," ELECTRIC FURY SAID AS CLAIR SLIPPED back into her own skin. "Make your choice!"

Clair blinked. For a second, the world settled oddly around her, disparate pieces that didn't seem to make sense. For a second, they didn't seem to have left the memory at all. There was the fermion oscillator, bubbling and crackling furiously, near critical. There was Electric Fury, feeding energy into its system.

And there was Jane. Standing right in line, controlled like a puppet, linked between Electric Fury and the fermion oscillator.

With a lurch that made her want to vomit, Clair understood what Electric Fury was doing. Jane or the city. With the super-charged device in her hand, she could stop Electric Fury from using Jane to trigger the oscillator, but not without destroying all of them. Mindsight—Amy—had made her choice last time, and look what it had done to her. Clair felt the presence of her, still hovering behind her shoulder. Watching. True, Amy's actions had saved thousands of lives, but at what cost? And if the Heroes truly don't kill, then what did it say about her if she chose to destroy Jane to save them? But what did it say if she allowed so many innocents to die instead? *There's always another way*, that was their motto, but was there, really? Always? It didn't seem like there had been, for Amy.

Clair looked across. Jane's eyes still sparked with the bolts of Electric Fury's energy, but somewhere in there, deep down past that, she could swear she found a hint of Jane. Watching her. Waiting. What would Jane have wanted?

It didn't matter, because how could Clair even consider it? There was no choice.

A hand rested flat across the top of Clair's shoulder. Comforting. Absolving.

"It's okay," Amy whispered. "You don't have to do this."

Clair reached up, placing her hand across Amy's. She gave a gentle squeeze. "I know."

The device clattered to the ground by their feet. Amy shut her eyes.

Electric Fury sighed. "Well, that's disappointing."

"Don't be," Clair said. "We're not finished." She tapped her earpiece. "Now."

Amy's eyes snapped back open. "What the—?" she started, but the answer arrived without words.

The howl of wind swept past their ears. A gleaming silver tear split the parking garage. The fermion oscillator sparked and spat, choking on itself, as the vibrant colors of Pixie Beats bloomed in midair, caught in a backflip. She landed with a fistful of wires, tossing them across just as a figure charged through the open gap of Rip-Shift's tear. Granite Girl, her stony arms protected inside a black rubberized suit, carried a lightning-rod device attached to a Ghostbusters-style backpack tank. She screamed as she plunged toward Electric Fury, lightning crackling and sparking all around them. The lightning rod collector had been modified since the last time they'd taken it out, so as not to hurt Jane, though this would be the first time they'd had a chance to test it. Clair would just need to have faith it would work.

Amy leaped back, boggling at the sight of it all.

Did she get it, now? Amy's mistake wasn't in making her choice. It was a horrible choice, impossible to make correctly. No, where Amy had failed was in isolating herself from the people around her in the first place. In thinking she didn't need anyone else, that she could go it alone. Amy had taken Jane's rejection and walled off her heart, and even the feelings she'd begun to have for Electric Fury were too little, too late.

What was the point of having powers, without love? What was the point in being a Hero, without trust? It was right there in the name: they were the Heroes of Hope—hope for the world, hope for humanity, hope for a better tomorrow. Hope for themselves.

They were never meant to face their threats alone.

Clair raced forward, joining her team. Rip-Shift dropped a pair of thick gloves through a tear above her, and Clair snatched them without even stopping. She slid them on as she caught Jane's collapsing form. Stray sparks trailed from Jane's hair as Clair brushed it away from her face, met Clair's lips as she kissed Jane's forehead. Pinpricks of Electric Fury's bitterness dissolved underneath the reassuring presence of Jane's consciousness, rising back to the surface. Clair swept her out of the way, even as the rest of the team tightened in on Electric Fury and the fermion oscillator. Lightning bristled past her, narrowly avoiding Clair's shoulder, close enough to raise hairs all over her body.

"You *bitch!*" Electric Fury screamed, and Clair whirled around.

The Heroes had her restrained, the last of her lightning sparking out around her. She tugged hard, but Granite Girl's grip was harder. Still, even with her powers sapped, her eyes were fire and rage, a thousand lightning bolts ready to strike.

Clair stood up, moving slowly over to her. "I'm sorry."

"I don't want your *apologies*," Electric Fury said. "I swear to god, Mindsight, I'm going to break free, and when I do—"

"I know." Clair shrugged. "You do what you need to do. And . . . I'll do what I need to do."

She reached out, her fingers resting against Electric Fury's temple.

Electric Fury flinched back, but Clair was not dissuaded.

"It's okay," she whispered, and then she shut her eyes. And she dug down deep.

Ever since she'd come back, there had been so many parts of Amy's past that were clouded from her. Hidden in the dark corners, tucked out of sight. So many things Amy had tried to keep hidden, tried to shield Clair from. But the time for that was over. *No more secrets,* Clair thought as she took a deep breath. As she plunged, headfirst, into the shadows.

That's where she found them. Every memory of Electric Fury, every good feeling, every afternoon Amy had spent daydreaming about her, every time she'd been caught smiling and staring off into space. Every night she'd laid there and watched Electric Fury sleep, every thrill that had coursed through her when she appeared. Every heartache when they parted. The anguish as she realized how things were about to unfold, just before they did. The terror at facing her in the parking garage. The sleepless nights spent running from her nightmares, after. The hollowness. The need with which she gave her life over to Clair, the desperate desire to free herself.

Clair reached in, gently scooping all of it into her arms. She cradled the experience like a newborn baby, and gently, so gently . . . she passed it over.

When she opened her eyes, Electric Fury was staring at her. So still, and so silent, that she may as well have been frozen in place. She didn't even breathe, not at first, as she processed this sudden influx of experiences.

"I hope this helps," Clair whispered, and then she backed away. Just one step, just enough to distance herself. She nodded at the rest of the team.

Electric Fury was still staring at her, even as the Heroes slapped cuffs on her. Even as they started to turn her away, to lead her off to her new containment cell. Clair watched her go, the glint of Electric Fury's silver catsuit winking off into the darkness.

"Clair?"

Clair spun around. Jane was just beginning to sit up, blinking in confusion.

"Jane!" Clair raced over, dropping to her knees as she slid the last few feet into Jane's embrace. She wrapped her tightly in her arms, buried her nose into the crook of Jane's neck, drowned herself in the smell of Jane's hair and the feel of Jane's arms and the surprise, then delight, then peace that settled over Jane as she relaxed into Clair.

"I'm sorry," Jane whispered. "I'm sorry, I didn't mean to doubt you, I didn't mean to let her take me, I was just, I was trying—"

"Shh," Clair said. She brushed a hand over Jane's hair, kissing the side of her head. "It's fine, Jane. It's fine. We're fine. I love you to pieces."

Jane's grip tightened around Clair. "Love you back together."

A pair of legs stepped in front of Clair. Mindsight's uniform. The coat closed around the front as Amy crouched down.

Clair peeked up, still holding Jane fast in a hug. Amy reached out, brushing a piece of Clair's bangs aside. A soft smile lit Amy's face, a shine of tears glimmering in the corners of her eyes.

She did not need to speak. Neither of them did. In a contest between Amy and Clair, there was no contest—they both knew who they'd rather be. Amy cupped Clair's cheek. *Thank you,* Amy mouthed.

And then she rose to her feet. Tugged at the hem of her shirt to straighten it. She was already fading, like a memory half forgotten. Two misty fingers raised to her forehead in a ghostly salute. "See you around, Clair Maxwell."

Clair stretched her hand out. "Amy . . ."

But by the time the name had escaped her lips, Amy was gone.

"Clair?" Jane asked. She was turning to look at her, her brow already wrinkled in concern. "Who are you talking to?"

Clair shut her eyes. She pressed her lips against Jane's forehead. She could have just answered the question with her powers, opening up the experience and letting it wash over Jane in an instant. But that kind of shortcut wasn't good enough for Jane. For Jane, Clair would share her experience the old-fashioned way: they'd *talk.* For hours, and days, and weeks. In stolen moments, and devoted conversations, and whispers as they lay in bed. For Jane, Clair would admit her truths out loud. Would own up to who she was, process her feelings verbally. No hiding, no half-truths. Just honesty and sharing and trading secrets. Facing the world together, as they should be.

For the rest of their lives.

"Come on," Clair said. She hauled Jane up to her feet, her arm solid around Jane's waist. Clair smiled at her. "We've got a lot of catching up to do."

"BY THE POWER VESTED IN ME FROM THE BYLAWS OF
Grand City, I now pronounce you wife and wife. You may kiss
your brides."

Cheers erupted in the packed room. Allison flinched back
from the sound of it as, at the front of the room, her sister dipped
Clair into an exaggerated kiss, like a sailor returning from a long
tour of duty.

Not really her sister.

Kind of her sister.

It didn't matter. Allison fixed the grin on her face, letting out
a whoop to join the chorus. Her hands tightened on Libby's legs,
holding her daughter in place on her shoulders as Libby laughed
and bounced against Allison's neck. She hated to admit it, but the
rejuve pod at the Heroes' headquarters had done a remarkable
job—she didn't even have a scar. If they hadn't been there? That

probably wasn't worth thinking about. Beside them, Gracie was hitched up on Alex like a backpack. Alex held her with one arm tucked back, the other holding his phone aloft so as to capture the moment on video.

Allison took a breath, held it for three seconds, let it out again. The crowd jostled around her. Fifty-seven people jammed into a room normally designed to host meetings of twenty, twenty-five max. But that wasn't even all of them. Guests spilled out into the hallway beyond, looking in through the plate glass walls of the conference room. Two exits to the room, plus a window three stories up from the ground. Four rooms across the hall with visibility into this one. Allison stood with her back toward most of the crowd, but even so, she could tell you every single person who stood between her and the elevator doors at the far end of the hall. Sixty-eight percent of them would go down without a fight, another fourteen percent were so out of shape as to be meaningless. Of the remainder, only a handful had experience in real-world combat, and most of those were the so-called Heroes, scattered like lost children through the crowd. There were no immediate threats, but that didn't relax Allison's guard. It never relaxed Allison's guard.

There was no pomp and circumstance this time. Jane and Clair's wedding ended up being a courthouse affair, tied off on a Tuesday afternoon, about a week after the debate. By rights, it shouldn't have been as big of a deal as it had turned into, but when the mayor's daughter gets married, most of City Hall turns up one way or another.

It seemed to suit the brides just fine. They posed for pictures, arms flexing, bunny-ear fingers snuck behind heads. Laughter spilled effortlessly across the room. Allison's lip twitched, almost enough to make her smile.

Her phone buzzed in her pocket.

Her mouth set back into a line. Allison didn't even need to take it out to know she had to answer it. This was her work phone, and only three people had the number. She plucked Libby from her shoulders, ignoring the squawks of protest. "Be right back," she whispered to Alex as she slid Libby's hand into his and planted a kiss on his cheek.

In a quiet corner, she swiped to accept the call. She didn't even say "hello."

"Agent Maxwell," the voice on the other end of the line said, as soon as she'd raised the phone to her ear. "Report."

Allison glanced diagonally across the room. Cal was beside Jane and Clair, talking animatedly as he accepted a piece of cake on a paper plate.

"There's still no indication that his memory or his powers have come back," Allison said now, watching him from her corner. Why they'd decided on *this* course of action, Allison couldn't even begin to understand, but by the time she'd finished healing, the job was already done. "The Heroes seem satisfied that, without being able to remember being corrupted by UltraViolet, he's back to the way he used to be."

"But the powers should still exist within him," the voice on the other side said.

"Maybe. Probably. Yes."

"Then he could still prove useful to our organization."

Allison chewed on her lip for a moment. "He *could* . . . ," she said. She picked through her words carefully, like trying to get gum out of Gracie's hair.

Instinctively, her eyes rose again, searching out a single face in the crowd. The cut of a vintage bob swung as Clair tipped her head back, laughing. A dot of chocolate frosting crowned her nose.

"But if I may make a suggestion, sir?" Allison said. "I don't think he's the Enhanced we should be keeping our eye on."

BLUE HAMILTON ALL BUT SKIPPED THROUGH THE EMPTY offices. All this space! She ran her hands gleefully over the surface of the desks, lined up and waiting like the first day of school. Already, the office brimmed with potential. She could only imagine the fun they were going to have here: Blue, scouting out the talent, bringing in fresh voices and unique skill; Jane, overseeing the vision, organizing the publications. Dream Sequence Comics. The logo was set to be painted on the walls tomorrow. It was really and finally happening. After months of planning, months of paperwork, months of early scouting and hiring.

But for now, the office was hers. Jane and Clair had disappeared on a delayed honeymoon, and Blue flounced between the desks, grinning and breathing in the smell of new upholstery.

In the corner, two offices overlooked the rest of the space. Blue stopped in front of them, running her fingers across the glass walls that separated them from the main floor. She traced the letters etched into the doors, first hers, then Jane's. Her face reflected in the glass, the pink of her hair catching the light. Blue wasn't *pretty*, and she always tried not to let it bother her, but— the sharp angles of her face, the overlarge gape of her nostrils, mirrored back to her above Jane's name. Blue swiped at the glass, as if she could smudge the image away.

She was just turning to leave when she spotted it.

Such a small bit of color, it might have easily gone unnoticed. But Blue was trained in seeing things that others overlooked. She walked over, pushing open the office door.

It sat in the middle of Jane's desk. A green orb in a rough metal frame. Light pulsed through it, filling the office with a faint, sickly glow. Blue frowned at it as she approached. Was it some kind of device, left behind by the techs who'd been in to set up the wifi? It didn't look like a router, not any kind Blue had ever seen anyway, but she'd ordered a lot of new equipment, and who knows what designers were up to these days?

Even as she considered the possibility, though, something about it felt . . . *wrong*. The device seemed to call to her, urging her forward. She couldn't take her eyes off it. The very air of the office seemed to crackle with excitement. More than anything, it actually reminded her of the drawings she'd found on Jane's computer one day, an old comic that seemed to have been about the Heroes of Hope. Blue had never asked her about it—mainly because doing so would mean admitting she'd gone snooping— but Blue had raced through those few digital issues, breathless as she pawed through the history of Grand City's foremost team of superheroes. Their backstory had something a lot like this, sitting on a generator behind an old chemical factory. So . . . what, was this some sort of scale model? Had Jane had it commissioned, to honor that early work she'd done?

Blue reached out.

She couldn't *not*. The possibility never occurred to her. She'd stepped into the room, she'd spotted the orb. She was always going to touch it.

The last thing Blue heard, before she lost consciousness, was the sound of glass shattering. The office wall, the one with Jane's name on it, collapsing against the force of Blue's back.

A few moments later, unbeknownst to Blue, a pair of shoes clicked across the office floor. Through the tangle of desks, around the central ball pit. They paused as their wearer regarded the mess, then resumed again. Toward Blue.

At the desk, they stopped. A woman's hand, smooth with treatments and not youth, carefully scooped the orb from where it lay. The power had gone out of it now, the lights dimming until it was nothing more than a paperweight. It looked like nothing so much as gray stone, now.

The woman pocketed it, then turned. She approached Blue cautiously. Glass crunched beneath her shoes. The woman crouched down in front of Blue, knees tucking to the side in her tight gray pencil skirt. The hand reached out again, running through the bristles of Blue's bubble-gum pink hair. Crackles of green electricity jumped between the strands. The woman's delicate fingers checked for a pulse, and pulled back in satisfaction when they found one.

A soft sigh filled the office. The woman straightened up, letting herself out. She pulled a phone from her purse and tapped out a quick text.

Across the city, beneath the open sky of a beautiful park, another phone trilled as a text came in. This phone was thinner than anything else on the market, almost see-through. The text popped up, bright and cheerful, hovering just above the glass. A finger tapped the message, the screen pulling up a conversation with a single text: *It's done.*

The cold slice of a smile reflected off the screen. A keyboard popped up.

Excellent news. Your payment will be forwarded at once. Thank you for your service, as always.

Three dots hovered beneath the reply. They didn't last long. The phone chimed, another message appearing. Laughter spilled across the park as the owner of the phone read the incoming text from Olivia.

Fuck you.

TO BE CONTINUED...

Photo by Corie Kelley

ABOUT THE AUTHOR

If JENN GOTT could have any power in the world, it would be superjumps. Lacking that, she fills her days writing stories about people with extraordinary abilities and tragic pasts. Her weaknesses are parallel worlds, time travel, and girl heroes. She lives in New England with her equally nerdy husband and their spoiled snuggle-cat.

🌐 jenngott.com
🐦 @gottwords
📷 @jenngottbooks
✉ jenn@jenngott.com

Sign up for the latest news and updates at:
jenngott.com/newsletter